SELECTED SHORT STORIES

SELECTED
SHORT STORIES

Joseph Conrad

WORDSWORTH CLASSICS

This edition published 1997 by
Wordsworth Editions Limited
Cumberland House, Crib Street
Ware, Hertfordshire SG12 9ET

ISBN 1 85326 190 4

Typeset by Antony Gray
Printed and bound in Great Britain by
Mackays of Chatham plc, Chatham Kent

CONTENTS

INTRODUCTION

The eleven short stories in this edition are taken from six of Conrad's seven collections of stories, tales, and nouvelles or long short stories.[1] Looseness of definitions here is deliberate because Conrad, like his publishers and such contemporaries as Henry James, used them unsystematically for any fiction where concision and rigorous selection were operative principles. Moreover, it is still evident today that subsequent attempts either to arrive at firm definitions of, or to distinguish between, 'tale', 'sketch' and 'short story', are impossible (Shaw, 20–1) and, I think, unrewarding. I prefer 'short story' because 'short' alerts us to the formal shaping, wroughtness and brevity treasured by Conrad and by such different practitioners as Poe, James and Kipling; and because 'story' retains a sense of the human teller and listener so characteristic of Conrad's framed narratives. I take 'short', following Poe, to refer to any story that can be read comfortably in 'from a half-hour to one or two hours . . . at one sitting', which is, perhaps, the most important and defining characteristic of this flexible and hybrid genre.[2] Thus the shortest I have chosen is 'The Lagoon' (5,700 words) and the longest is 'Karain' (16,000), and seven of the others are between 6,550 and 10,000 words.[3] Three other criteria governed my choice: these eleven are the best of the nineteen he wrote; they illustrate the range of his subjects and settings; and, more

---

1   For good formal descriptions of the various types of short story, see Abrams and Shaw (1–28). As Shaw notes 'the English language has no equivalent to "nouvelle" or "novella" other than "novelette", which has acquired a disparaging connotation' (20). Whenever possible, as here, I use only the author's name to identify a title. For full details turn to 'Works Cited' at the end of this Introduction. I thank Owen Knowles for his helpful critique of this Introduction.

2   Poe, 'Nathaniel Hawthorne', 572.

3   All the remaining ten tales gathered in Conrad's seven collections are long short stories or nouvelles; the shortest, 'Gaspar Ruiz', is nearly 19,000 words and the longest, 'The End of the Tether', is 47,000.

importantly, they demonstrate his radical and deliberate testing of the different 'ways of telling a tale' during the twenty years (1896–1916) that he devoted to the possibilities of the form.[4] As we shall see, Conrad was from the beginning a restless experimenter whose great distinction lies in his ingenious and rigorous exploration of the undiscovered possibilities latent in one of the genre's most familiar forms, namely the framed short story in which a first-person narrator (who is sometimes the member of a group) introduces, comments on and encloses another's tale. This form proved most amenable to his vision of the artist's task, man's fate, and to his sense of his reader's role and functions. (Precisely because these stories are often teasing and enigmatic, I strongly advise readers who do not know them to read them first and then to return to this Introduction.)

I

Conrad's first three short stories, 'The Idiots', 'An Outpost of Progress' and 'The Lagoon', were written successively in May, July and August 1896 in order to earn ready cash in the lucrative magazine market.[5] They represent his earliest experiments in the 'several ways of telling a tale'. 'The Idiots' is clearly modelled on Maupassant's example in that it has an anonymous first-person narrator who composes his story out of the 'listless answers to my questions' and 'indifferent words heard in wayside inns or on the very roads the idiots haunted' and who is used, initially, to guide our responses to 'a tale formidable and simple . . . endured by ignorant hearts'.[6] Thereafter, however, the narrator sequentially unfurls the violent events of *his* lurid tale and, as in 'The Lagoon' which is told in the third person, there is no closing frame and, consequently, little interaction between the tellers, listeners and the reader.

4 Author's Note (1920) to *Within the Tides* (1916), p. ix.
5 For details of the burgeoning market for short stories see Keating, 34–5. On 3 June 1896, the *Cornhill* solicited short stories from Conrad stipulating 'a general rule' of '6000 or 8000 words' and offering a 'remuneration' of 'one guinea' for every page of 'about 450 words' (*A Portrait in Letters*, 24). He earned £50 for 'An Outpost' from *Cosmopolis*, £12 10s. for 'The Lagoon' from the *Cornhill*, and £40 for 'Karain' from *Blackwood's*. These are huge sums, given that the average wage per annum of an adult male in 1897 was £56 and Conrad received only £20 for *Almayer's Folly* (1895). Until the unlikely success of *Chance* in 1913, Conrad's debts rose inexorably; and it is, perhaps, no accident that he ceased writing short stories in the autumn of 1916.
6 *Tales of Unrest*, p. 58. All page references to the works of Conrad (other than the short stories in this edition) are to the Dent Collected Edition (1946–9).

In his Author's Note (1919) to *Tales of Unrest* (1898), Conrad referred to 'An Outpost' as 'the lightest part of the loot I carried off from Central Africa', the main portion being of course 'Heart of Darkness', begun over two years later (ix).[7] Conrad had worked in the Belgian Congo in 1890 and both stories are pervaded with 'All the bitterness of those days, all my puzzled wonder as to the meaning of all I saw – all my indignation at masquerading philanthropy' (1, 294).[8] The greatness of 'An Outpost' is inseparable from its narrative method. Conrad achieves 'a scrupulous unity of tone' arising from (as Lothe and Hawthorn demonstrate) an ironic method (perfected by Flaubert), that he never used again in his short stories, but that characterises two of his finest novels, *Nostromo* (1904) and *The Secret Agent* (1907).[9] All three works combine an Olympian omniscience which works for detachment and thematic suggestiveness with a rich exploitation of the free indirect style which renders the characters' thoughts in their own idiom, initially evoking the reader's scorn but also arousing sympathy for their desperation and bewilderment – most noticeable in 'An Outpost' in the depiction of Kayerts' confusion after his accidental killing of Carlier. Like its great successors, 'An Outpost' is also remarkable for its 'merciless vividness of detail' (1, 303) and for the sheer intelligence and inclusiveness of its commentary which embraces not only the two insignificant 'pioneers of trade and progress', but all 'whose existence is only rendered possible through

7   Although Conrad was acutely aware that 'I must do something to live', and although he appreciated 'the general rule' governing the length of the short story, his 'effort at conciseness' in 'An Outpost of Progress' ran to 10,000 words (*The Collected Letters of Joseph Conrad*, vol. 1, 297. There are now five volumes; hereafter the appropriate number and page will appear in parentheses after the quotation). *Cosmopolis*, therefore, insisted on 'cutting it in two'; and, as he rightly feared, 'the first half read by itself' does 'appear strangely pointless' because, following one criterion for the short story, he had ensured that 'all the sting . . . is in the tail' (1, 299).

8   Cedric Watts in his fine Introduction to *Heart of Darkness and Other Tales*, quotes from an article in the July 1897 number of *Cosmopolis* which praises British imperialism in the year of Queen Victoria's Diamond Jubilee. The sardonic radicalism of Conrad's tale depicting the 'civilising mission' as 'an avidity for commercial profit' contradicts the ethos of the magazine (viii–ix).

9   As he worked on *The Secret Agent*, Conrad chose 'An Outpost' in 1906 for *Grand Magazine*'s 'My Best Story' series, highlighting both its 'unity of tone' and his 'inflexible and solemn resolve not to be led astray by my subject' (Lothe, 48–9). For Conrad's conscious homage to Flaubert see his letter to Garnett (1, 292), and Graver (11). Garnett's critique of 'An Outpost' probably (alas!) convinced Conrad to eschew omniscient narration in all his future short stories (1, 300).

the high organisation of civilised crowds' (89). And while we readily concur with Kayerts' shocked reaction to Henry Price's bartering of natives for ivory – 'Slavery is an awful thing' – we, also, are doomed to believe in 'words' because 'Everybody shows a respectful deference to certain sounds that he and his fellows can make': and, as we watch the appalling, drolly rendered disintegration of the hapless pair, we are asked to accept the terrible, quintessential Conradian belief that 'about feelings people really know nothing' (105).

'The Lagoon' was a deliberate attempt to accommodate the demands of the magazines and, as Conrad wryly informed Garnett, it 'is very much Malay indeed' (1, 296), containing 'the usual forests river – stars – wind sunrise . . . and lots of secondhand Conradese' (1, 301). Like 'Karain', it taps and stimulates the late-Victorian appetite for the exotic so expertly fostered by Stevenson and Kipling. The two violent, melodramatic tales of tribal conflict, passionate love, and betrayal, told by Malay warriors to white listeners, delighted Conrad's reviewers because they juxtaposed opposing racial cultures, instincts and beliefs and 'brought the East to our very doors' (Sherry, *The Critical Heritage*, 110).

Conrad thought of both stories as pot-boilers. He composed 'The Lagoon' quickly; but 'Karain', which he began in February 1897, thinking it would 'be easy', because it would fit the mould of 'seven to eight thousand words' (1, 358), proved 'a painful task' (1, 342). He discovered, however, like Henry James, that 'the rude prescription of brevity at any cost' was at odds with the complex narrative strategies of this experimental tale.[10] 'Karain' is in fact a key story in the history of Conrad's development as a writer, because he exploits more fully the teasing ending of 'The Lagoon' and builds upon its embryonic teller-listener structure, turning it into a fully-fledged tale within a tale. Thus his use of both a narrative audience and a characterised frame-narrator who introduces, comments on, and encloses another's tale anticipates the strategies of novels such as *Lord Jim* (1900) and *Chance* (1913), of long short stories such as 'Heart of Darkness' and 'Falk', and of all the remaining stories in this volume, except for 'The Secret Sharer'. As these elaborate structures show, once Conrad's imagination seizes a subject, 'a purely temperamental' imperative ensures that their evolution will manifest 'my unconventional grouping and . . '. perspective wherein almost all my "art" consists' (Jean-Aubry, 2, 316). They confirm James's intuition that Conrad's 'wandering, circling, yearning, imaginative faculty' sponsors narratives that usually enact 'a prolonged

10   Preface to 'The Lesson of the Master' (1908), 1227.

hovering flight of the subjective over the outstretched ground of the case exposed'.[11]

Conrad's indirect narrative strategies show that – in marked contrast to most practitioners of the genre – he did not aim at 'pure story telling'. Rather, as he told Blackwood, 'I am *modern*', because his work is based not on action and facts alone, but on 'action observed, felt and interpreted' (2, 418): felt in 'the light of a sincere mood' (Preface to *The Nigger of the 'Narcissus'*), and construed through the consciousness of the listener-narrator who functions as 'a medium of illumination' for the reader (Levenson, 21). Inevitably, therefore, his hovering narrators lack the pace and robustness of (say) Kipling's first-person 'special correspondent' narrator in the tales of the common soldier in India gathered in *Life's Handicap* (1891); and, correspondingly, the careful often elaborate framings of Conrad's short stories ensure that the 'episode' cannot become (as James noted in 'Rudyard Kipling') a 'detachable, compressible "case" ', making for an immediate and 'vivid picture' (1131).

The hovering flights of all Conrad's first-person narrators as they strive to interpret the strange and complex cases of (say) Karain, of Paul ('An Anarchist'), of the Count ('Il Conde'), and the Northman ('The Tale'), inevitably foreground an authorial self-consciousness, especially with regard to the motivation, justification, transmission and processes of the stories and to the inherent duplicity of language and of humankind's 'gift of expression' so marvellously captured in 'Heart of Darkness' (113). Correspondingly, almost all of Conrad's narratives are presented as transmitted orally, so that 'hearing and telling are the ground of the story . . . and the measure of its duration' (Said, 94). Thus, as we shall see, Conrad strives to make his readers 'collaborate with the author' (2, 394) because we function as overhearers of all the voices (whether tellers or listeners) and are obliged both to negotiate and weigh their competing, often partial interpretations.

'Karain: A Memory', is a typically mischievous title. It draws attention to three memories: to the 'subjective' musings of the reminiscing white, unnamed frame-narrator; to the 'case' of the titular character's memory of betrayal which attests also to the power of memory, fuelled by shame and guilt, to invoke 'noiseless phantoms' (55) that render even 'the ruler of a conquered land, a lover of war and danger . . . the slave of the dead' (59); and, as the framing coda (set seven years later in London) reveals, to Jackson's memory of Karain,

---

11 'The New Novel' (1914), 151, 149. James's remarks refer to Marlow's role and functions in *Chance*.

which is so vivid and disturbing that he finds the visible phenomena of metropolitan life to which the narrator appeals more phantasmal than either the native chief's dramatic spectacle of heroic life or his haunting tale of possession. Hence the last line of the story ('I think that, decidedly, he [Jackson] had been too long away from home') teases the reader, simultaneously confirming the frame-narrator's Western scepticism and raising the alarming possibility that 'the anger and the fear of a struggle against a thought, an idea', 'preys upon life', whether native or Western (31).

Conrad's narrative strategies, therefore, throw the burden of interpretation upon 'what the reader thinks' (74). Do we concur with the narrator's invocations of 'Greenwich Time' as 'a protection and a relief' (55–6) and of the activity of the metropolis as bulwarks against the unsettling re-definitions of the real raised by Karain's memory? Or do we agree with Jackson's sense that 'the noiseless phantoms' evoked by Karain are more real than the civility and order of Western life manifest in the image of 'a policeman, helmeted and dark, stretching out a rigid arm at the crossing of the streets' (78)? The very oppositions in this typical description ('helmeted and dark' and 'rigid') suggest the story's 'crossing' of unknowability and menace with the narrator's need to 'think . . . decidedly' (79) in order to control and ward off the darkness. Thus, in Wollaeger's fine formulation, the reader is persuaded to respond to ways in which 'The narrative holds in suspension a complex set of conflicting attitudes toward the question of what lies in the mysterious "elsewhere" beyond the empirical' (50). Our uncertain response is, therefore, fitting for several reasons: we enact Karain's swings between belief and unbelief in invisible forces and the white man's power to banish them; the narrative's between 'the fear of outer darkness' (52) – which embraces the native teller and Jackson the Western listener and rememberer – and our own submission to, and reliance on, the surface truth sustained by the ongoing, threatening activity of the busy metropolis; and, finally, we acknowledge the ambiguous stance of the sceptical author who, demonstrating his own haunting relation to the world, claims the power to haunt us with the ghosts of his own creation.

II

Gratified by publication in *Blackwood's* of 'Karain' in its entirety, Conrad in June 1898 dispatched 'Youth' (13,000 words), which was published complete in September. 'Youth' is an important development for two interrelated reasons: as he records in his Author's Note

(1917), it is the first to draw upon his own personal 'experience' and 'marks the first appearance in the world of the man Marlow', Conrad's most important story-teller who would appear later in 'Heart of Darkness', *Lord Jim* (1900) and *Chance* (1913). Conrad employs Marlow as a *persona* in order to distance himself from the actions and facts of his life and to observe, shape and interpret the 'bit of life' (2, 67) surveyed:[12] and he enables Conrad to avail himself of a flexible conversational voice that combines the 'intimately felt' (2, 375) and the lyric intensity of poetry.

Garnett's description of the story – 'a modern English epic of the Sea' (Sherry, *Critical Heritage*, 131) – is apt for several interrelated reasons: 1. the frame narrator's opening words ('This could have occurred nowhere but in England, where men and sea interpenetrate') and Marlow's paean to the 'something inborn and subtle and everlasting' that characterises English as opposed to 'French or German merchant-man', sound the national and patriotic notes of the 'chronicle' (32);[13] 2. the devotion of the stalwart men and their protracted struggle to save the *Judea* – 'all rust, dust, grime' with her boy's own 'motto "Do or Die"' inscribed underneath 'some sort of a coat of arms' – enlarges our conception of heroism; 3. 'Youth' 'like the *Odyssey* is a long voyage fraught with a seemingly endless and insurmountable series of hazards or tests' (Renner, 302); 4. correspondingly, Marlow invites his hearers to see the voyage as one 'ordered for the illustration of life . . . a symbol of existence'. And generations of readers, including most recently and thrillingly, Gavin Young, have responded to Marlow's determination to discover 'how good a man I was' and to his celebration of youth's 'feeling that I could outlast the sea, the earth, and all men' (41).[14]

'Youth' is, however, 'modern' because it is also a mock-epic. The tonal interplay of these two perspectives is wonderfully managed; and the reader simultaneously responds to the young Marlow's almost infinite capacity for action and to the older self's amused and searing

12 The story closely follows Conrad's adventures as second mate of the *Palestine*, which left Newcastle for Bangkok on 29 November 1881, and after grotesque ill-luck arrived at the port of Muntok on Bangka Island off the coast of Java on 15 March 1882. For details see Najder, 73–7.

13 Graver, among others, suggests that Conrad 'may have been deliberately catering to the patriotic ultraconservative point of view for which *Blackwood's* was so famous' (76). Significantly, Conrad changed the *Palestine's* multinational crew to an all-British one in the story.

14 Young was inspired to go *In Search of Conrad* (1991) by his headmaster's reading of this sequence.

recognition of humankind's ephemeral struggle for significance and meaning while 'surrounded by an impenetrable night' (33).[15]

III

In the autumn of 1900 Conrad ceased to play a direct role in the selling of his own fiction when he engaged J. B. Pinker, the literary agent, to manage his affairs. In search of advances and aware of Pinker's ability to place stories quickly, Conrad completed 'Typhoon', 'Falk' and 'Amy Foster' between September 1900 and June 1901. Pinker looked to popular magazines of high circulation and low quality such as *Pall Mall Magazine* and the *Illustrated London News* because they paid better than *Blackwood's*. Conrad promised Pinker that 'Amy Foster' would be 'really short this time' (2, 331); but it turned out to be 11,000 words long and (unlike 'Youth') was butchered into three weekly segments in December 1901 by the *Illustrated London News*.

After the story appeared in *Typhoon, and Other Stories* (1903), George Gissing acknowledged that it 'takes great hold upon me – as pathetic a thing as can be found in literature' (*A Portrait in Letters*, 41) and an anonymous reviewer boldly called it 'one of the most perfect short stories we have ever read'.[16] 'Amy Foster' is, I think, Conrad's best short story, not least because in it his vision of 'all the irreconcilable antagonisms that make our life' and constitute 'the only fundamental truth of fiction' finds its purest and most surprising expression (2, 348-49). Once again, Conrad reworks the strategies of his earlier stories, employing an unnamed frame-narrator, who introduces and comments on the main story, which is narrated by a Marlovian figure called Dr Kennedy, who gathers and shapes the local gossip. This time, however, Conrad locates 'the essential differences of the races' (2, 402) neither in the East nor Africa; rather, in a unique experiment, he records 'the simply tragic' fate of a shipwrecked Pole, Yanko Goorall, in Romney Marsh, Kent, thereby enabling him to present England itself as 'an undiscovered country'.[17]

I have written elsewhere about the interrelation between setting,

---

15 One anonymous early reviewer balked at 'the barren and not very pretty philosophy of "Youth"'; and John Masefield, accustomed to the 'vigorous, direct, effective' narratives of Kipling, objected to the 'page after page of stately and brilliant prose' of 'Youth' (Sherry, *Critical Heritage*, 137,142).
16 *Speaker*, 8, 6 June 1903; reprinted in Carabine, *Critical Assessments*, 1, 302.
17 Not surprisingly, therefore, many Conradians regard it as 'a work of spiritual autobiography, embodying his ever-present feelings of loneliness, foreignness, and isolation, and his sense of exile from Poland' (Herndon, 549).

narration and perspectives in the story. Suffice it to note here that
Kennedy shares Marlow's 'confounded democratic quality of vision'
(*Lord Jim*, 94) and articulates, with an intensity unmatched in English
literature since Wordsworth, Conrad's awareness of 'people of obscure
minds, of imperfect speech' who await 'the fertilising touch' of the
story-teller to transmute their 'imperfect speech' into the language of
art.[18] Yanko's broken speech and naïvety ensure that England becomes
(as it had for the Romans in 'Heart of Darkness') 'one of the dark places
of the earth' (48). And his dejected vision of English 'faces' as from 'the
other world – dead people' (141) echoes the frame-narrator's commentary on the still, sad music of humanity and prepares us for his terrible
death. Yanko's fate is more 'simply tragic' than any in Conrad's fiction
because it is bounded by Amy's two basic actions. In an 'act of
impulsive pity' she offers him 'such bread as the rich eat in my country'
and then when he is delirious and pleading in Polish 'for water – only a
little water', she is frightened and flees with their child in her arms;
'Lying face down and his body in a puddle' (154) Yanko reminds us of
Kurtz in 'Heart of Darkness' who is buried 'in a muddy hole' (150).
Both return to the 'powdered clods' from which all life once emerged
and both, in Kennedy's closing words, 'perish' (for very different
reasons) 'in the supreme disaster of loneliness and despair' (156).

IV

After finishing 'The End of the Tether' in November 1902, Conrad
began what he imagined would be a short story called 'Nostromo' that
soon manifested in extreme form the unforeseen principle of growth so
characteristic of his creative habits. He eventually finished his longest
and greatest novel in September 1904 and his letters throughout this
period and beyond are a catalogue of personal and familial illnesses, of
writing blocks, and ever-expanding debts. Lured by the promise of
quick returns, Conrad proclaimed in May 1905 that 'Short stories – is
the watchword now' (3, 243). Thus by November he finished the long
short story 'Gaspar Ruiz' and then in less than two months he wrote
'An Anarchist', 'The Brute' and 'The Informer'.

Conrad loathed these pressures: 'What cuts me to the quick is the
forced deterioration of my work produced hastily, carelessly in a temper
of desperation' (3, 300). His need for commercial success and popularity
led him to denigrate and to *misrepresent* these short stories, as his reply

18 I quote from the manuscript of 'The Husband' (Conrad's early name for
the story), Carabine, 'Irreconcilable Differences', 192.

to his publisher's request for 'a general definition of the stories' that he could use to advertise the forthcoming *A Set of Six* reveals:

> All the stories are stories of incident – action – not of analysis. All are dramatic in a measure but by no means of the gloomy sort. All, but two, draw their significance from the love interest – though of course they are not love stories in the conventional meaning. They are not studies – they touch no problem. They are just stories in which I've tried my best to be *simply entertaining*. [4, 29–30]

'Il Conde' centres on a single action and both 'An Anarchist' and 'The Informer' are packed full of incident, with the latter even having a 'love interest'. They are, however, neither '*simply entertaining*' nor can they be understood, as Graver maintains, as 'pot-boilers' (144). On the contrary they are unconventional precisely because they *are* stories of analysis; and the entertainment they offer is inseparable from their elaborate structures, baffled frame-narrators, curious tellers and riddling endings, which once again foreground problems of interpretation.

'The Informer', for example, is one of Conrad's most complicated narratives. It is told by an unnamed frame-narrator, a collector 'of Chinese bronzes and porcelain', who receives a visit from 'Mr X', another connoisseur, who is 'preceded by a letter of introduction from a good friend of mine in Paris' who 'collects acquaintances' (79).[19] Mr X is his prime specimen because 'He is the greatest rebel . . . of modern times' (80). The fastidious narrator admits that he doesn't 'understand anarchists', (81) but is curious about their underground activities. One evening over dinner Mr X casually remarks, 'There's no amendment to be got out of mankind except by terror and violence' (83), and then tells his shocked listener an elaborate, contemptuous tale of his successful staging of 'A conspiracy within a conspiracy' (94) designed to flush out 'the most systematic of informers' (100). That informer turns out to be Sevrin, who gives himself away because of his love for 'a charming, generous' upper-class girl whose involvement with anarchism, love for Sevrin, and subsequent 'retreat into a monastery' are cynically dismissed by Mr X as 'Gestures! Mere gestures of her class' (108). Mr X ends and frames his tale with the withering remark, 'That is why their kind is fated to perish' (109).

The narrative, however, ends with a brief coda in which the frame-narrator expresses his disgust both at X's cynicism and his Parisian

19 Sherry argues persuasively that 'The Informer' is based on Conrad's knowledge of the anarchist activities of Ford Madox Ford's juvenile relatives, Olive, Henry and Arthur Rossetti, *Conrad's Western World*, 205–18.

friend's enthusiastic pride in X. The friend agrees that X's cynicism is 'abominable':

> 'And then, you know, he likes to have his little joke sometimes,' he added in a confidential tone.
>
> I fail to understand the connection of this last remark. I have been utterly unable to discover where in all this the joke comes in. [102]

Clearly, the 'entertainment' in this Chinese-box narrative resides in the reader's willingness to discover the joke that evades its uncomprehending teller. As we have seen, this is typical of framed narratives that presume and incorporate listeners. The ending, I think, prompts two main and opposing lines of enquiry: one that concentrates on Mr X's relationship to his bemused and outraged auditor and another that concentrates on the doubly framed narrative and its juxtaposed voices. If we pursue the first line, then several possibilities emerge. That X is a surrogate for the author who enjoys his teller's jokes at the expense of his bourgeois auditor, who finds (say) his presentation of the girl 'intolerable to my sentiment of womanhood' (96); and delights in X's playful choice of 'a *bombe glacée*' as he begins his tale of anarchists who hide explosives in tins of 'Stone's Dried Soup' (88). Such absurd details are as 'entertaining' as the 'sort of theatrical expedient' (93) X uses to unmask the informer. This line suggests, then, that X's cynicism is perhaps a pose, an act designed to offend his auditor and to express Conrad's contempt for the radical political chic of 'that class . . . used to the feeling of being specially protected' whose members include the socialist lawyer in 'An Anarchist'.

If we consider 'all this', however, the joke illuminates Conrad's preference for the title 'Gestures' as 'the proper one, as bearing not on the facts but on the moral satirical idea' (3, 305). Following this line, X inadvertently puns on the title and *informs* against himself; like the girl he detests, he too knows 'little of anything except of words' (92).[20] Thus, compared to 'the Professor', 'the true spirit of an extreme revolutionist', X's framing glosses on his own tale which advocate terror and prophesy the death of 'that class' are revealed as 'sham meaning'; and his life, like the connoisseurs of chaos he despises, is also 'all a matter of pose and gesture' (84). From this angle X, 'safe within

20 Conrad feared and suspected revolutionaries and anarchists because they could not see that 'words should be handled with care lest the picture, the image of truth abiding in facts should become distorted – or blurred' (2, 200) – with disastrous consequences for action and, we might add, for interpretation.

his reputation of merely the greatest destructive publicist who ever lived' (80), is truly terrifying because his contempt is only matched by his complacency; his words inspire both 'the amateurs of emotion' he despises (84) and 'fanatics of social revolution' such as Horne (89); and he is admired by the Parisian 'collector of acquaintances'. Again, seen from this bleak perspective, the frame-narrator's judgement that X's 'cynicism was simply abominable' is fully justified (101). Moreover, such thoughts prompt the recognition that his 'cynicism' distorts his tale *and* is humanly disabling. All seems jaundiced to his jaundiced eye. He fails, therefore, to see 'the bitterest contradictions' in his own tale: that Sevrin informs 'from conviction' and then confesses to save the girl he truly loves and wishes to protect; and that the girl's 'gestures' may be misconceived but, none the less, she is heart-broken by her lover's betrayal and suicide. Thus buried in X's tale and the uncomprehending frame-narrator's narrative, is an alternative and untold story of thwarted love and genuine misery, revealing X's inability either to interpret or to love humankind whether viewed individually, or, as an anarchist, collectively. We still await a comprehensive appreciation of 'An Anarchist' and 'The Informer'. They are, *contra* Graver, distinctly 'modern' reworkings of 'the conventions of popular fiction' and radical experiments in handling 'time-honored formula[s]' of 'melodrama and murder' and of 'political intrigue of the cops-and-robbers sort' (125). Compared to *The Secret Agent* and *Under Western Eyes* they do 'lack "quality" '; but Conrad's 'fear they are but superficial' is, surely, a harsh self-critique (3, 346).

Conrad finished 'Il Conde' in early December 1906. On 18 August 1908, shortly after *A Set of Six* was published, he wrote to Ada Galsworthy: 'I am so glad you had . . . several good words for the Conde. Truth is I am rather proud of that little trick. It took me ten days' (4, 106). He glossed the 'trick' twelve years later in his Author's Note to the volume:

> . . . the last story in the volume, the one I call Pathetic, whose first title is Il Conde . . . is an almost verbatim transcript of the tale told me by a very charming old gentleman whom I met in Italy . . . Anyone can see that it is something more than a verbatim report, but where he left off and where I began must be left to the acute discrimination of the reader who may be interested in the problem . . . What I am certain of, however, is that it is not to be solved, for I am not at all clear about it myself by this time. All I can say is that the personality of the narrator was extremely suggestive quite apart from the story he was telling me. [vii]

Surprisingly, these teasing hints were ignored for over fifty years and as late as 1969 Graver praised the story because 'it exploits some of the most familiar conventions of magazine fiction: direct narrative, a suspenseful plot, a simple hero, and an undifferentiated villain' (144). A more egregious misreading is impossible to imagine. Why? Basically, Graver failed to see that the Count's tale is not a 'direct' 'verbatim report', but a carefully constructed collusion between the unnamed frame-narrator and the Count. In marked contrast to the tales of Paul ('An Anarchist') and X, therefore, the Count's account of 'the young man' who robs him is appropriated by the listener and told as reported speech and we are asked to accept that 'the poor Count' returns home to die because 'He was shocked at being the selected victim, not of robbery so much as of contempt' (305). In fact, every aspect of the short story subtly invites the discriminating reader to construct an alternative explanation against the grain of both the latter's telling and the former's empathetic commentary: the fastidious, moderate Count is unable to admit his homosexual inclinations and the gullible, sympathetic frame-narrator is unable to detect them.

I only have space to sketch the ways in which Conrad's 'trick' works. As several critics have noticed, every reference to the customs of the ancient Romans, to the places they inhabited, and to the statues they built, all of which are associated with the Count, are 'suggestive of decadence and immorality' (Hughes, 19). Thus, for example, the story opens with the narrator's fastidious encomium on 'that marvellous legacy of antique art whose delicate perfection has been preserved for us by the catastrophic fury of a volcano', and we learn that the 'perfectly unaffected' Count first addresses him 'over the celebrated Resting Hermes' (289). Neither, however, understands the powerful forces of fertility, phallus worship, lewdness, death, thievery and duplicity associated with this Roman god. Hence, from the outset, Conrad detaches himself from his tellers, and prefigures the destruction of the Count's 'delicate perfection' at the hands of the furious young thief.

Similarly, at every point in both the Count's tale and the narrator's summary of it, we note inconsistencies and contradictions. Thus, for example, the Count returns obsessively to 'the South Italian type of young man with . . . red lips . . . and liquid black eyes so wonderfully effective in leering or scowling' (298); and the narrator imagines the Count 'enjoying to the full, but with his usual tranquillity, the balminess of this southern night' (299), whereas the reader notes that he approaches the youth in the dark alley three times. The Count's story, then, is more 'deucedly queer' (more dubious and suspicious) than the narrator realises, for to be robbed is not 'dishonouring'; and aged seventy, rich and respectable, he could hardly be construed a robber! The sick Count finally announces that he must return home for 'I am a marked man'. In ways the narrator fails to understand the Count is now a mark for all the unscrupulous 'young men' who prey upon and blackmail fastidious gentlemen who find their type attractive. And this prospect is truly terrible for the Count because the 'contempt' of the brutal, beautiful youth triggered a traumatic 'confrontation with an aspect of his nature that he may have avoided looking at before' (Hughes, 86).

We are now in a position to recognise the extraordinary democracy of vision concealed in Conrad's 'little trick': the carefully-wrought collusion permits a sympathetic identification with the Count's appalling identity crisis; and the latter's hesitant, ambiguous tale enables Conrad to dramatise his own 'belief' (so memorably articulated by Marlow with regard to Jim's traumatising jump from the *Patna*) that 'no man ever understands quite his own artful dodges to escape from the grim shadow of self-knowledge' (*Lord Jim*, 80). Thus, even as he invites 'the discriminating reader' to decode 'Il Conde', our respect for the 'personality' of the 'extremely suggestive', tortured Count is never diminished: and the haunting 'problem' of 'where he left off and where I began' becomes part of our reading experience once we become 'interested in' it.

V

'Prince Roman' proved to be the only fiction set in Conrad's native Poland. He wrote a first draft in late 1908 and rewrote it in late 1910. Originally he planned to incorporate the material in his 'Reminiscences' which he began in the summer of 1908, during an *impasse* in the writing of *Under Western Eyes*.[21] The story is based on Conrad's memory of meeting the ancient Prince at his Uncle Tadeusz's estate in 1868, when he was only ten years old, and on his reading of Polish literature and his uncle's *Memoirs*.[22] Its structure largely follows the pattern of 'Karain' and its successors and, as in 'Il Conde', the unnamed frame-narrator and the anonymous teller collude. In 'Prince Roman', however, the reader's

21 They were first published in the *English Review* (December 1908–June 1909), founded by Conrad's friend, Ford Madox Ford; and then as *A Personal Record* (1912).

22 Nina Taylor is fine on this huge topic. She demonstrates how 'the private and public life of Prince Roman Sangusko . . . represents a certain typology of the Polish national fate' including 'martyrology' and 'the quintessentially Polish virtues of honour, duty and patriotism' (33–4).

relation to the narrative is much more direct, and the effects achieved much less equivocal than in its predecessors; and we are never induced to query where the teller ends and the author begins. This is basically because Conrad, so to speak, splits himself in two: he hands over his childhood memories of the Prince and his family history to a middle-aged Pole, who addresses a group of compatriots, which includes a narrator who introduces (but does not finally frame) the tale. From the beginning the two tellers collaborate: the primary speaker recalls the abortive Polish Uprising (against the Russians) in 1831, 'which happened seventy years ago . . . when in the presence of the world's passive indignation and eloquent sympathies we had once more to murmur *"Vae Victis"* and count the cost in sorrow' (91); and his listener mournfully chimes, 'that nationality . . . which persists in thinking, breathing, speaking, hoping, and suffering in its grave, railed in by a million of bayonets and triple-sealed with the seas of three great empires' (92). At such moments, Conrad the Polish patriot is painfully aware that his English readers may share their statesmen's fear and distrust of 'fanaticism'. He, therefore, demands of his readers either 'a certain greatness of soul' or 'a sincerity of feeling denied to the vulgar refinement of modern thought', because only then can we 'interpret worthily' 'the august simplicity of a sentiment [patriotism] proceeding from the very nature of things and men' (93). Chastened and forewarned, the reader is prepared for this direct, heroic tale, steeped in filial piety, of the Prince's passionate, doomed love for a beautiful wife and a gallant nation.

'Prince Roman' is a minor work: but it is worth reading because both its subject, and its consequent demand for the enlargement of the reader's sympathies, set it apart from the tradition of English letters. Indeed, Conrad's recognition that 'fanaticism is human' and can express moral motives 'springing from the secret needs and the unexpressed aspiration of the believers' (136) is central to his most un-English *appreciation* of the Professor in *The Secret Agent*, Sevrin in 'The Anarchist', and of Haldin and Sophia Antonovna, the Russian revolutionaries, in *Under Western Eyes*.

VI

Conrad wrote 'The Secret Sharer' in the first weeks of December 1909, during a break from *Under Western Eyes* which he was poised to finish. It was prompted by 'a visit from a man out of the Malay seas', Captain Marris, who moved Conrad deeply because he reported that 'all of these men of 22 years ago feel kindly to the chronicler of their lives and adventures. They shall have more of the stories they like' (4, 277-8). Hence he returned to the eastern seas of his earliest fiction, combining a stirring initiation story of a young seaman (compare 'Youth' and *Lord Jim*) with a reshaping of the notorious case of the mate of the *Cutty Sark* who killed an insubordinate black seaman with a capstan bar and was helped by his captain to escape from the law (Sherry, *Conrad's Eastern World*, 254–6).[23]

Formally, however, the story marks a new departure for it is the first fiction Conrad wrote from the first-person, autobiographical point of view. No longer, therefore, are the interrelations between hearing and telling the ground of the story, and we have no framing-voice either to introduce, observe and interpret another's oral tale, or to comment on its motivation and transmission. Rather, the captain's tale begins in *media res*: and the reader, locked into his viewpoint, is immediately gripped by a narrative that combines (in his strange encounter with his 'secret sharer') the dramatic force, tension and mystery of a psychological thriller with the huge moral, ethical and legal implications of crime and punishment raised by both Leggatt's tale and the captain's protection of him.

Every aspect of this fine story has generated an extraordinary range of confusing and conflicting debate.[24] Is the captain-narrator reliable or unreliable? Does the author endorse or subvert his teller's view of his 'secret sharer', Leggatt? Is the latter to be understood, as the captain insists, as a figure who enables him to live up to 'that ideal conception of one's own personality every man sets up for himself secretly' (104)? or does he embody his 'own potential criminality' (Guerard)? Are we meant to admire or to criticise the captain's calm acceptance of Leggatt's version of the killing of the crew-member and his own risky manoeuvre at the end of the story that puts at risk the lives of his crew? What are we to make of the suggestive details of the story (such as the L-shaped room or the floating hat) that have prompted a variety of symbolic readings?

While these questions will never be answered simply and unambiguously, readings such as Guerard's nevertheless strike me as untenable because, unlike any other story about an encounter with one's double, such as E. T. A. Hoffman's 'The Sandman', Poe's 'William Wilson', Dostoevsky's *The Double* and Stevenson's *Dr Jekyll and Mr Hyde*, 'The Secret Sharer' does not end with either the death or madness

23 In his Author's Note (1920) to *'Twixt Land and Sea*, Conrad discusses the Cutty Sark incident, remarking that 'It was . . . the common possession of the whole fleet of merchant ships trading to India, China, and Australia' (viii).
24 Harkness (1962) and Carabine, *Critical Assessments* (3, 274–346), contain representative essays.

of the protagonist.[25] Relatedly, and in marked contrast to 'William Wilson' (and all Poe's other first-person autobiographical horror tales), the captain is sane and neither denies nor represses his double: rather, in 'a familiar Conradian paradox' his story explores the ways in which his 'sympathy for the outlaw conflicts with his need to achieve solidarity with his . . . crew' (Fraser, 40). Thus at the close he discovers an authentic self and integrates with the crew through his acceptance of his responsibility for another human being. Furthermore, most of Conrad's short stories deal 'with matters outside the general run of everyday experience'; and from this point of view the captain's calm and surprisingly unreflective account constitutes Conrad's main solution to the eternal 'problem' of making 'unfamiliar things credible' (Author's Note to *Within the Tides*, vii). Finally, if we place 'The Secret Sharer' alongside *Under Western Eyes* it works, as several critics have pointed out, as a 'romantic counterpart' to Conrad's tragic novel (Ressler, 81). Hence, in marked contrast to Razumov's sense that he no longer belongs to himself and that his double, Haldin, will not cease haunting him until he confesses his crime of betrayal, the captain, after his initial 'horrid frost-bound sensation'(109), admires and is inspired by his secret sharer's self-possession and resolve. Thus, as Conrad drew to the close of the novel that tested his inner resources to the limit (and that led to his breakdown on its completion in January 1910), and as he was poised to record the terrible price Razumov pays for his independence, he grants both the young captain and his double happier fates.

VII

Conrad began his 'new' (and last) 'short story', 'The Tale', 'on a sudden impulse' in October 1916, shortly after he had been 'out mine sweeping' as a guest of the British Navy (5, 668). It is an appropriate finale to Conrad's career as a short-story writer, because as its generic title spotlights, it is a self-conscious artifice. Indeed, both in form and subject, it is a tale about tales, about their construction, reception and meaning, and the intricate relation between tellers, listeners and readers. And because it is built up out of a series of misprisions, centring around the Commanding Officer's account of his drastic construing of the Northman's tale, it foregrounds the difficulties and

25 Incidentally, all the external evidence clearly indicates that Conrad thought his narrator was reliable. Thus, for example, in a letter to Galsworthy he expresses his outrage that a reviewer called Leggatt 'a murderous ruffian . . . I was simply knocked over – for indeed I meant him to be what you have seen at once he was' (4, 121) – presumably, a figure worthy of the captain's admiration.

consequences of (mis)reading and (mis)interpretation.[26]

'The Tale', like the subtitle of 'Karain' ('A Memory') and titles such as 'The Informer', is mischievous, alerting us to the several tales that make up the narrative. There are at least three concentric tales and two lies: a shadowy, omniscient voice insists on the 'murmurs of infinite sadness' (155) that characterise the relationship of the Commanding Officer and his mistress-listener (155); with her request, 'Why not tell me a tale?' (157) he presents a tale in the third person about a Commanding Officer's encounter in a 'deceitful' fog (168) with a neutral ship that he suspects is secretly supplying German submarines. The Officer's interrogation sponsors the Northman's tale; but the former proves a poor listener because he has already decided against his addressee and because he attends to an 'inward voice, a grave murmur in the depth of his very own self, telling another tale' (188) that is prompted by his very English, gentlemanly indignation at profiteers masquerading as neutrals; and this 'inward voice', subsequently, leads him to give false information (another tale) to the Northman. Finally, he confesses to his mistress that his tale to her constitutes a confession because he was the Officer in his own tale: 'They [the Northman and his crew] all went down; and I don't know whether I have done stern retribution – or murder . . . I shall never know' (204).

The Commanding Officer, then, like the frame-narrator of 'Karain', Mr X in 'The Informer' and both the narrator and the Count in 'Il Conde', attempts to reduce interpretive possibilities, only to discover (as the narratives that contain them suggest) that we can 'never know' either the truth about the tales we tell ourselves or the truth in the tales others tell us about themselves. Thus, fittingly, Conrad's last short story dramatises, on the one hand, the folly of reaching after certainty that besets tellers, listeners and readers, and, on the other, reminds us that all his characteristic fictions are modernist, remaining tantalisingly open and unresolved.

DR KEITH CARABINE
University of Kent, Canterbury

---

26 Not surprisingly, 'The Tale', after years of neglect, is now a great favourite of narrative theorists such as Bonney, Lothe, Hawthorn and Rundle, all of whom concentrate on issues of (mis)interpretation and of reading.

WORKS CITED

M. H. Abrams, *A Glossary of Literary Terms* (6th edition), Harcourt Brace, Fort Worth 1993

Jocelyn Baines, *Joseph Conrad: A Critical Biography*, Weidenfeld & Nicolson, London 1960

William Bonney, *Thorns and Arabesques*, Johns Hopkins University Press, Baltimore 1980

Keith Carabine, *Joseph Conrad: Critical Assessments* (4 vols), Helm International, Robertsbridge 1992

Keith Carabine, ' "Irreconcilable Differences": England as an "Undiscovered Country" in Conrad's "Amy Foster" ', in Simon Gattrell (ed.), *The Ends of the Earth*, London-Atlantic Highlands, NJ, The Ashfield Press, 187–217

Gail Fraser, 'The Short Fiction', in John H. Stape (ed.), *The Cambridge Companion to Joseph Conrad*, Cambridge University Press, 1996, 25–44

Lawrence Graver, *Conrad's Short Fiction*, University of California Press, Berkeley 1969

Albert Guerard, *Conrad the Novelist*, Harvard University Press, Cambridge, Mass. 1958

Bruce Harkness, *Conrad's 'Secret Sharer' and the Critics*, Wadsworth Publishing Company, Belmont 1962

Jeremy Hawthorn, *Joseph Conrad: Narrative Technique and Ideological Commitment*, Edward Arnold, London 1990

Richard Herndon, 'The Genesis of Conrad's "Amy Foster" ', in *Studies in Philology*, 57 (1960), 549–66

Douglas A. Hughes, 'Conrad's "Il Conde": A Deucedly Queer Story', *Conradiana*, 7/1 (1975), 17–25

Henry James, 'The New Novel' (1914) and 'Rudyard Kipling' (1891), *Essays on Literature, American Writers, English Writers*, The Library of America, New York 1984, 124–59, 1122–31

Henry James, Preface to 'The Lesson of the Master', in *French Writers, Other European Writers, Prefaces to the New York Edition*, The Library of America, New York, 1984, 1225–37

G. Jean-Aubry, *Joseph Conrad: Life and Letters* (2 vols), Heinemann, London 1927

Frederick R. Karl and Laurence Davies (eds), *The Collected Letters of Joseph Conrad* (5 vols), Cambridge University Press, 1983–96

Peter Keating, *The Haunted Study*, Secker and Warburg, London 1989

Michael Levenson, *A Genealogy of Modernism: A Study of English Literary Doctrine, 1908–1922*, Cambridge University Press, 1979

Jakob Lothe, *Conrad's Narrative Method*, Clarendon Press, Oxford 1989

Thomas Moser, *Joseph Conrad: Achievement and Decline*, Harvard University Press, Cambridge, Mass. 1957

Z. Najder, *Joseph Conrad: A Chronicle*, Cambridge University Press, 1983

Edgar Allen Poe, Review of Nathaniel Hawthorne's *Twice-Told Tales*, in *Essays and Reviews*, The Library of America, New York 1984, 569–77

Stanley Renner, ' "Youth" and the Sinking Ship of Faith: Conrad's Miniature Nineteenth-Century Epic', in *Ball State University Forum*, 28 (1987), 57–73

Steve Ressler, *Joseph Conrad: Consciousness and Integrity*, New York University Press, 1988

Vivienne Rundle, ' "The Tale" and the Ethics of Interpretation', *The Conradian*, 17/1 (1992), 17–36

Edward W. Said, 'Conrad: The Presentation of Narrative', in *The World, The Text, The Critic*, Faber and Faber, London 1984

Valerie Shaw, *The Short Story: A Critical Introduction*, Longman, London and New York 1983

Norman Sherry, *Conrad's Eastern World*, Cambridge University Press, 1966

Norman Sherry, *Conrad's Western World*, Cambridge University Press, 1971

Norman Sherry, *Conrad: The Critical Heritage*, Routledge & Kegan Paul, London 1973

J. H. Stape & Owen Knowles (eds), *A Portrait in Letters: Correspondence to and about Conrad*, The Conradian, 19/1 and 2 (1995)

Nina Taylor, 'Landscapes of "Prince Roman" ', *The Conradian*, 15/2 (1991), 33-67

Cedric Watts, *Conrad's 'Heart of Darkness': A Critical and Contextual Study*, Mursia International, Milan 1977

Cedric Watts, *A Preface to Conrad*, Preface Books, Longman, London and New York 1982

Mark Wollaeger, *Joseph Conrad and the Fictions of Skepticism*, Stanford University Press 1990

BIBLIOGRAPHY

The eleven stories were first published in the following magazines: 'The Lagoon', *The Cornhill*, third series, vol. 2 (January 1897), 59–71; 'An Outpost of Progress', *Cosmopolis*, vol. 6 (June 1897), 609–20 and vol. 7 (July), 1–15; 'Karain: A Memory', *Blackwood's Magazine*, vol. 162 (November 1897), 630–56; 'Youth', *Blackwood's Magazine*, vol. 164 (September 1898), 309–30; 'Amy Foster', *Illustrated London News*, vol. 119 (14, 21, 28 December 1901), 915–16, 965–66, 1007–08; 'An Anarchist', *Harper's Magazine*, vol. 113 (August 1906), 406–16; 'The Informer', *Harper's Magazine*, vol. 114 (December 1906), 131–42; 'Il Conde', *Cassell's Magazine*, vol. 46 (August 1908), 243–53; 'The Secret Sharer', *Harper's Magazine*, vol. 121 (August and September 1910), 349–59, 530–41); 'Prince Roman', *Oxford and Cambridge Review*, no. 16 (October 1911), 201–26, and entitled 'The Aristocrat', *Metropolitan Magazine*, vol. 35 (January 1912), 19–22, 56, 58; and 'The Tale', *Strand Magazine*, vol. 54 (October 1917), 345–53.

TEXTUAL NOTE

All the stories, in keeping with Wordsworth Editions' aim to produce accessible modern texts, have undergone a 'Moderate Modernisation Programme'. Thus, for example, single quotes with double quotes within, replace double quotes with single quotes within; the old-fashioned em dash (—) is replaced with the en dash (–) with space before and after; and ellipses always have three dots (. . .). Printer's hyphens are removed, but many of the hyphenated words, of which Conrad was so fond, are retained.

After consulting the first English editions and the Dent Collected Edition, I silently corrected printing errors and missing punctuation marks in the first-edition texts. There are only a few substantive changes: in 'Amy Foster', 'would be startled' not 'should' (145) and 'wicket-gate' not 'wicker-gate' (154); commas follow after 'grave' (297) and 'heap' (304) in 'Il Conde', and after 'very elusive' (176) in 'The Tale'.

SELECTED SHORT STORIES

An Outpost of Progress

I

There were two white men in charge of the trading station. Kayerts, the chief, was short and fat; Carlier, the assistant, was tall, with a large head and a very broad trunk perched upon a long pair of thin legs. The third man on the staff was a Sierra Leone nigger, who maintained that his name was Henry Price. However, for some reason or other, the natives down the river had given him the name of Makola, and it stuck to him through all his wanderings about the country. He spoke English and French with a warbling accent, wrote a beautiful hand, understood bookkeeping, and cherished in his innermost heart the worship of evil spirits. His wife was a negress from Loanda, very large and very noisy. Three children rolled about in sunshine before the door of his low, shed-like dwelling. Makola, taciturn and impenetrable, despised the two white men. He had charge of a small clay storehouse with a dried-grass roof, and pretended to keep a correct account of beads, cotton cloth, red kerchiefs, brass wire, and other trade goods it contained. Besides the storehouse and Makola's hut, there was only one large building in the cleared ground of the station. It was built neatly of reeds, with a verandah on all the four sides. There were three rooms in it. The one in the middle was the living-room, and had two rough tables and a few stools in it. The other two were the bedrooms for the white men. Each had a bedstead and a mosquito net for all furniture. The plank floor was littered with the belongings of the white men: open half-empty boxes, torn wearing apparel, old boots; all the things dirty, and all the things broken, that accumulate mysteriously round untidy men. There was also another dwelling-place some distance away from the buildings. In it, under a tall cross much out of the perpendicular, slept the man who had seen the beginning of all this; who had planned and had watched the construction of this outpost of progress. He had been, at home, an unsuccessful painter who, weary of pursuing fame on an empty stomach, had gone out there through high protections. He had been the first chief of that station. Makola had watched the energetic artist die of fever in the just finished house with his usual kind of 'I told you so' indifference. Then, for a time, he dwelt alone with his family, his account books, and the Evil Spirit that rules the lands under the equator. He got on very well with his god. Perhaps he had propitiated him by a promise of more white men to play with, by and by. At any rate the director of the Great Trading Company, coming up in a steamer that resembled an enormous sardine box with a flat-roofed shed erected on it, found the station in good order, and Makola as usual quietly diligent. The director had the cross put up over the first agent's grave, and appointed Kayerts to the post. Carlier was told off as second in charge. The director was a man ruthless and efficient, who at times, but very imperceptibly, indulged in grim humour. He made a speech to Kayerts and Carlier, pointing out to them the promising aspect of their station. The nearest trading-post was about three hundred miles away. It was an exceptional opportunity for them to distinguish themselves and to earn percentages on the trade. This appointment was a favour done to beginners. Kayerts was moved almost to tears by his director's kindness. He would, he said, by doing his best, try to justify the flattering confidence, etc., etc. Kayerts had been in the Administration of the Telegraphs, and knew how to express himself correctly. Carlier, an ex-non-commissioned officer of cavalry in an army guaranteed from harm by several European Powers, was less impressed. If there were commissions to get, so much the better; and, trailing a sulky glance over the river, the forests, the impenetrable bush that seemed to cut off the station from the rest of the world, he muttered between his teeth, 'We shall see, very soon.'

Next day, some bales of cotton goods and a few cases of provisions having been thrown on shore, the sardine-box steamer went off, not to return for another six months. On the deck the director touched his cap to the two agents, who stood on the bank waving their hats, and turning to an old servant of the company on his passage to head-quarters, said, 'Look at those two imbeciles. They must be mad at home to send me such specimens. I told those fellows to plant a vegetable garden, build new storehouses and fences, and construct a landing-stage. I bet nothing will be done! They won't know how to begin. I always thought the station on this river useless, and they just fit the station!'

'They will form themselves there,' said the old stager with a quiet smile.

'At any rate, I am rid of them for six months,' retorted the director.

The two men watched the steamer round the bend, then, ascending arm in arm the slope of the bank, returned to the station. They had been in this vast and dark country only a very short time, and as yet always in the midst of other white men, under the eye and guidance of their superiors. And now, dull as they were to the subtle influences of surroundings, they felt themselves very much alone when suddenly left unassisted to face the wilderness: a wilderness rendered more strange, more incomprehensible by the mysterious glimpses of the vigorous life it contained. They were two perfectly insignificant and incapable individuals, whose existence is only rendered possible through the high organisation of civilised crowds. Few men realise that their life, the very essence of their character, their capabilities and their audacities, are only the expression of their belief in the safety of their surroundings. The courage, the composure, the confidence; the emotions and principles; every great and every insignificant thought belongs not to the individual but to the crowd: to the crowd that believes blindly in the irresistible force of its institutions and of its morals, in the power of its police and of its opinion. But the contact with pure unmitigated savagery, with primitive nature and primitive man, brings sudden and profound trouble into the heart. To the sentiment of being alone of one's kind, to the clear perception of the loneliness of one's thoughts, of one's sensations – to the negation of the habitual, which is safe, there is added the affirmation of the unusual, which is dangerous; a suggestion of things vague, uncontrollable, and repulsive, whose discomposing intrusion excites the imagination and tries the civilised nerves of the foolish and the wise alike.

Kayerts and Carlier walked arm in arm drawing close to one another as children do in the dark; and they had the same, not altogether unpleasant, sense of danger which one half suspects to be imaginary. They chatted persistently in familiar tones. 'Our station is prettily situated,' said one. The other assented with enthusiasm, enlarging volubly on the beauties of the situation. Then they passed near the grave. 'Poor devil!' said Kayerts. 'He died of fever, didn't he?' muttered Carlier, stopping short. 'Why,' retorted Kayerts, with indignation, 'I've been told that the fellow exposed himself recklessly to the sun. The climate here, everybody says, is not at all worse than at home, as long as you keep out of the sun. Do you hear that, Carlier? I am chief here, and my orders are that you should not expose yourself to the sun!' He assumed his superiority jocularly, but his meaning was serious. The idea that he would, perhaps, have to bury Carlier and remain alone, gave him an inward shiver. He felt suddenly that this Carlier was more precious to him here, in the centre of Africa, than a brother could be anywhere else. Carlier, entering into the spirit of the thing, made a military salute and answered in a brisk tone, 'Your orders shall be attended to, chief!' Then he burst out laughing, slapped Kayerts on the back, and shouted, 'We shall let life run easily here! Just sit still and gather in the ivory those savages will bring. This country has its good points, after all!' They both laughed loudly while Carlier thought: That poor Kayerts; he is so fat and unhealthy. It would be awful if I had to bury him here. He is a man I respect . . . Before they reached the verandah of their house they called one another 'my dear fellow'.

The first day they were very active, pottering about with hammers and nails and red calico, to put up curtains, make their house habitable and pretty; resolved to settle down comfortably to their new life. For them an impossible task. To grapple effectually with even purely material problems requires more serenity of mind and more lofty courage than people generally imagine. No two beings could have been more unfitted for such a struggle. Society, not from any tenderness, but because of its strange needs, had taken care of those two men, forbidding them all independent thought, all initiative, all departure from routine; and forbidding it under pain of death. They could only live on condition of being machines. And now, released from the fostering care of men with pens behind the ears, or of men with gold lace on the sleeves, they were like those lifelong prisoners who, liberated after many years, do not know what use to make of their freedom. They did not know what use to make of their faculties, being both, through want of practice, incapable of independent thought.

At the end of two months Kayerts often would say, 'If it was not for my Melie, you wouldn't catch me here.' Melie was his daughter. He had thrown up his post in the Administration of the Telegraphs, though he had been for seventeen years perfectly happy there, to earn a dowry for his girl. His wife was dead, and the child was being brought up by his sisters. He regretted the streets, the pavements, the cafés, his friends of many years; all the things he used to see, day after day; all the thoughts suggested by familiar things – the thoughts effortless, mo-notonous, and soothing of a government clerk; he regretted all the gossip, the small enmities, the mild venom, and the little jokes of government offices. 'If I had had a decent brother-in-law,' Carlier would remark, 'a fellow with a heart, I would not be here.' He had left the army and had made himself so obnoxious to his family by his laziness and impudence, that an exasperated brother-in-law had made superhuman efforts to procure him an appointment in the Company as a second-class agent. Having not a penny in the world, he was compelled to accept this means of livelihood as soon as it became quite clear to him that there was nothing more to squeeze out of his relations. He, like Kayerts, regretted his old life. He regretted the clink of sabre and spurs on a fine afternoon, the barrack-room witticisms, the girls of garrison towns; but, besides, he had also a sense of grievance. He was evidently a much ill-used man. This made him moody, at times. But the two men got on well together in the fellowship of their stupidity and laziness. Together they did nothing, absolutely nothing, and enjoyed the sense of the idleness for which they were paid. And in time they came to feel something resembling affection for one another.

They lived like blind men in a large room, aware only of what came in contact with them (and of that only imperfectly), but unable to see the general aspect of things. The river, the forest, all the great land throbbing with life, were like a great emptiness. Even the brilliant sunshine disclosed nothing intelligible. Things appeared and disappeared before their eyes in an unconnected and aimless kind of way. The river seemed to come from nowhere and flow nowhither. It flowed through a void. Out of that void, at times, came canoes, and men with spears in their hands would suddenly crowd the yard of the station. They were naked, glossy black, ornamented with snowy shells and glistening brass wire, perfect of limb. They made an uncouth babbling noise when they spoke, moved in a stately manner, and sent quick, wild glances out of their startled, never-resting eyes. Those warriors would squat in long rows, four or more deep, before the verandah, while their chiefs bargained for hours with Makola over an elephant tusk. Kayerts sat on his chair and looked down on the proceedings, understanding nothing. He stared at them with his round blue eyes, called out to Carlier, 'Here, look! look at that fellow there – and that other one, to the left. Did you ever see such a face? Oh, the funny brute!'

Carlier, smoking native tobacco in a short wooden pipe, would swagger up twirling his moustaches, and, surveying the warriors with haughty indulgence, would say –

'Fine animals. Brought any bone? Yes? It's not any too soon. Look at the muscles of that fellow – third from the end. I wouldn't care to get a punch on the nose from him. Fine arms, but legs no good below the knee. Couldn't make cavalry men of them.' And after glancing down complacently at his own shanks, he always concluded: 'Pah! Don't they stink! You, Makola! Take that herd over to the fetish' (the storehouse was in every station called the fetish, perhaps because of the spirit of civilisation it contained) 'and give them up some of the rubbish you keep there. I'd rather see it full of bone than full of rags.'

Kayerts approved.

'Yes, yes! Go and finish that palaver over there, Mr Makola. I will come round when you are ready, to weigh the tusk. We must be careful.' Then, turning to his companion: 'This is the tribe that lives down the river; they are rather aromatic. I remember, they have been once before here. D'ye hear that row? What a fellow has got to put up with in this dog of a country! My head is split.'

Such profitable visits were rare. For days the two pioneers of trade and progress would look on their empty courtyard in the vibrating brilliance of vertical sunshine. Below the high bank, the silent river flowed on, glittering and steady. On the sands in the middle of the stream, hippos and alligators sunned themselves side by side. And stretching away in all directions, surrounding the insignificant cleared spot of the trading post, immense forests, hiding fateful complications of fantastic life, lay in the eloquent silence of mute greatness. The two men understood nothing, cared for nothing but for the passage of days that separated them from the steamer's return. Their predecessor had left some torn books. They took up these wrecks of novels, and, as they had never read anything of the kind before, they were surprised and amused. Then during long days there were interminable and silly discussions about plots and personages. In the centre of Africa they made the acquaintance of Richelieu and of d'Artagnan, of Hawk's Eye and of Father Goriot, and of many other people. All these imaginary personages became subjects for gossip as if they had been living friends. They discounted their virtues, suspected their motives, decried their successes; were scandalised at their duplicity or were doubtful about their courage. The accounts of crimes filled them with indignation, while tender or pathetic passages moved them deeply. Carlier cleared his throat and said in a soldierly voice, 'What nonsense!' Kayerts, his round eyes suffused with tears, his fat cheeks quivering, rubbed his bald head, and declared, 'This is a splendid book. I had no idea there were such clever fellows in the world.' They also found some old copies of a home paper. That print discussed what it was pleased to call 'Our Colonial Expansion' in high-flown language. It spoke much of the rights and duties of civilisation, of the sacredness of the civilising work, and extolled the merits of those who went about bringing light, and faith, and commerce to the dark places of the earth. Carlier and Kayerts read, wondered, and began to think better of themselves. Carlier said one evening, waving his hand about, 'In a hundred years, there will be perhaps a town here. Quays, and warehouses, and barracks, and – and – billiard-rooms. Civilisation, my boy, and virtue – and all. And then, chaps will read that two good fellows, Kayerts and Carlier, were the first civilised men to live in this very spot!' Kayerts nodded, 'Yes, it is a consolation to think of that.' They seemed to forget their dead predecessor; but, early one day, Carlier went out and replanted the cross firmly. 'It used to make me squint whenever I walked that way,' he explained to Kayerts over the morning coffee. 'It made me squint, leaning over so much. So I just planted it upright. And solid, I promise you! I suspended myself with both hands to the cross-piece. Not a move. Oh, I did that properly.'

At times Gobila came to see them. Gobila was the chief of the neighbouring villages. He was a grey-headed savage, thin and black, with a white cloth round his loins and a mangy panther skin hanging over his back. He came up with long strides of his skeleton legs, swinging a staff as tall as himself, and, entering the common room of the station, would squat on his heels to the left of the door. There he sat, watching Kayerts, and now and then making a speech which the other did not understand. Kayerts, without interrupting his occupation, would from time to time say in a friendly manner: 'How goes it, you old image?' and they would smile at one another. The two whites had a liking for that old and incomprehensible creature, and called him Father Gobila. Gobila's manner was paternal, and he seemed really to love all white men. They all appeared to him very young, indistinguishably alike (except for stature), and he knew that they were all brothers, and also immortal. The death of the artist, who was the first white man whom he knew intimately, did not disturb this belief, because he was firmly convinced that the white stranger had pretended to die and got himself buried for some mysterious purpose of his own, into which it was useless to enquire. Perhaps it was his way of going home to his own country? At any rate, these were his brothers, and he transferred his absurd affection to them. They returned it in a way. Carlier slapped him on the back, and recklessly struck off matches for his amusement. Kayerts was always ready to let him have a sniff at the ammonia bottle. In short, they behaved just like that other white creature that had hidden itself in a hole in the ground. Gobila considered them attentively. Perhaps they were the same being with the other – or one of them was. He couldn't decide – clear up that mystery; but he remained always very friendly. In consequence of that friendship the women of Gobila's village walked in single file through the reedy grass, bringing every morning to the station, fowls, and sweet potatoes, and palm wine, and sometimes a goat. The Company never provisioned the stations fully, and the agents required those local supplies to live. They had them through the good-will of Gobila, and lived well. Now and then one of them had a bout of fever, and the other nursed him with gentle devotion. They did not think much of it. It left them weaker, and their appearance changed for the worse. Carlier was hollow-eyed and irritable. Kayerts showed a drawn, flabby face above the rotundity of his stomach, which gave him a weird aspect.

But being constantly together, they did not notice the change that took place gradually in their appearance, and also in their dispositions.

Five months passed in that way.

Then, one morning, as Kayerts and Carlier, lounging in their chairs under the verandah, talked about the approaching visit of the steamer, a knot of armed men came out of the forest and advanced towards the station. They were strangers to that part of the country. They were tall, slight, draped classically from neck to heel in blue fringed cloths, and carried percussion muskets over their bare right shoulders. Makola showed signs of excitement, and ran out of the storehouse (where he spent all his days) to meet these visitors. They came into the courtyard and looked about them with steady, scornful glances. Their leader, a powerful and determined-looking negro with bloodshot eyes, stood in front of the verandah and made a long speech. He gesticulated much, and ceased very suddenly.

There was something in his intonation, in the sounds of the long sentences he used, that startled the two whites. It was like a reminiscence of something not exactly familiar, and yet resembling the speech of civilised men. It sounded like one of those impossible languages which sometimes we hear in our dreams.

'What lingo is that?' said the amazed Carlier. 'In the first moment I fancied the fellow was going to speak French. Anyway, it is a different kind of gibberish to what we ever heard.'

'Yes,' replied Kayerts. 'Hey, Makola, what does he say? Where do they come from? Who are they?'

But Makola, who seemed to be standing on hot bricks, answered hurriedly, 'I don't know. They come from very far. Perhaps Mrs Price will understand. They are perhaps bad men.'

The leader, after waiting for a while, said something sharply to Makola, who shook his head. Then the man, after looking round, noticed Makola's hut and walked over there. The next moment Mrs Makola was heard speaking with great volubility. The other strangers – they were six in all – strolled about with an air of ease, put their heads through the door of the store-room, congregated round the grave, pointed understandingly at the cross, and generally made themselves at home.

'I don't like those chaps – and, I say, Kayerts, they must be from the coast; they've got firearms,' observed the sagacious Carlier.

Kayerts also did not like those chaps. They both, for the first time, became aware that they lived in conditions where the unusual may be dangerous, and that there was no power on earth outside of themselves to stand between them and the unusual. They became uneasy, went in and loaded their revolvers. Kayerts said, 'We must order Makola to tell them to go away before dark.'

The strangers left in the afternoon, after eating a meal prepared for them by Mrs Makola. The immense woman was excited, and talked much with the visitors. She rattled away shrilly, pointing here and pointing there at the forests and at the river. Makola sat apart and watched. At times he got up and whispered to his wife. He accompanied the strangers across the ravine at the back of the station-ground, and returned slowly looking very thoughtful. When questioned by the white men he was very strange, seemed not to understand, seemed to have forgotten French – seemed to have forgotten how to speak altogether. Kayerts and Carlier agreed that the nigger had had too much palm wine.

There was some talk about keeping a watch in turn, but in the evening everything seemed so quiet and peaceful that they retired as usual. All night they were disturbed by a lot of drumming in the villages. A deep, rapid roll near by would be followed by another far off – then all ceased. Soon short appeals would rattle out here and there, then all mingle together, increase, become vigorous and sustained, would spread out over the forest, roll through the night, unbroken and ceaseless, near and far, as if the whole land had been one immense drum booming out steadily an appeal to heaven. And through the deep and tremendous noise sudden yells that resembled snatches of songs from a madhouse darted shrill and high in discordant jets of sound which seemed to rush far above the earth and drive all peace from under the stars.

Carlier and Kayerts slept badly. They both thought they had heard shots fired during the night – but they could not agree as to the direction. In the morning Makola was gone somewhere. He returned about noon with one of yesterday's strangers, and eluded all Kayerts' attempts to close with him: had become deaf apparently. Kayerts wondered. Carlier, who had been fishing off the bank, came back and remarked while he showed his catch, 'The niggers seem to be in a deuce of a stir; I wonder what's up. I saw about fifteen canoes cross the river during the two hours I was there fishing.' Kayerts, worried, said, 'Isn't this Makola very queer today?' Carlier advised, 'Keep all our men together in case of some trouble.'

II

There were ten station men who had been left by the director. Those fellows, having engaged themselves to the Company for six months (without having any idea of a month in particular and only a very faint notion of time in general), had been serving the cause of progress for upwards of two years. Belonging to a tribe from a very distant part of this land of darkness and sorrow, they did not run away, naturally supposing that as wandering strangers they would be killed by the inhabitants of the country; in which they were right. They lived in straw huts on the slope of a ravine overgrown with reedy grass, just behind the station buildings. They were not happy, regretting the festive incantations, the sorceries, the human sacrifices of their own land; where they also had parents, brothers, sisters, admired chiefs, respected magicians, loved friends, and other ties supposed generally to be human. Besides, the rice rations served out by the Company did not agree with them, being a food unknown to their land, and to which they could not get used. Consequently they were unhealthy and miserable. Had they been of any other tribe they would have made up their minds to die – for nothing is easier to certain savages than suicide – and so have escaped from the puzzling difficulties of existence. But belonging, as they did, to a warlike tribe with filed teeth, they had more grit, and went on stupidly living through disease and sorrow. They did very little work, and had lost their splendid physique. Carlier and Kayerts doctored them assiduously without being able to bring them back into condition again. They were mustered every morning and told off to different tasks – grass-cutting, fence-building, tree-felling, etc., etc., which no power on earth could induce them to execute efficiently. The two whites had practically very little control over them.

In the afternoon Makola came over to the big house and found Kayerts watching three heavy columns of smoke rising above the forests. 'What is that?' asked Kayerts. 'Some villages burn,' answered Makola, who seemed to have regained his wits. Then he said abruptly: 'We have got very little ivory; bad six months' trading. Do you like get a little more ivory?'

'Yes,' said Kayerts eagerly. He thought of percentages which were low.

'Those men who came yesterday are traders from Loanda who have got more ivory than they can carry home. Shall I buy? I know their camp.'

'Certainly,' said Kayerts, 'What are those traders?'

'Bad fellows,' said Makola indifferently. 'They fight with people, and catch women and children. They are bad men, and got guns. There is a great disturbance in the country. Do you want ivory?'

'Yes,' said Kayerts. Makola said nothing for a while. Then: 'Those workmen of ours are no good at all,' he muttered, looking round. 'Station in very bad order, sir. Director will growl. Better get a fine lot of ivory, then he say nothing.'

'I can't help it; the men won't work,' said Kayerts. 'When will you get that ivory?'

'Very soon,' said Makola. 'Perhaps tonight. You leave it to me, and keep indoors, sir. I think you had better give some palm wine to our men to make a dance this evening. Enjoy themselves. Work better tomorrow. There's plenty palm wine – gone a little sour.'

Kayerts said yes, and Makola, with his own hands, carried the big calabashes to the door of his hut. They stood there till the evening, and Mrs Makola looked into every one. The men got them at sunset. When Kayerts and Carlier retired, a big bonfire was flaring before the men's huts. They could hear their shouts and drumming. Some men from Gobila's village had joined the station hands, and the entertainment was a great success.

In the middle of the night, Carlier, waking suddenly, heard a man shout loudly; then a shot was fired. Only one. Carlier ran out and met Kayerts on the verandah. They were both startled. As they went across the yard to call Makola, they saw shadows moving in the night. One of them cried, 'Don't shoot! It's me, Price.' Then Makola appeared close to them. 'Go back, go back, please,' he urged, 'you spoil all.' 'There are strange men about,' said Carlier. 'Never mind; I know,' said Makola. Then he whispered, 'All right. Bring ivory. Say nothing! I know my business.' The two white men reluctantly went back to the house, but did not sleep. They heard footsteps, whispers, some groans. It seemed as if a lot of men came in, dumped heavy things on the ground, squabbled a long time, then went away. They lay on their hard beds and thought: 'This Makola is invaluable.' In the morning Carlier came out, very sleepy, and pulled at the cord of the big bell. The station hands mustered every morning to the sound of the bell. That morning nobody came. Kayerts turned out also, yawning. Across the yard they saw Makola come out of his hut, a tin basin of soapy water in his hand. Makola, a civilised nigger, was very neat in his person. He threw the soapsuds skilfully over a wretched little yellow cur he had, then turning his face to the agent's house, he shouted from the distance, 'All the men gone last night!'

They heard him plainly, but in their surprise they both yelled out together: 'What!' Then they stared at one another. 'We are in a proper fix now,' growled Carlier. 'It's incredible!' muttered Kayerts. 'I will go to the huts and see,' said Carlier, striding off. Makola coming up found Kayerts standing alone.

'I can hardly believe it,' said Kayerts tearfully. 'We took care of them as if they had been our children.'

'They went with the coast people,' said Makola after a moment of hesitation.

'What do I care with whom they went – the ungrateful brutes!' exclaimed the other. Then with sudden suspicion, and looking hard at Makola, he added: 'What do you know about it?'

Makola moved his shoulders, looking down on the ground. 'What do I know? I think only. Will you come and look at the ivory I've got there? It is a fine lot. You never saw such.'

He moved towards the store. Kayerts followed him mechanically, thinking about the incredible desertion of the men. On the ground before the door of the fetish lay six splendid tusks.

'What did you give for it?' asked Kayerts, after surveying the lot with satisfaction.

'No regular trade,' said Makola. 'They brought the ivory and gave it to me. I told them to take what they most wanted in the station. It is a beautiful lot. No station can show such tusks. Those traders wanted carriers badly, and our men were no good here. No trade, no entry in books; all correct.'

Kayerts nearly burst with indignation. 'Why!' he shouted, 'I believe you have sold our men for these tusks!' Makola stood impassive and silent. 'I – I – will – I,' stuttered Kayerts. 'You fiend!' he yelled out.

'I did the best for you and the Company,' said Makola imperturbably. 'Why you shout so much? Look at this tusk.'

'I dismiss you! I will report you – I won't look at the tusk. I forbid you to touch them. I order you to throw them into the river. You – you!'

'You very red, Mr Kayerts. If you are so irritable in the sun, you will get fever and die – like the first chief!' pronounced Makola impressively.

They stood still, contemplating one another with intense eyes, as if they had been looking with effort across immense distances. Kayerts shivered. Makola had meant no more than he said, but his words seemed to Kayerts full of ominous menace! He turned sharply and went away to the house. Makola retired into the bosom of his family; and the tusks, left lying before the store, looked very large and valuable in the sunshine.

Carlier came back on the verandah. 'They're all gone, hey?' asked Kayerts from the far end of the common room in a muffled voice. 'You did not find anybody?'

'Oh, yes,' said Carlier, 'I found one of Gobila's people lying dead before the huts – shot through the body. We heard that shot last night.'

Kayerts came out quickly. He found his companion staring grimly over the yard at the tusks, away by the store. They both sat in silence for a while. Then Kayerts related his conversation with Makola. Carlier said nothing. At the midday meal they ate very little. They hardly exchanged a word that day. A great silence seemed to lie heavily over the station and press on their lips. Makola did not open the store; he spent the day playing with his children. He lay full-length on a mat outside his door, and the youngsters sat on his chest and clambered all over him. It was a touching picture. Mrs Makola was busy cooking all day as usual. The white men made a somewhat better meal in the evening. Afterwards, Carlier smoking his pipe strolled over to the store; he stood for a long time over the tusks, touched one or two with his foot, even tried to lift the largest one by its small end. He came back to his chief, who had not stirred from the verandah, threw himself in the chair and said –

'I can see it! They were pounced upon while they slept heavily after drinking all that palm wine you'd allowed Makola to give them. A put-up job! See? The worst is, some of Gobila's people were there, and got carried off too, no doubt. The least drunk woke up, and got shot for his sobriety. This is a funny country. What will you do now?'

'We can't touch it, of course,' said Kayerts.

'Of course not,' assented Carlier.

'Slavery is an awful thing,' stammered out Kayerts in an unsteady voice.

'Frightful – the sufferings,' grunted Carlier, with conviction.

They believed their words. Everybody shows a respectful deference to certain sounds that he and his fellows can make. But about feelings people really know nothing. We talk with indignation or enthusiasm; we talk about oppression, cruelty, crime, devotion, self-sacrifice, virtue, and we know nothing real beyond the words. Nobody knows what suffering or sacrifice mean – except, perhaps, the victims of the mysterious purpose of these illusions.

Next morning they saw Makola very busy setting up in the yard the big scales used for weighing ivory. By and by Carlier said: 'What's that filthy scoundrel up to?' and lounged out into the yard. Kayerts followed. They stood by watching. Makola took no notice. When the balance was swung true, he tried to lift a tusk into the scale. It was too heavy. He looked up helplessly without a word, and for a minute they stood round that balance as mute and still as three statues. Suddenly Carlier said: 'Catch hold of the other end, Makola – you beast!' and together they swung the tusk up. Kayerts trembled in every limb. He muttered, 'I say! Oh! I say!' and putting his hand in his pocket found there a dirty bit of paper and the stump of a pencil. He turned his back on the others, as if about to do something tricky, and noted stealthily the weights which Carlier shouted out to him with unnecessary loudness. When all was over, Makola whispered to himself: 'The sun's very strong here for the tusks.' Carlier said to Kayerts in a careless tone: 'I say, chief, I might just as well give him a lift with this lot into the store.'

As they were going back to the house Kayerts observed with a sigh: 'It had to be done.' And Carlier said: 'It's deplorable, but, the men being Company's men, the ivory is Company's ivory. We must look after it.'

'I will report to the director, of course,' said Kayerts. 'Of course; let him decide,' approved Carlier.

At midday they made a hearty meal. Kayerts sighed from time to time. Whenever they mentioned Makola's name they always added to it an opprobrious epithet. It eased their conscience. Makola gave himself a half-holiday, and bathed his children in the river. No one from Gobila's villages came near the station that day. No one came the next day, and the next, nor for a whole week. Gobila's people might have all been dead and buried for any sign of life they gave. But they were only mourning for those they had lost by the witchcraft of white men, who had brought wicked people into their country. The wicked people were gone, but fear remained. Fear always remains. A man may destroy everything within himself, love and hate and belief, and even doubt; but as long as he clings to life he cannot destroy fear: the fear, subtle, indestructible, and terrible, that pervades his being; that tinges his thoughts; that lurks in his heart; that watches on his lips the struggle of his last breath. In his fear, the mild old Gobila offered extra human sacrifices to all the evil spirits that had taken possession of his white friends. His heart was heavy. Some warriors spoke about burning and killing, but the cautious old savage dissuaded them. Who could foresee the woe those mysterious creatures, if irritated, might bring? They should be left alone. Perhaps in time they would disappear into the earth as the first one had disappeared. His people must keep away from them, and hope for the best.

Kayerts and Carlier did not disappear, but remained above on this earth, that, somehow, they fancied had become bigger and very empty.

It was not the absolute and dumb solitude of the post that impressed them so much as an inarticulate feeling that something from within them was gone, something that worked for their safety, and had kept the wilderness from interfering with their hearts. The images of home; the memory of people like them, of men that thought and felt as they used to think and feel, receded into distances made indistinct by the glare of unclouded sunshine. And out of the great silence of the surrounding wilderness, its very hopelessness and savagery seemed to approach them nearer, to draw them gently, to look upon them, to envelop them with a solicitude irresistible, familiar, and disgusting.

Days lengthened into weeks, then into months. Gobila's people drummed and yelled to every new moon, as of yore, but kept away from the station. Makola and Carlier tried once in a canoe to open communications, but were received with a shower of arrows, and had to fly back to the station for dear life. That attempt set the country up and down the river into an uproar that could be very distinctly heard for days. The steamer was late. At first they spoke of delay jauntily, then anxiously, then gloomily. The matter was becoming serious. Stores were running short. Carlier cast his lines off the bank, but the river was low, and the fish kept out in the stream. They dared not stroll far away from the station to shoot. Moreover, there was no game in the impenetrable forest. Once Carlier shot a hippo in the river. They had no boat to secure it, and it sank. When it floated up it drifted away, and Gobila's people secured the carcase. It was the occasion for a national holiday, but Carlier had a fit of rage over it, and talked about the necessity of exterminating all the niggers before the country could be made habitable. Kayerts mooned about silently; spent hours looking at the portrait of his Melie. It represented a little girl with long bleached tresses and a rather sour face. His legs were much swollen, and he could hardly walk. Carlier, undermined by fever, could not swagger any more, but kept tottering about, still with a devil-may-care air, as became a man who remembered his crack regiment. He had become hoarse, sarcastic, and inclined to say unpleasant things. He called it 'being frank with you'. They had long ago reckoned their percentages on trade, including in them that last deal of 'this infamous Makola'. They had also concluded not to say anything about it. Kayerts hesitated at first – was afraid of the director.

'He has seen worse things done on the quiet,' maintained Carlier, with a hoarse laugh. 'Trust him! He won't thank you if you blab. He is no better than you or me. Who will talk if we hold our tongues? There is nobody here.'

That was the root of the trouble! There was nobody there; and being left there alone with their weakness, they became daily more like a pair of accomplices than like a couple of devoted friends. They had heard nothing from home for eight months. Every evening they said, 'Tomorrow we shall see the steamer.' But one of the Company's steamers had been wrecked, and the director was busy with the other, relieving very distant and important stations on the main river. He thought that the useless station, and the useless men, could wait. Meantime Kayerts and Carlier lived on rice boiled without salt, and cursed the Company, all Africa, and the day they were born. One must have lived on such diet to discover what ghastly trouble the necessity of swallowing one's food may become. There was literally nothing else in the station but rice and coffee; they drank the coffee without sugar. The last fifteen lumps Kayerts had solemnly locked away in his box, together with a half-bottle of Cognac, 'in case of sickness', he explained. Carlier approved. 'When one is sick,' he said, 'any little extra like that is cheering.'

They waited. Rank grass began to sprout over the courtyard. The bell never rang now. Days passed, silent, exasperating, and slow. When the two men spoke, they snarled; and their silences were bitter, as if tinged by the bitterness of their thoughts.

One day after a lunch of boiled rice, Carlier put down his cup untasted, and said: 'Hang it all! Let's have a decent cup of coffee for once. Bring out that sugar, Kayerts!'

'For the sick,' muttered Kayerts, without looking up.

'For the sick,' mocked Carlier. 'Bosh! . . . Well! I am sick.'

'You are no more sick than I am, and I go without,' said Kayerts in a peaceful tone.

'Come! out with that sugar, you stingy old slave-dealer.'

Kayerts looked up quickly. Carlier was smiling with marked insolence. And suddenly it seemed to Kayerts that he had never seen that man before. Who was he? He knew nothing about him. What was he capable of? There was a surprising flash of violent emotion within him, as if in the presence of something undreamt of, dangerous, and final. But he managed to pronounce with composure –

'That joke is in very bad taste. Don't repeat it.'

'Joke!' said Carlier, hitching himself forward on his seat. 'I am hungry – I am sick – I don't joke! I hate hypocrites. You are a hypocrite. You are a slave-dealer. I am a slave-dealer. There's nothing but slave-dealers in this cursed country. I mean to have sugar in my coffee today, anyhow!'

'I forbid you to speak to me in that way,' said Kayerts with a fair show of resolution.

'You! – What?' shouted Carlier, jumping up.

Kayerts stood up also. 'I am your chief,' he began, trying to master the shakiness of his voice.

'What?' yelled the other. 'Who's chief? There's no chief here. There's nothing here: there's nothing but you and I. Fetch the sugar – you pot-bellied ass.'

'Hold your tongue. Go out of this room,' screamed Kayerts. 'I dismiss you – you scoundrel!'

Carlier swung a stool. All at once he looked dangerously in earnest. 'You flabby, good-for-nothing civilian – take that!' he howled.

Kayerts dropped under the table, and the stool struck the grass inner wall of the room. Then, as Carlier was trying to upset the table, Kayerts in desperation made a blind rush, head low, like a cornered pig would do, and overturning his friend, bolted along the verandah and into his room. He locked the door, snatched his revolver, and stood panting. In less than a minute Carlier was kicking at the door furiously, howling, 'If you don't bring out that sugar, I will shoot you at sight, like a dog. Now then – one – two – three. You won't? I will show you who's the master.'

Kayerts thought the door would fall in, and scrambled through the square hole that served for a window in his room. There was then the whole breadth of the house between them. But the other was apparently not strong enough to break in the door, and Kayerts heard him running round. Then he also began to run laboriously on his swollen legs. He ran as quickly as he could, grasping the revolver, and unable yet to understand what was happening to him. He saw in succession Makola's house, the store, the river, the ravine, and the low bushes; and he saw all those things again as he ran for the second time round the house. Then again they flashed past him. That morning he could not have walked a yard without a groan.

And now he ran. He ran fast enough to keep out of sight of the other man.

Then as, weak and desperate, he thought 'Before I finish the next round I shall die,' he heard the other man stumble heavily, then stop. He stopped also. He had the back and Carlier the front of the house, as before. He heard him drop into a chair cursing, and suddenly his own legs gave way, and he slid down into a sitting posture with his back to the wall. His mouth was as dry as a cinder, and his face was wet with perspiration – and tears. What was it all about? He thought it must be a horrible illusion; he thought he was dreaming; he thought he was going mad! After a while he collected his senses. What did they quarrel about? That sugar! How absurd! He would give it to him – didn't want it himself. And he began scrambling to his feet with a sudden feeling of security. But before he had fairly stood upright, a common-sense reflection occurred to him and drove him back into despair. He thought: If I give way now to that brute of a soldier, he will begin this horror again tomorrow – and the day after – every day – raise other pretensions, trample on me, torture me, make me his slave – and I will be lost! Lost! The steamer may not come for days – may never come. He shook so that he had to sit down on the floor again. He shivered forlornly. He felt he could not, would not move any more. He was completely distracted by the sudden perception that the position was without issue – that death and life had in a moment become equally difficult and terrible.

All at once he heard the other push his chair back; and he leaped to his feet with extreme facility. He listened and got confused. Must run again! Right or left? He heard footsteps. He darted to the left, grasping his revolver, and at the very same instant, as it seemed to him, they came into violent collision. Both shouted with surprise. A loud explosion took place between them; a roar of red fire, thick smoke; and Kayerts, deafened and blinded, rushed back thinking: I am hit – it's all over. He expected the other to come round – to gloat over his agony. He caught hold of an upright of the roof – 'All over!' Then he heard a crashing fall on the other side of the house, as if somebody had tumbled headlong over a chair – then silence. Nothing more happened. He did not die. Only his shoulder felt as if it had been badly wrenched, and he had lost his revolver. He was disarmed and helpless! He waited for his fate. The other man made no sound. It was stratagem. He was stalking him now! Along what side? Perhaps he was taking aim this very minute!

After a few moments of an agony frightful and absurd, he decided to go and meet his doom. He was prepared for every surrender. He turned the corner, steadying himself with one hand on the wall, made a few paces, and nearly swooned. He had seen on the floor, protruding past the other corner, a pair of turned-up feet. A pair of white naked feet in red slippers. He felt deadly sick, and stood for a time in profound darkness. Then Makola appeared before him, saying quietly: 'Come along, Mr Kayerts. He is dead.' He burst into tears of gratitude; a loud, sobbing fit of crying. After a time he found himself sitting in a chair and looking at Carlier, who lay stretched on his back. Makola was kneeling over the body.

'Is this your revolver?' asked Makola, getting up.

'Yes,' said Kayerts; then he added very quickly, 'He ran after me to shoot me – you saw!'

'Yes, I saw,' said Makola. 'There is only one revolver; where's his?'

'Don't know,' whispered Kayerts in a voice that had become suddenly very faint.

'I will go and look for it,' said the other gently. He made the round along the verandah, while Kayerts sat still and looked at the corpse. Makola came back empty-handed, stood in deep thought, then stepped quietly into the dead man's room, and came out directly with a revolver, which he held up before Kayerts. Kayerts shut his eyes. Everything was going round. He found life more terrible and difficult than death. He had shot an unarmed man.

After meditating for a while, Makola said softly, pointing at the dead man who lay there with his right eye blown out –

'He died of fever.' Kayerts looked at him with a stony stare. 'Yes,' repeated Makola thoughtfully, stepping over the corpse, 'I think he died of fever. Bury him tomorrow.'

And he went away slowly to his expectant wife, leaving the two white men alone on the verandah.

Night came, and Kayerts sat unmoving on his chair. He sat quiet as if he had taken a dose of opium. The violence of the emotions he had passed through produced a feeling of exhausted serenity. He had plumbed in one short afternoon the depths of horror and despair, and now found repose in the conviction that life had no more secrets for him: neither had death! He sat by the corpse thinking; thinking very actively, thinking very new thoughts. He seemed to have broken loose from himself altogether. His old thoughts, convictions, likes and dislikes, things he respected and things he abhorred, appeared in their true light at last! Appeared contemptible and childish, false and ridiculous. He revelled in his new wisdom while he sat by the man he had killed. He argued with himself about all things under heaven with that kind of wrong-headed lucidity which may be observed in some lunatics. Incidentally he reflected that the fellow dead there had been a noxious beast anyway; that men died every day in thousands; perhaps in hundreds of thousands – who could tell? – and that, in the number, that one death could not possibly make any difference; couldn't have any importance, at least to a thinking creature. He, Kayerts, was a thinking creature. He had been all his life, till that moment, a believer in a lot of nonsense like the rest of mankind – who are fools; but now he thought! He knew! He was at peace; he was familiar with the highest wisdom! Then he tried to imagine himself dead, and Carlier sitting in his chair watching him; and his attempt met with such unexpected success, that in a very few moments he became not at all sure who was dead and who was alive. This extraordinary achievement of his fancy startled him, however, and by a clever and timely effort of mind he saved himself just in time from becoming Carlier. His heart thumped, and he felt hot all over at the thought of that danger. Carlier! What a beastly thing! To compose his now disturbed nerves – and no wonder! – he tried to whistle a little. Then, suddenly, he fell asleep, or thought he had slept; but at any rate there was a fog, and somebody had whistled in the fog.

He stood up. The day had come, and a heavy mist had descended upon the land: the mist penetrating, enveloping, and silent; the morning mist of tropical lands; the mist that clings and kills; the mist white and deadly, immaculate and poisonous. He stood up, saw the body, and threw his arms above his head with a cry like that of a man who, waking from a trance, finds himself immured for ever in a tomb. '*Help!* . . . *My God!*'

A shriek, inhuman, vibrating and sudden, pierced like a sharp dart the white shroud of that land of sorrow. Three short, impatient screeches followed, and then, for a time, the fog-wreaths rolled on, undisturbed, through a formidable silence. Then many more shrieks, rapid and piercing, like the yells of some exasperated and ruthless creature, rent the air. Progress was calling to Kayerts from the river. Progress and civilisation and all the virtues. Society was calling to its accomplished child to come, to be taken care of, to be instructed, to be judged, to be condemned; it called him to return to that rubbish heap from which he had wandered away, so that justice could be done.

Kayerts heard and understood. He stumbled out of the verandah, leaving the other man quite alone for the first time since they had been thrown there together. He groped his way through the fog, calling in his ignorance upon the invisible heaven to undo its work. Makola flitted by in the mist, shouting as he ran –

'Steamer! Steamer! They can't see. They whistle for the station. I go ring the bell. Go down to the landing, sir. I ring.'

He disappeared. Kayerts stood still. He looked upwards; the fog rolled low over his head. He looked round like a man who has lost his way; and he saw a dark smudge, a cross-shaped stain, upon the shifting purity of the mist. As he began to stumble towards it, the station bell rang in a tumultuous peal its answer to the impatient clamour of the steamer.

The managing director of the Great Civilising Company (since we know that civilisation follows trade) landed first, and incontinently lost sight of the steamer. The fog down by the river was exceedingly dense; above, at the station, the bell rang unceasing and brazen.

The director shouted loudly to the steamer: 'There is nobody down to meet us; there may be something wrong, though they are ringing. You had better come, too!'

And he began to toil up the steep bank. The captain and the engine-driver of the boat followed behind. As they scrambled up the fog thinned, and they could see their director a good way ahead. Suddenly they saw him start forward, calling to them over his shoulder: 'Run! Run to the house! I've found one of them. Run, look for the other!'

He had found one of them! And even he, the man of varied and startling experience, was somewhat discomposed by the manner of this finding. He stood and fumbled in his pockets (for a knife) while he faced Kayerts, who was hanging by a leather strap from the cross. He had evidently climbed the grave, which was high and narrow, and after tying the end of the strap to the arm, had swung himself off. His toes were only a couple of inches above the ground; his arms hung stiffly down; he seemed to be standing rigidly at attention, but with one purple cheek playfully posed on the shoulder. And, irreverently, he was putting out a swollen tongue at his managing director.

The Lagoon

The white man, leaning with both arms over the roof of the little house in the stern of the boat, said to the steersman –

'We will pass the night in Arsat's clearing. It is late.'

The Malay only grunted, and went on looking fixedly at the river. The white man rested his chin on his crossed arms and gazed at the wake of the boat. At the end of the straight avenue of forests cut by the intense glitter of the river, the sun appeared unclouded and dazzling, poised low over the water that shone smoothly like a band of metal. The forests, sombre and dull, stood motionless and silent on each side of the broad stream. At the foot of big, towering trees, trunkless nipa palms rose from the mud of the bank, in bunches of leaves enormous and heavy, that hung unstirring over the brown swirl of eddies. In the stillness of the air every tree, every leaf, every bough, every tendril of creeper and every petal of minute blossoms seemed to have been bewitched into an immobility perfect and final. Nothing moved on the river but the eight paddles that rose flashing regularly, dipped together with a single splash; while the steersman swept right and left with a periodic and sudden flourish of his blade describing a glinting semicircle above his head. The churned-up water frothed alongside with a confused murmur. And the white man's canoe, advancing upstream in the short-lived disturbance of its own making, seemed to enter the portals of a land from which the very memory of motion had for ever departed.

The white man, turning his back upon the setting sun, looked along the empty and broad expanse of the sea-reach. For the last three miles of its course the wandering, hesitating river, as if enticed irresistibly by the freedom of an open horizon, flows straight into the sea, flows straight to the east – to the east that harbours both light and darkness. Astern of the boat the repeated call of some bird, a cry discordant and feeble, skipped along over the smooth water and lost itself, before it could reach the other shore, in the breathless silence of the world.

The steersman dug his paddle into the stream, and held hard with stiffened arms, his body thrown forward. The water gurgled aloud; and suddenly the long straight reach seemed to pivot on its centre, the forests swung in a semicircle, and the slanting beams of sunset touched the broadside of the canoe with a fiery glow, throwing the slender and distorted shadows of its crew upon the streaked glitter of the river. The white man turned to look ahead. The course of the boat had been altered at right-angles to the stream, and the carved dragon-head of its prow was pointing now at a gap in the fringing bushes of the bank. It glided through, brushing the overhanging twigs, and disappeared from the river like some slim and amphibious creature leaving the water for its lair in the forests.

The narrow creek was like a ditch: tortuous, fabulously deep; filled with gloom under the thin strip of pure and shining blue of the heaven. Immense trees soared up, invisible behind the festooned draperies of creepers. Here and there, near the glistening blackness of the water, a twisted root of some tall tree showed amongst the tracery of small ferns, black and dull, writhing and motionless, like an arrested snake. The short words of the paddlers reverberated loudly between the thick and sombre walls of vegetation. Darkness oozed out from between the trees, through the tangled maze of the creepers, from behind the great fantastic and unstirring leaves; the darkness, mysterious and invincible; the darkness scented and poisonous of impenetrable forests.

The men poled in the shoaling water. The creek broadened, opening out into a wide sweep of a stagnant lagoon. The forests receded from the marshy bank, leaving a level strip of bright green, reedy grass to frame the reflected blueness of the sky. A fleecy pink cloud drifted high above, trailing the delicate colouring of its image under the floating leaves and the silvery blossoms of the lotus. A little house, perched on high piles, appeared black in the distance. Near it, two tall nibong palms, that seemed to have come out of the forests in the background, leaned slightly over the ragged roof, with a suggestion of sad tenderness and care in the droop of their leafy and soaring heads.

The steersman, pointing with his paddle, said, 'Arsat is there. I see his canoe fast between the piles.'

The polers ran along the sides of the boat glancing over their shoulders at the end of the day's journey. They would have preferred to spend the night somewhere else than on this lagoon of weird aspect and ghostly reputation. Moreover, they disliked Arsat, first as a stranger, and also because he who repairs a ruined house, and dwells in it, proclaims that he is not afraid to live amongst the spirits that haunt the places abandoned by mankind. Such a man can disturb the course of fate by glances or words; while his familiar ghosts are not easy to propitiate by casual wayfarers upon whom they long to wreak the malice of their human master. White men care not for such things, being unbelievers and in league with the Father of Evil, who leads them unharmed through the invisible dangers of this world. To the warnings of the righteous they oppose an offensive pretence of disbelief. What is there to be done?

So they thought, throwing their weight on the end of their long poles. The big canoe glided on swiftly, noiselessly, and smoothly, towards Arsat's clearing, till, in a great rattling of poles thrown down, and the loud murmurs of 'Allah be praised!' it came with a gentle knock against the crooked piles below the house.

The boatmen with uplifted faces shouted discordantly, 'Arsat! O Arsat!' Nobody came. The white man began to climb the rude ladder giving access to the bamboo platform before the house. The juragan of the boat said sulkily, 'We will cook in the sampan, and sleep on the water.'

'Pass my blankets and the basket,' said the white man curtly.

He knelt on the edge of the platform to receive the bundle. Then the boat shoved off, and the white man, standing up, confronted Arsat, who had come out through the low door of his hut. He was a man young, powerful, with a broad chest and muscular arms. He had nothing on but his sarong. His head was bare. His big, soft eyes stared eagerly at the white man, but his voice and demeanour were composed as he asked, without any words of greeting –

'Have you medicine, Tuan?'

'No,' said the visitor in a startled tone. 'No. Why? Is there sickness in the house?'

'Enter and see,' replied Arsat, in the same calm manner, and turning short round, passed again through the small doorway. The white man, dropping his bundles, followed.

In the dim light of the dwelling he made out on a couch of bamboos a woman stretched on her back under a broad sheet of red cotton cloth. She lay still, as if dead; but her big eyes, wide open, glittered in the gloom, staring upwards at the slender rafters, motionless and unseeing. She was in a high fever, and evidently unconscious. Her cheeks were sunk slightly, her lips were partly open, and on the young face there was the ominous and fixed expression – the absorbed, contemplating expression of the unconscious who are going to die. The two men stood looking down at her in silence.

'Has she been long ill?' asked the traveller.

'I have not slept for five nights,' answered the Malay, in a deliberate tone. 'At first she heard voices calling her from the water and struggled against me who held her. But since the sun of today rose she hears nothing – she hears not me. She sees nothing. She sees not me – me!'

He remained silent for a minute, then asked softly –

'Tuan, will she die?'

'I fear so,' said the white man sorrowfully. He had known Arsat years ago, in a far country in times of trouble and danger, when no friendship is to be despised. And since his Malay friend had come unexpectedly to dwell in the hut on the lagoon with a strange woman, he had slept many times there, in his journeys up and down the river. He liked the man who knew how to keep faith in council and how to fight without fear by the side of his white friend. He liked him – not so much perhaps as a man likes his favourite dog – but still he liked him well enough to help and ask no questions, to think sometimes vaguely and hazily in the midst of his own pursuits, about the lonely man and the long-haired woman with audacious face and triumphant eyes, who lived together hidden by the forests – alone and feared.

The white man came out of the hut in time to see the enormous conflagration of sunset put out by the swift and stealthy shadows that, rising like a black and impalpable vapour above the tree-tops, spread over the heaven, extinguishing the crimson glow of floating clouds and the red brilliance of departing daylight. In a few moments all the stars came out above the intense blackness of the earth, and the great lagoon gleaming suddenly with reflected lights resembled an oval patch of night sky flung down into the hopeless and abysmal night of the wilderness. The white man had some supper out of the basket, then collecting a few sticks that lay about the platform, made up a small fire, not for warmth, but for the sake of the smoke, which would keep off the mosquitos. He wrapped himself in his blankets and sat with his back against the reed wall of the house, smoking thoughtfully.

Arsat came through the doorway with noiseless steps and squatted down by the fire. The white man moved his outstretched legs a little.

'She breathes,' said Arsat in a low voice, anticipating the expected question. 'She breathes and burns as if with a great fire. She speaks not; she hears not – and burns!'

He paused for a moment, then asked in a quiet, incurious tone –

'Tuan . . . will she die?'

The white man moved his shoulders uneasily, and muttered in a hesitating manner –

'If such is her fate.'

'No, Tuan,' said Arsat calmly. 'If such is my fate. I hear, I see, I wait. I remember . . . Tuan, do you remember the old days? Do you remember my brother?'

'Yes,' said the white man. The Malay rose suddenly and went in. The other, sitting still outside, could hear the voice in the hut. Arsat said: 'Hear me! Speak!' His words were succeeded by a complete silence. 'O

Diamelen!' he cried suddenly. After that cry there was a deep sigh. Arsat came out and sank down again in his old place.

They sat in silence before the fire. There was no sound within the house, there was no sound near them; but far away on the lagoon they could hear the voices of the boatmen ringing fitful and distinct on the calm water. The fire in the bows of the sampan shone faintly in the distance with a hazy red glow. Then it died out. The voices ceased. The land and the water slept invisible, unstirring and mute. It was as though there had been nothing left in the world but the glitter of stars streaming, ceaseless and vain, through the black stillness of the night.

The white man gazed straight before him into the darkness with wide-open eyes. The fear and fascination, the inspiration and the wonder of death – of death near, unavoidable, and unseen, soothed the unrest of his race and stirred the most indistinct, the most intimate of his thoughts. The ever-ready suspicion of evil, the gnawing suspicion that lurks in our hearts, flowed out into the stillness round him – into the stillness profound and dumb, and made it appear untrustworthy and infamous like the placid and impenetrable mask of an unjustifiable violence. In that fleeting and powerful disturbance of his being the earth enfolded in the starlight peace became a shadowy country of inhuman strife, a battle-field of phantoms terrible and charming, august or ignoble, struggling ardently for the possession of our helpless hearts. An unquiet and mysterious country of inextinguishable desires and fears.

A plaintive murmur rose in the night; a murmur saddening and startling, as if the great solitudes of surrounding woods had tried to whisper into his ear the wisdom of their immense and lofty indifference. Sounds hesitating and vague floated in the air round him, shaped themselves slowly into words; and at last flowed on gently in a murmuring stream of soft and monotonous sentences. He stirred like a man waking up and changed his position slightly. Arsat, motionless and shadowy, sitting with bowed head under the stars, was speaking in a low and dreamy tone –

' . . . for where can we lay down the heaviness of our trouble but in a friend's heart? A man must speak of war and of love. You, Tuan, know what war is, and you have seen me in time of danger seek death as other men seek life! A writing may be lost; a lie may be written; but what the eye has seen is truth and remains in the mind!'

'I remember,' said the white man quietly. Arsat went on with mournful composure –

'Therefore I shall speak to you of love. Speak in the night. Speak before both night and love are gone – and the eye of day looks upon my sorrow and my shame; upon my blackened face; upon my burnt-up heart.'

A sigh, short and faint, marked an almost imperceptible pause, and then his words flowed on, without a stir, without a gesture.

'After the time of trouble and war was over and you went away from my country in the pursuit of your desires, which we, men of the islands, cannot understand, I and my brother became again, as we had been before, the sword-bearers of the Ruler. You know we were men of family, belonging to a ruling race, and more fit than any to carry on our right shoulder the emblem of power. And in the time of prosperity Si Dendring showed us favour, as we, in time of sorrow, had showed to him the faithfulness of our courage. It was a time of peace. A time of deer-hunts and cock-fights; of idle talks and foolish squabbles between men whose bellies are full and weapons are rusty. But the sower watched the young rice-shoots grow up without fear, and the traders came and went, departed lean and returned fat into the river of peace. They brought news too. Brought lies and truth mixed together, so that no man knew when to rejoice and when to be sorry. We heard from them about you also. They had seen you here and had seen you there. And I was glad to hear, for I remembered the stirring times, and I always remembered you, Tuan, till the time came when my eyes could see nothing in the past, because they had looked upon the one who is dying there – in the house.'

He stopped to exclaim in an intense whisper, 'O Mara bahia! O Calamity!' then went on speaking a little louder.

'There's no worse enemy and no better friend than a brother, Tuan, for one brother knows another, and in perfect knowledge is strength for good or evil. I loved my brother. I went to him and told him that I could see nothing but one face, hear nothing but one voice. He told me: "Open your heart so that she can see what is in it – and wait. Patience is wisdom. Inchi Midah may die or our Ruler may throw off his fear of a woman!" . . . I waited! . . . You remember the lady with the veiled face, Tuan, and the fear of our Ruler before her cunning and temper. And if she wanted her servant, what could I do? But I fed the hunger of my heart on short glances and stealthy words. I loitered on the path to the bath-houses in the daytime, and when the sun had fallen behind the forest I crept along the jasmine hedges of the women's courtyard. Unseeing, we spoke to one another through the scent of flowers, through the veil of leaves, through the blades of long grass that stood still before our lips; so great was our prudence, so faint was the murmur of our great longing. The time passed swiftly. . . and there were whispers amongst women – and our enemies watched – my brother was gloomy, and I began to think of killing and of a fierce death . . . We are of a people who take what they want – like you whites. There is a time when a man should forget loyalty and respect. Might and authority are given to rulers, but to all men is given love and strength and courage. My brother said, "You shall take her from their midst. We are two who are like one." And I answered, "Let it be soon, for I find no warmth in sunlight that does not shine upon her." Our time came when the Ruler and all the great people went to the mouth of the river to fish by torchlight. There were hundreds of boats, and on the white sand, between the water and the forests, dwellings of leaves were built for the households of the Rajahs. The smoke of cooking-fires was like a blue mist of the evening, and many voices rang in it joyfully. While they were making the boats ready to beat up the fish, my brother came to me and said, "Tonight!" I looked to my weapons, and when the time came our canoe took its place in the circle of boats carrying the torches. The lights blazed on the water, but behind the boats there was darkness. When the shouting began and the excite-ment made them like mad we dropped out. The water swallowed our fire, and we floated back to the shore that was dark with only here and there the glimmer of embers. We could hear the talk of slave-girls amongst the sheds. Then we found a place deserted and silent. We waited there. She came. She came running along the shore, rapid and leaving no trace, like a leaf driven by the wind into the sea. My brother said gloomily, "Go and take her; carry her into our boat." I lifted her in my arms. She panted. Her heart was beating against my breast. I said, "I take you from those people. You came to the cry of my heart, but my arms take you into my boat against the will of the great!" "It is right," said my brother. "We are men who take what we want and can hold it against many. We should have taken her in daylight." I said, "Let us be off," for since she was in my boat I began to think of our ruler's many men. "Yes. Let us be off," said my brother. "We are cast out and this boat is our country now – and the sea is our refuge." He lingered with his foot on the shore, and I entreated him to hasten, for I remembered the strokes of her heart against my breast and thought that two men cannot withstand a hundred. We left, paddling downstream close to the bank; and as we passed by the creek where they were fishing, the great shouting had ceased, but the murmur of voices was loud like the humming of insects flying at noonday. The boats floated, clustered together, in the red light of torches, under a black roof of smoke; and men talked of their sport. Men that boasted, and praised, and jeered – men that would have been our friends in the morning, but on that night were already our enemies. We paddled swiftly past. We had no more friends in the country of our birth. She sat in the middle of the canoe with covered face; silent as she is now; unseeing as she is now – and I had no regret at what I was leaving because I could hear her breathing close to me – as I can hear her now.'

He paused, listened with his ear turned to the doorway, then shook his head and went on.

'My brother wanted to shout the cry of challenge – one cry only – to let the people know we were freeborn robbers who trusted our arms and the great sea. And again I begged him in the name of our love to be silent. Could I not hear her breathing close to me? I knew the pursuit would come quick enough. My brother loved me. He dipped his paddle without a splash. He only said, "There is half a man in you now – the other half is in that woman. I can wait. When you are a whole man again, you will come back with me here to shout defiance. We are sons of the same mother." I made no answer. All my strength and all my spirit were in my hands that held the paddle – for I longed to be with her in a safe place beyond the reach of men's anger and of women's spite. My love was so great, that I thought it could guide me to a country where death was unknown, if I could only escape from Inchi Midah's fury and from our Ruler's sword. We paddled with haste, breathing through our teeth. The blades bit deep into the smooth water. We passed out of the river; we flew in clear channels amongst the shallows. We skirted the black coast; we skirted the sand beaches where the sea speaks in whispers to the land; and the gleam of white sand flashed back past our boat, so swiftly she ran upon the water. We spoke not. Only once I said, "Sleep, Diamelen, for soon you may want all your strength." I heard the sweetness of her voice, but I never turned my head. The sun rose and still we went on. Water fell from my face like rain from a cloud. We flew in the light and heat. I never looked back, but I knew that my brother's eyes, behind me, were looking steadily ahead, for the boat went as straight as a bushman's dart, when it leaves the end of the sumpitan. There was no better paddler, no better steersman than my brother. Many times, together, we had won races in that canoe. But we never had put out our strength as we did then – then, when for the last time we paddled together! There was no braver or stronger man in our country than my brother. I could not spare the strength to turn my head and look at him, but every moment I heard the hiss of his breath getting louder behind me. Still he did not speak. The sun was high. The heat clung to my back like a flame of fire. My ribs were ready to burst, but I could no longer get enough air into my chest. And then I felt I must cry out with my last breath, "Let us rest!" . . . "Good!" he answered; and his voice was firm. He was strong. He was brave. He knew not fear and no fatigue . . . My brother!'

A murmur powerful and gentle, a murmur vast and faint; the murmur of trembling leaves, of stirring boughs, ran through the tangled depths of the forests, ran over the starry smoothness of the lagoon, and the water between the piles lapped the slimy timber once with a sudden splash. A breath of warm air touched the two men's faces and passed on with a mournful sound – a breath loud and short like an uneasy sigh of the dreaming earth.

Arsat went on in an even, low voice.

'We ran our canoe on the white beach of a little bay close to a long tongue of land that seemed to bar our road; a long wooded cape going far into the sea. My brother knew that place. Beyond the cape a river has its entrance, and through the jungle of that land there is a narrow path. We made a fire and cooked rice. Then we lay down to sleep on the soft sand in the shade of our canoe, while she watched. No sooner had I closed my eyes than I heard her cry of alarm. We leaped up. The sun was halfway down the sky already, and coming in sight in the opening of the bay we saw a prau manned by many paddlers. We knew it at once; it was one of our Rajah's praus. They were watching the shore, and saw us. They beat the gong, and turned the head of the prau into the bay. I felt my heart become weak within my breast. Diamelen sat on the sand and covered her face. There was no escape by sea. My brother laughed. He had the gun you had given him, Tuan, before you went away, but there was only a handful of powder. He spoke to me quickly: "Run with her along the path. I shall keep them back, for they have no firearms, and landing in the face of a man with a gun is certain death for some. Run with her. On the other side of that wood there is a fisherman's house – and a canoe. When I have fired all the shots I will follow. I am a great runner, and before they can come up we shall be gone. I will hold out as long as I can, for she is but a woman – that can neither run nor fight, but she has your heart in her weak hands." He dropped behind the canoe. The prau was coming. She and I ran, and as we rushed along the path I heard shots. My brother fired – once – twice – and the booming of the gong ceased. There was silence behind us. That neck of land is narrow. Before I heard my brother fire the third shot I saw the shelving shore, and I saw the water again: the mouth of a broad river. We crossed a grassy glade. We ran down to the water. I saw a low hut above the black mud, and a small canoe hauled up. I heard another shot behind me. I thought, "That is his last charge." We rushed down to the canoe; a man came running from the hut, but I leaped on him, and we rolled together in the mud. Then I got up, and he lay still at my feet. I don't know whether I had killed him or not. I and Diamelen pushed the canoe afloat. I heard yells behind me, and I saw my brother run across the glade. Many men were bounding after him, I took her in my arms and threw her into the boat, then leaped in myself. When I looked back I saw that my brother had fallen. He fell and was up again, but the men were closing round him. He shouted, "I am coming!" The men were close to him. I looked. Many men. Then I looked at her. Tuan, I pushed the canoe! I pushed it into deep water. She was kneeling forward looking at me, and I said, "Take your paddle," while I struck the water with mine. Tuan, I heard him cry. I heard him cry my name twice; and I heard voices shouting, "Kill! Strike!" I never turned back. I heard him calling my name again with a great shriek, as when life is going out together with the voice – and I never turned my head. My own name! . . . My brother! Three times he called – but I was not afraid of life. Was she not there in that canoe? And could I not with her find a country where death is forgotten – where death is unknown!'

The white man sat up. Arsat rose and stood, an indistinct and silent figure above the dying embers of the fire. Over the lagoon a mist drifting and low had crept, erasing slowly the glittering images of the stars. And now a great expanse of white vapour covered the land: it flowed cold and grey in the darkness, eddied in noiseless whirls round the tree-trunks and about the platform of the house, which seemed to float upon a restless and impalpable illusion of a sea. Only far away the tops of the trees stood outlined on the twinkle of heaven, like a sombre and forbidding shore – a coast deceptive, pitiless and black.

Arsat's voice vibrated loudly in the profound peace.

'I had her there! I had her! To get her I would have faced all mankind. But I had her – and – '

His words went out ringing into the empty distances. He paused, and seemed to listen to them dying away very far – beyond help and beyond recall. Then he said quietly –

'Tuan, I loved my brother.'

A breath of wind made him shiver. High above his head, high above the silent sea of mist the drooping leaves of the palms rattled together with a mournful and expiring sound. The white man stretched his legs. His chin rested on his chest, and he murmured sadly without lifting his head –

'We all love our brothers.'

Arsat burst out with an intense whispering violence –

'What did I care who died? I wanted peace in my own heart.'

He seemed to hear a stir in the house – listened – then stepped in noiselessly. The white man stood up. A breeze was coming in fitful puffs. The stars shone paler as if they had retreated into the frozen depths of immense space. After a chill gust of wind there were a few seconds of perfect calm and absolute silence. Then from behind the black and wavy line of the forests a column of golden light shot up into the heavens and spread over the semi-circle of the eastern horizon. The sun had risen. The mist lifted, broke into drifting patches, vanished into thin flying wreaths; and the unveiled lagoon lay, polished and black, in the heavy shadows at the foot of the wall of trees. A white eagle rose over it with a slanting and ponderous flight, reached the clear sunshine and appeared dazzlingly brilliant for a moment, then soaring higher, became a dark and motionless speck before it vanished into the blue as if it had left the earth for ever. The white man, standing gazing upwards before the doorway, heard in the hut a confused and broken murmur of distracted words ending with a loud groan. Suddenly Arsat stumbled out with outstretched hands, shivered, and stood still for some time with fixed eyes. Then he said –

'She burns no more.'

Before his face the sun showed its edge above the tree-tops, rising steadily. The breeze freshened; a great brilliance burst upon the lagoon, sparkled on the rippling water. The forests came out of the clear shadows of the morning, became distinct, as if they had rushed nearer – to stop short in a great stir of leaves, of nodding boughs, of swaying branches. In the merciless sunshine the whisper of unconscious life grew louder, speaking in an incomprehensible voice round the dumb darkness of that human sorrow. Arsat's eyes wandered slowly, then stared at the rising sun.

'I can see nothing,' he said half aloud to himself.

'There is nothing,' said the white man, moving to the edge of the platform and waving his hand to his boat. A shout came faintly over the lagoon and the sampan began to glide towards the abode of the friend of ghosts.

'If you want to come with me, I will wait all the morning,' said the white man, looking away upon the water.

'No, Tuan,' said Arsat softly. 'I shall not eat or sleep in this house, but I must first see my road. Now I can see nothing – see nothing! There is no light and no peace in the world; but there is death – death for many. We were sons of the same mother – and I left him in the midst of enemies; but I am going back now.'

He drew a long breath and went on in a dreamy tone.

'In a little while I shall see clear enough to strike – to strike. But she has died, and . . . now . . . darkness.'

He flung his arms wide open, let them fall along his body, then stood still with unmoved face and stony eyes, staring at the sun. The white man got down into his canoe. The polers ran smartly along the sides of the boat, looking over their shoulders at the beginning of a weary journey. High in the stern, his head muffled up in white rags, the juragan sat moody, letting his paddle trail in the water. The white man, leaning with both arms over the grass roof of the little cabin, looked back at the shining ripple of the boat's wake. Before the sampan passed out of the lagoon into the creek he lifted his eyes. Arsat had not moved. He stood lonely in the searching sunshine; and he looked beyond the great light of a cloudless day into the darkness of a world of illusions.

Karain: A Memory

I

We knew him in those unprotected days when we were content to hold in our hands our lives and our property. None of us, l believe, has any property now, and I hear that many, negligently, have lost their lives; but I am sure that the few who survive are not yet so dim-eyed as to miss in the befogged respectability of their newspapers the intelligence of various native risings in the Eastern Archipelago. Sunshine gleams between the lines of those short paragraphs – sunshine and the glitter of the sea. A strange name wakes up memories; the printed words scent the smoky atmosphere of today faintly, with the subtle and penetrating perfume as of land breezes breathing through the starlight of bygone nights; a signal fire gleams like a jewel on the high brow of a sombre cliff; great trees, the advanced sentries of immense forests, stand watchful and still over sleeping stretches of open water; a line of white surf thunders on an empty beach, the shallow water foams on the reefs; and green islets scattered through the calm of noonday lie upon the level of a polished sea, like a handful of emeralds on a buckler of steel.

There are faces too – faces dark, truculent, and smiling; the frank audacious faces of men barefooted, well armed and noiseless. They thronged the narrow length of our schooner's decks with their ornamented and barbarous crowd, with the variegated colours of checkered sarongs, red turbans, white jackets, embroideries; with the gleam of scabbards, gold rings, charms, armlets, lance blades, and jewelled handles of their weapons. They had an independent bearing, resolute eyes, a restrained manner; and we seem yet to hear their soft voices speaking of battles, travels, and escapes; boasting with composure, joking quietly; sometimes in well-bred murmurs extolling their own valour, our generosity; or celebrating with loyal enthusiasm the virtues of their ruler. We remember the faces, the eyes, the voices, we see again the gleam of silk and metal; the murmuring stir of that crowd, brilliant, festive, and martial; and we seem to feel the touch of friendly brown hands that, after one short grasp, return to rest on a chased hilt. They were Karain's people – a devoted following. Their movements hung on his lips; they read their thoughts in his eyes; he murmured to them nonchalantly of life and death, and they accepted his words humbly, like gifts of fate. They were all free men, and when speaking to him said, 'Your slave.' On his passage voices died out as though he had walked guarded by silence; awed whispers followed him. They called him their war-chief. He was the ruler of three villages on a narrow plain; the master of an insignificant foothold on the earth – of a conquered foothold that, shaped like a young moon, lay ignored between the hills and the sea.

From the deck of our schooner, anchored in the middle of the bay, he indicated by a theatrical sweep of his arm along the jagged outline of the hills the whole of his domain; and the ample movement seemed to drive back its limits, augmenting it suddenly into something so immense and vague that for a moment it appeared to be bounded only by the sky. And really, looking at that place, landlocked from the sea and shut off from the land by the precipitous slopes of mountains, it was difficult to believe in the existence of any neighbourhood. It was still, complete, unknown, and full of a life that went on stealthily with a troubling effect of solitude; of a life that seemed unaccountably empty of anything that would stir the thought, touch the heart, give a hint of the ominous sequence of days. It appeared to us a land without memories, regrets, and hopes; a land where nothing could survive the coming of the night, and where each sunrise, like a dazzling act of special creation, was disconnected from the eve and the morrow.

Karain swept his hand over it. 'All mine!' He struck the deck with his long staff; the gold head flashed like a falling star; very close behind him a silent old fellow in a richly embroidered black jacket alone of all the Malays around did not follow the masterful gesture with a look. He did not even lift his eyelids. He bowed his head behind his master, and without stirring held hilt up over his right shoulder a long blade in a silver scabbard. He was there on duty, but without curiosity, and seemed weary, not with age, but with the possession of a burdensome secret of existence. Karain, heavy and proud, had a lofty pose and breathed calmly. It was our first visit, and we looked about curiously.

The bay was like a bottomless pit of intense light. The circular sheet of water reflected a luminous sky, and the shores enclosing it made an opaque ring of earth floating in an emptiness of transparent blue. The hills, purple and arid, stood out heavily on the sky: their summits seemed to fade into a coloured tremble as of ascending vapour; their steep sides were streaked with the green of narrow ravines; at their foot lay rice-fields, plantain-patches, yellow sands. A torrent wound about like a dropped thread. Clumps of fruit-trees marked the villages; slim palms put their nodding heads together above the low houses; dried-

palm-leaf roofs shone afar, like roofs of gold, behind the dark colon-
nades of tree-trunks; figures passed vivid and vanishing; the smoke of
fires stood upright above the masses of flowering bushes; bamboo
fences glittered, running away in broken lines between the fields. A
sudden cry on the shore sounded plaintive in the distance, and ceased
abruptly, as if stifled in the downpour of sunshine; a puff of breeze
made a flash of darkness on the smooth water, touched our faces, and
became forgotten. Nothing moved. The sun blazed down into a
shadowless hollow of colours and stillness.

It was the stage where, dressed splendidly for his part, he strutted,
incomparably dignified, made important by the power he had to
awaken an absurd expectation of something heroic going to take
place – a burst of action or song – upon the vibrating tone of a
wonderful sunshine. He was ornate and disturbing, for one could not
imagine what depth of horrible void such an elaborate front could be
worthy to hide. He was not masked – there was too much life in him,
and a mask is only a lifeless thing; but he presented himself essentially
as an actor, as a human being aggressively disguised. His smallest acts
were prepared and unexpected, his speeches grave, his sentences
ominous like hints and complicated like arabesques. He was treated
with a solemn respect accorded in the irreverent West only to the
monarchs of the stage, and he accepted the profound homage with a
sustained dignity seen nowhere else but behind the footlights and in
the condensed falseness of some grossly tragic situation. It was almost
impossible to remember who he was – only a petty chief of a
conveniently isolated corner of Mindanao, where we could in comparative safety break the law against the traffic in firearms and ammunition
with the natives. What would happen should one of the moribund
Spanish gun-boats be suddenly galvanised into a flicker of active life
did not trouble us, once we were inside the bay – so completely did it
appear out of the reach of a meddling world; and besides, in those days
we were imaginative enough to look with a kind of joyous equanimity
on any chance there was of being quietly hanged somewhere out of the
way of diplomatic remonstrance. As to Karain, nothing could happen
to him unless what happens to all – failure and death; but his quality
was to appear clothed in the illusion of unavoidable success. He seemed
too effective, too necessary there, too much of an essential condition
for the existence of his land and his people, to be destroyed by anything
short of an earthquake. He summed up his race, his country, the
elemental force of ardent life, of tropical nature. He had its luxuriant
strength, its fascination; and, like it, he carried the seed of peril within.

In many successive visits we came to know his stage well – the purple semicircle of hills, the slim trees leaning over houses, the yellow sands, the streaming green of ravines. All that had the crude and blended colouring, the appropriateness almost excessive, the suspicious immobility of a painted scene; and it enclosed so perfectly the accomplished acting of his amazing pretences that the rest of the world seemed shut out for ever from the gorgeous spectacle. There could be nothing outside. It was as if the earth had gone on spinning, and had left that crumb of its surface alone in space. He appeared utterly cut off from everything but the sunshine, and that even seemed to be made for him alone. Once when asked what was on the other side of the hills, he said, with a meaning smile, 'Friends and enemies – many enemies; else why should I buy your rifles and powder?' He was always like this – word-perfect in his part, playing up faithfully to the mysteries and certitudes of his surroundings. 'Friends and enemies – ' nothing else. It was impalpable and vast. The earth had indeed rolled away from under his land, and he, with his handful of people, stood surrounded by a silent tumult as of contending shades. Certainly no sound came from outside. 'Friends and enemies!' He might have added, 'and memories', at least as far as he himself was concerned; but he neglected to make that point then. It made itself later on, though; but it was after the daily performance – in the wings, so to speak, and with the lights out. Meantime he filled the stage with barbarous dignity. Some ten years ago he had led his people – a scratch lot of wandering Bugis – to the conquest of the bay, and now in his august care they had forgotten all the past, and had lost all concern for the future. He gave them wisdom, advice, reward, punishment, life or death, with the same serenity of attitude and voice. He understood irrigation and the art of war – the qualities of weapons and the craft of boat-building. He could conceal his heart; had more endurance; he could swim longer, and steer a canoe better than any of his people; he could shoot straighter, and negotiate more tortuously than any man of his race I knew. He was an adventurer of the sea, an outcast, a ruler – and my very good friend. I wish him a quick death in a stand-up fight, a death in sunshine; for he had known remorse and power, and no man can demand more from life. Day after day he appeared before us, incomparably faithful to the illusions of the stage, and at sunset the night descended upon him quickly, like a falling curtain. The seamed hills became black shadows towering high upon a clear sky; above them the glittering confusion of stars resembled a mad turmoil stilled by a gesture; sounds ceased, men slept, forms vanished – and the reality of the universe alone remained – a marvellous thing of darkness and glimmers.

II

But it was at night that he talked openly, forgetting the exactions of his stage. In the daytime there were affairs to be discussed in state. There were at first between him and me his own splendour, my shabby suspicions, and the scenic landscape that intruded upon the reality of our lives by its motionless fantasy of outline and colour. His followers thronged round him; above his head the broad blades of their spears made a spiked halo of iron points, and they hedged him from humanity by the shimmer of silks, the gleam of weapons, the excited and respectful hum of eager voices. Before sunset he would take leave with ceremony, and go off sitting under a red umbrella, and escorted by a score of boats. All the paddles flashed and struck together with a mighty splash that reverberated loudly in the monumental amphitheatre of hills. A broad stream of dazzling foam trailed behind the flotilla. The canoes appeared very black on the white hiss of water; turbaned heads swayed back and forth; a multitude of arms in crimson and yellow rose and fell with one movement; the spearmen upright in the bows of canoes had variegated sarongs and gleaming shoulders like bronze statues; the muttered strophes of the paddlers' song ended periodically in a plaintive shout. They diminished in the distance; the song ceased; they swarmed on the beach in the long shadows of the western hills. The sunlight lingered on the purple crests, and we could see him leading the way to his stockade, a burly bareheaded figure walking far in advance of a straggling *cortège*, and swinging regularly an ebony staff taller than himself. The darkness deepened fast; torches gleamed fitfully, passing behind bushes; a long hail or two trailed in the silence of the evening; and at last the night stretched its smooth veil over the shore, the lights, and the voices.

Then, just as we were thinking of repose, the watchmen of the schooner would hail a splash of paddles away in the starlit gloom of the bay; a voice would respond in cautious tones, and our serang, putting his head down the open skylight, would inform us without surprise, 'That Rajah, he coming. He here now.' Karain appeared noiselessly in the doorway of the little cabin. He was simplicity itself then; all in white; muffled about his head; for arms only a kriss with a plain buffalo-horn handle, which he would politely conceal within a fold of his sarong before stepping over the threshold. The old sword-bearer's face, the worn-out and mournful face so covered with wrinkles that it seemed to look out through the meshes of a fine dark net, could be seen close above his shoulder. Karain never moved without that attendant, who stood or squatted close at his back. He had a dislike of an open space behind him. It was more than a dislike – it resembled fear, a nervous preoccupation of what went on where he could not see. This, in view of the evident and fierce loyalty that surrounded him, was inexplicable. He was there alone in the midst of devoted men; he was safe from neighbourly ambushes, from fraternal ambitions; and yet more than one of our visitors had assured us that their ruler could not bear to be alone. They said, 'Even when he eats and sleeps there is always one on the watch near him who has strength and weapons.' There was indeed always one near him, though our informants had no conception of that watcher's strength and weapons, which were both shadowy and terrible. We knew, but only later on, when we had heard the story. Meantime we noticed that, even during the most important interviews, Karain would often give a start, and interrupting his discourse, would sweep his arm back with a sudden movement, to feel whether the old fellow was there. The old fellow, impenetrable and weary, was always there. He shared his food, his repose, and his thoughts; he knew his plans, guarded his secrets; and, impassive behind his master's agitation, without stirring the least bit, murmured above his head in a soothing tone some words difficult to catch.

It was only on board the schooner, when surrounded by white faces, by unfamiliar sights and sounds, that Karain seemed to forget the strange obsession that wound like a black thread through the gorgeous pomp of his public life. At night we treated him in a free and easy manner, which just stopped short of slapping him on the back, for there are liberties one must not take with a Malay. He said himself that on such occasions he was only a private gentleman coming to see other gentlemen whom he supposed as well born as himself. I fancy that to the last he believed us to be emissaries of Government, darkly official persons furthering by our illegal traffic some dark scheme of high statecraft. Our denials and protestations were unavailing. He only smiled with discreet politeness and enquired about the Queen. Every visit began with that enquiry; he was insatiable of details; he was fascinated by the holder of a sceptre the shadow of which, stretching from the westward over the earth and over the seas, passed far beyond his own hand's-breadth of conquered land. He multiplied questions; he could never know enough of the monarch of whom he spoke with wonder and chivalrous respect – with a kind of affectionate awe! Afterwards, when we had learned that he was the son of a woman who had many years ago ruled a small Bugis state, we came to suspect that the memory of his mother (of whom he spoke with enthusiasm) mingled somehow in his mind with the image he tried to form for himself of the far-off Queen whom he called great, invincible, pious, and fortunate. We had to invent details at last to satisfy his craving curiosity; and our loyalty must be pardoned, for we tried to make them fit for his august and resplendent ideal. We talked. The night slipped over us, over the still schooner, over the sleeping land, and over the sleepless sea that thundered amongst the reefs outside the bay. His paddlers, two trustworthy men, slept in the canoe at the foot of our side-ladder. The old confidant, relieved from duty, dozed on his heels, with his back against the companion-doorway; and Karain sat squarely in the ship's wooden armchair, under the slight sway of the cabin lamp, a cheroot between his dark fingers, and a glass of lemonade before him. He was amused by the fizz of the thing, but after a sip or two would let it get flat, and with a courteous wave of his hand ask for a fresh bottle. He decimated our slender stock; but we did not begrudge it to him, for, when he began, he talked well. He must have been a great Bugis dandy in his time, for even then (and when we knew him he was no longer young) his splendour was spotlessly neat, and he dyed his hair a light shade of brown. The quiet dignity of his bearing transformed the dim-lit cuddy of the schooner into an audience-hall. He talked of inter-island politics with an ironic and melancholy shrewdness. He had travelled much, suffered not a little, intrigued, fought. He knew native courts, European settlements, the forests, the sea, and, as he said himself, had spoken in his time to many great men. He liked to talk with me because I had known some of these men: he seemed to think that I could understand him, and, with a fine confidence, assumed that I, at least, could appreciate how much greater he was himself. But he preferred to talk of his native country – a small Bugis state on the island of Celebes. I had visited it some time before, and he asked eagerly for news. As men's names came up in conversation he would say, 'We swam against one another when we were boys;' or, 'We hunted the deer together – he could use the noose and the spear as well as I.' Now and then his big dreamy eyes would roll restlessly; he frowned or smiled, or he would become pensive, and, staring in silence, would nod slightly for a time at some regretted vision of the past.

His mother had been the ruler of a small semi-independent state on the sea-coast at the head of the Gulf of Boni. He spoke of her with pride. She had been a woman resolute in affairs of state and of her own heart. After the death of her first husband, undismayed by the turbulent opposition of the chiefs, she married a rich trader, a Korinchi man of no family. Karain was her son by that second marriage, but his unfortunate descent had apparently nothing to do with his exile. He said nothing as to its cause, though once he let slip with a sigh, 'Ha! my land will not feel any more the weight of my body.' But he related winningly the story of his wanderings, and told us all about the conquest of the bay. Alluding to the people beyond the hills, he would murmur gently, with a careless wave of the hand, 'They came over the hills once to fight us, but those who got away never came again.' He thought for a while, smiling to himself. 'Very few got away,' he added, with proud serenity. He cherished the recollections of his successes; he had an exulting eagerness for endeavour; when he talked, his aspect was warlike, chivalrous, and uplifting. No wonder his people admired him. We saw him once walking in daylight amongst the houses of the settlement. At the doors of huts groups of women turned to look after him, warbling softly, and with gleaming eyes; armed men stood out of the way, submissive and erect; others approached from the side, bending their backs to address him humbly; an old woman stretched out a draped lean arm – 'Blessings on thy head!' she cried from a dark doorway; a fiery-eyed man showed above the low fence of a plantain-patch a streaming face, a bare breast scarred in two places, and bellowed out pantingly after him, 'God give victory to our master!' Karain walked fast, and with firm long strides; he answered greetings right and left by quick piercing glances. Children ran forward between the houses, peeped fearfully round corners; young boys kept up with him, gliding between bushes: their eyes gleamed through the dark leaves. The old sword-bearer, shouldering the silver scabbard, shuffled hastily at his heels with bowed head, and his eyes on the ground. And in the midst of a great stir they passed swift and absorbed, like two men hurrying through a great solitude.

In his council hall he was surrounded by the gravity of armed chiefs, while two long rows of old headmen dressed in cotton stuffs squatted on their heels, with idle arms hanging over their knees. Under the thatch roof supported by smooth columns, of which each one had cost the life of a straight-stemmed young palm, the scent of flowering hedges drifted in warm waves. The sun was sinking. In the open courtyard suppliants walked through the gate, raising, when yet far off, their joined hands above bowed heads, and bending low in the bright stream of sunlight. Young girls, with flowers in their laps, sat under the wide-spreading boughs of a big tree. The blue smoke of wood fires spread in a thin mist above the high-pitched roofs of houses that had glistening walls of woven reeds, and all round them rough wooden pillars under the sloping eaves. He dispensed justice in the shade; from a high seat he gave orders, advice, reproof. Now and then the hum of approbation rose louder, and idle spearmen that lounged listlessly against the posts, looking at the girls, would turn their heads slowly. To no man had been given the shelter of so much respect, confidence, and awe. Yet at times he would lean forward and appear to listen as for a far-off note of discord as if expecting to hear some faint voice, the sound of light footsteps; or he would start half up in his seat, as though he had been familiarly touched on the shoulder. He glanced back with apprehension; his aged follower whispered inaudibly at his ear; the chiefs turned their eyes away in silence, for the old wizard, the man who could command ghosts and send evil spirits against enemies, was speaking low to their ruler. Around the short stillness of the open place the trees rustled faintly, the soft laughter of girls playing with the flowers rose in clear bursts of joyous sound. At the end of upright spear-shafts the long tufts of dyed horse-hair waved crimson and filmy in the gust of wind; and beyond the blaze of hedges the brook of limpid quick water ran invisible and loud under the drooping grass of the bank, with a great murmur, passionate and gentle.

After sunset, far across the fields and over the bay, clusters of torches could be seen burning under the high roofs of the council shed. Smoky red flames swayed on high poles, and the fiery blaze flickered over faces, clung to the smooth trunks of palm-trees, kindled bright sparks on the rims of metal dishes standing on fine floor-mats. That obscure adventurer feasted like a king. Small groups of men crouched in tight circles round the wooden platters; brown hands hovered over snowy heaps of rice. Sitting upon a rough couch apart from the others, he leaned on his elbow with inclined head; and near him a youth improvised in a high tone a song that celebrated his valour and wisdom. The singer rocked himself to and fro, rolling frenzied eyes; old women hobbled about with dishes, and men, squatting low, lifted their heads to listen gravely without ceasing to eat. The song of triumph vibrated in the night, and the stanzas rolled out mournfully and fiery like the thoughts of a hermit. He silenced it with a sign, 'Enough!' An owl hooted far away, exulting in the delight of deep gloom in dense foliage; overhead lizards ran in the attap thatch, calling softly; the dry leaves of the roof rustled; the rumour of mingled voices grew louder suddenly. After a circular and startled glance, as of a man waking up abruptly to the sense of danger, he would throw himself back, and under the downward gaze of the old sorcerer take up, wide-eyed, the slender thread of his dream. They watched his moods; the swelling rumour of animated talk subsided like a wave on a sloping beach. The chief is pensive. And above the spreading whisper of lowered voices only a light rattle of weapons would be heard, a single louder word distinct and alone, or the grave ring of a big brass tray.

III

For two years at short intervals we visited him. We came to like him, to trust him, almost to admire him. He was plotting and preparing a war with patience, with foresight – with a fidelity to his purpose and with a steadfastness of which I would have thought him racially incapable. He seemed fearless of the future, and in his plans displayed a sagacity that was only limited by his profound ignorance of the rest of the world. We tried to enlighten him, but our attempts to make clear the irresistible nature of the forces which he desired to arrest failed to discourage his eagerness to strike a blow for his own primitive ideas. He did not understand us, and replied by arguments that almost drove one to desperation by their childish shrewdness. He was absurd and unanswerable. Sometimes we caught glimpses of a sombre, glowing fury within him – a brooding and vague sense of wrong, and a concentrated lust of violence which is dangerous in a native. He raved like one inspired. On one occasion, after we had been talking to him late in his campong, he jumped up. A great, clear fire blazed in the grove; lights and shadows danced together between the trees; in the still night bats flitted in and out of the boughs like fluttering flakes of denser darkness. He snatched the sword from the old man, whizzed it out of the scabbard, and thrust the point into the earth. Upon the thin, upright blade the silver hilt, released, swayed before him like something alive. He stepped back a pace, and in a deadened tone spoke fiercely to the vibrating steel: 'If there is virtue in the fire, in the iron, in the hand that forged thee, in the words spoken over thee, in the desire of my heart, and in the wisdom of thy makers – then we shall be victorious together!' He drew it out, looked along the edge. 'Take,' he said over his shoulder to the old sword-bearer. The other, unmoved on his hams, wiped the point with a corner of his sarong, and returning the weapon to its scabbard, sat nursing it on his knees without a single look upwards. Karain, suddenly very calm, reseated himself with dignity. We gave up remonstrating after this, and let him go his way to an honourable disaster. All we could do for him was to see to it that the powder was good for the money and the rifles serviceable, if old.

But the game was becoming at last too dangerous; and if we, who had faced it pretty often, thought little of the danger, it was decided for us by some very respectable people sitting safely in counting-houses that the risks were too great, and that only one more trip could be made. After giving in the usual way many misleading hints as to our destination, we slipped away quietly, and after a very quick passage entered the bay. It was early morning, and even before the anchor went to the bottom the schooner was surrounded by boats.

The first thing we heard was that Karain's mysterious sword-bearer had died a few days ago. We did not attach much importance to the news. It was certainly difficult to imagine Karain without his inseparable follower; but the fellow was old, he had never spoken to one of us, we hardly ever had heard the sound of his voice; and we had come to look upon him as something inanimate, as part of our friend's trappings of state – like that sword he had carried, or the fringed red umbrella displayed during an official progress. Karain did not visit us in the afternoon as usual. A message of greeting and a present of fruit and vegetables came off for us before sunset. Our friend paid us like a banker, but treated us like a prince. We sat up for him till midnight. Under the stern awning bearded Jackson jingled an old guitar and sang, with an execrable accent, Spanish love-songs; while young Hollis and I, sprawling on the deck, had a game of chess by the light of a cargo lantern. Karain did not appear. Next day we were busy unloading, and heard that the Rajah was unwell. The expected invitation to visit him ashore did not come. We sent friendly messages, but, fearing to intrude upon some secret council, remained on board. Early on the third day we had landed all the powder and rifles, and also a six-pounder brass gun with its carriage, which we had subscribed together for a present to our friend. The afternoon was sultry. Ragged edges of black clouds peeped over the hills, and invisible thunderstorms circled outside, growling like wild beasts. We got the schooner ready for sea, intending to leave next morning at daylight. All day a merciless sun blazed down into the bay, fierce and pale, as if at white heat. Nothing moved on the land. The beach was empty, the villages seemed deserted; the trees far off stood in unstirring clumps, as if painted; the white smoke of some invisible bush-fire spread itself low over the shores of the bay like a settling fog. Late in the day three of Karain's chief men, dressed in their best and armed to the teeth, came off in a canoe, bringing a case of dollars. They were gloomy and languid, and told us they had not seen their Rajah for five days. No one had seen him! We settled all accounts, and after shaking hands in turn and in profound silence, they descended one after another into their boat, and were paddled to the shore, sitting close together, clad in vivid colours, with hanging heads: the gold embroideries of their jackets flashed dazzlingly as they went away gliding on the smooth water, and not one of them looked back once. Before sunset the growling clouds carried with a rush the ridge of hills, and came tumbling down the inner slopes. Everything disappeared;

black whirling vapours filled the bay, and in the midst of them the schooner swung here and there in the shifting gusts of wind. A single clap of thunder detonated in the hollow with a violence that seemed capable of bursting into small pieces the ring of high land, and a warm deluge descended. The wind died out. We panted in the close cabin; our faces streamed; the bay outside hissed as if boiling; the water fell in perpendicular shafts as heavy as lead; it swished about the deck, poured off the spars, gurgled, sobbed, splashed, murmured in the blind night. Our lamp burned low. Hollis, stripped to the waist, lay stretched out on the lockers, with closed eyes and motionless like a despoiled corpse; at his head Jackson twanged the guitar, and gasped out in sighs a mournful dirge about hopeless love and eyes like stars. Then we heard startled voices on deck crying in the rain, hurried footsteps overhead, and suddenly Karain appeared in the doorway of the cabin. His bare breast and his face glistened in the light; his sarong, soaked, clung about his legs; he had his sheathed kriss in his left hand; and wisps of wet hair, escaping from under his red kerchief, stuck over his eyes and down his cheeks. He stepped in with a headlong stride and looking over his shoulder like a man pursued. Hollis turned on his side quickly and opened his eyes. Jackson clapped his big hand over the strings and the jingling vibration died suddenly. I stood up.

'We did not hear your boat's hail!' I exclaimed.

'Boat! The man's swum off,' drawled out Hollis from the locker. 'Look at him!'

He breathed heavily, wild-eyed, while we looked at him in silence. Water dripped from him, made a dark pool, and ran crookedly across the cabin floor. We could hear Jackson, who had gone out to drive away our Malay seamen from the doorway of the companion; he swore menacingly in the patter of a heavy shower, and there was a great commotion on deck. The watchmen, scared out of their wits by the glimpse of a shadowy figure leaping over the rail, straight out of the night as it were, had alarmed all hands.

Then Jackson, with glittering drops of water on his hair and beard, came back looking angry, and Hollis, who, being the youngest of us, assumed an indolent superiority, said without stirring, 'Give him a dry sarong – give him mine; it's hanging up in the bathroom.' Karain laid the kriss on the table, hilt inwards, and murmured a few words in a strangled voice.

'What's that?' asked Hollis, who had not heard.

'He apologises for coming in with a weapon in his hands,' I said, dazedly.

'Ceremonious beggar. Tell him we forgive a friend . . . on such a night,' drawled out Hollis. 'What's wrong?'

Karain slipped the dry sarong over his head, dropped the wet one at his feet, and stepped out of it. I pointed to the wooden armchair – his armchair. He sat down very straight, said 'Ha!' in a strong voice; a short shiver shook his broad frame. He looked over his shoulder uneasily, turned as if to speak to us, but only stared in a curious blind manner, and again looked back. Jackson bellowed out, 'Watch well on deck there!' heard a faint answer from above, and reaching out with his foot slammed-to the cabin door.

'All right now,' he said.

Karain's lips moved slightly. A vivid flash of lightning made the two round sternports facing him glimmer like a pair of cruel and phosphorescent eyes. The flame of the lamp seemed to wither into brown dust for an instant, and the looking-glass over the little sideboard leaped out behind his back in a smooth sheet of livid light. The roll of thunder came near, crashed over us; the schooner trembled, and the great voice went on, threatening terribly, into the distance. For less than a minute a furious shower rattled on the decks. Karain looked slowly from face to face, and then the silence became so profound that we all could hear distinctly the two chronometers in my cabin ticking along with unflagging speed against one another.

And we three, strangely moved, could not take our eyes from him. He had become enigmatical and touching, in virtue of that mysterious cause that had driven him through the night and through the thunder-storm to the shelter of the schooner's cuddy. Not one of us doubted that we were looking at a fugitive, incredible as it appeared to us. He was haggard, as though he had not slept for weeks; he had become lean, as though he had not eaten for days. His cheeks were hollow, his eyes sunk, the muscles of his chest and arms twitched slightly as if after an exhausting contest. Of course, it had been a long swim off to the schooner; but his face showed another kind of fatigue, the tormented weariness, the anger and the fear of a struggle against a thought, an idea – against something that cannot be grappled, that never rests – a shadow, a nothing, unconquerable and immortal, that preys upon life. We knew it as though he had shouted it at us. His chest expanded time after time, as if it could not contain the beating of his heart. For a moment he had the power of the possessed – the power to awaken in the beholders wonder, pain, pity, and a fearful near sense of things invisible, of things dark and mute, that surround the loneliness of mankind. His eyes roamed about aimlessly for a moment, then became still. He said with effort –

'I came here . . . I leaped out of my stockade as after a defeat. I ran in the night. The water was black. I left him calling on the edge of black water . . . I left him standing alone on the beach. I swam . . . he called out after me . . . I swam . . . '

He trembled from head to foot, sitting very upright and gazing straight before him. Left whom? Who called? We did not know. We could not understand. I said at all hazards –

'Be firm.'

The sound of my voice seemed to steady him into a sudden rigidity, but otherwise he took no notice. He seemed to listen, to expect something for a moment, then went on –

'He cannot come here – therefore I sought you. You men with white faces who despise the invisible voices. He cannot abide your unbelief and your strength.'

He was silent for a while, then exclaimed softly –

'Oh! the strength of unbelievers!'

'There's no one here but you – and we three,' said Hollis, quietly. He reclined with his head supported on his elbow and did not budge.

'I know,' said Karain. 'He has never followed me here. Was not the wise man ever by my side? But since the old wise man, who knew of my trouble, has died, I have heard the voice every night. I shut myself up – for many days – in the dark. I can hear the sorrowful murmurs of women, the whisper of the wind, of the running waters; the clash of weapons in the hands of faithful men, their footsteps – and his voice! . . . Near . . . So! In my ear! I felt him near . . . His breath passed over my neck. I leaped out without a cry. All about me men slept quietly. I ran to the sea. He ran by my side without footsteps, whispering, whispering old words – whispering into my ear in his old voice. I ran into the sea; I swam off to you, with my kriss between my teeth. I, armed, I fled before a breath – to you. Take me away to your land. The wise old man has died, and with him is gone the power of his words and charms. And I can tell no one. No one. There is no one here faithful enough and wise enough to know. It is only near you, unbelievers, that my trouble fades like a mist under the eye of day.'

He turned to me.

'With you I go!' he cried in a contained voice. 'With you, who know so many of us. I want to leave this land – my people . . . and him – there!'

He pointed a shaking finger at random over his shoulder. It was hard for us to bear the intensity of that undisclosed distress. Hollis stared at him hard. I asked gently –

'Where is the danger?'

'Everywhere outside this place,' he answered, mournfully. 'In every place where I am. He waits for me on the paths, under the trees, in the place where I sleep – everywhere but here.'

He looked round the little cabin, at the painted beams, at the tarnished varnish of bulkheads; he looked round as if appealing to all its shabby strangeness, to the disorderly jumble of unfamiliar things that belong to an inconceivable life of stress, of power, of endeavour, of unbelief – to the strong life of white men, which rolls on irresistible and hard on the edge of outer darkness. He stretched out his arms as if to embrace it and us. We waited. The wind and rain had ceased, and the stillness of the night round the schooner was as dumb and complete as if a dead world had been laid to rest in a grave of clouds. We expected him to speak. The necessity within him tore at his lips. There are those who say that a native will not speak to a white man. Error. No man will speak to his master; but to a wanderer and a friend, to him who does not come to teach or to rule, to him who asks for nothing and accepts all things, words are spoken by the camp-fires, in the shared solitude of the sea, in riverside villages, in resting-places surrounded by forests – words are spoken that take no account of race or colour. One heart speaks – another one listens; and the earth, the sea, the sky, the passing wind and the stirring leaf, hear also the futile tale of the burden of life.

He spoke at last. It is impossible to convey the effect of his story. It is undying, it is but a memory, and its vividness cannot be made clear to another mind any more than the vivid emotions of a dream. One must have seen his infinite splendour, one must have known him before – looked at him then. The wavering gloom of the little cabin; the breathless stillness outside, through which only the lapping of water against the schooner's sides could be heard; Hollis's pale face, with steady dark eyes; the energetic head of Jackson held up between two big palms, and with the long yellow hair of his beard flowing over the strings of the guitar lying on the table; Karain's upright and motionless pose, his tone – all this made an impression that cannot be forgotten. He faced us across the table. His dark head and bronze torso appeared above the tarnished slab of wood, gleaming and still as if cast in metal. Only his lips moved, and his eyes glowed, went out, blazed again, or stared mournfully. His expressions came straight from his tormented heart. His words sounded low, in a sad murmur as of running water; at times they rang loud like the clash of a war-gong – or trailed slowly like weary travellers – or rushed forward with the speed of fear.

IV

This is, imperfectly, what he said –

'It was after the great trouble that broke the alliance of the four states of Wajo. We fought amongst ourselves, and the Dutch watched from afar till we were weary. Then the smoke of their fire-ships was seen at the mouth of our rivers, and their great men came in boats full of soldiers to talk to us of protection and peace. We answered with caution and wisdom, for our villages were burnt, our stockades weak, the people weary, and the weapons blunt. They came and went; there had been much talk, but after they went away everything seemed to be as before, only their ships remained in sight from our coast, and very soon their traders came amongst us under a promise of safety. My brother was a Ruler, and one of those who had given the promise. I was young then, and had fought in the war, and Pata Matara had fought by my side. We had shared hunger, danger, fatigue, and victory. His eyes saw my danger quickly, and twice my arm had preserved his life. It was his destiny. He was my friend. And he was great amongst us – one of those who were near my brother, the ruler. He spoke in council, his courage was great, he was the chief of many villages round the great lake that is in the middle of our country as the heart is in the middle of a man's body. When his sword was carried into a campong in advance of his coming, the maidens whispered wonderingly under the fruit-trees, the rich men consulted together in the shade, and a feast was made ready with rejoicing and songs. He had the favour of the Ruler and the affection of the poor. He loved war, deer hunts, and the charms of women. He was the possessor of jewels, of lucky weapons, and of men's devotion. He was a fierce man; and I had no other friend.

'I was the chief of a stockade at the mouth of the river, and collected tolls for my brother from the passing boats. One day I saw a Dutch trader go up the river. He went up with three boats, and no toll was demanded from him, because the smoke of Dutch warships stood out from the open sea, and we were too weak to forget treaties. He went up under the promise of safety, and my brother gave him protection. He said he came to trade. He listened to our voices, for we are men who speak openly and without fear; he counted the number of our spears, he examined the trees, the running waters, the grasses of the bank, the slopes of our hills. He went up to Matara's country and obtained permission to build a house. He traded and planted. He despised our joys, our thoughts, and our sorrows. His face was red, his hair like flame, and his eyes pale, like a river mist; he moved heavily, and spoke with a deep voice; he laughed aloud like a fool, and knew no courtesy in his speech. He was a big, scornful man, who looked into women's faces and put his hand on the shoulders of free men as though he had been a noble-born chief. We bore with him. Time passed.

'Then Pata Matara's sister fled from the campong and went to live in the Dutchman's house. She was a great and wilful lady: I had seen her once carried high on slaves' shoulders amongst the people, with uncovered face, and I had heard all men say that her beauty was extreme, silencing the reason and ravishing the heart of the beholders. The people were dismayed; Matara's face was blackened with that disgrace, for she knew she had been promised to another man. Matara went to the Dutchman's house, and said, "Give her up to die – she is the daughter of chiefs." The white man refused, and shut himself up, while his servants kept guard night and day with loaded guns. Matara raged. My brother called a council. But the Dutch ships were near, and watched our coast greedily. My brother said, "If he dies now our land will pay for his blood. Leave him alone till we grow stronger and the ships are gone." Matara was wise; he waited and watched. But the white man feared for her life and went away.

'He left his house, his plantations, and his goods! He departed, armed and menacing, and left all – for her! She had ravished his heart! From my stockade I saw him put out to sea in a big boat. Matara and I watched him from the fighting platform behind the pointed stakes. He sat cross-legged, with his gun in his hands, on the roof at the stern of his prau. The barrel of his rifle glinted aslant before his big, red face. The broad river was stretched under him – level, smooth, shining, like a plain of silver; and his prau, looking very short and black from the shore, glided along the silver plain and over into the blue of the sea.

'Thrice Matara, standing by my side, called aloud her name with grief and imprecations. He stirred my heart. It leaped three times; and three times with the eye of my mind I saw in the gloom within the enclosed space of the prau a woman with streaming hair going away from her land and her people. I was angry – and sorry. Why? And then I also cried out insults and threats. Matara said, "Now they have left our land their lives are mine. I shall follow and strike – and, alone, pay the price of blood." A great wind was sweeping towards the setting sun over the empty river. I cried, "By your side I will go!" He lowered his head in sign of assent. It was his destiny. The sun had set, and the trees swayed their boughs with a great noise above our heads.

'On the third night we two left our land together in a trading prau.

'The sea met us – the sea, wide, pathless, and without voice. A sailing prau leaves no track. We went south. The moon was full; and, looking up, we said to one another, "When the next moon shines as this one, we shall return and they will be dead." It was fifteen years ago. Many moons have grown full and withered, and I have not seen my land since. We sailed south; we overtook many praus; we examined the creeks and the bays; we saw the end of our coast, of our island – a steep cape over a disturbed strait, where drift the shadows of shipwrecked praus and drowned men clamour in the night. The wide sea was all round us now. We saw a great mountain burning in the midst of water; we saw thousands of islets scattered like bits of iron fired from a big gun; we saw a long coast of mountain and lowlands stretching away in sunshine from west to east. It was Java. We said, "They are there; their time is near, and we shall return or die cleansed from dishonour."

'We landed. Is there anything good in that country? The paths run straight and hard and dusty. Stone campongs, full of white faces, are surrounded by fertile fields, but every man you meet is a slave. The rulers live under the edge of a foreign sword. We ascended mountains, we traversed valleys; at sunset we entered villages. We asked everyone, 'Have you seen such a white man?' Some stared; others laughed; women gave us food, sometimes, with fear and respect, as though we had been distracted by the visitation of God; but some did not understand our language, and some cursed us, or, yawning, asked with contempt the reason of our quest. Once, as we were going away, an old man called after us, "Desist!"

'We went on. Concealing our weapons, we stood humbly aside before the horsemen on the road; we bowed low in the courtyards of chiefs who were no better than slaves. We lost ourselves in the fields, in the jungle; and one night, in a tangled forest, we came upon a place where crumbling old walls had fallen amongst the trees, and where strange stone idols – carved images of devils with many arms and legs, with snakes twined round their bodies, with twenty heads and holding a hundred swords – seemed to live and threaten in the light of our camp-fire. Nothing dismayed us. And on the road, by every fire, in resting-places, we always talked of her and of him. Their time was near. We spoke of nothing else. No! not of hunger, thirst, weariness, and faltering hearts. No! we spoke of him and her! Of her! And we thought of them – of her! Matara brooded by the fire. I sat and thought and thought, till suddenly I could see again the image of a woman, beautiful, and young, and great, and proud, and tender, going away from her land and her people. Matara said, "When we find them we shall kill her first to cleanse the dishonour – then the man must die." I would say, "It shall be so; it is your vengeance." He stared long at me with his big sunken eyes.

'We came back to the coast. Our feet were bleeding, our bodies thin. We slept in rags under the shadow of stone enclosures; we prowled, soiled and lean, about the gateways of white men's courtyards. Their hairy dogs barked at us, and their servants shouted from afar, "Begone!" Low-born wretches, that keep watch over the streets of stone campongs, asked us who we were. We lied, we cringed, we smiled with hate in our hearts, and we kept looking here, looking there, for them – for the white man with hair like flame, and for her, for the woman who had broken faith, and therefore must die. We looked. At last in every woman's face I thought I could see hers. We ran swiftly. No! Sometimes Matara would whisper, "Here is the man," and we waited, crouching. He came near. It was not the man – those Dutchmen are all alike. We suffered the anguish of deception. In my sleep I saw her face, and was both joyful and sorry . . . Why? . . . I seemed to hear a whisper near me. I turned swiftly. She was not there! And as we trudged wearily from stone city to stone city I seemed to hear a light footstep near me. A time came when I heard it always, and I was glad. I thought, walking dizzy and weary in sunshine on the hard paths of white men – I thought, She is there – with us! . . . Matara was sombre. We were often hungry.

'We sold the carved sheaths of our krisses – the ivory sheaths with golden ferules. We sold the jewelled hilts. But we kept the blades – for them. The blades that never touch but kill – we kept the blades for her . . . Why? She was always by our side . . . We starved. We begged. We left Java at last.

'We went West, we went East. We saw many lances, crowds of strange faces, men that live in trees and men who eat their old people. We cut rattans in the forest for a handful of rice, and for a living swept the decks of big ships and heard curses heaped upon our heads. We toiled in villages; we wandered upon the seas with the Bajow people, who have no country. We fought for pay; we hired ourselves to work for Goram men, and were cheated; and under the orders of rough white-faces we dived for pearls in barren bays, dotted with black rocks, upon a coast of sand and desolation. And everywhere we watched, we listened, we asked. We asked traders, robbers, white men. We heard jeers, mockery, threats – words of wonder and words of contempt. We never knew rest; we never thought of home, for our work was not done. A year passed, then another. I ceased to count the number of nights, of moons, of years. I watched over Matara. He had my last handful of rice; if there was water enough for one he drank it; I covered him up when he shivered with cold; and when the hot sickness came upon him I sat sleepless through many nights and fanned his face. He was a fierce man, and my friend. He spoke of her with fury in the daytime, with sorrow in the dark; he remembered her in health, in sickness. I said nothing; but I saw her every day always! At first I saw only her head, as of a woman walking in the low mist on a river bank. Then she sat by our fire. I saw her! I looked at her! She had tender eyes and a ravishing face. I murmured to her in the night. Matara said sleepily sometimes, "To whom are you talking? Who is there?" I answered quickly, "No one" . . . It was a lie! She never left me. She shared the warmth of our fire, she sat on my couch of leaves, she swam on the sea to follow me . . . I saw her! . . . I tell you I saw her long black hair spread behind her upon the moonlit water as she struck out with bare arms by the side of a swift prau. She was beautiful, she was faithful, and in the silence of foreign countries she spoke to me very low in the language of my people. No one saw her; no one heard her; she was mine only! In daylight she moved with a swaying walk before me upon the weary paths; her figure was straight and flexible like the stem of a slender tree; the heels of her feet were round and polished like shells of eggs; with her round arm she made signs. At night she looked into my face. And she was sad! Her eyes were tender and frightened; her voice soft and pleading. Once I murmured to her, "You shall not die," and she smiled . . . ever after she smiled! . . . She gave me courage to bear weariness and hardships. Those were times of pain, and she soothed me. We wandered patient in our search. We knew deception, false hopes; we knew captivity, sickness, thirst, misery, despair . . . Enough! We found them! . . . '

He cried out the last words and paused. His face was impassive, and he kept still like a man in a trance. Hollis sat up quickly, and spread his elbows on the table. Jackson made a brusque movement, and accidentally touched the guitar. A plaintive resonance filled the cabin with confused vibrations and died out slowly. Then Karain began to speak again. The restrained fierceness of his tone seemed to rise like a voice from outside, like a thing unspoken but heard; it filled the cabin and enveloped in its intense and deadened murmur the motionless figure in the chair.

'We were on our way to Atjeh, where there was war; but the vessel ran on a sandbank, and we had to land in Delli. We had earned a little money, and had bought a gun from some Selangore traders; only one gun, which was fired by the spark of a stone: Matara carried it. We landed. Many white men lived there, planting tobacco on conquered plains, and Matara . . . But no matter. He saw him! . . . The Dutchman! . . . At last! . . . We crept and watched. Two nights and a day we watched. He had a house – a big house in a clearing in the midst of his fields; flowers and bushes grew around; there were narrow paths of yellow earth between the cut grass, and thick hedges to keep people out. The third night we came armed, and lay behind a hedge.

'A heavy dew seemed to soak through our flesh and made our very entrails cold. The grass, the twigs, the leaves, covered with drops of water, were grey in the moonlight. Matara, curled up in the grass, shivered in his sleep. My teeth rattled in my head so loud that I was afraid the noise would wake up all the land. Afar, the watchmen of white men's houses struck wooden clappers and hooted in the darkness. And, as every night, I saw her by my side. She smiled no more! . . . The fire of anguish burned in my breast, and she whispered to me with compassion, with pity, softly – as women will; she soothed the pain of my mind; she bent her face over me – the face of a woman who ravishes the hearts and silences the reason of men. She was all mine, and no one could see her – no one of living mankind! Stars shone through her bosom, through her floating hair. I was overcome with regret, with tenderness, with sorrow. Matara slept . . . Had I slept? Matara was shaking me by the shoulder, and the fire of the sun was drying the grass, the bushes, the leaves. It was day. Shreds of white mist hung between the branches of trees.

'Was it night or day? I saw nothing again till I heard Matara breathe quickly where he lay, and then outside the house I saw her. I saw them both. They had come out. She sat on a bench under the wall, and twigs laden with flowers crept high above her head, hung over her hair. She had a box on her lap, and gazed into it, counting the increase of her pearls. The Dutchman stood by looking on; he smiled down at her; his white teeth flashed; the hair on his lip was like two twisted flames. He was big and fat, and joyous, and without fear. Matara tipped fresh priming from the hollow of his palm, scraped the flint with his thumbnail, and gave the gun to me. To me! I took it . . . O fate!

'He whispered into my ear, lying on his stomach, "I shall creep close and then amok . . . let her die by my hand. You take aim at the fat swine there. Let him see me strike my shame off the face of the earth – and then . . . you are my friend – kill with a sure shot." I said nothing; there was no air in my chest – there was no air in the world. Matara had gone suddenly from my side. The grass nodded. Then a bush rustled. She lifted her head.

'I saw her! The consoler of sleepless nights, of weary days; the companion of troubled years! I saw her! She looked straight at the place where I crouched. She was there as I had seen her for years – a faithful wanderer by my side. She looked with sad eyes and had smiling lips; she looked at me . . . Smiling lips! Had I not promised that she should not die!

'She was far off and I felt her near. Her touch caressed me, and her voice murmured, whispered above me, around me, "Who shall be thy companion, who shall console thee if I die?" I saw a flowering thicket to the left of her stir a little . . . Matara was ready . . . I cried aloud – "Return!"

'She leaped up; the box fell; the pearls streamed at her feet. The big Dutchman by her side rolled menacing eyes through the still sunshine. The gun went up to my shoulder. I was kneeling and I was firm – firmer than the trees, the rocks, the mountains. But in front of the steady long barrel the fields, the house, the earth, the sky swayed to and fro like shadows in a forest on a windy day. Matara burst out of the thicket; before him the petals of torn flowers whirled high as if driven by a tempest. I heard her cry; I saw her spring with open arms in front of the white man. She was a woman of my country and of noble blood. They are so! I heard her shriek of anguish and fear – and all stood still! The fields, the house, the earth, the sky stood still – while Matara leaped at her with uplifted arm. I pulled the trigger, saw a spark, heard nothing; the smoke drove back into my face, and then I could see Matara roll over head first and lie with stretched arms at her feet. Ha! A sure shot! The sunshine fell on my back colder than the running water. A sure shot! I flung the gun after the shot. Those two stood over the dead man as though they had been bewitched by a charm. I shouted at her, "Live and remember!" Then for a time I stumbled about in a cold darkness.

'Behind me there were great shouts, the running of many feet; strange men surrounded me, cried meaningless words into my face, pushed me, dragged me, supported me . . . I stood before the big Dutchman: he stared as if bereft of his reason. He wanted to know, he talked fast, he spoke of gratitude, he offered me food, shelter, gold – he asked many questions. I laughed in his face. I said, "I am a Korinchi traveller from Perak over there, and know nothing of that dead man. I was passing along the path when I heard a shot, and your senseless people rushed out and dragged me here." He lifted his arms, he wondered, he could not believe, he could not understand, he clamoured in his own tongue! She had her arms clasped round his neck, and over her shoulder stared back at me with wide eyes. I smiled and looked at her; I smiled and waited to hear the sound of her voice. The white man asked her suddenly, "Do you know him?" I listened – my life was in my ears! She looked at me long, she looked at me with unflinching eyes, and said aloud, "No! I never saw him before." . . .

What! Never before? Had she forgotten already? Was it possible? Forgotten already – after so many years – so many years of wandering, of companionship, of trouble, of tender words! Forgotten already! . . . I tore myself out from the hands that held me and went away without a word . . . They let me go.

'I was weary. Did I sleep? I do not know. I remember walking upon a broad path under a clear starlight; and that strange country seemed so big, the rice-fields so vast, that, as I looked around, my head swam with the fear of space. Then I saw a forest. The joyous starlight was heavy upon me. I turned off the path and entered the forest, which was very sombre and very sad.'

V

Karain's tone had been getting lower and lower, as though he had been going away from us, till the last words sounded faint but clear, as if shouted on a calm day from a very great distance. He moved not. He stared fixedly past the motionless head of Hollis, who faced him, as still as himself. Jackson had turned sideways, and with elbow on the table shaded his eyes with the palm of his hand. And I looked on, surprised and moved; I looked at that man, loyal to a vision, betrayed by his dream, spurned by his illusion, and coming to us unbelievers for help – against a thought. The silence was profound; but it seemed full of noiseless phantoms, of things sorrowful, shadowy, and mute, in whose invisible presence the firm, pulsating beat of the two ship's chronometers ticking off steadily the seconds of Greenwich Time seemed to me a protection and a relief. Karain stared stonily; and looking at his rigid figure, I thought of his wanderings, of that obscure odyssey of revenge, of all the men that wander amongst illusions; of the illusions as restless as men; of the illusions faithful, faithless; of the illusions that give joy, that give sorrow, that give pain, that give peace; of the invincible illusions that can make life and death appear serene, inspiring, tormented, or ignoble.

A murmur was heard; that voice from outside seemed to flow out of a dreaming world into the lamplight of the cabin. Karain was speaking.

'I lived in the forest.

'She came no more. Never! Never once! I lived alone. She had forgotten. It was well. I did not want her; I wanted no one. I found an abandoned house in an old clearing. Nobody came near. Sometimes I heard in the distance the voices of people going along a path. I slept; I rested; there was wild rice, water from a running stream and peace!

Every night I sat alone by my small fire before the hut. Many nights passed over my head.

'Then, one evening, as I sat by my fire after having eaten, I looked down on the ground and began to remember my wanderings. I lifted my head. I had heard no sound, no rustle, no footsteps – but I lifted my head. A man was coming towards me across the small clearing. I waited. He came up without a greeting and squatted down into the firelight. Then he turned his face to me. It was Matara. He stared at me fiercely with his big sunken eyes. The night was cold; the heat died suddenly out of the fire, and he stared at me. I rose and went away from there, leaving him by the fire that had no heat.

'I walked all that night, all next day, and in the evening made up a big blaze and sat down to wait for him. He did not come into the light. I heard him in the bushes here and there, whispering, whispering. I understood at last – I had heard the words before, "You are my friend – kill with a sure shot."

'I bore it as long as I could then leaped away, as on this very night I leaped from my stockade and swam to you. I ran – I ran crying like a child left alone and far from the houses. He ran by my side, without footsteps, whispering, whispering – invisible and heard. I sought people – I wanted men around me! Men who had not died! And again we two wandered. I sought danger, violence and death. I fought in the Atjeh war, and a brave people wondered at the valiance of a stranger. But we were two; he warded off the blows . . . Why? I wanted peace, not life. And no one could see him; no one knew – I dared tell no one. At times he would leave me, but not for long; then he would return and whisper or stare. My heart was torn with a strange fear, but could not die. Then I met an old man.

'You all knew him. People here called him my sorcerer, my servant and sword-bearer; but to me he was father, mother, protection, refuge, and peace. When I met him he was returning from a pilgrimage, and I heard him intoning the prayer of sunset. He had gone to the holy place with his son, his son's wife, and a little child; and on their return, by the favour of the Most High, they all died: the strong man, the young mother, the little child – they died; and the old man reached his country alone. He was a pilgrim serene and pious, very wise and very lonely. I told him all. For a time we lived together. He said over me words of compassion, of wisdom, of prayer. He warded from me the shade of the dead. I begged him for a charm that would make me safe. For a long time he refused; but at last, with a sigh and a smile, he gave me one. Doubtless he could command a spirit stronger than the unrest of my dead friend, and again I had peace; but I had become restless, and a lover of turmoil and danger. The old man never left me. We travelled together. We were welcomed by the great; his wisdom and my courage are remembered where your strength, O white men, is forgotten! We served the Sultan of Sula. We fought the Spaniards. There were victories, hopes, defeats, sorrow, blood, women's tears . . . What for? . . . We fled. We collected wanderers of a warlike race and came here to fight again. The rest you know. I am the ruler of a conquered land, a lover of war and danger, a fighter and a plotter. But the old man has died, and I am again the slave of the dead. He is not here now to drive away the reproachful shade – to silence the lifeless voice! The power of his charm has died with him. And I know fear; and I hear the whisper, "Kill! kill! kill!" . . . Have I not killed enough? . . . '

For the first time that night a sudden convulsion of madness and rage passed over his face. His wavering glances darted here and there like scared birds in a thunderstorm. He jumped up, shouting –

'By the spirits that drink blood: by the spirits that cry in the night: by all the spirits of fury, misfortune, and death, I swear some day I will strike into every heart I meet – I . . . '

He looked so dangerous that we all three leaped to our feet, and Hollis, with the back of his hand, sent the kriss flying off the table. I believe we shouted together. It was a short scare, and the next moment he was again composed in his chair, with three white men standing over him in rather foolish attitudes. We felt a little ashamed of ourselves. Jackson picked up the kriss, and, after an enquiring glance at me, gave it to him. He received it with a stately inclination of the head and stuck it in the twist of his sarong, with punctilious care to give his weapon a pacific position. Then he looked up at us with an austere smile. We were abashed and reproved. Hollis sat sideways on the table and, holding his chin in his hand, scrutinised him in pensive silence. I said –

'You must abide with your people. They need you. And there is forgetfulness in life. Even the dead cease to speak in time.'

'Am I a woman, to forget long years before an eyelid has had the time to beat twice?' he exclaimed, with bitter resentment. He startled me. It was amazing. To him his life – that cruel mirage of love and peace – seemed as real, as undeniable, as theirs would be to any saint, philosopher, or fool of us all. Hollis muttered –

'You won't soothe him with your platitudes.'

Karain spoke to me.

'You know us. You have lived with us. Why? – we cannot know; but you understand our sorrows and thoughts. You have lived with my people, and you understand our desires and our fears. With you I will go. To your land – to your people. To your people, who live in unbelief; to whom day is day and night is night – nothing more, because you understand all things seen, and despise all else! To your land of unbelief, where the dead do not speak, where every man is wise, and alone – and at peace!'

'Capital description,' murmured Hollis, with the flicker of a smile.

Karain hung his head.

'I can toil, and fight – and be faithful,' he whispered, in a weary tone, 'but I cannot go back to him who waits for me on the shore. No! Take me with you . . . Or else give me some of your strength – of your unbelief . . . A charm! . . . '

He seemed utterly exhausted.

'Yes, take him home,' said Hollis, very low, as if debating with himself. 'That would be one way. The ghosts there are in society, and talk affably to ladies and gentlemen, but would scorn a naked human being – like our princely friend . . . Naked . . . Flayed! I should say. I am sorry for him. Impossible – of course. The end of all this shall be,' he went on, looking up at us – 'the end of this shall be, that some day he will run amok amongst his faithful subjects and send *ad patres* ever so many of them before they make up their minds to the disloyalty of knocking him on the head.'

I nodded. I thought it more than probable that such would be the end of Karain. It was evident that he had been hunted by his thought along the very limit of human endurance, and very little more pressing was needed to make him swerve over into the form of madness peculiar to his race. The respite he had had during the old man's life made the return of the torment unbearable. That much was clear.

He lifted his head suddenly; we had imagined for a moment that he had been dozing.

'Give me your protection – or your strength!' he cried. 'A charm . . . a weapon!'

Again his chin fell on his breast. We looked at him, then looked at one another with suspicious awe in our eyes, like men who come unexpectedly upon the scene of some mysterious disaster. He had given himself up to us; he had thrust into our hands his errors and his torment, his life and his peace; and we did not know what to do with that problem from the outer darkness. We three white men, looking at that Malay, could not find one word to the purpose amongst us – if indeed there existed a word that could solve that problem. We pondered, and our hearts sank. We felt as though we three had been called to the very gate of Infernal Regions to judge, to decide the fate of a wanderer coming suddenly from a world of sunshine and illusions.

'By Jove, he seems to have a great idea of our power,' whispered

Hollis, hopelessly. And then again there was a silence, the feeble plash of water, the steady tick of chronometers. Jackson, with bare arms crossed, leaned his shoulders against the bulkhead of the cabin. He was bending his head under the deck beam, his fair beard spread out magnificently over his chest; he looked colossal, ineffectual, and mild. There was something lugubrious in the aspect of the cabin; the air in it seemed to become slowly charged with the cruel chill of helplessness, with the pitiless anger of egoism against the incomprehensible form of an intruding pain. We had no idea what to do; we began to resent bitterly the hard necessity to get rid of him.

Hollis mused, muttered suddenly with a short laugh, 'Strength. . . Protection. . . Charm.' He slipped off the table and left the cuddy without a look at us. It seemed a base desertion. Jackson and I exchanged indignant glances. We could hear him rummaging in his pigeon-hole of a cabin. Was the fellow actually going to bed? Karain sighed. It was intolerable!

Then Hollis reappeared, holding in both hands a small leather box. He put it down gently on the table and looked at us with a queer gasp, we thought, as though he had from some cause become speechless for a moment, or were ethically uncertain about producing that box. But in an instant the insolent and unerring wisdom of his youth gave him the needed courage. He said, as he unlocked the box with a very small key, 'Look as solemn as you can, you fellows.'

Probably we looked only surprised and stupid, for he glanced over his shoulder, and said angrily –

'This is no play; I am going to do something for him. Look serious. Confound it! . . . Can't you lie a little . . . for a friend!'

Karain seemed to take no notice of us, but when Hollis threw open the lid of the box his eyes flew to it – and so did ours. The quilted crimson satin of the inside put a violent patch of colour into the sombre atmosphere; it was something positive to look at – it was fascinating.

VI

Hollis looked smiling into the box. He had lately made a dash home through the Canal. He had been away six months, and only joined us again just in time for this last trip. We had never seen the box before. His hands hovered above it; and he talked to us ironically, but his face became as grave as though he were pronouncing a powerful incantation over the things inside.

'Every one of us,' he said, with pauses that somehow were more offensive than his words – 'every one of us, you'll admit, has been haunted by some woman . . . And . . . as to friends . . . dropped by the way . . . Well! . . . ask yourselves . . .'

He paused. Karain stared. A deep rumble was heard high up under the deck. Jackson spoke seriously –

'Don't be so beastly cynical.'

'Ah! You are without guile,' said Hollis, sadly. 'You will learn . . . Meantime this Malay has been our friend . . .'

He repeated several times thoughtfully, 'Friend . . . Malay. Friend, Malay,' as though weighing the words against one another, then went on more briskly –

'A good fellow – a gentleman in his way. We can't, so to speak, turn our backs on his confidence and belief in us. Those Malays are easily impressed – all nerves, you know – therefore . . .

He turned to me sharply.

'You know him best,' he said, in a practical tone. 'Do you think he is fanatical – I mean very strict in his faith?'

I stammered in profound amazement that 'I did not think so.'

'It's on account of its being a likeness – an engraved image,' muttered Hollis, enigmatically, turning to the box. He plunged his fingers into it. Karain's lips were parted and his eyes shone. We looked into the box.

There were there a couple of reels of cotton, a packet of needles, a bit of silk ribbon, dark blue; a cabinet photograph, at which Hollis stole a glance before laying it on the table face downwards. A girl's portrait, I could see. There were, amongst a lot of various small objects, a bunch of flowers, a narrow white glove with many buttons, a slim packet of letters carefully tied up. Amulets of white men! Charms and talismans! Charms that keep them straight, that drive them crooked, that have the power to make a young man sigh, an old man smile. Potent things that procure dreams of joy, thoughts of regret; that soften hard hearts, and can temper a soft one to the hardness of steel. Gifts of heaven – things of earth.

Hollis rummaged in the box.

And it seemed to me, during that moment of waiting, that the cabin of the schooner was becoming filled with a stir invisible and living as of subtle breaths. All the ghosts driven out of the unbelieving West by men who pretend to be wise and alone and at peace – all the homeless ghosts of an unbelieving world – appeared suddenly round the figure of Hollis bending over the box; all the exiled and charming shades of loved women; all the beautiful and tender ghosts of ideals, remembered, forgotten, cherished, execrated; all the cast-out and reproachful ghosts of friends admired, trusted, traduced, betrayed, left dead by the way – they all seemed to come from the inhospitable regions of the earth to crowd into the gloomy cabin, as though it had been a refuge and, in all the unbelieving world, the only place of avenging belief . . . It lasted a second – all disappeared. Hollis was facing us alone with something small that glittered between his fingers. It looked like a coin.

'Ah! here it is,' he said.

He held it up. It was a sixpence – a Jubilee sixpence. It was gilt; it had a hole punched near the rim. Hollis looked towards Karain.

'A charm for our friend,' he said to us. 'The thing itself is of great power – money, you know – and his imagination is struck. A loyal vagabond; if only his puritanism doesn't shy at a likeness . . .'

We said nothing. We did not know whether to be scandalised, amused, or relieved. Hollis advanced towards Karain, who stood up as if startled, and then, holding the coin up, spoke in Malay.

'This is the image of the Great Queen, and the most powerful thing the white men know,' he said, solemnly.

Karain covered the handle of his kriss in sign of respect, and stared at the crowned head.

'The Invincible, the Pious,' he muttered.

'She is more powerful than Suleiman the Wise, who commanded the genii, as you know,' said Hollis, gravely. 'I shall give this to you.'

He held the sixpence in the palm of his hand, and looking at it thoughtfully, spoke to us in English.

'She commands a spirit, too – the spirit of her nation; a masterful, conscientious, unscrupulous, unconquerable devil . . . that does a lot of good – incidentally . . . a lot of good . . . at times – and wouldn't stand any fuss from the best ghost out for such a little thing as our friend's shot. Don't look thunderstruck, you fellows. Help me to make him believe – everything's in that.'

'His people will be shocked,' I murmured.

Hollis looked fixedly at Karain, who was the incarnation of the very essence of still excitement. He stood rigid, with head thrown back; his eyes rolled wildly, flashing; the dilated nostrils quivered.

'Hang it all!' said Hollis at last, 'he is a good fellow. I'll give him something that I shall really miss.'

He took the ribbon out of the box, smiled at it scornfully, then with a pair of scissors cut out a piece from the palm of the glove.

'I shall make him a thing like those Italian peasants wear, you know.'

He sewed the coin in the delicate leather, sewed the leather to the ribbon, tied the ends together. He worked with haste. Karain watched his fingers all the time.

'Now then,' he said – then stepped up to Karain. They looked close into one another's eyes. Those of Karain stared in a lost glance, but Hollis's seemed to grow darker and looked out masterful and compelling. They were in violent contrast together – one motionless and the colour of bronze, the other dazzling white and lifting his arms, where the powerful muscles rolled slightly under a skin that gleamed like satin. Jackson moved near with the air of a man closing up to a chum in a tight place. I said impressively, pointing to Hollis –

'He is young, but he is wise. Believe him!'

Karain bent his head: Hollis threw lightly over it the dark-blue ribbon and stepped back.

'Forget, and be at peace!' I cried.

Karain seemed to wake up from a dream. He said, 'Ha!' shook himself as if throwing off a burden. He looked round with assurance. Someone on deck dragged off the skylight cover, and a flood of light fell into the cabin. It was morning already.

'Time to go on deck,' said Jackson.

Hollis put on a coat, and we went up, Karain leading.

The sun had risen beyond the hills, and their long shadows stretched far over the bay in the pearly light. The air was clear, stainless, and cool. I pointed at the curved line of yellow sands.

'He is not there,' I said, emphatically, to Karain. 'He waits no more. He has departed for ever.'

A shaft of bright hot rays darted into the bay between the summits of two hills, and the water all round broke out as if by magic into a dazzling sparkle.

'No! He is not there waiting,' said Karain, after a long look over the beach. 'I do not hear him,' he went on, slowly. 'No!'

He turned to us.

'He has departed again – for ever!' he cried.

We assented vigorously, repeatedly, and without compunction. The great thing was to impress him powerfully; to suggest absolute safety – the end of all trouble. We did our best; and I hope we affirmed our faith in the power of Hollis's charm efficiently enough to put the matter beyond the shadow of a doubt. Our voices rang around him joyously in the still air, and above his head the sky, pellucid, pure, stainless, arched its tender blue from shore to shore and over the bay, as if to envelop the water, the earth, and the man in the caress of its light.

The anchor was up, the sails hung still, and half a dozen big boats were seen sweeping over the bay to give us a tow out. The paddlers in the first one that came alongside lifted their heads and saw their ruler standing amongst us. A low murmur of surprise arose then a shout of greeting.

He left us, and seemed straightway to step into the glorious splendour of his stage, to wrap himself in the illusion of unavoidable success. For a moment he stood erect, one foot over the gangway, one hand on the hilt of his kriss, in a martial pose; and, relieved from the fear of outer darkness, he held his head high, he swept a serene look over his conquered foothold on the earth. The boats far off took up the cry of greeting; a great clamour rolled on the water; the hills echoed it, and seemed to toss back at him the words invoking life and victories.

He descended into a canoe, and as soon as he was clear of the side we gave him three cheers. They sounded faint and orderly after the wild tumult of his loyal subjects, but it was the best we could do. He stood up in the boat, lifted up both his arms, then pointed to the infallible charm. We cheered again; and the Malays in the boats stared – very much puzzled and impressed. I wonder what they thought; what he thought . . . what the reader thinks?

We towed out slowly. We saw him land and watch us from the beach. A figure approached him humbly but openly – not at all like a ghost with a grievance. We could see other men running towards him. Perhaps he had been missed? At any rate there was a great stir. A group formed itself rapidly near him, and he walked along the sands, followed by a growing *cortège*, and kept nearly abreast of the schooner. With our glasses we could see the blue ribbon on his neck and a patch of white on his brown chest. The bay was waking up. The smoke of morning fires stood in faint spirals higher than the heads of palms; people moved between the houses; a herd of buffaloes galloped clumsily across a green slope; the slender figures of boys brandishing sticks appeared black and leaping in the long grass; a coloured line of women, with water bamboos on their heads, moved swaying through a thin grove of fruit-trees. Karain stopped in the midst of his men and waved his hand; then, detaching himself from the splendid group, walked alone to the water's edge and waved his hand again. The schooner passed out to sea between the steep headlands that shut in the bay, and at the same instant Karain passed out of our life for ever.

But the memory remains. Some years afterwards I met Jackson, in the Strand. He was magnificent as ever. His head was high above the crowd. His beard was gold, his face red, his eyes blue; he had a wide-brimmed grey hat and no collar or waistcoat; he was inspiring; he had just come home – had landed that very day! Our meeting caused an eddy in the current of humanity. Hurried people would run against us, then walk round us, and turn back to look at that giant. We tried to compress seven years of life into seven exclamations; then, suddenly

appeased, walked sedately along, giving one another the news of
yesterday. Jackson gazed about him, like a man who looks for land-
marks, then stopped before Bland's window. He always had a passion
for firearms; so he stopped short and contemplated the row of
weapons, perfect and severe, drawn up in a line behind the black-
framed panes. I stood by his side. Suddenly he said –

'Do you remember Karain?'

I nodded.

'The sight of all this made me think of him,' he went on, with his face
near the glass . . . and I could see another man, powerful and bearded,
peering at him intently from amongst the dark and polished tubes that
can cure so many illusions. 'Yes; it made me think of him,' he
continued, slowly. 'I saw a paper this morning; they are fighting over
there again. He's sure to be in it. He will make it hot for the caballeros.
Well, good luck to him, poor devil! He was perfectly stunning.'

We walked on.

'I wonder whether the charm worked – you remember Hollis's
charm, of course. If it did . . . never was a sixpence wasted to better
advantage! Poor devil! I wonder whether he got rid of that friend of his.
Hope so . . . Do you know, I sometimes think that – '

I stood still and looked at him.

'Yes . . . I mean, whether the thing was so, you know . . . whether it
really happened to him . . . What do you think?'

'My dear chap,' I cried, 'you have been too long away from home.
What a question to ask! Only look at all this.'

A watery gleam of sunshine flashed from the west and went out
between two long lines of walls; and then the broken confusion of
roofs, the chimney-stacks, the gold letters sprawling over the fronts of
houses, the sombre polish of windows, stood resigned and sullen under
the falling gloom. The whole length of the street, deep as a well and
narrow like a corridor, was full of a sombre and ceaseless stir. Our ears
were filled by a headlong shuffle and beat of rapid footsteps and an
underlying rumour – a rumour vast, faint, pulsating, as of panting
breaths, of beating hearts, of gasping voices. Innumerable eyes stared
straight in front, feet moved hurriedly, blank faces flowed, arms swung.
Over all, a narrow ragged strip of smoky sky wound about between the
high roofs, extended and motionless, like a soiled streamer flying above
the rout of a mob.

'Ye–e–e–s,' said Jackson, meditatively.

The big wheels of hansoms turned slowly along the edge of side-
walks; a pale-faced youth strolled, overcome by weariness, by the side
of his stick and with the tails of his overcoat flapping gently near his

heels; horses stepped gingerly on the greasy pavement, tossing their heads; two young girls passed by, talking vivaciously and with shining eyes; a fine old fellow strutted, red-faced, stroking a white moustache; and a line of yellow boards with blue letters on them approached us slowly, tossing on high behind one another like some queer wreckage adrift upon a river of hats.

'Ye–e–es,' repeated Jackson. His clear blue eyes looked about, contemptuous, amused and hard, like the eyes of a boy. A clumsy string of red, yellow, and green omnibuses rolled swaying, monstrous and gaudy; two shabby children ran across the road; a knot of dirty men with red neckerchiefs round their bare throats lurched along, discussing filthily; a ragged old man with a face of despair yelled horribly in the mud the name of a paper; while far off, amongst the tossing heads of horses, the dull flash of harnesses, the jumble of lustrous panels and roofs of carriages, we could see a policeman, helmeted and dark, stretching out a rigid arm at the crossing of the streets.

'Yes; I see it,' said Jackson, slowly. 'It is there; it pants, it runs, it rolls; it is strong and alive; it would smash you if you didn't look out; but I'll be hanged if it is yet as real to me as . . . as the other thing . . . say, Karain's story.'

I think that, decidedly, he had been too long away from home.

Youth: a Narrative

This could have occurred nowhere but in England, where men and sea interpenetrate, so to speak – the sea entering into the life of most men, and the men knowing something or everything about the sea, in the way of amusement, of travel, or of bread-winning.

We were sitting round a mahogany table that reflected the bottle, the claret-glasses, and our faces as we leaned on our elbows. There was a director of companies, an accountant, a lawyer, Marlow, and myself. The director had been a *Conway* boy, the accountant had served four years at sea, the lawyer – a fine crusted Tory, High Churchman, the best of old fellows, the soul of honour – had been chief officer in the P & O service in the good old days when mail-boats were square-rigged at least on two masts, and used to come down the China Sea before a fair monsoon with stun'-sails set alow and aloft. We all began life in the merchant service. Between the five of us there was the strong bond of the sea, and also the fellowship of the craft, which no amount of enthusiasm for yachting, cruising, and so on can give, since one is only the amusement of life and the other is life itself.

Marlow (at least I think that is how he spelt his name) told the story, or rather the chronicle, of a voyage:

'Yes, I have seen a little of the Eastern seas; but what I remember best is my first voyage there. You fellows know there are those voyages that seem ordered for the illustration of life, that might stand for a symbol of existence. You fight, work, sweat, nearly kill yourself, sometimes do kill yourself, trying to accomplish something – and you can't. Not from any fault of yours. You simply can do nothing, neither great nor little – not a thing in the world – not even marry an old maid, or get a wretched six-hundred-ton cargo of coal to its port of destination.

'It was altogether a memorable affair. It was my first voyage to the East, and my first voyage as second mate; it was also my skipper's first command. You'll admit it was time. He was sixty if a day; a little man, with a broad, not very straight back, with bowed shoulders and one leg more bandy than the other, he had that queer twisted-about appearance you see so often in men who work in the fields. He had a nut-cracker face – chin and nose trying to come together over a sunken mouth – and it was framed in iron-grey fluffy hair, that looked like a chin-strap of cotton-wool sprinkled with coal-dust. And he had blue eyes in that old face of his, which were amazingly like a boy's, with that candid expression some quite common men preserve to the end of their days by a rare internal gift of simplicity of heart and rectitude of soul. What induced him to accept me was a wonder. I had come out of a crack Australian clipper, where I had been third officer, and he seemed to have a prejudice against crack clippers as aristocratic and high-toned. He said to me, 'You know, in this ship you will have to work.' I said I had to work in every ship I had ever been in. 'Ah, but this is different, and you gentlemen out of them big ships; . . . but there! I dare say you will do. Join tomorrow.'

'I joined tomorrow. It was twenty-two years ago; and I was just twenty. How time passes! It was one of the happiest days of my life. Fancy! Second mate for the first time – a really responsible officer! I wouldn't have thrown up my new billet for a fortune. The mate looked me over carefully. He was also an old chap, but of another stamp. He had a Roman nose, a snow-white, long beard, and his name was Mahon, but he insisted that it should be pronounced Mann. He was well connected; yet there was something wrong with his luck, and he had never got on.

'As to the captain, he had been for years in coasters, then in the Mediterranean, and last in the West Indian trade. He had never been round the Capes. He could just write a kind of sketchy hand, and didn't care for writing at all. Both were thorough good seamen of course, and between those two old chaps I felt like a small boy between two grandfathers.

'The ship also was old. Her name was the *Judea*. Queer name, isn't it? She belonged to a man Wilmer, Wilcox – some name like that; but he has been bankrupt and dead these twenty years or more, and his name don't matter. She had been laid up in Shadwell basin for ever so long. You may imagine her state. She was all rust, dust, grime – soot aloft, dirt on deck. To me it was like coming out of a palace into a ruined cottage. She was about four hundred tons, had a primitive windlass, wooden latches to the doors, not a bit of brass about her, and a big square stern. There was on it, below her name in big letters, a lot of scrollwork, with the gilt off, and some sort of a coat of arms, with the motto "Do or Die" underneath. I remember it took my fancy immensely. There was a touch of romance in it, something that made me love the old thing – something that appealed to my youth!

'We left London in ballast – sand ballast – to load a cargo of coal in a northern port for Bankok. Bankok! I thrilled. I had been six years at sea, but had only seen Melbourne and Sydney, very good places, charming places in their way – but Bankok!

'We worked out of the Thames under canvas, with a North Sea pilot on board. His name was Jermyn, and he dodged all day long about the galley drying his handkerchief before the stove. Apparently he never slept. He was a dismal man, with a perpetual tear sparkling at the end of his nose, who either had been in trouble, or was in trouble, or expected to be in trouble – couldn't be happy unless something went wrong. He mistrusted my youth, my common-sense, and my seaman-ship, and made a point of showing it in a hundred little ways. I dare say he was right. It seems to me I knew very little then, and I know not much more now; but I cherish a hate for that Jermyn to this day.

'We were a week working up as far as Yarmouth Roads, and then we got into a gale – the famous October gale of twenty-two years ago. It was wind, lightning, sleet, snow, and a terrific sea. We were flying light, and you may imagine how bad it was when I tell you we had smashed bulwarks and a flooded deck. On the second night she shifted her ballast into the lee bow, and by that time we had been blown off somewhere on the Dogger Bank. There was nothing for it but go below with shovels and try to right her, and there we were in that vast hold, gloomy like a cavern, the tallow dips stuck and flickering on the beams, the gale howling above, the ship tossing about like mad on her side; there we all were, Jermyn, the captain, everyone, hardly able to keep our feet, engaged on that gravedigger's work, and trying to toss shovelfuls of wet sand up to windward. At every tumble of the ship you could see vaguely in the dim light men falling down with a great flourish of shovels. One of the ship's boys (we had two), impressed by the weirdness of the scene, wept as if his heart would break. We could hear him blubbering somewhere in the shadows.

'On the third day the gale died out, and by and by a north-country tug picked us up. We took sixteen days in all to get from London to the Tyne! When we got into dock we had lost our turn for loading, and they hauled us off to a tier where we remained for a month. Mrs Beard (the captain's name was Beard) came from Colchester to see the old man. She lived on board. The crew of runners had left, and there remained only the officers, one boy, and the steward, a mulatto who answered to the name of Abraham. Mrs Beard was an old woman with a face all wrinkled and ruddy like a winter apple, and the figure of a young girl. She caught sight of me once, sewing on a button, and insisted on having my shirts to repair. This was something different from the captains' wives I had known on board crack clippers. When I brought her the shirts, she said: "And the socks? They want mending, I am sure, and John's – Captain Beard's – things are all in order now. I would be glad of something to do." Bless the old woman. She overhauled my outfit for me, and meantime I read for the first time *Sartor Resartus* and Burnaby's *Ride to Khiva*. I didn't understand much of the first then; but I remember I preferred the soldier to the philosopher at the time; a preference which life has only confirmed. One was a man, and the other was either more – or less. However, they are both dead, and Mrs Beard is dead, and youth, strength, genius, thoughts, achievements, simple hearts – all die . . . No matter.

'They loaded us at last. We shipped a crew. Eight able seamen and two boys. We hauled off one evening to the buoys at the dock-gates, ready to go out, and with a fair prospect of beginning the voyage next day. Mrs Beard was to start for home by a late train. When the ship was fast we went to tea. We sat rather silent through the meal – Mahon, the old couple, and I. I finished first, and slipped away for a smoke, my cabin being in a deck-house just against the poop. It was high water, blowing fresh with a drizzle; the double dock-gates were opened, and the steam-colliers were going in and out in the darkness with their lights burning bright, a great plashing of propellers, rattling of winches, and a lot of hailing on the pier-heads. I watched the procession of head-lights gliding high and of green lights gliding low in the night, when suddenly a red gleam flashed at me, vanished, came into view again, and remained. The fore-end of a steamer loomed up close. I shouted down the cabin, "Come up, quick!" and then heard a startled voice saying afar in the dark, "Stop her, sir." A bell jingled. Another voice cried warningly, "We are going right into that barque, sir." The answer to this was a gruff "All right," and the next thing was a heavy crash as the steamer struck a glancing blow with the bluff of her bow about our fore-rigging. There was a moment of confusion, yelling, and running about. Steam roared. Then somebody was heard saying, "All clear, sir." . . . "Are you all right?" asked the gruff voice. I had jumped forward to see the damage, and hailed back, "I think so." "Easy astern," said the gruff voice. A bell jingled. "What steamer is that?" screamed Mahon. By that time she was no more to us than a bulky shadow manoeuvring a little way off. They shouted at us some name – a woman's name, Miranda or Melissa – or some such thing. "This means another month in this beastly hole," said Mahon to me, as we peered with lamps about the splintered bulwarks and broken braces. "But where's the captain?"

'We had not heard or seen anything of him all that time. We went aft to look. A doleful voice arose hailing somewhere in the middle of the dock, "*Judea* ahoy!" . . . How the devil did he get there? . . . "Hallo!" we shouted. "I am adrift in our boat without oars," he cried. A belated water-man offered his services, and Mahon struck a bargain with him for half-a-crown to tow our skipper alongside; but it was Mrs Beard that came up the ladder first. They had been floating about the dock in that mizzly cold rain for nearly an hour. I was never so surprised in my life.

'It appears that when he heard my shout "Come up" he understood at once what was the matter, caught up his wife, ran on deck, and across, and down into our boat, which was fast to the ladder. Not bad for a sixty-year-old. Just imagine that old fellow saving heroically in his arms that old woman – the woman of his life. He set her down on a thwart, and was ready to climb back on board when the painter came adrift somehow, and away they went together. Of course in the confusion we did not hear him shouting. He looked abashed. She said cheerfully, "I suppose it does not matter my losing the train now?" "No, Jenny – you go below and get warm," he growled. Then to us: "A sailor has no business with a wife – I say. There I was, out of the ship. Well, no harm done this time. Let's go and look at what that fool of a steamer smashed."

'It wasn't much, but it delayed us three weeks. At the end of that time, the captain being engaged with his agents, I carried Mrs Beard's bag to the railway-station and put her all comfy into a third-class carriage. She lowered the window to say, "You are a good young man. If you see John – Captain Beard – without his muffler at night, just remind him from me to keep his throat well wrapped up." "Certainly, Mrs Beard," I said. "You are a good young man; I noticed how attentive you are to John – to Captain – " The train pulled out suddenly; I took my cap off to the old woman: I never saw her again . . . Pass the bottle.

'We went to sea next day. When we made that start for Bankok we had been already three months out of London. We had expected to be a fortnight or so – at the outside.

'It was January, and the weather was beautiful – the beautiful sunny winter weather that has more charm than in the summer-time, because it is unexpected, and crisp, and you know it won't, it can't, last long. It's like a windfall, like a godsend, like an unexpected piece of luck.

'It lasted all down the North Sea, all down Channel; and it lasted till we were three hundred miles or so to the westward of the Lizards: then the wind went round to the sou'west and began to pipe up. In two days it blew a gale. The *Judea*, hove to, wallowed on the Atlantic like an old candlebox. It blew day after day: it blew with spite, without interval, without mercy, without rest. The world was nothing but an immensity of great foaming waves rushing at us, under a sky low enough to touch with the hand and dirty like a smoked ceiling. In the stormy space surrounding us there was as much flying spray as air. Day after day and night after night there was nothing round the ship but the howl of the wind, the tumult of the sea, the noise of water pouring over her deck. There was no rest for her and no rest for us. She tossed, she pitched, she stood on her head, she sat on her tail, she rolled, she groaned, and we had to hold on while on deck and cling to our bunks when below, in a constant effort of body and worry of mind.

'One night Mahon spoke through the small window of my berth. It opened right into my very bed, and I was lying there sleepless, in my boots, feeling as though I had not slept for years, and could not if I tried. He said excitedly – "You got the sounding-rod in here, Marlow? I can't get the pumps to suck. By God! it's no child's play."

'I gave him the sounding-rod and lay down again, trying to think of various things – but I thought only of the pumps. When I came on deck they were still at it, and my watch relieved at the pumps. By the light of the lantern brought on deck to examine the sounding-rod I caught a glimpse of their weary, serious faces. We pumped all the four hours. We pumped all night, all day, all the week – watch and watch. She was working herself loose, and leaked badly – not enough to drown us at once, but enough to kill us with the work at the pumps. And while we pumped the ship was going from us piecemeal: the bulwarks went, the stanchions were torn out, the ventilators smashed, the cabin-door burst in. There was not a dry spot in the ship. She was being gutted bit by bit. The long-boat changed, as if by magic, into matchwood where she stood in her gripes. I had lashed her myself, and was rather proud of my handiwork, which had withstood so long the malice of the sea. And we pumped. And there was no break in the weather. The sea was white like a sheet of foam, like a caldron of boiling milk; there was not a break in the clouds, no – not the size of a man's hand – no, not for so much as ten seconds. There was for us no sky, there were for us no stars, no sun, no universe – nothing but angry clouds and an infuriated sea. We pumped watch and watch, for dear life; and it seemed to last for months, for years, for all eternity, as though we had been dead and gone to a hell for sailors. We forgot the day of the week, the name of the month, what year it was, and whether we had ever been ashore. The sails blew away, she lay broadside on under a weather-cloth, the ocean poured over her, and we did not care. We turned those handles, and had the eyes of idiots. As soon as we had crawled on deck I used to take a round turn with a rope about the men, the pumps, and the mainmast, and we turned, we turned incessantly, with the water to our waists, to our necks, over our heads. It was all one. We had forgotten how it felt to be dry.

'And there was somewhere in me the thought: By Jove! this is the deuce of an adventure – something you read about; and it is my first voyage as second mate – and I am only twenty – and here I am lasting it out as well as any of these men, and keeping my chaps up to the mark. I was pleased. I would not have given up the experience for worlds. I had moments of exultation. Whenever the old dismantled craft pitched heavily with her counter high in the air, she seemed to me to throw up, like an appeal, like a defiance, like a cry to the clouds without mercy, the words written on her stern: "*Judea*, London. Do or Die."

'O youth! The strength of it, the faith of it, the imagination of it! To me she was not an old rattle-trap carting about the world a lot of coal for a freight – to me she was the endeavour, the test, the trial of life. I think of her with pleasure, with affection, with regret – as you would think of someone dead you have loved. I shall never forget her . . . Pass the bottle.

'One night when tied to the mast, as I explained, we were pumping on, deafened with the wind, and without spirit enough in us to wish ourselves dead, a heavy sea crashed aboard and swept clean over us. As soon as I got my breath I shouted, as in duty bound, "Keep on, boys!" when suddenly I felt something hard floating on deck strike the calf of my leg. I made a grab at it and missed. It was so dark we could not see each other's faces within a foot – you understand.

'After that thump the ship kept quiet for a while, and the thing, whatever it was, struck my leg again. This time I caught it – and it was a saucepan. At first, being stupid with fatigue and thinking of nothing but the pumps, I did not understand what I had in my hand. Suddenly it dawned upon me, and I shouted, "Boys, the house on deck is gone. Leave this, and let's look for the cook."

'There was a deck-house forward, which contained the galley, the cook's berth, and the quarters of the crew. As we had expected for days to see it swept away, the hands had been ordered to sleep in the cabin – the only safe place in the ship. The steward, Abraham, however, persisted in clinging to his berth, stupidly, like a mule – from sheer fright I believe, like an animal that won't leave a stable falling in an earthquake. So we went to look for him. It was chancing death, since once out of our lashings we were as exposed as if on a raft. But we went. The house was shattered as if a shell had exploded inside. Most of it had gone overboard – stove, men's quarters, and their property, all was gone; but two posts, holding a portion of the bulkhead to which

Abraham's bunk was attached, remained as if by a miracle. We groped in the ruins and came upon this, and there he was, sitting in his bunk, surrounded by foam and wreckage, jabbering cheerfully to himself. He was out of his mind; completely and for ever mad, with this sudden shock coming upon the fag-end of his endurance. We snatched him up, lugged him aft, and pitched him head-first down the cabin companion. You understand there was no time to carry him down with infinite precautions and wait to see how he got on. Those below would pick him up at the bottom of the stairs all right. We were in a hurry to go back to the pumps. That business could not wait. A bad leak is an inhuman thing.

'One would think that the sole purpose of that fiendish gale had been to make a lunatic of that poor devil of a mulatto. It eased before morning, and next day the sky cleared, and as the sea went down the leak took up. When it came to bending a fresh set of sails the crew demanded to put back – and really there was nothing else to do. Boats gone, decks swept clean, cabin gutted, men without a stitch but what they stood in, stores spoiled, ship strained. We put her head for home, and – would you believe it? The wind came east right in our teeth. It blew fresh, it blew continuously. We had to beat up every inch of the way, but she did not leak so badly, the water keeping comparatively smooth. Two hours' pumping in every four is no joke – but it kept her afloat as far as Falmouth.

'The good people there live on casualties of the sea, and no doubt were glad to see us. A hungry crowd of shipwrights sharpened their chisels at the sight of that carcass of a ship. And, by Jove! they had pretty pickings off us before they were done. I fancy the owner was already in a tight place. There were delays. Then it was decided to take part of the cargo out and caulk her topsides. This was done, the repairs finished, cargo reshipped; a new crew came on board, and we went out – for Bankok. At the end of a week we were back again. The crew said they weren't going to Bankok – a hundred and fifty days' passage – in a something hooker that wanted pumping eight hours out of the twenty-four; and the nautical papers inserted again the little paragraph: "*Judea*. Barque. Tyne to Bankok; coals; put back to Falmouth leaky and with crew refusing duty."

'There were more delays – more tinkering. The owner came down for a day, and said she was as right as a little fiddle. Poor old Captain Beard looked like the ghost of a Geordie skipper – through the worry and humiliation of it. Remember he was sixty, and it was his first command. Mahon said it was a foolish business, and would end badly. I loved the ship more than ever, and wanted awfully to get to Bankok.

To Bankok! Magic name, blessed name. Mesopotamia wasn't a patch on it. Remember I was twenty, and it was my first second mate's billet, and the East was waiting for me.

'We went out and anchored in the outer roads with a fresh crew – the third. She leaked worse than ever. It was as if those confounded shipwrights had actually made a hole in her. This time we did not even go outside. The crew simply refused to man the windlass.

'They towed us back to the inner harbour, and we became a fixture, a feature, an institution of the place. People pointed us out to visitors as "That 'ere barque that's going to Bankok – has been here six months – put back three times." On holidays the small boys pulling about in boats would hail, "*Judea*, ahoy!" and if a head showed above the rail shouted, "Where you bound to? – Bankok?" and jeered. We were only three on board. The poor old skipper mooned in the cabin. Mahon undertook the cooking, and unexpectedly developed all a Frenchman's genius for preparing nice little messes. I looked languidly after the rigging. We became citizens of Falmouth. Every shopkeeper knew us. At the barber's or tobacconist's they asked familiarly, "Do you think you will ever get to Bankok?" Meantime the owner, the underwriters, and the charterers squabbled amongst themselves in London, and our pay went on . . . Pass the bottle.

'It was horrid. Morally it was worse than pumping for life. It seemed as though we had been forgotten by the world, belonged to nobody, would get nowhere; it seemed that, as if bewitched, we would have to live for ever and ever in that inner harbour, a derision and a byword to generations of long-shore loafers and dishonest boatmen. I obtained three months' pay and a five days' leave, and made a rush for London. It took me a day to get there and pretty well another to come back – but three months' pay went all the same. I don't know what I did with it. I went to a music-hall, I believe, lunched, dined, and supped in a swell place in Regent Street, and was back to time, with nothing but a complete set of Byron's works and a new railway rug to show for three months' work. The boatman who pulled me off to the ship said: "Hallo! I thought you had left the old thing. *She* will never get to Bankok." "That's all *you* know about it," I said, scornfully – but I didn't like that prophecy at all.

'Suddenly a man, some kind of agent to somebody, appeared with full powers. He had grog-blossoms all over his face, an indomitable energy, and was a jolly soul. We leaped into life again. A hulk came alongside, took our cargo, and then we went into dry dock to get our copper stripped. No wonder she leaked. The poor thing, strained beyond endurance by the gale, had, as if in disgust, spat out all the oakum of her lower seams. She was recaulked, new coppered, and made as tight as a bottle. We went back to the hulk and reshipped our cargo.

'Then, on a fine moonlight night, all the rats left the ship.

'We had been infested with them. They had destroyed our sails, consumed more stores than the crew, affably shared our beds and our dangers, and now, when the ship was made seaworthy, concluded to clear out. I called Mahon to enjoy the spectacle. Rat after rat appeared on our rail, took a last look over his shoulder, and leaped with a hollow thud into the empty hulk. We tried to count them, but soon lost the tale. Mahon said: "Well, well! don't talk to me about the intelligence of rats. They ought to have left before, when we had that narrow squeak from foundering. There you have the proof how silly is the superstition about them. They leave a good ship for an old rotten hulk, where there is nothing to eat, too, the fools! . . . I don't believe they know what is safe or what is good for them, any more than you or I."

'And after some more talk we agreed that the wisdom of rats had been grossly overrated, being in fact no greater than that of men.

'The story of the ship was known, by this, all up the Channel from Land's End to the Forelands, and we could get no crew on the south coast. They sent us one all complete from Liverpool, and we left once more – for Bankok.

'We had fair breezes, smooth water right into the tropics, and the old *Judea* lumbered along in the sunshine. When she went eight knots everything cracked aloft, and we tied our caps to our heads; but mostly she strolled on at the rate of three miles an hour. What could you expect? She was tired – that old ship. Her youth was where mine is – where yours is – you fellows who listen to this yarn; and what friend would throw your years and your weariness in your face? We didn't grumble at her. To us aft, at least, it seemed as though we had been born in her, reared in her, had lived in her for ages, had never known any other ship. I would just as soon have abused the old village church at home for not being a cathedral.

'And for me there was also my youth to make me patient. There was all the East before me, and all life, and the thought that I had been tried in that ship and had come out pretty well. And I thought of men of old who, centuries ago, went that road in ships that sailed no better, to the land of palms, and spices, and yellow sands, and of brown nations ruled by kings more cruel than Nero the Roman and more splendid than Solomon the Jew. The old bark lumbered on, heavy with her age and the burden of her cargo, while I lived the life of youth in ignorance and hope. She lumbered on through an interminable procession of days;

and the fresh gilding flashed back at the setting sun, seemed to cry out over the darkening sea the words painted on her stern, "*Judea*, London. Do or Die."

'Then we entered the Indian Ocean and steered northerly for Java Head. The winds were light. Weeks slipped by. She crawled on, do or die, and people at home began to think of posting us as overdue.

'One Saturday evening, I being off duty, the men asked me to give them an extra bucket of water or so – for washing clothes. As I did not wish to screw on the fresh-water pump so late, I went forward whistling and with a key in my hand to unlock the forepeak scuttle, intending to serve the water out of a spare tank we kept there.

'The smell down below was as unexpected as it was frightful. One would have thought hundreds of paraffin-lamps had been flaring and smoking in that hole for days. I was glad to get out. The man with me coughed and said, "Funny smell, sir." I answered negligently, "It's good for the health they say," and walked aft.

'The first thing I did was to put my head down the square of the midship ventilator. As I lifted the lid a visible breath, something like a thin fog, a puff of faint haze, rose from the opening. The ascending air was hot, and had a heavy, sooty, paraffiny smell. I gave one sniff, and put down the lid gently. It was no use choking myself. The cargo was on fire.

'Next day she began to smoke in earnest. You see it was to be expected, for though the coal was of a safe kind, that cargo had been so handled, so broken up with handling, that it looked more like smithy coal than anything else. Then it had been wetted – more than once. It rained all the time we were taking it back from the hulk, and now with this long passage it got heated, and there was another case of spontaneous combustion.

'The captain called us into the cabin. He had a chart spread on the table, and looked unhappy. He said, "The coast of West Australia is near, but I mean to proceed to our destination. It is the hurricane month too; but we will just keep her head for Bankok, and fight the fire. No more putting back anywhere, if we all get roasted. We will try first to stifle this 'ere damned combustion by want of air."

'We tried. We battened down everything, and still she smoked. The smoke kept coming out through imperceptible crevices; it forced itself through bulkheads and covers; it oozed here and there and everywhere in slender threads, in an invisible film, in an incomprehensible manner. It made its way into the cabin, into the forecastle; it poisoned the sheltered places on the deck, it could be sniffed as high as the mainyard. It was clear that if the smoke came out the air came in. This was disheartening. This combustion refused to be stifled.

'We resolved to try water, and took the hatches off. Enormous volumes of smoke, whitish, yellowish, thick, greasy, misty, choking, ascended as high as the trucks. All hands cleared out aft. Then the poisonous cloud blew away, and we went back to work in a smoke that was no thicker now than that of an ordinary factory chimney.

'We rigged the force-pump, got the hose along, and by and by it burst. Well, it was as old as the ship – a prehistoric hose, and past repair. Then we pumped with the feeble head-pump, drew water with buckets, and in this way managed in time to pour lots of Indian Ocean into the main hatch. The bright stream flashed in sunshine, fell into a layer of white crawling smoke, and vanished on the black surface of coal. Steam ascended mingling with the smoke. We poured salt water as into a barrel without a bottom. It was our fate to pump in that ship, to pump out of her, to pump into her; and after keeping water out of her to save ourselves from being drowned, we frantically poured water into her to save ourselves from being burnt.

'And she crawled on, do or die, in the serene weather. The sky was a miracle of purity, a miracle of azure. The sea was polished, was blue, was pellucid, was sparkling like a precious stone, extending on all sides, all round to the horizon – as if the whole terrestrial globe had been one jewel, one colossal sapphire, a single gem fashioned into a planet. And on the lustre of the great calm waters the *Judea* glided imperceptibly, enveloped in languid and unclean vapours, in a lazy cloud that drifted to leeward, light and slow: a pestiferous cloud defiling the splendour of sea and sky.

'All this time of course we saw no fire. The cargo smouldered at the bottom somewhere. Once Mahon, as we were working side by side, said to me with a queer smile: "Now, if she only would spring a tidy leak – like that time when we first left the Channel – it would put a stopper on this fire. Wouldn't it?" I remarked irrelevantly, "Do you remember the rats?"

'We fought the fire and sailed the ship too as carefully as though nothing had been the matter. The steward cooked and attended on us. Of the other twelve men, eight worked while four rested. Everyone took his turn, captain included. There was equality, and if not exactly fraternity, then a deal of good feeling. Sometimes a man, as he dashed a bucketful of water down the hatchway, would yell out, "Hurrah for Bankok!" and the rest laughed. But generally we were taciturn and serious – and thirsty. Oh! how thirsty! And we had to be careful with the water. Strict allowance. The ship smoked, the sun blazed . . . Pass the bottle.

'We tried everything. We even made an attempt to dig down to the fire. No good, of course. No man could remain more than a minute below. Mahon, who went first, fainted there, and the man who went to fetch him out did likewise. We lugged them out on deck. Then I leaped down to show how easily it could be done. They had learned wisdom by that time, and contented themselves by fishing for me with a chain-hook tied to a broom-handle, I believe. I did not offer to go and fetch up my shovel, which was left down below.

'Things began to look bad. We put the long-boat into the water. The second boat was ready to swing out. We had also another, a fourteen-foot thing, on davits aft, where it was quite safe.

'Then, behold, the smoke suddenly decreased. We redoubled our efforts to flood the bottom of the ship. In two days there was no smoke at all. Everybody was on the broad grin. This was on a Friday. On Saturday no work, but sailing the ship of course, was done. The men washed their clothes and their faces for the first time in a fortnight, and had a special dinner given them. They spoke of spontaneous combustion with contempt, and implied *they* were the boys to put out combustions. Somehow we all felt as though we each had inherited a large fortune. But a beastly smell of burning hung about the ship. Captain Beard had hollow eyes and sunken cheeks. I had never noticed so much before how twisted and bowed he was. He and Mahon prowled soberly about hatches and ventilators, sniffing. It struck me suddenly poor Mahon was a very, very old chap. As to me, I was as pleased and proud as though I had helped to win a great naval battle. O! Youth!

'The night was fine. In the morning a homeward-bound ship passed us hull down – the first we had seen for months; but we were nearing the land at last, Java Head being about a hundred and ninety miles off, and nearly due north.

'Next day it was my watch on deck from eight to twelve. At breakfast the captain observed, "It's wonderful how that smell hangs about the cabin." About ten, the mate being on the poop, I stepped down on the main-deck for a moment. The carpenter's bench stood abaft the mainmast: I leaned against it sucking at my pipe, and the carpenter, a young chap, came to talk to me. He remarked, "I think we have done very well, haven't we?" and then I perceived with annoyance the fool was trying to tilt the bench. I said curtly, "Don't, Chips," and immediately became aware of a queer sensation, of an absurd delusion – I seemed somehow to be in the air. I heard all round me like a pent-up breath released – as if a thousand giants simultaneously had said Phoo! – and felt a dull concussion which made my ribs ache suddenly. No doubt about it – I was in the air, and my body was describing a short parabola. But short as it was, I had the time to think several thoughts in, as far as I can remember, the following order: "This can't be the carpenter – What is it? – Some accident – Submarine volcano? – Coals, gas! – By Jove! we are being blown up – Everybody's dead – I am falling into the after-hatch – I see fire in it."

'The coal-dust suspended in the air of the hold had glowed dull-red at the moment of the explosion. In the twinkling of an eye, in an infinitesimal fraction of a second since the first tilt of the bench, I was sprawling full length on the cargo. I picked myself up and scrambled out. It was quick like a rebound. The deck was a wilderness of smashed timber, lying crosswise like trees in a wood after a hurricane; an immense curtain of soiled rags waved gently before me – it was the mainsail blown to strips. I thought, The masts will be toppling over directly; and to get out of the way bolted on all-fours towards the poop-ladder. The first person I saw was Mahon, with eyes like saucers, his mouth open, and the long white hair standing straight on end round his head like a silver halo. He was just about to go down when the sight of the main-deck stirring, heaving up, and changing into splinters before his eyes, petrified him on the top step. I stared at him in unbelief, and he stared at me with a queer kind of shocked curiosity. I did not know that I had no hair, no eyebrows, no eyelashes, that my young moustache was burnt off, that my face was black, one cheek laid open, my nose cut, and my chin bleeding. I had lost my cap, one of my slippers, and my shirt was torn to rags. Of all this I was not aware. I was amazed to see the ship still afloat, the poop-deck whole – and, most of all, to see anybody alive. Also the peace of the sky and the serenity of the sea were distinctly surprising. I suppose I expected to see them convulsed with horror . . . Pass the bottle.

'There was a voice hailing the ship from somewhere – in the air, in the sky – I couldn't tell. Presently I saw the captain – and he was mad. He asked me eagerly, "Where's the cabin-table?" and to hear such a question was a frightful shock. I had just been blown up, you understand, and vibrated with that experience – I wasn't quite sure whether I was alive. Mahon began to stamp with both feet and yelled at him, "Good God! don't you see the deck's blown out of her?" I found my voice, and stammered out as if conscious of some gross neglect of duty, "I don't know where the cabin-table is." It was like an absurd dream.

'Do you know what he wanted next? Well, he wanted to trim the yards. Very placidly, and as if lost in thought, he insisted on having the foreyard squared. "I don't know if there's anybody alive," said Mahon, almost tearfully. "Surely," he said, gently, "there will be enough left to square the foreyard."

'The old chap, it seems, was in his own berth, winding up the chronometers, when the shock sent him spinning. Immediately it occurred to him – as he said afterwards – that the ship had struck something, and he ran out into the cabin. There, he saw, the cabin-table had vanished somewhere. The deck being blown up, it had fallen down into the lazarette of course. Where we had our breakfast that morning he saw only a great hole in the floor. This appeared to him so awfully mysterious, and impressed him so immensely, that what he saw and heard after he got on deck were mere trifles in comparison. And, mark, he noticed directly the wheel deserted and his barque off her course – and his only thought was to get that miserable, stripped, undecked, smouldering shell of a ship back again with her head pointing at her port of destination. Bankok! That's what he was after. I tell you this quiet, bowed, bandy-legged, almost deformed little man was immense in the singleness of his idea and in his placid ignorance of our agitation. He motioned us forward with a commanding gesture, and went to take the wheel himself.

'Yes; that was the first thing we did – trim the yards of that wreck! No one was killed, or even disabled, but everyone was more or less hurt. You should have seen them! Some were in rags, with black faces, like coalheavers, like sweeps, and had bullet heads that seemed closely cropped, but were in fact singed to the skin. Others, of the watch below, awakened by being shot out from their collapsing bunks, shivered incessantly, and kept on groaning even as we went about our work. But they all worked. That crew of Liverpool hard cases had in them the right stuff. It's my experience they always have. It is the sea that gives it – the vastness, the loneliness surrounding their dark stolid souls. Ah! Well! we stumbled, we crept, we fell, we barked our shins on the wreckage, we hauled. The masts stood, but we did not know how much they might be charred down below. It was nearly calm, but a long swell ran from the west and made her roll. They might go at any moment. We looked at them with apprehension. One could not foresee which way they would fall.

'Then we retreated aft and looked about us. The deck was a tangle of planks on edge, of planks on end, of splinters, of ruined woodwork. The masts rose from that chaos like big trees above a matted undergrowth. The interstices of that mass of wreckage were full of something whitish, sluggish, stirring – of something that was like a greasy fog. The smoke of the invisible fire was coming up again, was trailing, like a poisonous thick mist in some valley choked with dead wood. Already lazy wisps were beginning to curl upwards amongst the mass of splinters. Here and there a piece of timber, stuck upright, resembled a post. Half of a fife-rail had been shot through the foresail, and the sky made a patch of glorious blue in the ignobly soiled canvas. A portion of several boards holding together had fallen across the rail, and one end protruded overboard, like a gangway leading upon nothing, like a gangway leading over the deep sea, leading to death – as if inviting us to walk the plank at once and be done with our ridiculous troubles. And still the air, the sky – a ghost, something invisible was hailing the ship.

'Someone had the sense to look over, and there was the helmsman, who had impulsively jumped overboard, anxious to come back. He yelled and swam lustily like a merman, keeping up with the ship. We threw him a rope, and presently he stood amongst us streaming with water and very crestfallen. The captain had surrendered the wheel, and apart, elbow on rail and chin in hand, gazed at the sea wistfully. We asked ourselves, What next? I thought, Now, this is something like. This is great. I wonder what will happen. O youth!

'Suddenly Mahon sighted a steamer far astern. Captain Beard said, "We may do something with her yet." We hoisted two flags, which said in the international language of the sea, "On fire. Want immediate assistance." The steamer grew bigger rapidly, and by and by spoke with two flags on her foremast, "I am coming to your assistance."

'In half an hour she was abreast, to windward, within hail, and rolling slightly, with her engines stopped. We lost our composure, and yelled all together with excitement, "We've been blown up." A man in a white helmet, on the bridge, cried, "Yes! All right! all right!" and he nodded his head, and smiled, and made soothing motions with his hand as though at a lot of frightened children. One of the boats dropped in the water, and walked towards us upon the sea with her long oars. Four Calashes pulled a swinging stroke. This was my first sight of Malay seamen. I've known them since, but what struck me then was their unconcern: they came alongside, and even the bowman standing up and holding to our main-chains with the boat-hook did not deign to lift his head for a glance. I thought people who had been blown up deserved more attention.

'A little man, dry like a chip and agile like a monkey, clambered up. It was the mate of the steamer. He gave one look, and cried, "O boys – you had better quit."

'We were silent. He talked apart with the captain for a time – seemed to argue with him. Then they went away together to the steamer.

'When our skipper came back we learned that the steamer was the *Sommerville*, Captain Nash, from West Australia to Singapore *via*

Batavia with mails, and that the agreement was she should tow us to Anjer or Batavia, if possible, where we could extinguish the fire by scuttling, and then proceed on our voyage to Bankok! The old man seemed excited. "We will do it yet," he said to Mahon, fiercely. He shook his fist at the sky. Nobody else said a word.

'At noon the steamer began to tow. She went ahead slim and high, and what was left of the *Judea* followed at the end of seventy fathom of tow-rope – followed her swiftly like a cloud of smoke with mastheads protruding above. We went aloft to furl the sails. We coughed on the yards, and were careful about the bunts. Do you see the lot of us there, putting a neat furl on the sails of that ship doomed to arrive nowhere? There was not a man who didn't think that at any moment the masts would topple over. From aloft we could not see the ship for smoke, and they worked carefully, passing the gaskets with even turns. "Harbour furl – aloft there!" cried Mahon from below.

'You understand this? I don't think one of those chaps expected to get down in the usual way. When we did I heard them saying to each other, "I thought we would come down overboard, in a lump – sticks and all – blame me if I didn't." "That's what I was thinking to myself," would answer wearily another battered and bandaged scarecrow. And, mind, these were men without the drilled-in habit of obedience. To an onlooker they would be a lot of profane scallywags without a redeeming point. What made them do it – what made them obey me when I, thinking consciously how fine it was, made them drop the bunt of the foresail twice to try and do it better? What? They had no professional reputation – no examples, no praise. It wasn't a sense of duty; they all knew well enough how to shirk, and laze, and dodge – when they had a mind to it – and mostly they had. Was it the two pounds ten a month that sent them there? They didn't think their pay half good enough. No; it was something in them, something inborn and subtle and everlasting. I don't say positively that the crew of a French or German merchantman wouldn't have done it, but I doubt whether it would have been done in the same way. There was a completeness in it, something solid like a principle, and masterful like an instinct – a disclosure of something secret – of that hidden something, that gift of good or evil that makes racial difference, that shapes the fate of nations.

'It was that night at ten that, for the first time since we had been fighting it, we saw the fire. The speed of the towing had fanned the smouldering destruction. A blue gleam appeared forward, shining below the wreck of the deck. It wavered in patches, it seemed to stir and creep like the light of a glowworm. I saw it first, and told Mahon. "Then the game's up," he said. "We had better stop this towing, or she will burst out suddenly fore and aft before we can clear out." We set up a yell; rang bells to attract their attention; they towed on. At last Mahon and I had to crawl forward and cut the rope with an axe. There was no time to cast off the lashings. Red tongues could be seen licking the wilderness of splinters under our feet as we made our way back to the poop.

'Of course they very soon found out in the steamer that the rope was gone. She gave a loud blast of her whistle, her lights were seen sweeping in a wide circle, she came up ranging close alongside, and stopped. We were all in a tight group on the poop looking at her. Every man had saved a little bundle or a bag. Suddenly a conical flame with a twisted top shot up forward and threw upon the black sea a circle of light, with the two vessels side by side and heaving gently in its centre. Captain Beard had been sitting on the gratings still and mute for hours, but now he rose slowly and advanced in front of us, to the mizzen-shrouds. Captain Nash hailed: "Come along! Look sharp. I have mailbags on board. I will take you and your boats to Singapore."

'"Thank you! No!" said our skipper. "We must see the last of the ship."

'"I can't stand by any longer," shouted the other. "Mails – you know."

'"Ay! ay! We are all right."

'"Very well! I'll report you in Singapore. . . Goodbye!"

'He waved his hand. Our men dropped their bundles quietly. The steamer moved ahead, and passing out of the circle of light, vanished at once from our sight, dazzled by the fire which burned fiercely. And then I knew that I would see the East first as commander of a small boat. I thought it fine; and the fidelity to the old ship was fine. We should see the last of her. Oh, the glamour of youth! Oh, the fire of it, more dazzling than the flames of the burning ship, throwing a magic light on the wide earth, leaping audaciously to the sky, presently to be quenched by time, more cruel, more pitiless, more bitter than the sea – and like the flames of the burning ship surrounded by an impenetrable night.'

*   *   *

'The old man warned us in his gentle and inflexible way that it was part of our duty to save for the underwriters as much as we could of the ship's gear. Accordingly we went to work aft, while she blazed forward to give us plenty of light. We lugged out a lot of rubbish. What didn't we save? An old barometer fixed with an absurd quantity of screws nearly cost me my life: a sudden rush of smoke came upon me, and I just got away in time. There were various stores, bolts of canvas, coils of rope; the poop looked like a marine bazaar, and the boats were lumbered to the gunwales. One would have thought the old man wanted to take as much as he could of his first command with him. He was very, very quiet, but off his balance evidently. Would you believe it? He wanted to take a length of old stream-cable and a kedge-anchor with him in the long-boat. We said, "Ay, ay, sir," deferentially, and on the quiet let the things slip overboard. The heavy medicine-chest went that way, two bags of green coffee, tins of paint – fancy, paint! – a whole lot of things. Then I was ordered with two hands into the boats to make a stowage and get them ready against the time it would be proper for us to leave the ship.

'We put everything straight, stepped the long-boat's mast for our skipper, who was to take charge of her, and I was not sorry to sit down for a moment. My face felt raw, every limb ached as if broken, I was aware of all my ribs, and would have sworn to a twist in the backbone. The boats, fast astern, lay in a deep shadow, and all around I could see the circle of the sea lighted by the fire. A gigantic flame arose forward straight and clear. It flared fierce, with noises like the whirr of wings, with rumbles as of thunder. There were cracks, detonations, and from the cone of flame the sparks flew upwards, as man is born to trouble, to leaky ships, and to ships that burn.

'What bothered me was that the ship, lying broadside to the swell and to such wind as there was – a mere breath – the boats would not keep astern where they were safe, but persisted, in a pig-headed way boats have, in getting under the counter and then swinging alongside. They were knocking about dangerously and coming near the flame, while the ship rolled on them, and, of course, there was always the danger of the masts going over the side at any moment. I and my two boat-keepers kept them off as best we could, with oars and boat-hooks; but to be constantly at it became exasperating, since there was no reason why we should not leave at once. We could not see those on board, nor could we imagine what caused the delay. The boat-keepers were swearing feebly, and I had not only my share of the work but also had to keep at it two men who showed a constant inclination to lay themselves down and let things slide.

'At last I hailed, "On deck there," and someone looked over. "We're ready here," I said. The head disappeared, and very soon popped up again. "The captain says, All right, sir, and to keep the boats well clear of the ship."

'Half an hour passed. Suddenly there was a frightful racket, rattle, clanking of chain, hiss of water, and millions of sparks flew up into the shivering column of smoke that stood leaning slightly above the ship. The cat-heads had burned away, and the two red-hot anchors had gone to the bottom, tearing out after them two hundred fathom of red-hot chain. The ship trembled, the mass of flame swayed as if ready to collapse, and the fore top-gallant-mast fell. It darted down like an arrow of fire, shot under, and instantly leaping up within an oar's-length of the boats, floated quietly, very black on the luminous sea. I hailed the deck again. After some time a man in an unexpectedly cheerful but also muffled tone, as though he had been trying to speak with his mouth shut, informed me, "Coming directly, sir," and vanished. For a long time I heard nothing but the whirr and roar of the fire. There were also whistling sounds. The boats jumped, tugged at the painters, ran at each other playfully, knocked their sides together, or, do what we would, swung in a bunch against the ship's side. I couldn't stand it any longer, and swarming up a rope, clambered aboard over the stern.

'It was as bright as day. Coming up like this, the sheet of fire facing me was a terrifying sight, and the heat seemed hardly bearable at first. On a settee cushion dragged out of the cabin, Captain Beard, his legs drawn up and one arm under his head, slept with the light playing on him. Do you know what the rest were busy about? They were sitting on deck right aft, round an open case, eating bread and cheese and drinking bottled stout.

'On the background of flames twisting in fierce tongues above their heads they seemed at home like salamanders, and looked like a band of desperate pirates. The fire sparkled in the whites of their eyes, gleamed on patches of white skin seen through the torn shirts. Each had the marks as of a battle about him – bandaged heads, tied-up arms, a strip of dirty rag round a knee – and each man had a bottle between his legs and a chunk of cheese in his hand. Mahon got up. With his handsome and disreputable head, his hooked profile, his long white beard, and with an uncorked bottle in his hand, he resembled one of those reckless sea-robbers of old making merry amidst violence and disaster. "The last meal on board," he explained solemnly. "We've had nothing to eat all day, and it was no use leaving all this." He flourished the bottle and indicated the sleeping skipper. "He said he couldn't swallow anything, so I got him to lie down," he went on; and as I stared, "I don't know whether you are aware, young fellow, the man has had no sleep to speak of for days – and there will be dam' little sleep in the boats." "There will be no boats by and by if you fool about much longer," I said, indignantly. I walked up to the skipper and shook him by the shoulder. At last he opened his eyes, but did not move. "Time to leave her, sir," I said, quietly.

'He got up painfully, looked at the flames, at the sea sparkling round the ship, and black, black as ink farther away; he looked at the stars shining dim through a thin veil of smoke in a sky black, black as Erebus.

' "Youngest first," he said.

'And the ordinary seaman, wiping his mouth with the back of his hand, got up, clambered over the taffrail, and vanished. Others followed. One, on the point of going over, stopped short to drain his bottle, and with a great swing of his arm flung it at the fire. "Take this!" he cried.

'The skipper lingered disconsolately, and we left him to commune alone for a while with his first command. Then I went up again and brought him away at last. It was time. The ironwork on the poop was hot to the touch.

'Then the painter of the long-boat was cut, and the three boats, tied together, drifted clear of the ship. It was just sixteen hours after the explosion when we abandoned her. Mahon had charge of the second boat, and I had the smallest – the fourteen-foot thing. The long-boat would have taken the lot of us; but the skipper said we must save as much property as we could – for the underwriters – and so I got my first command. I had two men with me, a bag of biscuits, a few tins of meat, and a breaker of water. I was ordered to keep close to the long-boat, that in case of bad weather we might be taken into her.

'And do you know what I thought? I thought I would part company as soon as I could. I wanted to have my first command all to myself. I wasn't going to sail in a squadron if there were a chance for independent cruising. I would make land by myself. I would beat the other boats. Youth! All youth! The silly, charming, beautiful youth.

'But we did not make a start at once. We must see the last of the ship. And so the boats drifted about that night, heaving and setting on the swell. The men dozed, waked, sighed, groaned. I looked at the burning ship.

'Between the darkness of earth and heaven she was burning fiercely upon a disc of purple sea shot by the blood-red play of gleams; upon a disc of water glittering and sinister. A high, clear flame, an immense and lonely flame, ascended from the ocean, and from its summit the black smoke poured continuously at the sky. She burned furiously, mournful and imposing like a funeral pile kindled in the night, surrounded by the sea, watched over by the stars. A magnificent death had come like a grace, like a gift, like a reward to that old ship at the end of her laborious days. The surrender of her weary ghost to the keeping of stars and sea was stirring like the sight of a glorious triumph.

The masts fell just before daybreak, and for a moment there was a burst and turmoil of sparks that seemed to fill with flying fire the night patient and watchful, the vast night lying silent upon the sea. At daylight she was only a charred shell, floating still under a cloud of smoke and bearing a glowing mass of coal within.

'Then the oars were got out, and the boats forming in a line moved round her remains as if in procession – the long-boat leading. As we pulled across her stern a slim dart of fire shot out viciously at us, and suddenly she went down, head first, in a great hiss of steam. The unconsumed stern was the last to sink; but the paint had gone, had cracked, had peeled off, and there were no letters, there was no word, no stubborn device that was like her soul, to flash at the rising sun her creed and her name.

'We made our way north. A breeze sprang up, and about noon all the boats came together for the last time. I had no mast or sail in mine, but I made a mast out of a spare oar and hoisted a boat-awning for a sail, with a boat-hook for a yard. She was certainly over-masted, but I had the satisfaction of knowing that with the wind aft I could beat the other two. I had to wait for them. Then we all had a look at the captain's chart, and, after a sociable meal of hard bread and water, got our last instructions. These were simple: steer north, and keep together as much as possible. "Be careful with that jury-rig, Marlow," said the captain; and Mahon, as I sailed proudly past his boat, wrinkled his curved nose and hailed, "You will sail that ship of yours under water, if you don't look out, young fellow." He was a malicious old man – and may the deep sea where he sleeps now rock him gently, rock him tenderly to the end of time!

'Before sunset a thick rain-squall passed over the two boats, which were far astern, and that was the last I saw of them for a time. Next day I sat steering my cockle-shell – my first command – with nothing but water and sky around me. I did sight in the afternoon the upper sails of a ship far away, but said nothing, and my men did not notice her. You see I was afraid she might be homeward bound, and I had no mind to turn back from the portals of the East. I was steering for Java – another blessed name – like Bankok, you know. I steered many days.

'I need not tell you what it is to be knocking about in an open boat. I remember nights and days of calm, when we pulled, we pulled, and the boat seemed to stand still, as if bewitched within the circle of the sea horizon. I remember the heat, the deluge of rain-squalls that kept us baling for dear life (but filled our water-cask), and I remember sixteen hours on end with a mouth dry as a cinder and a steering-oar over the stern to keep my first command head on to a breaking sea. I did not know how good a man I was till then. I remember the drawn faces, the dejected figures of my two men, and I remember my youth and the feeling that will never come back any more – the feeling that I could last for ever, outlast the sea, the earth, and all men; the deceitful feeling that lures us on to joys, to perils, to love, to vain effort – to death; the triumphant conviction of strength, the heat of life in the handful of dust, the glow in the heart that with every year grows dim, grows cold, grows small, and expires – and expires, too soon, too soon – before life itself.

'And this is how I see the East. I have seen its secret places and have looked into its very soul; but now I see it always from a small boat, a high outline of mountains, blue and afar in the morning; like faint mist at noon; a jagged wall of purple at sunset. I have the feel of the oar in my hand, the vision of a scorching blue sea in my eyes. And I see a bay, a wide bay, smooth as glass and polished like ice, shimmering in the dark. A red light burns far off upon the gloom of the land, and the night is soft and warm. We drag at the oars with aching arms, and suddenly a puff of wind, a puff faint and tepid and laden with strange odours of blossoms, of aromatic wood, comes out of the still night – the first sigh of the East on my face. That I can never forget. It was impalpable and enslaving, like a charm, like a whispered promise of mysterious delight.

'We had been pulling this finishing spell for eleven hours. Two pulled, and he whose turn it was to rest sat at the tiller. We had made out the red light in that bay and steered for it, guessing it must mark some small coasting port. We passed two vessels, outlandish and high-sterned, sleeping at anchor, and, approaching the light, now very dim, ran the boat's nose against the end of a jutting wharf. We were blind with fatigue. My men dropped the oars and fell off the thwarts as if dead. I made fast to a pile. A current rippled softly. The scented obscurity of the shore was grouped into vast masses, a density of colossal clumps of vegetation, probably – mute and fantastic shapes. And at their foot the semicircle of a beach gleamed faintly, like an illusion. There was not a light, not a stir, not a sound. The mysterious East faced me, perfumed like a flower, silent like death, dark like a grave.

'And I sat weary beyond expression, exulting like a conqueror, sleepless and entranced as if before a profound, a fateful enigma.

'A splashing of oars, a measured dip reverberating on the level of water, intensified by the silence of the shore into loud claps, made me jump up. A boat, a European boat, was coming in. I invoked the name of the dead; I hailed: *Judea* ahoy! A thin shout answered.

'It was the captain. I had beaten the flagship by three hours, and I was glad to hear the old man's voice again, tremulous and tired. "Is it you, Marlow?" "Mind the end of that jetty, sir," I cried.

'He approached cautiously, and brought up with the deep-sea lead-line which we had saved – for the underwriters. I eased my painter and fell alongside. He sat, a broken figure at the stern, wet with dew, his hands clasped in his lap. His men were asleep already. "I had a terrible time of it," he murmured. "Mahon is behind – not very far." We conversed in whispers, in low whispers, as if afraid to wake up the land. Guns, thunder, earthquakes would not have awakened the men just then.

'Looking round as we talked, I saw away at sea a bright light travelling in the night. "There's a steamer passing the bay," I said. She was not passing, she was entering, and she even came close and anchored. "I wish," said the old man, "you would find out whether she is English. Perhaps they could give us a passage somewhere." He seemed nervously anxious. So by dint of punching and kicking I started one of my men into a state of somnambulism, and giving him an oar, took another and pulled towards the lights of the steamer.

'There was a murmur of voices in her, metallic hollow clangs of the engine-room, footsteps on the deck. Her ports shone, round like dilated eyes. Shapes moved about, and there was a shadowy man high up on the bridge. He heard my oars.

'And then, before I could open my lips, the East spoke to me, but it was in a Western voice. A torrent of words was poured into the enigmatical, the fateful silence; outlandish, angry words, mixed with words and even whole sentences of good English, less strange but even more surprising. The voice swore and cursed violently; it riddled the solemn peace of the bay by a volley of abuse. It began by calling me Pig, and from that went crescendo into unmentionable adjectives – in English. The man up there raged aloud in two languages, and with a sincerity in his fury that almost convinced me I had, in some way, sinned against the harmony of the universe. I could hardly see him, but began to think he would work himself into a fit.

'Suddenly he ceased, and I could hear him snorting and blowing like a porpoise. I said –

'"What steamer is this, pray?"

'"Eh? What's this? And who are you?"

'"Castaway crew of an English barque burnt at sea. We came here tonight. I am the second mate. The captain is in the long-boat, and wishes to know if you would give us a passage somewhere."

'"Oh, my goodness! I say . . . This is the *Celestial* from Singapore on her return trip. I'll arrange with your captain in the morning . . . and . . . I say . . . did you hear me just now?"

'"I should think the whole bay heard you."

'"I thought you were a shore-boat. Now, look here – this infernal lazy scoundrel of a caretaker has gone to sleep again – curse him. The light is out, and I nearly ran foul of the end of this damned jetty. This is the third time he plays me this trick. Now, I ask you, can anybody stand this kind of thing? It's enough to drive a man out of his mind. I'll report him . . . I'll get the Assistant Resident to give him the sack, by . . . ! See – there's no light. It's out, isn't it? I take you to witness the light's out. There should be a light, you know. A red light on the – "

'"There was a light," I said, mildly.

'"But it's out, man! What's the use of talking like this? You can see for yourself it's out – don't you? If you had to take a valuable steamer along this God-forsaken coast you would want a light too. I'll kick him from end to end of his miserable wharf. You'll see if I don't. I will – "

'"So I may tell my captain you'll take us?" I broke in.

'"Yes, I'll take you. Good-night," he said, brusquely.

'I pulled back, made fast again to the jetty, and then went to sleep at last. I had faced the silence of the East. I had heard some of its language. But when I opened my eyes again the silence was as complete as though it had never been broken. I was lying in a flood of light, and the sky had never looked so far, so high, before. I opened my eyes and lay without moving.

'And then I saw the men of the East – they were looking at me. The whole length of the jetty was full of people. I saw brown, bronze, yellow faces, the black eyes, the glitter, the colour of an Eastern crowd. And all these beings stared without a murmur, without a sigh, without a movement. They stared down at the boats, at the sleeping men who at night had come to them from the sea. Nothing moved. The fronds of palms stood still against the sky. Not a branch stirred along the shore, and the brown roofs of hidden houses peeped through the green foliage, through the big leaves that hung shining and still like leaves forged of heavy metal. This was the East of the ancient navigators, so old, so mysterious, resplendent and sombre, living and unchanged, full of danger and promise. And these were the men. I sat up suddenly. A wave of movement passed through the crowd from end to end, passed along the heads, swayed the bodies, ran along the jetty like a ripple on the water, like a breath of wind on a field – and all was still again. I see it now – the wide sweep of the bay, the glittering sands, the wealth of green infinite and varied, the sea blue like the sea of a dream, the crowd of attentive faces, the blaze of vivid colour – the water reflecting it all, the curve of the shore, the jetty, the high-sterned outlandish craft floating still, and the three boats with the tired men from the West sleeping, unconscious of the land and the people and of the violence of sunshine. They slept thrown across the thwarts, curled on bottom-boards, in the careless attitudes of death. The head of the old skipper, leaning back in the stern of the long-boat, had fallen on his breast, and he looked as though he would never wake. Farther out old Mahon's face was upturned to the sky, with the long white beard spread out on his breast, as though he had been shot where he sat at the tiller; and a man, all in a heap in the bows of the boat, slept with both arms embracing the stem-head and with his cheek laid on the gunwale. The East looked at them without a sound.

'I have known its fascination since; I have seen the mysterious shores, the still water, the lands of brown nations, where a stealthy Nemesis lies in wait, pursues, overtakes so many of the conquering race, who are proud of their wisdom, of their knowledge, of their strength. But for me all the East is contained in that vision of my youth. It is all in that moment when I opened my young eyes on it. I came upon it from a tussle with the sea – and I was young – and I saw it looking at me. And this is all that is left of it! Only a moment; a moment of strength, of romance, of glamour – of youth! . . . A flick of sunshine upon a strange shore, the time to remember, the time for a sigh, and – goodbye! – Night – Goodbye . . .!'

He drank.

'Ah! The good old time – the good old time. Youth and the sea. Glamour and the sea! The good, strong sea, the salt, bitter sea, that could whisper to you and roar at you and knock your breath out of you.'

He drank again.

'By all that's wonderful it is the sea, I believe, the sea itself – or is it youth alone? Who can tell? But you here – you all had something out of life: money, love – whatever one gets on shore – and, tell me, wasn't that the best time, that time when we were young at sea; young and had nothing, on the sea that gives nothing, except hard knocks – and sometimes a chance to feel your strength – that only – what you all regret?'

And we all nodded at him: the man of finance, the man of accounts, the man of law, we all nodded at him over the polished table that like a still sheet of brown water reflected our faces, lined, wrinkled; our faces marked by toil, by deceptions, by success, by love; our weary eyes looking still, looking always, looking anxiously for something out of life, that while it is expected is already gone – has passed unseen, in a sigh, in a flash – together with the youth, with the strength, with the romance of illusions.

Amy Foster

Kennedy is a country doctor, and lives in Colebrook, on the shores of Eastbay. The high ground rising abruptly behind the red roofs of the little town crowds the quaint High Street against the wall which defends it from the sea. Beyond the sea-wall there curves for miles in a vast and regular sweep the barren beach of shingle, with the village of Brenzett standing out darkly across the water, a spire in a clump of trees; and still further out the perpendicular column of a lighthouse, looking in the distance no bigger than a lead-pencil, marks the vanishing-point of the land. The country at the back of Brenzett is low and flat; but the bay is fairly well sheltered from the seas, and occasionally a big ship, windbound or through stress of weather, makes use of the anchoring ground a mile and a half due north from you as you stand at the back door of the Ship Inn in Brenzett. A dilapidated windmill near by lifting its shattered arms from a mound no loftier than a rubbish-heap, and a Martello tower squatting at the water's edge half a mile to the south of the coastguard cottages, are familiar to the skippers of small craft. These are the official sea marks for the patch of trustworthy bottom represented on the Admiralty charts by an irregular oval of dots enclosing several figures six, with a tiny anchor engraved among them, and the legend 'mud and shells' over all.

The brow of the upland overtops the square tower of the Colebrook Church. The slope is green and looped by a white road. Ascending along this road, you open a valley broad and shallow, a wide green trough of pastures and hedges merging inland into a vista of purple tints and flowing lines closing the view.

In this valley down to Brenzett and Colebrook and up to Darnford, the market town fourteen miles away, lies the practice of my friend Kennedy. He had begun life as a surgeon in the Navy, and afterwards had been the companion of a famous traveller, in the days when there were continents with unexplored interiors. His papers on the fauna and flora made him known to scientific societies. And now he had come to a country practice – from choice. The penetrating power of his mind, acting like a corrosive fluid, had destroyed his ambition, I fancy. His intelligence is of a scientific order, of an investigating habit, and of that unappeasable curiosity which believes that there is a particle of a general truth in every mystery.

A good many years ago now, on my return from abroad, he invited me to stay with him. I came readily enough, and as he could not neglect his patients to keep me company, he took me on his rounds – thirty miles or so of an afternoon, sometimes. I waited for him on the roads; the horse reached after the leafy twigs, and, sitting high in the dogcart, I could hear Kennedy's laugh through the half-open door of some cottage. He had a big, hearty laugh that would have fitted a man twice his size, a brisk manner, a bronzed face, and a pair of grey, profoundly attentive eyes. He had the talent of making people talk to him freely, and an inexhaustible patience in listening to their tales.

One day, as we trotted out of a large village into a shady bit of road, I saw on our left hand a low, black cottage, with diamond panes in the windows, a creeper on the end wall, a roof of shingle, and some roses climbing on the rickety trellis-work of the tiny porch. Kennedy pulled up to a walk. A woman, in full sunlight, was throwing a dripping blanket over a line stretched between two old apple-trees. And as the bobtailed, long-necked chestnut, trying to get his head, jerked the left hand, covered by a thick dogskin glove, the doctor raised his voice over the hedge: 'How's your child, Amy?'

I had the time to see her dull face, red, not with a mantling blush, but as if her flat cheeks had been vigorously slapped, and to take in the squat figure, the scanty, dusty brown hair drawn into a tight knot at the back of the head. She looked quite young. With a distinct catch in her breath, her voice sounded low and timid.

'He's well, thank you.'

We trotted again. 'A young patient of yours,' I said; and the doctor, flicking the chestnut absently, muttered, 'Her husband used to be.'

'She seems a dull creature,' I remarked listlessly.

'Precisely,' said Kennedy. 'She is very passive. It's enough to look at the red hands hanging at the end of those short arms, at those slow, prominent brown eyes, to know the inertness of her mind – an inertness that one would think made it everlastingly safe from all the surprises of imagination. And yet which of us is safe? At any rate, such as you see her, she had enough imagination to fall in love. She's the daughter of one Isaac Foster, who from a small farmer has sunk into a shepherd; the beginning of his misfortunes dating from his runaway marriage with the cook of his widowed father – a well-to-do, apoplectic grazier, who passionately struck his name off his will, and had been heard to utter threats against his life. But this old affair, scandalous enough to serve as a motive for a Greek tragedy, arose from the similarity of their characters. There are other tragedies, less scandalous and of a subtler poignancy, arising from irreconcilable differences and from that fear of the Incomprehensible that hangs over all our heads – over all our heads . . . '

The tired chestnut dropped into a walk; and the rim of the sun, all red in a speckless sky, touched familiarly the smooth top of a ploughed rise near the road as I had seen it times innumerable touch the distant horizon of the sea. The uniform brownness of the harrowed field glowed with a rosy tinge, as though the powdered clods had sweated out in minute pearls of blood the toil of uncounted ploughmen. From the edge of a copse a waggon with two horses was rolling gently along the ridge. Raised above our heads upon the sky-line, it loomed up against the red sun, triumphantly big, enormous, like a chariot of giants drawn by two slow-stepping steeds of legendary proportions. And the clumsy figure of the man plodding at the head of the leading horse projected itself on the background of the Infinite with a heroic uncouthness. The end of his carter's whip quivered high up in the blue. Kennedy discoursed –

'She's the eldest of a large family. At the age of fifteen they put her out to service at the New Barns Farm. I attended Mrs Smith, the tenant's wife, and saw that girl there for the first time. Mrs Smith, a genteel person with a sharp nose, made her put on a black dress every afternoon. I don't know what induced me to notice her at all. There are faces that call your attention by a curious want of definiteness in their whole aspect, as, walking in a mist, you peer attentively at a vague shape which, after all, may be nothing more curious or strange than a signpost. The only peculiarity I perceived in her was a slight hesitation in her utterance, a sort of preliminary stammer which passes away with the first word. When sharply spoken to, she was apt to lose her head at once; but her heart was of the kindest. She had never been heard to express a dislike for a single human being, and she was tender to every living creature. She was devoted to Mrs Smith, to Mr Smith, to their dogs, cats, canaries; and as to Mrs Smith's grey parrot, its peculiarities exercised upon her a positive fascination. Nevertheless, when that outlandish bird, attacked by the cat, shrieked for help in human accents, she ran out into the yard stopping her ears, and did not prevent the crime. For Mrs Smith this was another evidence of her stupidity; on the other hand, her want of charm, in view of Smith's well-known frivolousness, was a great recommendation. Her short-sighted eyes would swim with pity for a poor mouse in a trap, and she had been seen once by some boys on her knees in the wet grass helping a toad in difficulties. If it's true, as some German fellow has said, that without phosphorus there is no thought, it is still more true that there is no kindness of heart without a certain amount of imagination. She had some. She had even more than is necessary to understand suffering and to be moved by pity. She fell in love under circumstances that leave no room for doubt in the matter; for you need imagination to form a notion of beauty at all, and still more to discover your ideal in an unfamiliar shape.

'How this aptitude came to her, what it did feed upon, is an inscrutable mystery. She was born in the village, and had never been further away from it than Colebrook or perhaps Darnford. She lived for four years with the Smiths. New Barns is an isolated farmhouse a mile away from the road, and she was content to look day after day at the same fields, hollows, rises; at the trees and the hedgerows; at the faces of the four men about the farm, always the same – day after day, month after month, year after year. She never showed a desire for conversation, and, as it seemed to me, she did not know how to smile. Sometimes of a fine Sunday afternoon she would put on her best dress, a pair of stout boots, a large grey hat trimmed with a black feather (I've seen her in that finery), seize an absurdly slender parasol, climb over two stiles, tramp over three fields and along two hundred yards of road – never further. There stood Foster's cottage. She would help her mother to give their tea to the younger children, wash up the crockery, kiss the little ones, and go back to the farm. That was all. All the rest, all the change, all the relaxation. She never seemed to wish for anything more. And then she fell in love. She fell in love silently, obstinately – perhaps helplessly. It came slowly, but when it came it worked like a powerful spell; it was love as the Ancients understood it: an irresistible and fateful impulse – a possession! Yes, it was in her to become haunted and possessed by a face, by a presence, fatally, as though she had been a pagan worshipper of form under a joyous sky – and to be awakened at last from that mysterious forgetfulness of self, from that enchantment, from that transport, by a fear resembling the unaccountable terror of a brute . . . '

With the sun hanging low on its western limit, the expanse of the grasslands framed in the counterscarps of the rising ground took on a gorgeous and sombre aspect. A sense of penetrating sadness, like that inspired by a grave strain of music, disengaged itself from the silence of the fields. The men we met walked past, slow, unsmiling, with downcast eyes, as if the melancholy of an over-burdened earth had weighted their feet, bowed their shoulders, borne down their glances.

'Yes,' said the doctor to my remark, 'one would think the earth is under a curse, since of all her children these that cling to her the closest are uncouth in body and as leaden of gait as if their very hearts were loaded with chains. But here on this same road you might have seen amongst these heavy men a being lithe, supple and long-limbed, straight like a pine, with something striving upwards in his appearance as though the heart within him had been buoyant. Perhaps it was only the force of the contrast, but when he was passing one of these villagers here, the soles of his feet did not seem to me to touch the dust of the road. He vaulted over the stiles, paced these slopes with a long elastic stride that made him noticeable at a great distance, and had lustrous black eyes. He was so different from the mankind around that, with his freedom of movement, his soft – a little startled, glance, his olive complexion and graceful bearing, his humanity suggested to me the nature of a woodland creature. He came from there.'

The doctor pointed with his whip, and from the summit of the descent seen over the rolling tops of the trees in a park by the side of the road, appeared the level sea far below us, like the floor of an immense edifice inlaid with bands of dark ripple, with still trails of glitter, ending in a belt of glassy water at the foot of the sky. The light blur of smoke, from an invisible steamer, faded on the great clearness of the horizon like the mist of a breath on a mirror; and, inshore, the white sails of a coaster, with the appearance of disentangling themselves slowly from under the branches, floated clear of the foliage of the trees.

'Shipwrecked in the bay?' I said.

'Yes; he was a castaway. A poor emigrant from central Europe bound to America and washed ashore here in a storm. And for him, who knew nothing of the earth, England was an undiscovered country. It was some time before he learned its name; and for all I know he might have expected to find wild beasts or wild men here, when, crawling in the dark over the sea-wall, he rolled down the other side into a dyke, where it was another miracle he didn't get drowned. But he struggled instinctively like an animal under a net, and this blind struggle threw him out into a field. He must have been, indeed, of a tougher fibre than he looked to withstand without expiring such buffetings, the violence of his exertions, and so much fear. Later on, in his broken English that resembled curiously the speech of a young child, he told me himself that he put his trust in God, believing he was no longer in this world. And truly – he would add – how was he to know? He fought his way against the rain and the gale on all fours, and crawled at last among some sheep huddled close under the lee of a hedge. They ran off in all directions, bleating in the darkness, and he welcomed the first familiar sound he heard on these shores. It must have been two in the morning then. And this is all we know of the manner of his landing, though he did not arrive unattended by any means. Only his grisly company did not begin to come ashore till much later in the day . . . '

The doctor gathered the reins, clicked his tongue; we trotted down the hill. Then turning, almost directly, a sharp corner into the High Street, we rattled over the stones and were home.

Late in the evening Kennedy, breaking a spell of moodiness that had come over him, returned to the story. Smoking his pipe, he paced the long room from end to end. A reading-lamp concentrated all its light upon the papers on his desk; and, sitting by the open window, I saw, after the windless, scorching day, the frigid splendour of a hazy sea lying motionless under the moon. Not a whisper, not a splash, not a stir of the shingle, not a footstep, not a sigh came up from the earth below – never a sign of life but the scent of climbing jasmine; and Kennedy's voice, speaking behind me, passed through the wide casement, to vanish outside in a chill and sumptuous stillness.

' . . . The relations of shipwrecks in the olden time tell us of much suffering. Often the castaways were only saved from drowning to die miserably from starvation on a barren coast; others suffered violent death or else slavery, passing through years of precarious existence with people to whom their strangeness was an object of suspicion, dislike or fear. We read about these things, and they are very pitiful. It is indeed hard upon a man to find himself a lost stranger, helpless, incomprehensible, and of a mysterious origin, in some obscure corner of the earth. Yet amongst all the adventurers shipwrecked in all the wild parts of the world, there is not one, it seems to me, that ever had to suffer a fate so simply tragic as the man I am speaking of, the most innocent of adventurers cast out by the sea in the bight of this bay, almost within sight from this very window.

'He did not know the name of his ship. Indeed, in the course of time we discovered he did not even know that ships had names – 'like Christian people'; and when, one day, from the top of the Talfourd Hill, he beheld the sea lying open to his view, his eyes roamed afar, lost in an air of wild surprise, as though he had never seen such a sight before. And probably he had not. As far as I could make out, he had been hustled together with many others on board an emigrant ship lying at the mouth of the Elbe, too bewildered to take note of his surroundings, too weary to see anything, too anxious to care. They were driven below into the 'tween-deck and battened down from the very start. It was a low timber dwelling – he would say – with wooden beams overhead, like the houses in his country, but you went into it down a ladder. It was very large, very cold, damp and sombre, with places in the manner of wooden boxes where people had to sleep one above another, and it kept on rocking all ways at once all the time. He crept into one of these boxes and lay down there in the clothes in which he had left his home many days before, keeping his bundle and his stick by his side. People groaned, children cried, water dripped, the lights went out, the walls of the place creaked, and everything was being shaken so that in one's little box one dared not lift one's head. He had lost touch with his only companion (a young man from the same valley, he said), and all the time a great noise of wind went on outside and heavy blows fell – boom! boom! An awful sickness overcame him, even to the point of making him neglect his prayers. Besides, one could not tell whether it was morning or evening. It seemed always to be night in that place.

'Before that he had been travelling a long, long time on the iron track. He looked out of the window, which had a wonderfully clear glass in it, and the trees, the houses, the fields, and the long roads seemed to fly round and round about him till his head swam. He gave me to understand that he had on his passage beheld uncounted multitudes of people – whole nations – all dressed in such clothes as the rich wear. Once he was made to get out of the carriage, and slept through a night on a bench in a house of bricks with his bundle under his head; and once for many hours he had to sit on a floor of flat stones dozing, with his knees up and with his bundle between his feet. There was a roof over him, which seemed made of glass, and was so high that the tallest mountain-pine he had ever seen would have had room to grow under it. Steam-machines rolled in at one end and out at the other. People swarmed more than you can see on a feast-day round the miraculous Holy Image in the yard of the Carmelite Convent down in the plains where, before he left his home, he drove his mother in a wooden cart – a pious old woman who wanted to offer prayers and make a vow for his safety. He could not give me an idea of how large and lofty and full of noise and smoke and gloom, and clang of iron, the place was, but someone had told him it was called Berlin. Then they rang a bell, and another steam-machine came in, and again he was taken on and on through a land that wearied his eyes by its flatness without a single bit of a hill to be seen anywhere. One more night he spent shut up in a building like a good stable with a litter of straw on the floor, guarding his bundle amongst a lot of men, of whom not one could understand a single word he said. In the morning they were all led down to the stony shores of an extremely broad muddy river, flowing not between hills but between houses that seemed immense. There was a steam-machine that went on the water, and they all stood upon it packed tight, only now there were with them many women and children who made much noise. A cold rain fell, the wind blew in his face; he was wet through, and his teeth chattered. He and the young man from the same valley took each other by the hand.

'They thought they were being taken to America straight away, but suddenly the steam-machine bumped against the side of a thing like a great house on the water. The walls were smooth and black, and there uprose, growing from the roof as it were, bare trees in the shape of crosses, extremely high. That's how it appeared to him then, for he had never seen a ship before. This was the ship that was going to swim all the way to America. Voices shouted, everything swayed; there was a ladder dipping up and down. He went up on his hands and knees in mortal fear of falling into the water below, which made a great splashing. He got separated from his companion, and when he descended into the bottom of that ship his heart seemed to melt suddenly within him.

'It was then also, as he told me, that he lost contact for good and all with one of those three men who the summer before had been going about through all the little towns in the foothills of his country. They would arrive on market-days driving in a peasant's cart, and would set up an office in an inn or some other Jew's house. There were three of them, of whom one with a long beard looked venerable; and they had red cloth collars round their necks and gold lace on their sleeves like Government officials. They sat proudly behind a long table; and in the next room, so that the common people shouldn't hear, they kept a cunning telegraph machine, through which they could talk to the Emperor of America. The fathers hung about the door, but the young men of the mountains would crowd up to the table asking many questions, for there was work to be got all the year round at three dollars a day in America, and no military service to do.

'But the American Kaiser would not take everybody. Oh no! He himself had great difficulty in getting accepted, and the venerable man in uniform had to go out of the room several times to work the telegraph on his behalf. The American Kaiser engaged him at last at three dollars, he being young and strong. However, many able young men backed out, afraid of the great distance; besides, those only who had some money could be taken. There were some who had sold their huts and their land because it cost a lot of money to get to America; but then, once there, you had three dollars a day, and if you were clever you could find places where true gold could be picked up on the ground. His father's house was getting over full. Two of his brothers were married and had children. He promised to send money home from America by post twice a year. His father sold an old cow, a pair of piebald mountain ponies of his own raising, and a cleared plot of fair pasture land on the sunny slope of a pine-clad pass to a Jew inn-keeper, in order to pay the people of the ship that took men to America to get rich in a short time.

'He must have been a real adventurer at heart, for how many of the greatest enterprises in the conquest of the earth had for their beginning just such a bargaining away of the paternal cow for the mirage of true gold far away! I have been telling you more or less in my own words what I learned fragmentarily in the course of two or three years, during which I seldom missed an opportunity of a friendly chat with him. He told me this story of his adventure with many flashes of white teeth and lively glances of black eyes, at first in a sort of anxious baby-talk, then, as he acquired the language, with great fluency, but always with that singing, soft, and at the same time vibrating intonation that instilled a strangely penetrating power into the sound of the most familiar English words, as if they had been the words of an unearthly language. And he always would come to an end, with many emphatic shakes of his head, upon that awful sensation of his heart melting within him directly he set foot on board that ship. Afterwards there seemed to come for him a period of blank ignorance, at any rate as to facts. No doubt he must have been abominably seasick and abominably unhappy – this soft and passionate adventurer, taken thus out of his knowledge, and feeling bitterly as he lay in his emigrant bunk his utter loneliness; for his was a highly sensitive nature. The next thing we know of him for certain is that he had been hiding in Hammond's pig-pound by the side of the road to Norton, six miles, as the crow flies, from the sea. Of these experiences he was unwilling to speak: they seemed to have seared into his soul a sombre sort of wonder and indignation. Through the rumours of the countryside, which lasted for a good many days after his arrival, we know that the fishermen of West Colebrook had been disturbed and startled by heavy knocks against the walls of weatherboard cottages, and by a voice crying piercingly strange words in the night. Several of them turned out even, but, no doubt, he had fled in sudden alarm at their rough angry tones hailing each other in the darkness. A sort of frenzy must have helped him up the steep Norton Hill. It was he, no doubt, who early the following morning had been seen lying (in a swoon, I should say) on the roadside grass by the Brenzett carrier, who actually got down to have a nearer look, but drew back, intimidated by the perfect immobility, and by something queer in the aspect of that tramp, sleeping so still under the showers. As the day advanced, some children came dashing into school at Norton in such a fright that the schoolmistress went out and spoke indignantly to a "horrid-looking man" on the road. He edged away, hanging his head, for a few steps, and then suddenly ran off with extraordinary fleetness. The driver of Mr Bradley's milk-cart made no secret of it that he had lashed with his whip at a hairy sort of gypsy fellow who, jumping up at a turn of the road by the Vents, made a snatch at the pony's bridle. And he caught him a good one too, right over the face, he said, that made him drop down in the mud a jolly sight quicker than he had jumped up; but it was a good half a mile before he could stop the pony. Maybe that in his desperate endeavours to get help, and in his need to get in touch with someone, the poor devil had tried to stop the cart. Also three boys confessed afterwards to throwing stones at a funny tramp, knocking about all wet and muddy, and, it seemed, very drunk, in the narrow deep lane by the limekilns. All this was the talk of three villages for days; but we have Mrs Finn's (the wife of Smith's waggoner) unimpeachable testimony that she saw him get over the low wall of Hammond's pig-pound and lurch straight at her, babbling aloud in a voice that was enough to make one die of fright. Having the baby with her in a perambulator, Mrs Finn called out to him to go away, and as he persisted in coming nearer, she hit him courageously with her umbrella over the head, and, without once looking back, ran like the wind with the perambulator as far as the first house in the village. She stopped then, out of breath, and spoke to old Lewis, hammering there at a heap of stones; and the old chap, taking off his immense black wire goggles, got up on his shaky legs to look where she pointed. Together they followed with their eyes the figure of the man running over a field; they saw him fall down, pick himself up, and run on again, staggering and waving his long arms above his head, in the direction of the New Barns Farm. From that moment he is plainly in the toils of his obscure and touching destiny. There is no doubt after this of what happened to him. All is certain now: Mrs Smith's intense terror; Amy Foster's stolid conviction held against the other's nervous attack, that the man "meant no harm"; Smith's exasperation (on his return from Darnford Market) at finding the dog barking himself into a fit, the back-door locked, his wife in hysterics; and all for an unfortunate dirty tramp, supposed to be even then lurking in his stackyard. Was he? He would teach him to frighten women.

'Smith is notoriously hot-tempered, but the sight of some nonde-script and miry creature sitting cross-legged amongst a lot of loose straw, and swinging itself to and fro like a bear in a cage, made him pause. Then this tramp stood up silently before him, one mass of mud and filth from head to foot. Smith, alone amongst his stacks with this apparition, in the stormy twilight ringing with the infuriated barking of the dog, felt the dread of an inexplicable strangeness. But when that being, parting with his black hands the long matted locks that hung before his face, as you part the two halves of a curtain, looked out at him with glistening, wild, black-and-white eyes, the weirdness of this silent encounter fairly staggered him. He has admitted since (for the story has been a legitimate subject of conversation about here for years) that he made more than one step backwards. Then a sudden burst of rapid, senseless speech persuaded him at once that he had to do with an escaped lunatic. In fact, that impression never wore off completely. Smith has not in his heart given up his secret conviction of the man's essential insanity to this very day.

'As the creature approached him, jabbering in a most discomposing manner, Smith (unaware that he was being addressed as "gracious lord", and adjured in God's name to afford food and shelter) kept on speaking firmly but gently to it, and retreating all the time into the other yard. At last, watching his chance, by a sudden charge he bundled him headlong into the wood-lodge, and instantly shot the bolt. Thereupon he wiped his brow, though the day was cold. He had done his duty to the community by shutting up a wandering and probably dangerous maniac. Smith isn't a hard man at all, but he had room in his brain only for that one idea of lunacy. He was not imaginative enough to ask himself whether the man might not be perishing with cold and hunger. Meantime, at first, the maniac made a great deal of noise in the lodge. Mrs Smith was screaming upstairs, where she had locked herself in her bedroom; but Amy Foster sobbed piteously at the kitchen-door, wringing her hands and muttering, "Don't! don't!" I dare say Smith had a rough time of it that evening with one noise and another, and this insane, disturbing voice crying obstinately through the door only added to his irritation. He couldn't possibly have connected this troublesome lunatic with the sinking of a ship in Eastbay, of which there had been a rumour in the Darnford market-place. And I dare say the man inside had been very near to insanity on that night. Before his excitement collapsed and he became unconscious he was throwing himself violently about in the dark, rolling on some dirty sacks, and biting his fists with rage, cold, hunger, amazement, and despair.

'He was a mountaineer of the eastern range of the Carpathians, and the vessel sunk the night before in Eastbay was the Hamburg emigrant ship *Herzogin Sophia-Dorothea*, of appalling memory.

'A few months later we could read in the papers the accounts of the bogus "Emigration Agencies" among the Sclavonian peasantry in the more remote provinces of Austria. The object of these scoundrels was to get hold of the poor ignorant people's homesteads, and they were in league with the local usurers. They exported their victims through Hamburg mostly. As to the ship, I had watched her out of this very window, reaching close-hauled under short canvas into the bay on a dark, threatening afternoon. She came to an anchor, correctly by the chart, off the Brenzett coastguard station. I remember before the night fell looking out again at the outlines of her spars and rigging that stood out dark and pointed on a background of ragged, slaty clouds like another and a slighter spire to the left of the Brenzett church-tower. In the evening the wind rose. At midnight I could hear in my bed the terrific gusts and the sounds of a driving deluge.

'About that time the coastguardmen thought they saw the lights of a steamer over the anchoring-ground. In a moment they vanished; but it is clear that another vessel of some sort had tried for shelter in the bay on that awful, blind night, had rammed the German ship amidships (a breach – as one of the divers told me afterwards – 'that you could sail a Thames barge through'), and then had gone out either scathless or damaged, who shall say; but had gone out, unknown, unseen, and fatal, to perish mysteriously at sea. Of her nothing ever came to light, and yet the hue and cry that was raised all over the world would have found her out if she had been in existence anywhere on the face of the waters.

'A completeness without a clue, and a stealthy silence as of a neatly executed crime, characterise this murderous disaster, which, as you may remember, had its gruesome celebrity. The wind would have prevented the loudest outcries from reaching the shore; there had been evidently no time for signals of distress. It was death without any sort of fuss. The Hamburg ship, filling all at once, capsized as she sank, and at daylight there was not even the end of a spar to be seen above water. She was missed, of course, and at first the coastguardmen surmised that she had either dragged her anchor or parted her cable some time during the night, and had been blown out to sea. Then, after the tide turned, the wreck must have shifted a little and released some of the bodies, because a child – a little fair-haired child in a red frock – came ashore abreast of the Martello tower. By the afternoon you could see along three miles of beach dark figures with bare legs dashing in and out of the tumbling foam, and rough-looking men, women with hard faces, children, mostly fair-haired, were being carried, stiff and dripping, on stretchers, on wattles, on ladders, in a long procession past the door of the Ship Inn, to be laid out in a row under the north wall of the Brenzett Church.

'Officially, the body of the little girl in the red frock is the first thing that came ashore from that ship. But I have patients amongst the seafaring population of West Colebrook, and, unofficially, I am informed that very early that morning two brothers, who went down to look after their cobble hauled up on the beach, found, a good way from Brenzett, an ordinary ship's hencoop lying high and dry on the shore, with eleven drowned ducks inside. Their families ate the birds, and the hencoop was split into firewood with a hatchet. It is possible that a man (supposing he happened to be on deck at the time of the accident) might have floated ashore on that hencoop. He might. I admit it is improbable, but there was the man – and for days, nay, for weeks – it didn't enter our heads that we had amongst us the only living soul that had escaped from that disaster. The man himself, even when he learned to speak intelligibly, could tell us very little. He remembered he had felt better (after the ship had anchored, I suppose), and that the darkness, the wind, and the rain took his breath away. This looks as if he had been on deck some time during that night. But we mustn't forget he had been taken out of his knowledge, that he had been sea-sick and battened down below for four days, that he had no general notion of a ship or of the sea, and therefore could have no definite idea of what was happening to him. The rain, the wind, the darkness he knew; he understood the bleating of the sheep, and he remembered the pain of his wretchedness and misery, his heartbroken astonishment that it was neither seen nor understood, his dismay at finding all the men angry and all the women fierce. He had approached them as a beggar, it is true, he said; but in his country, even if they gave nothing, they spoke gently to beggars. The children in his country were not taught to throw stones at those who asked for compassion. Smith's strategy overcame him completely. The wood-lodge presented the horrible aspect of a dungeon. What would be done to him next? . . . No wonder that Amy Foster appeared to his eyes with the aureole of an angel of light. The girl had not been able to sleep for thinking of the poor man, and in the morning, before the Smiths were up, she slipped out across the back yard. Holding the door of the wood-lodge ajar, she looked in and extended to him half a loaf of white bread – "such bread as the rich eat in my country," he used to say.

'At this he got up slowly from amongst all sorts of rubbish, stiff, hungry, trembling, miserable, and doubtful. "Can you eat this?" she asked in her soft and timid voice. He must have taken her for a "gracious lady". He devoured ferociously, and tears were falling on the crust. Suddenly he dropped the bread, seized her wrist, and imprinted a kiss on her hand. She was not frightened. Through his forlorn condition she had observed that he was good-looking. She shut the door and walked back slowly to the kitchen. Much later on, she told

Mrs Smith, who shuddered at the bare idea of being touched by that creature.

'Through this act of impulsive pity he was brought back again within the pale of human relations with his new surroundings. He never forgot it – never.

'That very same morning old Mr Swaffer (Smith's nearest neighbour) came over to give his advice, and ended by carrying him off. He stood, unsteady on his legs, meek, and caked over in half-dried mud, while the two men talked around him in an incomprehensible tongue. Mrs Smith had refused to come downstairs till the madman was off the premises; Amy Foster, from far within the dark kitchen, watched through the open back door; and he obeyed the signs that were made to him to the best of his ability. But Smith was full of mistrust. "Mind, sir! It may be all his cunning," he cried repeatedly in a tone of warning. When Mr Swaffer started the mare, the deplorable being sitting humbly by his side, through weakness, nearly fell out over the back of the high two-wheeled cart. Swaffer took him straight home. And it is then that I come upon the scene.

'I was called in by the simple process of the old man beckoning to me with his forefinger over the gate of his house as I happened to be driving past. I got down, of course.

"I've got something here,' he mumbled, leading the way to an outhouse at a little distance from his other farm-buildings.

'It was there that I saw him first, in a long low room taken upon the space of that sort of coach-house. It was bare and whitewashed, with a small square aperture glazed with one cracked, dusty pane at its further end. He was lying on his back upon a straw pallet; they had given him a couple of horse-blankets, and he seemed to have spent the remainder of his strength in the exertion of cleaning himself. He was almost speechless; his quick breathing under the blankets pulled up to his chin, his glittering, restless black eyes reminded me of a wild bird caught in a snare. While I was examining him, old Swaffer stood silently by the door, passing the tips of his fingers along his shaven upper lip. I gave some directions, promised to send a bottle of medicine, and naturally made some enquiries.

'Smith caught him in the stackyard at New Barns,' said the old chap in his deliberate, unmoved manner, and as if the other had been indeed a sort of wild animal, 'That's how I came by him. Quite a curiosity, isn't he? Now tell me, doctor – you've been all over the world – don't you think that's a bit of a Hindu we've got hold of here?'

'I was greatly surprised. His long black hair scattered over the straw bolster contrasted with the olive pallor of his face. It occurred to me he might be a Basque. It didn't necessarily follow that he should understand Spanish; but I tried him with the few words I know, and also with some French. The whispered sounds I caught by bending my ear to his lips puzzled me utterly. That afternoon the young ladies from the rectory (one of them read Goethe with a dictionary, and the other had struggled with Dante for years), coming to see Miss Swaffer, tried their German and Italian on him from the doorway. They retreated, just the least bit scared by the flood of passionate speech which, turning on his pallet, he let out at them. They admitted that the sound was pleasant, soft, musical – but, in conjunction with his looks perhaps, it was startling – so excitable, so utterly unlike anything one had ever heard. The village boys climbed up the bank to have a peep through the little square aperture. Everybody was wondering what Mr Swaffer would do with him.

'He simply kept him.

'Swaffer would be called eccentric were he not so much respected. They will tell you that Mr Swaffer sits up as late as ten o'clock at night to read books, and they will tell you also that he can write a cheque for two hundred pounds without thinking twice about it. He himself would tell you that the Swaffers have owned land between this and Darnford for these three hundred years. He must be eighty-five today, but he does not look a bit older than when I first came here. He is a great breeder of sheep, and deals extensively in cattle. He attends market days for miles around in every sort of weather, and drives sitting bowed low over the reins, his lank grey hair curling over the collar of his warm coat, and with a green plaid rug round his legs. The calmness of advanced age gives a solemnity to his manner. He is clean-shaved; his lips are thin and sensitive; something rigid and monachal in the set of his features lends a certain elevation to the character of his face. He has been known to drive miles in the rain to see a new kind of rose in somebody's garden, or a monstrous cabbage grown by a cottager. He loves to hear tell of or to be shown something what he calls "outlandish". Perhaps it was just that outlandishness of the man which influenced old Swaffer. Perhaps it was only an inexplicable caprice. All I know is that at the end of three weeks I caught sight of Smith's lunatic digging in Swaffer's kitchen garden. They had found out he could use a spade. He dug barefooted.

'His black hair flowed over his shoulders. I suppose it was Swaffer who had given him the striped old cotton shirt; but he wore still the national brown cloth trousers (in which he had been washed ashore) fitting to the leg almost like tights; was belted with a broad leathern belt studded with little brass discs; and had never yet ventured into the village. The land he looked upon seemed to him kept neatly, like the grounds round a landowner's house; the size of the cart-horses struck him with astonishment; the roads resembled garden walks, and the aspect of the people, especially on Sundays, spoke of opulence. He wondered what made them so hardhearted and their children so bold. He got his food at the back door, carried it in both hands, carefully, to his outhouse, and, sitting alone on his pallet, would make the sign of the cross before he began. Beside the same pallet, kneeling in the early darkness of the short days, he recited aloud the Lord's Prayer before he slept. Whenever he saw old Swaffer he would bow with veneration from the waist, and stand erect while the old man, with his fingers over his upper lip, surveyed him silently. He bowed also to Miss Swaffer, who kept house frugally for her father – a broad-shouldered, big-boned woman of forty-five, with the pocket of her dress full of keys, and a grey, steady eye. She was Church – as people said (while her father was one of the trustees of the Baptist Chapel) – and wore a little steel cross at her waist. She dressed severely in black, in memory of one of the innumerable Bradleys of the neighbourhood, to whom she had been engaged some twenty-five years ago – a young farmer who broke his neck out hunting on the eve of the wedding-day. She had the unmoved countenance of the deaf, spoke very seldom, and her lips, thin like her father's, astonished one sometimes by a mysteriously ironic curl.

'These were the people to whom he owed allegiance, and an overwhelming loneliness seemed to fall from the leaden sky of that winter without sunshine. All the faces were sad. He could talk to no one, and had no hope of ever understanding anybody. It was as if these had been the faces of people from the other world – dead people – he used to tell me years afterwards. Upon my word, I wonder he did not go mad. He didn't know where he was. Somewhere very far from his mountains – somewhere over the water. Was this America, he wondered?

'If it hadn't been for the steel cross at Miss Swaffer's belt he would not, he confessed, have known whether he was in a Christian country at all. He used to cast stealthy glances at it, and feel comforted. There was nothing here the same as in his country! The earth and the water were different; there were no images of the Redeemer by the roadside. The very grass was different, and the trees. All the trees but the three old Norway pines on the bit of lawn before Swaffer's house, and these reminded him of his country. He had been detected once, after dusk, with his forehead against the trunk of one of them, sobbing, and talking to himself. They had been like brothers to him at that time, he affirmed. Everything else was strange. Conceive you the kind of an existence over-shadowed, oppressed, by the everyday material appearances, as if by the visions of a nightmare. At night, when he could not sleep, he kept on thinking of the girl who gave him the first piece of bread he had eaten in this foreign land. She had been neither fierce nor angry, nor frightened. Her face he remembered as the only comprehensible face amongst all these faces that were as closed, as mysterious, and as mute as the faces of the dead who are possessed of a knowledge beyond the comprehension of the living. I wonder whether the memory of her compassion prevented him from cutting his throat. But there! I suppose I am an old sentimentalist, and forget the instinctive love of life which it takes all the strength of an uncommon despair to overcome.

'He did the work which was given him with an intelligence which surprised old Swaffer. By and by it was discovered that he could help at the ploughing, could milk the cows, feed the bullocks in the cattle-yard, and was of some use with the sheep. He began to pick up words, too, very fast; and suddenly, one fine morning in spring, he rescued from an untimely death a grandchild of old Swaffer.

'Swaffer's younger daughter is married to Willcox, a solicitor and the Town Clerk of Colebrook. Regularly twice a year they come to stay with the old man for a few days. Their only child, a little girl not three years old at the time, ran out of the house alone in her little white pinafore, and, toddling across the grass of a terraced garden, pitched herself over a low wall head first into the horsepond in the yard below.

'Our man was out with the waggoner and the plough in the field nearest to the house, and as he was leading the team round to begin a fresh furrow, he saw, through the gap of a gate, what for anybody else would have been a mere flutter of something white. But he had straight-glancing, quick, far-reaching eyes, that only seemed to flinch and lose their amazing power before the immensity of the sea. He was barefooted, and looking as outlandish as the heart of Swaffer could desire. Leaving the horses on the turn, to the inexpressible disgust of the waggoner he bounded off, going over the ploughed ground in long leaps, and suddenly appeared before the mother, thrust the child into her arms, and strode away.

'The pond was not very deep; but still, if he had not had such good eyes, the child would have perished – miserably suffocated in the foot or so of sticky mud at the bottom. Old Swaffer walked out slowly into the field, waited till the plough came over to his side, had a good look at him, and without saying a word went back to the house. But from that time they laid out his meals on the kitchen table; and at first, Miss Swaffer, all in black and with an inscrutable face, would come and stand in the doorway of the living-room to see him make a big sign of the cross before he fell to. I believe that from that day, too, Swaffer began to pay him regular wages.

'I can't follow step by step his development. He cut his hair short, was seen in the village and along the road going to and fro his work like any other man. Children ceased to shout after him. He became aware of social differences, but remained for a long time surprised at the bare poverty of the churches among so much wealth. He couldn't understand either why they were kept shut up on weekdays. There was nothing to steal in them. Was it to keep people from praying too often? The rectory took much notice of him about that time, and I believe the young ladies attempted to prepare the ground for his conversion. They could not, however, break him of his habit of crossing himself, but he went so far as to take off the string with a couple of brass medals the size of a sixpence, a tiny metal cross, and a square sort of scapulary which he wore round his neck. He hung them on the wall by the side of his bed, and he was still to be heard every evening reciting the Lord's Prayer, in incomprehensible words and in a slow, fervent tone, as he had heard his old father do at the head of all the kneeling family, big and little, on every evening of his life. And though he wore corduroys at work, and a slop-made pepper-and-salt suit on Sundays, strangers would turn round to look after him on the road. His foreignness had a peculiar and indelible stamp. At last people became used to see him. But they never became used to him. His rapid, skimming walk; his swarthy complexion; his hat cocked on the left ear; his habit, on warm evenings, of wearing his coat over one shoulder, like a hussar's dolman; his manner of leaping over the stiles, not as a feat of agility, but in the ordinary course of progression – all these peculiarities were, as one may say, so many causes of scorn and offence to the inhabitants of the village. *They* wouldn't in their dinner hour lie flat on their backs on the grass to stare at the sky. Neither did they go about the fields screaming dismal tunes. Many times have I heard his high-pitched voice from behind the ridge of some sloping sheep-walk, a voice light and soaring, like a lark's, but with a melancholy human note, over our fields that hear only the song of birds. And I would be startled myself. Ah! He was different: innocent of heart, and full of good will, which nobody wanted, this castaway, that, like a man transplanted into another planet, was separated by an immense space from his past and by an immense ignorance from his future. His quick, fervent utterance positively shocked everybody. "An excitable devil", they called him. One evening, in the tap-room of the Coach and Horses (having drunk some whisky), he upset them all by singing a love-song of his country. They hooted him down, and he was pained; but Preble, the lame wheelwright, and

Vincent, the fat blacksmith, and the other notables too, wanted to drink their evening beer in peace. On another occasion he tried to show them how to dance. The dust rose in clouds from the sanded floor; he leaped straight up amongst the deal tables, struck his heels together, squatted on one heel in front of old Preble, shooting out the other leg, uttered wild and exulting cries, jumped up to whirl on one foot, snapping his fingers above his head – and a strange carter who was having a drink in there began to swear, and cleared out with his half-pint in his hand into the bar. But when suddenly he sprang upon a table and continued to dance among the glasses, the landlord interfered. He didn't want any "acrobat tricks in the tap-room". They laid their hands on him. Having had a glass or two, Mr Swaffer's foreigner tried to expostulate: was ejected forcibly: got a black eye.

'I believe he felt the hostility of his human surroundings. But he was tough – tough in spirit, too, as well as in body. Only the memory of the sea frightened him, with that vague terror that is left by a bad dream. His home was far away; and he did not want now to go to America. I had often explained to him that there is no place on earth where true gold can be found lying ready and to be got for the trouble of the picking up. How then, he asked, could he ever return home with empty hands when there had been sold a cow, two ponies, and a bit of land to pay for his going? His eyes would fill with tears, and, averting them from the immense shimmer of the sea, he would throw himself face down on the grass. But sometimes, cocking his hat with a little conquering air, he would defy my wisdom. He had found his bit of true gold. That was Amy Foster's heart; which was "a golden heart, and soft to people's misery", he would say in the accents of overwhelming conviction.

'He was called Yanko. He had explained that this meant Little John; but as he would also repeat very often that he was a mountaineer (some word sounding in the dialect of his country like Goorall) he got it for his surname. And this is the only trace of him that the succeeding ages may find in the marriage register of the parish. There it stands – Yanko Goorall – in the rector's handwriting. The crooked cross made by the castaway, a cross whose tracing no doubt seemed to him the most solemn part of the whole ceremony, is all that remains now to perpetuate the memory of his name.

'His courtship had lasted some time – ever since he got his precarious footing in the community. It began by his buying for Amy Foster a green satin ribbon in Darnford. This was what you did in his country. You bought a ribbon at a Jew's stall on a fair-day. I don't suppose the girl knew what to do with it, but he seemed to think that his honourable intentions could not be mistaken.

'It was only when he declared his purpose to get married that I fully understood how, for a hundred futile and inappreciable reasons, how – shall I say odious? – he was to all the countryside. Every old woman in the village was up in arms. Smith, coming upon him near the farm, promised to break his head for him if he found him about again. But he twisted his little black moustache with such a bellicose air and rolled such big, black fierce eyes at Smith that this promise came to nothing. Smith, however, told the girl that she must be mad to take up with a man who was surely wrong in his head. All the same, when she heard him in the gloaming whistle from beyond the orchard a couple of bars of a weird and mournful tune, she would drop whatever she had in her hand – she would leave Mrs Smith in the middle of a sentence – and she would run out to his call. Mrs Smith called her a shameless hussy. She answered nothing. She said nothing at all to anybody, and went on her way as if she had been deaf. She and I alone in all the land, I fancy, could see his very real beauty. He was very good-looking, and most graceful in his bearing, with that something wild as of a woodland creature in his aspect. Her mother moaned over her dismally whenever the girl came to see her on her day out. The father was surly, but pretended not to know; and Mrs Finn once told her plainly that "this man, my dear, will do you some harm some day yet". And so it went on. They could be seen on the roads, she tramping stolidly in her finery – grey dress, black feather, stout boots, prominent white cotton gloves that caught your eye a hundred yards away; and he, his coat slung picturesquely over one shoulder, pacing by her side, gallant of bearing and casting tender glances upon the girl with the golden heart. I wonder whether he saw how plain she was. Perhaps, among types so different from what he had ever seen, he had not the power to judge; or perhaps he was seduced by the divine quality of her pity.

'Yanko was in great trouble meantime. In his country you get an old man for an ambassador in marriage affairs. He did not know how to proceed. However, one day in the midst of sheep in a field (he was now Swaffer's under-shepherd with Foster) he took off his hat to the father and declared himself humbly. "I dare say she's fool enough to marry you," was all Foster said. "And then," he used to relate, "he puts his hat on his head, looks black at me as if he wanted to cut my throat, whistles the dog, and off he goes, leaving me to do the work." The Fosters, of course, didn't like to lose the wages the girl earned: Amy used to give all her money to her mother. But there was in Foster a very genuine aversion to that match. He contended that the fellow was very good with sheep, but was not fit for any girl to marry. For one thing, he used to go along the hedges muttering to himself like a dam' fool; and then, these foreigners behave very queerly to women sometimes. And perhaps he would want to carry her off somewhere – or run off himself. It was not safe. He preached it to his daughter that the fellow might ill-use her in some way. She made no answer. It was, they said in the village, as if the man had done something to her. People discussed the matter. It was quite an excitement, and the two went on "walking out" together in the face of opposition. Then something unexpected happened.

'I don't know whether old Swaffer ever understood how much he was regarded in the light of a father by his foreign retainer. Anyway the relation was curiously feudal. So when Yanko asked formally for an interview – "and the Miss too" (he called the severe, deaf Miss Swaffer simply *Miss*) – it was to obtain their permission to marry. Swaffer heard him unmoved, dismissed him by a nod, and then shouted the intelligence into Miss Swaffer's best ear. She showed no surprise, and only remarked grimly, in a veiled blank voice, "He certainly won't get any other girl to marry him."

'It is Miss Swaffer who has all the credit of the munificence: but in a very few days it came out that Mr Swaffer had presented Yanko with a cottage (the cottage you've seen this morning) and something like an acre of ground – had made it over to him in absolute property. Willcox expedited the deed, and I remember him telling me he had a great pleasure in making it ready. It recited: "In consideration of saving the life of my beloved grandchild, Bertha Willcox."

'Of course, after that no power on earth could prevent them from getting married.

'Her infatuation endured. People saw her going out to meet him in the evening. She stared with unblinking, fascinated eyes up the road where he was expected to appear, walking freely, with a swing from the hip, and humming one of the love-tunes of his country. When the boy was born, he got elevated at the Coach and Horses, essayed again a song and a dance, and was again ejected. People expressed their commiseration for a woman married to that Jack-in-the-box. He didn't care. There was a man now (he told me boastfully) to whom he could sing and talk in the language of his country, and show how to dance by and by.

'But I don't know. To me he appeared to have grown less springy of step, heavier in body, less keen of eye. Imagination, no doubt; but it seems to me now as if the net of fate had been drawn closer round him already.

'One day I met him on the footpath over the Talfourd Hill. He told me that "women were funny". I had heard already of domestic differences. People were saying that Amy Foster was beginning to find out what sort of man she had married. He looked upon the sea with indifferent, unseeing eyes. His wife had snatched the child out of his arms one day as he sat on the doorstep crooning to it a song such as the mothers sing to babies in his mountains. She seemed to think he was doing it some harm. Women are funny. And she had objected to him praying aloud in the evening. Why? He expected the boy to repeat the prayer aloud after him by and by, as he used to do after his old father when he was a child – in his own country. And I discovered he longed for their boy to grow up so that he could have a man to talk with in that language that to our ears sounded so disturbing, so passionate, and so bizarre. Why his wife should dislike the idea he couldn't tell. But that would pass, he said. And tilting his head knowingly, he tapped his breastbone to indicate that she had a good heart: not hard, not fierce, open to compassion, charitable to the poor!

'I walked away thoughtfully; I wondered whether his difference, his strangeness, were not penetrating with repulsion that dull nature they had begun by irresistibly attracting. I wondered . . . '

The doctor came to the window and looked out at the frigid splendour of the sea, immense in the haze, as if enclosing all the earth with all the hearts lost among the passions of love and fear.

'Physiologically, now,' he said, turning away abruptly, 'it was possible. It was possible.'

He remained silent. Then went on –

'At all events, the next time I saw him he was ill – lung trouble. He was tough, but I dare say he was not acclimatised as well as I had supposed. It was a bad winter; and, of course, these mountaineers do get fits of home sickness; and a state of depression would make him vulnerable. He was lying half dressed on a couch downstairs.

'A table covered with a dark oilcloth took up all the middle of the little room. There was a wicker cradle on the floor, a kettle spouting steam on the hob, and some child's linen lay drying on the fender. The room was warm, but the door opens right into the garden, as you noticed perhaps.

'He was very feverish, and kept on muttering to himself. She sat on a chair and looked at him fixedly across the table with her brown, blurred eyes. "Why don't you have him upstairs?" I asked. With a start and a confused stammer she said, "Oh! ah! I couldn't sit with him upstairs, sir."

'I gave her certain directions; and going outside, I said again that he ought to be in bed upstairs. She wrung her hands. "I couldn't. I couldn't. He keeps on saying something – I don't know what." With the memory of all the talk against the man that had been dinned into her ears, I looked at her narrowly. I looked into her short-sighted eyes, at her dumb eyes that once in her life had seen an enticing shape, but seemed, staring at me, to see nothing at all now. But I saw she was uneasy.

'"What's the matter with him?" she asked in a sort of vacant trepidation. "He doesn't look very ill. I never did see anybody look like this before . . . "

'"Do you think," I asked indignantly, "he is shamming?"

'"I can't help it, sir," she said stolidly. And suddenly she clapped her hands and looked right and left. "And there's the baby. I am so frightened. He wanted me just now to give him the baby. I can't understand what he says to it."

'"Can't you ask a neighbour to come in tonight?" I asked.

'"Please, sir, nobody seems to care to come," she muttered, dully resigned all at once.

'I impressed upon her the necessity of the greatest care, and then had to go. There was a good deal of sickness that winter. "Oh, I hope he won't talk!" she exclaimed softly just as I was going away.

'I don't know how it is I did not see – but I didn't. And yet, turning in my trap, I saw her lingering before the door, very still, and as if meditating a flight up the miry road.

'Towards the night his fever increased.

'He tossed, moaned, and now and then muttered a complaint. And she sat with the table between her and the couch, watching every movement and every sound, with the terror, the unreasonable terror, of that man she could not understand creeping over her. She had drawn the wicker cradle close to her feet. There was nothing in her now but the maternal instinct and that unaccountable fear.

'Suddenly coming to himself, parched, he demanded a drink of water. She did not move. She had not understood, though he may have thought he was speaking in English. He waited, looking at her, burning with fever, amazed at her silence and immobility, and then he shouted impatiently, "Water! Give me water!"

'She jumped to her feet, snatched up the child, and stood still. He spoke to her, and his passionate remonstrances only increased her fear of that strange man. I believe he spoke to her for a long time, entreating, wondering, pleading, ordering, I suppose. She says she bore it as long as she could. And then a gust of rage came over him.

'He sat up and called out terribly one word – some word. Then he got up as though he hadn't been ill at all, she says. And as in fevered dismay, indignation, and wonder he tried to get to her round the table, she simply opened the door and ran out with the child in her arms. She heard him call twice after her down the road in a terrible voice – and fled. . . . Ah! but you should have seen stirring behind the dull, blurred glance of those eyes the spectre of the fear which had hunted her on that night three miles and a half to the door of Foster's cottage! I did the next day.

'And it was I who found him lying face down and his body in a puddle, just outside the little wicket-gate.

'I had been called out that night to an urgent case in the village, and on my way home at daybreak passed by the cottage. The door stood open. My man helped me to carry him in. We laid him on the couch. The lamp smoked, the fire was out, the chill of the stormy night oozed from the cheerless yellow paper on the wall. "Amy!" I called aloud, and my voice seemed to lose itself in the emptiness of this tiny house as if I had cried in a desert. He opened his eyes. "Gone!" he said distinctly. "I had only asked for water – only for a little water . . ."

'He was muddy. I covered him up and stood waiting in silence, catching a painfully gasped word now and then. They were no longer in his own language. The fever had left him, taking with it the heat of life. And with his panting breast and lustrous eyes he reminded me again of a wild creature under the net; of a bird caught in a snare. She had left him. She had left him – sick – helpless – thirsty. The spear of the hunter had entered his very soul. "Why?" he cried in the penetrating and indignant voice of a man calling to a responsible Maker. A gust of wind and a swish of rain answered.

'And as I turned away to shut the door he pronounced the word "Merciful!" and expired.

'Eventually I certified heart-failure as the immediate cause of death. His heart must have indeed failed him, or else he might have stood this night of storm and exposure, too. I closed his eyes and drove away. Not very far from the cottage I met Foster walking sturdily between the dripping hedges with his collie at his heels.

'"Do you know where your daughter is?" I asked.

'"Don't I!" he cried. "I am going to talk to him a bit. Frightening a poor woman like this."

'"He won't frighten her any more," I said. "He is dead."

'He struck with his stick at the mud.

'"And there's the child."

'Then, after thinking deeply for a while –

'"I don't know that it isn't for the best."

'That's what he said. And she says nothing at all now. Not a word of him. Never. Is his image as utterly gone from her mind as his lithe and striding figure, his carolling voice are gone from our fields? He is no longer before her eyes to excite her imagination into a passion of love or fear; and his memory seems to have vanished from her dull brain as a shadow passes away upon a white screen. She lives in the cottage and works for Miss Swaffer. She is Amy Foster for everybody, and the child is "Amy Foster's boy". She calls him Johnny – which means Little John.

'It is impossible to say whether this name recalls anything to her. Does she ever think of the past? I have seen her hanging over the boy's cot in a very passion of maternal tenderness. The little fellow was lying on his back, a little frightened at me, but very still, with his big black eyes, with his fluttered air of a bird in a snare. And looking at him I seemed to see again the other one – the father, cast out mysteriously by the sea to perish in the supreme disaster of loneliness and despair.'

An Anarchist

That year I spent the best two months of the dry season on one of the estates – in fact, on the principal cattle estate – of a famous meat-extract manufacturing company.

BOS. Bos. You have seen the three magic letters on the advertisement pages of magazines and newspapers, in the windows of provision merchants, and on calendars for next year you receive by post in the month of November. They scatter pamphlets also, written in a sickly enthusiastic style and in several languages, giving statistics of slaughter and bloodshed enough to make a Turk turn faint. The 'art' illustrating that 'literature' represents in vivid and shining colours a large and enraged black bull stamping upon a yellow snake writhing in emerald-green grass, with a cobalt-blue sky for a background. It is atrocious and it is an allegory. The snake symbolises disease, weakness – perhaps mere hunger, which last is the chronic disease of the majority of mankind. Of course everybody knows the BOS Ltd, with its unrivalled products: Vinobos, Jellybos, and the latest unequalled perfection, Tribos, whose nourishment is offered to you not only highly concentrated, but already half digested. Such apparently is the love that limited company bears to its fellow-men – even as the love of the father and mother penguin for their hungry fledglings.

Of course the capital of a country must be productively employed. I have nothing to say against the company. But being myself animated by feelings of affection towards my fellow-men, I am saddened by the modern system of advertising. Whatever evidence it offers of enterprise, ingenuity, impudence, and resource in certain individuals, it proves to my mind the wide prevalence of that form of mental degradation which is called gullibility.

In various parts of the civilised and uncivilised world I have had to swallow BOS with more or less benefit to myself, though without great pleasure. Prepared with hot water and abundantly peppered to bring out the taste, this extract is not really unpalatable. But I have never swallowed its advertisements. Perhaps they have not gone far enough. As far as I can remember they make no promise of everlasting youth to the users of BOS, nor yet have they claimed the power of raising the dead for their estimable products. Why this austere reserve, I wonder!

But I don't think they would have had me even on these terms. Whatever form of mental degradation I may (being but human) be suffering from, it is not the popular form. I am not gullible.

I have been at some pains to bring out distinctly this statement about myself in view of the story which follows. I have checked the facts as far as possible. I have turned up the files of French newspapers, and I also talked with the officer who commands the military guard on the Ile Royale, when in the course of my travels I reached Cayenne. I believe the story to be in the main true. It is the sort of story that no man, I think, would ever invent about himself, for it is neither grandiose nor flattering, nor yet funny enough to gratify a perverted vanity.

It concerns the engineer of the steam-launch belonging to the Marañon cattle estate of BOS Co. Ltd. This estate is also an island – an island as big as a small province, lying in the estuary of a great South American river. It is wild and not beautiful, but the grass growing on its low plains seems to possess exceptionally nourishing and flavouring qualities. It resounds with the lowing of innumerable herds – a deep and distressing sound under the open sky, rising like a monstrous protest of prisoners condemned to death. On the mainland, across twenty miles of discoloured muddy water, there stands a city whose name, let us say, is Horta.

But the most interesting characteristic of this island (which seems like a sort of penal settlement for condemned cattle) consists in its being the only known habitat of an extremely rare and gorgeous butterfly. The species is even more rare than it is beautiful, which is not saying little. I have already alluded to my travels. I travelled at that time, but strictly for myself and with a moderation unknown in our days of round-the-world tickets. I even travelled with a purpose. As a matter of fact, I am – 'Ha, ha, ha! – a desperate butterfly-slayer. Ha, ha, ha!'

This was the tone in which Mr Harry Gee, the manager of the cattle station, alluded to my pursuits. He seemed to consider me the greatest absurdity in the world. On the other hand, the BOS Co. Ltd, represented to him the acme of the nineteenth century's achievement. I believe that he slept in his leggings and spurs. His days he spent in the saddle flying over the plains, followed by a train of half-wild horsemen, who called him Don Enrique, and who had no definite idea of the BOS Co. Ltd, which paid their wages. He was an excellent manager, but I don't see why, when we met at meals, he should have thumped me on the back, with loud derisive enquiries: 'How's the deadly sport today? Butterflies going strong? Ha, ha, ha!' – especially as he charged me two dollars *per diem* for the hospitality of the BOS

Co. Ltd (capital £1,500,000, fully paid up), in whose balance-sheet for that year those monies are no doubt included. 'I don't think I can make it anything less in justice to my company,' he had remarked, with extreme gravity, when I was arranging with him the terms of my stay on the island.

His chaff would have been harmless enough if intimacy of intercourse in the absence of all friendly feeling were not a thing detestable in itself. Moreover, his facetiousness was not very amusing. It consisted in the wearisome repetition of descriptive phrases applied to people with a burst of laughter. 'Desperate butterfly-slayer. Ha, ha, ha!' was one sample of his peculiar wit which he himself enjoyed so much. And in the same vein of exquisite humour he called my attention to the engineer of the steam-launch, one day, as we strolled on the path by the side of the creek.

The man's head and shoulders emerged above the deck, over which were scattered various tools of his trade and a few pieces of machinery. He was doing some repairs to the engines. At the sound of our footsteps he raised anxiously a grimy face with a pointed chin and a tiny fair moustache. What could be seen of his delicate features under the black smudges appeared to me wasted and livid in the greenish shade of the enormous tree spreading its foliage over the launch moored close to the bank.

To my great surprise, Harry Gee addressed him as 'Crocodile', in that half-jeering, half-bullying tone which is characteristic of self-satisfaction in his delectable kind: 'How does the work get on, Crocodile?'

I should have said before that the amiable Harry had picked up French of a sort somewhere in some colony or other – and that he pronounced it with a disagreeable forced precision as though he meant to guy the language. The man in the launch answered him quickly in a pleasant voice. His eyes had a liquid softness and his teeth flashed dazzlingly white between his thin, drooping lips.

The manager turned to me, very cheerful and loud, explaining: 'I call him Crocodile because he lives half in, half out of the creek. Amphibious – see? There's nothing else amphibious living on the island except crocodiles; so he must belong to the species eh? But in reality he's nothing less than *un citoyen anarchiste de Barcelone*.'

'A citizen anarchist from Barcelona?' I repeated, stupidly, looking down at the man.

He had turned to his work in the engine-well of the launch and presented his bowed back to us. In that attitude I heard him protest, very audibly: 'I do not even know Spanish.'

'Hey? What? You dare to deny you come from over there?' the accomplished manager was down on him truculently.

At this the man straightened himself up, dropping a spanner he had been using, and faced us; but he trembled in all his limbs.

'I deny nothing, nothing, nothing!' he said, excitedly.

He picked up the spanner and went to work again without paying any further attention to us. After looking at him for a minute or so, we went away.

'Is he really an anarchist?' I asked, when out of ear-shot.

'I don't care a hang what he is,' answered the humorous official of the BOS Co. 'I gave him the name because it suited me to label him in that way. It's good for the company.'

'For the company!' I exclaimed, stopping short.

'Aha!' he triumphed, tilting up his hairless pug face and straddling his thin, long legs. 'That surprises you. I am bound to do my best for my company. They have enormous expenses. Why – our agent in Horta tells me they spend fifty thousand pounds every year in advertising all over the world! One can't be too economical in working the show. Well, just you listen. When I took charge here the estate had no steam-launch. I asked for one, and kept on asking by every mail till I got it; but the man they sent out with it chucked his job at the end of two months, leaving the launch moored at the pontoon in Horta. Got a better screw at a sawmill up the river – blast him! And ever since it has been the same thing. Any Scotch or Yankee vagabond that likes to call himself a mechanic out here gets eighteen pounds a month, and the next you know he's cleared out, after smashing something as likely as not. I give you my word that some of the objects I've had for engine-drivers couldn't tell the boiler from the funnel. But this fellow understands his trade, and I don't mean him to clear out. See?'

And he struck me lightly on the chest for emphasis. Disregarding his peculiarities of manner, I wanted to know what all this had to do with the man being an anarchist.

'Come!' jeered the manager. 'If you saw suddenly a barefooted, unkempt chap slinking amongst the bushes on the sea face of the island, and at the same time observed less than a mile from the beach, a small schooner full of niggers hauling off in a hurry, you wouldn't think the man fell there from the sky, would you? And it could be nothing else but either that or Cayenne. I've got my wits about me. Directly I sighted this queer game I said to myself – "Escaped Convict". I was as certain of it as I am of seeing you standing here this minute. So I spurred on straight at him. He stood his ground for a bit on a sand hillock crying out: "*Monsieur! Monsieur! Arrêtez!*" then at the last moment broke and ran for life. Says I to myself, "I'll tame you before I'm done with you." So without a single word I kept on, heading him off here and there. I rounded him up towards the shore, and at last I had him corralled on a spit, his heels in the water and nothing but sea and sky at his back, with my horse pawing the sand and shaking his head within a yard of him.

'He folded his arms on his breast then and stuck his chin up in a sort of desperate way; but I wasn't to be impressed by the beggar's posturing.

'Says I, "You're a runaway convict."

'When he heard French, his chin went down and his face changed.

' "I deny nothing," says he, panting yet, for I had kept him skipping about in front of my horse pretty smartly. I asked him what he was doing there. He had got his breath by then, and explained that he had meant to make his way to a farm which he understood (from the schooner's people, I suppose) was to be found in the neighbourhood. At that I laughed aloud and he got uneasy. Had he been deceived? Was there no farm within walking distance?

'I laughed more and more. He was on foot, and of course the first bunch of cattle he came across would have stamped him to rags under their hoofs. A dismounted man caught on the feeding-grounds hasn't got the ghost of a chance.

' "My coming upon you like this has certainly saved your life," I said. He remarked that perhaps it was so; but that for his part he had imagined I had wanted to kill him under the hoofs of my horse. I assured him that nothing would have been easier had I meant it. And then we came to a sort of dead stop. For the life of me I didn't know what to do with this convict, unless I chucked him into the sea. It occurred to me to ask him what he had been transported for. He hung his head.

' "What is it?" says I. "Theft, murder, rape, or what?" I wanted to hear what he would have to say for himself, though of course I expected it would be some sort of lie. But all he said was –

' "Make it what you like. I deny nothing. It is no good denying anything."

'I looked him over carefully and a thought struck me.

' "They've got anarchists there, too," I said. 'Perhaps you're one of them."

' "I deny nothing whatever, monsieur," he repeats.

'This answer made me think that perhaps he was not an anarchist. I believe those damned lunatics are rather proud of themselves. If he had been one, he would have probably confessed straight out.

' "What were you before you became a convict?"

' "*Ouvrier*," he says. "And a good workman, too."

'At that I began to think he must be an anarchist, after all. That's the class they come mostly from, isn't it? I hate the cowardly bomb-throwing brutes. I almost made up my mind to turn my horse short round and leave him to starve or drown where he was, whichever he liked best. As to crossing the island to bother me again, the cattle would see to that. I don't know what induced me to ask –

' "What sort of workman?"

'I didn't care a hang whether he answered me or not. But when he said at once, "*Mécanicien, monsieur*," I nearly jumped out of the saddle with excitement. The launch had been lying disabled and idle in the creek for three weeks. My duty to the company was clear. He noticed my start, too, and there we were for a minute or so staring at each other as if bewitched.

' "Get up on my horse behind me," I told him. "You shall put my steam-launch to rights." '

These are the words in which the worthy manager of the Marañon estate related to me the coming of the supposed anarchist. He meant to keep him – out of a sense of duty to the company – and the name he had given him would prevent the fellow from obtaining employment anywhere in Horta. The *vaqueros* of the estate, when they went on leave, spread it all over the town. They did not know what an anarchist was, nor yet what Barcelona meant. They called him Anarchisto de Barcelona, as if it were his Christian name and surname. But the people in town had been reading in their papers about the anarchists in Europe and were very much impressed. Over the jocular addition of 'de Barcelona' Mr Harry Gee chuckled with immense satisfaction. 'That breed is particularly murderous, isn't it? It makes the sawmills crowd still more afraid of having anything to do with him – see?' he exulted, candidly. 'I hold him by that name better than if I had him chained up by the leg to the deck of the steam-launch.

'And mark,' he added, after a pause, 'he does not deny it. I am not wronging him in any way. He is a convict of some sort, anyhow.'

'But I suppose you pay him some wages, don't you?' I asked.

'Wages! What does he want with money here? He gets his food from my kitchen and his clothing from the store. Of course I'll give him something at the end of the year, but you don't think I'd employ a convict and give him the same money I would give an honest man? I am looking after the interests of my company first and last.'

I admitted that, for a company spending fifty thousand pounds every year in advertising, the strictest economy was obviously necessary. The manager of the Marañon Estancia grunted approvingly.

'And I'll tell you what,' he continued: 'if I were certain he's an anarchist and he had the cheek to ask me for money, I would give him the toe of my boot. However, let him have the benefit of the doubt. I am perfectly willing to take it that he has done nothing worse than to stick a knife into somebody – with extenuating circumstances – French fashion, don't you know. But that subversive sanguinary rot of doing away with all law and order in the world makes my blood boil. It's simply cutting the ground from under the feet of every decent, respectable, hard-working person. I tell you that the consciences of people who have them, like you or I, must be protected in some way; or else the first low scoundrel that came along would in every respect be just as good as myself. Wouldn't he, now? And that's absurd!'

He glared at me. I nodded slightly and murmured that doubtless there was much subtle truth in his view.

The principal truth discoverable in the views of Paul the engineer was that a little thing may bring about the undoing of a man.

'*Il ne faut pas beaucoup pour perdre un homme*,' he said to me, thoughtfully, one evening.

I report this reflection in French, since the man was of Paris, not of Barcelona at all. At the Marañon he lived apart from the station, in a small shed with a metal roof and straw walls, which he called *mon atelier*. He had a work-bench there. They had given him several horse-blankets and a saddle – not that he ever had occasion to ride, but because no other bedding was used by the working-hands, who were all *vaqueros* – cattlemen. And on this horseman's gear, like a son of the plains, he used to sleep amongst the tools of his trade, in a litter of rusty scrap-iron, with a portable forge at his head, under the work-bench sustaining his grimy mosquito-net.

Now and then I would bring him a few candle ends saved from the scant supply of the manager's house. He was very thankful for these. He did not like to lie awake in the dark, he confessed. He complained that sleep fled from him. '*Le sommeil me fuit*,' he declared, with his habitual air of subdued stoicism, which made him sympathetic and touching. I made it clear to him that I did not attach undue importance to the fact of his having been a convict.

Thus it came about that one evening he was led to talk about himself. As one of the bits of candle on the edge of the bench burned down to the end, he hastened to light another.

He had done his military service in a provincial garrison and returned to Paris to follow his trade. It was a well-paid one. He told me with some pride that in a short time he was earning no less than ten francs a day. He was thinking of setting up for himself by and by and of getting married.

Here he sighed deeply and paused. Then with a return to his stoical note: 'It seems I did not know enough about myself.'

On his twenty-fifth birthday two of his friends in the repairing shop where he worked proposed to stand him a dinner. He was immensely touched by this attention.

'I was a steady man,' he remarked, 'but I am not less sociable than any other body.'

The entertainment came off in a little café on the Boulevard de la Chapelle. At dinner they drank some special wine. It was excellent. Everything was excellent; and the world – in his own words – seemed a very good place to live in. He had good prospects, some little money laid by, and the affection of two excellent friends. He offered to pay for all the drinks after dinner, which was only proper on his part.

They drank more wine; they drank liqueurs, cognac, beer, then more liqueurs and more cognac. Two strangers sitting at the next table looked at him, he said, with so much friendliness, that he invited them to join the party.

He had never drunk so much in his life. His elation was extreme, and so pleasurable that whenever it flagged he hastened to order more drinks.

'It seemed to me,' he said, in his quiet tone and looking on the ground in the gloomy shed full of shadows, 'that I was on the point of just attaining a great and wonderful felicity. Another drink, I felt, would do it. The others were holding out well with me, glass for glass.'

But an extraordinary thing happened. At something the strangers said his elation fell. Gloomy ideas – *des idées noires* – rushed into his head. All the world outside the café appeared to him as a dismal, evil place where a multitude of poor wretches had to work and slave to the sole end that a few individuals should ride in carriages and live riotously in palaces. He became ashamed of his happiness. The pity of mankind's cruel lot wrung his heart. In a voice choked with sorrow he tried to express these sentiments. He thinks he wept and swore in turns.

The two new acquaintances hastened to applaud his humane indignation. Yes. The amount of injustice in the world was indeed scandalous. There was only one way of dealing with the rotten state of society. Demolish the whole *sacrée boutique*. Blow up the whole iniquitous show.

Their heads hovered over the table. They whispered to him elo-
quently; I don't think they quite expected the result. He was extremely
drunk – mad drunk. With a howl of rage he leaped suddenly upon the
table. Kicking over the bottles and glasses, he yelled: '*Vive l'anarchie!*
Death to the capitalists!' He yelled this again and again. All round him
broken glass was falling, chairs were being swung in the air, people were
taking each other by the throat. The police dashed in. He hit, bit,
scratched and struggled, till something crashed down upon his head . . .

He came to himself in a police cell, locked up on a charge of assault,
seditious cries, and anarchist propaganda.

He looked at me fixedly with his liquid, shining eyes, that seemed
very big in the dim light.

'That was bad. But even then I might have got off somehow,
perhaps,' he said, slowly.

I doubt it. But whatever chance he had was done away with by a
young socialist lawyer who volunteered to undertake his defence. In
vain he assured him that he was no anarchist; that he was a quiet,
respectable mechanic, only too anxious to work ten hours per day at his
trade. He was represented at the trial as the victim of society and his
drunken shoutings as the expression of infinite suffering. The young
lawyer had his way to make, and this case was just what he wanted for a
start. The speech for the defence was pronounced magnificent.

The poor fellow paused, swallowed, and brought out the statement:
'I got the maximum penalty applicable to a first offence.'

I made an appropriate murmur. He hung his head and folded his
arms.

'When they let me out of prison,' he began, gently, 'I made tracks, of
course, for my old workshop. My *patron* had a particular liking for me
before; but when he saw me he turned green with fright and showed
me the door with a shaking hand.'

While he stood in the street, uneasy and disconcerted, he was
accosted by a middle-aged man who introduced himself as an engineer's fitter, too. 'I know who you are,' he said. 'I have attended your
trial. You are a good comrade and your ideas are sound. But the devil of
it is that you won't be able to get work anywhere now. These
bourgeois'll conspire to starve you. That's their way. Expect no mercy
from the rich.'

To be spoken to so kindly in the street had comforted him very
much. His seemed to be the sort of nature needing support and
sympathy. The idea of not being able to find work had knocked him
over completely. If his *patron*, who knew him so well for a quiet,
orderly, competent workman, would have nothing to do with him

now – then surely nobody else would. That was clear. The police, keeping their eye on him, would hasten to warn every employer inclined to give him a chance. He felt suddenly very helpless, alarmed and idle; and he followed the middle-aged man to the *estaminet* round the corner where he met some other good companions. They assured him that he would not be allowed to starve, work or no work. They had drinks all round to the discomfiture of all employers of labour and to the destruction of society.

He sat biting his lower lip.

'That is, monsieur, how I became a *compagnon*,' he said. The hand he passed over his forehead was trembling. 'All the same, there's something wrong in a world where a man can get lost for a glass more or less.'

He never looked up, though I could see he was getting excited under his dejection. He slapped the bench with his open palm.

'No!' he cried. 'It was an impossible existence! Watched by the police, watched by the comrades, I did not belong to myself any more! Why, I could not even go to draw a few francs from my savings-bank without a comrade hanging about the door to see that I didn't bolt! And most of them were neither more nor less than housebreakers. The intelligent, I mean. They robbed the rich; they were only getting back their own, they said. When I had had some drink I believed them. There were also the fools and the mad. *Des exaltés – quoi!* When I was drunk I loved them. When I got more drink I was angry with the world. That was the best time. I found refuge from misery in rage. But one can't be always drunk – *n'est-ce pas, monsieur?* And when I was sober I was afraid to break away. They would have stuck me like a pig.'

He folded his arms again and raised his sharp chin with a bitter smile.

'By and by they told me it was time to go to work. The work was to rob a bank. Afterwards a bomb would be thrown to wreck the place. My beginner's part would be to keep watch in a street at the back and to take care of a black bag with the bomb inside till it was wanted. After the meeting at which the affair was arranged a trusty comrade did not leave me an inch. I had not dared to protest; I was afraid of being done away with quietly in that room; only, as we were walking together, I wondered whether it would not be better for me to throw myself suddenly into the Seine. But while I was turning it over in my mind we had crossed the bridge, and afterwards I had not the opportunity.'

In the light of the candle end, with his sharp features, fluffy little moustache, and oval face, he looked at times delicately and gaily young, and then appeared quite old, decrepit, full of sorrow, pressing his folded arms to his breast.

As he remained silent I felt bound to ask: 'Well! And how did it end?'
'Deportation to Cayenne,' he answered.

He seemed to think that somebody had given the plot away. As he
was keeping watch in the back street, bag in hand, he was set upon by
the police. 'These imbeciles,' had knocked him down without noticing
what he had in his hand. He wondered how the bomb failed to explode
as he fell. But it didn't explode.

'I tried to tell my story in court,' he continued. 'The president was
amused. There were in the audience some idiots who laughed.'

I expressed the hope that some of his companions had been caught,
too. He shuddered slightly before he told me that there were two –
Simon, called also Biscuit, the middle-aged fitter who spoke to him in
the street, and a fellow of the name of Mafile, one of the sympathetic
strangers who had applauded his sentiments and consoled his humani-
tarian sorrows when he got drunk in the café.

'Yes,' he went on, with an effort, 'I had the advantage of their
company over there on St Joseph's Island, amongst some eighty or
ninety other convicts. We were all classed as dangerous.'

St Joseph's Island is the prettiest of the Iles de Salut. It is rocky and
green, with shallow ravines, bushes, thickets, groves of mango-trees,
and many feathery palms. Six warders armed with revolvers and
carbines are in charge of the convicts kept there.

An eight-oared galley keeps up the communication in the daytime,
across a channel a quarter of a mile wide, with the Ile Royale, where
there is a military post. She makes the first trip at six in the morning. At
four in the afternoon her service is over, and she is then hauled up into
a little dock on the Ile Royale and a sentry put over her and a few
smaller boats. From that time till next morning the island of St Joseph
remains cut off from the rest of the world, with the warders patrolling
in turn the path from the warders' house to the convict huts, and a
multitude of sharks patrolling the waters all round.

Under these circumstances the convicts planned a mutiny. Such a
thing had never been known in the penitentiary's history before. But
their plan was not without some possibility of success. The warders
were to be taken by surprise and murdered during the night. Their
arms would enable the convicts to shoot down the people in the galley
as she came alongside in the morning. The galley once in their
possession, other boats were to be captured, and the whole company
was to row away up the coast.

At dusk the two warders on duty mustered the convicts as usual.
Then they proceeded to inspect the huts to ascertain that everything
was in order. In the second they entered they were set upon and

absolutely smothered under the numbers of their assailants. The twilight faded rapidly. It was a new moon; and a heavy black squall gathering over the coast increased the profound darkness of the night. The convicts assembled in the open space, deliberating upon the next step to be taken, argued amongst themselves in low voices.

'You took part in all this?' I asked.

'No. I knew what was going to be done, of course. But why should I kill these warders? I had nothing against them. But I was afraid of the others. Whatever happened, I could not escape from them. I sat alone on the stump of a tree with my head in my hands, sick at heart at the thought of a freedom that could be nothing but a mockery to me. Suddenly I was startled to perceive the shape of a man on the path near by. He stood perfectly still, then his form became effaced in the night. It must have been the chief warder coming to see what had become of his two men. No one noticed him. The convicts kept on quarrelling over their plans. The leaders could not get themselves obeyed. The fierce whispering of that dark mass of men was very horrible.

'At last they divided into two parties and moved off. When they had passed me I rose, weary and hopeless. The path to the warders' house was dark and silent, but on each side the bushes rustled slightly. Presently I saw a faint thread of light before me. The chief warder, followed by his three men, was approaching cautiously. But he had failed to close his dark lantern properly. The convicts had seen that faint gleam, too. There was an awful savage yell, a turmoil on the dark path, shots fired, blows, groans: and with the sound of smashed bushes, the shouts of the pursuers and the screams of the pursued, the man-hunt, the warder-hunt, passed by me into the interior of the island. I was alone. And I assure you, monsieur, I was indifferent to everything. After standing still for a while, I walked on along the path till I kicked something hard. I stooped and picked up a warder's revolver. I felt with my fingers that it was loaded in five chambers. In the gusts of wind I heard the convicts calling to each other far away, and then a roll of thunder would cover the soughing and rustling of the trees. Suddenly, a big light ran across my path very low along the ground. And it showed a woman's skirt with the edge of an apron.

'I knew that the person who carried it must be the wife of the head warder. They had forgotten all about her, it seems. A shot rang out in the interior of the island, and she cried out to herself as she ran. She passed on. I followed, and presently I saw her again. She was pulling at the cord of the big bell which hangs at the end of the landing-pier, with one hand, and with the other she was swinging the heavy lantern to and fro. This is the agreed signal for the Ile Royale should assistance be required at night. The wind carried the sound away from our island and the light she swung was hidden on the shore side by the few trees that grow near the warders' house.

'I came up quite close to her from behind. She went on without stopping, without looking aside, as though she had been all alone on the island. A brave woman, monsieur. I put the revolver inside the breast of my blue blouse and waited. A flash of lightning and a clap of thunder destroyed both the sound and the light of the signal for an instant, but she never faltered, pulling at the cord and swinging the lantern as regularly as a machine. She was a comely woman of thirty – no more. I thought to myself, "All that's no good on a night like this." And I made up my mind that if a body of my fellow-convicts came down to the pier – which was sure to happen soon – I would shoot her through the head before I shot myself. I knew the "comrades" well. This idea of mine gave me quite an interest in life, monsieur; and at once, instead of remaining stupidly exposed on the pier, I retreated a little way and crouched behind a bush. I did not intend to let myself be pounced upon unawares and be prevented perhaps from rendering a supreme service to at least one human creature before I died myself.

'But we must believe the signal was seen, for the galley from Ile Royale came over in an astonishingly short time. The woman kept right on till the light of her lantern flashed upon the officer in command and the bayonets of the soldiers in the boat. Then she sat down and began to cry.

'She didn't need me any more. I did not budge. Some soldiers were only in their shirt-sleeves, others without boots, just as the call to arms had found them. They passed by my bush at the double. The galley had been sent away for more; and the woman sat all alone crying at the end of the pier, with the lantern standing on the ground near her.

'Then suddenly I saw in the light at the end of the pier the red pantaloons of two more men. I was overcome with astonishment. They, too, started off at a run. Their tunics flapped unbuttoned and they were bare-headed. One of them panted out to the other, "Straight on, straight on!"

'Where on earth did they spring from, I wondered. Slowly I walked down the short pier. I saw the woman's form shaken by sobs and heard her moaning more and more distinctly, "Oh, my man! my poor man! my poor man!" I stole on quietly. She could neither hear nor see anything. She had thrown her apron over her head and was rocking herself to and fro in her grief. But I remarked a small boat fastened to the end of the pier.

'Those two men – they looked like *sous-officiers* – must have come in it, after being too late, I suppose, for the galley. It is incredible that they should have thus broken the regulations from a sense of duty. And it was a stupid thing to do. I could not believe my eyes in the very moment I was stepping into that boat.

'I pulled along the shore slowly. A black cloud hung over the Iles de Salut. I heard firing, shouts. Another hunt had begun – the convict-hunt. The oars were too long to pull comfortably. I managed them with difficulty, though the boat herself was light. But when I got round to the other side of the island the squall broke in rain and wind. I was unable to make head against it. I let the boat drift ashore and secured her.

'I knew the spot. There was a tumbledown old hovel standing near the water. Cowering in there I heard through the noises of the wind and the falling downpour some people tearing through the bushes. They came out on the strand. Soldiers perhaps. A flash of lightning threw everything near me into violent relief. Two convicts!

'And directly an amazed voice exclaimed, "It's a miracle!" It was the voice of Simon, otherwise Biscuit.

'And another voice growled, "What's a miracle?"

' "Why, there's a boat lying here!"

' "You must be mad, Simon! But there is, after all . . . A boat."

'They seemed awed into complete silence. The other man was Mafile. He spoke again, cautiously.

' "It is fastened up. There must be somebody here."

'I spoke to them from within the hovel: "I am here."

'They came in then, and soon gave me to understand that the boat was theirs, not mine. "There are two of us," said Mafile, "against you alone."

'I got out into the open to keep clear of them for fear of getting a treacherous blow on the head. I could have shot them both where they stood. But I said nothing. I kept down the laughter rising in my throat. I made myself very humble and begged to be allowed to go. They consulted in low tones about my fate, while with my hand on the revolver in the bosom of my blouse I had their lives in my power. I let them live. I meant them to pull that boat. I represented to them with abject humility that I understood the management of a boat, and that, being three to pull, we could get a rest in turns. That decided them at last. It was time. A little more and I would have gone into screaming fits at the drollness of it.'

At this point his excitement broke out. He jumped off the bench and gesticulated. The great shadows of his arms darting over roof and walls made the shed appear too small to contain his agitation.

'I deny nothing,' he burst out. 'I was elated, monsieur. I tasted a sort of felicity. But I kept very quiet. I took my turns at pulling all through the night. We made for the open sea, putting our trust in a passing ship. It was a foolhardy action. I persuaded them to it. When the sun rose the immensity of water was calm, and the Iles de Salut appeared only like dark specks from the top of each swell. I was steering then. Mafile, who was pulling bow, let out an oath and said, "We must rest."

'The time to laugh had come at last. And I took my fill of it, I can tell you. I held my sides and rolled in my seat, they had such startled faces. "What's got into him, the animal?" cries Mafile.

'And Simon, who was nearest to me, says over his shoulder to him, "Devil take me if I don't think he's gone mad!"

'Then I produced the revolver. Aha! In a moment they both got the stoniest eyes you can imagine. Ha, ha! They were frightened. But they pulled. Oh, yes, they pulled all day, sometimes looking wild and sometimes looking faint. I lost nothing of it because I had to keep my eyes on them all the time, or else – crack! – they would have been on top of me in a second. I rested my revolver hand on my knee all ready and steered with the other. Their faces began to blister. Sky and sea seemed on fire round us and the sea steamed in the sun. The boat made a sizzling sound as she went through the water. Sometimes Mafile foamed at the mouth and sometimes he groaned. But he pulled. He dared not stop. His eyes became blood-shot all over, and he had bitten his lower lip to pieces. Simon was as hoarse as a crow.

' "Comrade – " he begins.

' "There are no comrades here. I am your *patron*."

' "*Patron*, then," he says, "in the name of humanity let us rest."

'I let them. There was a little rainwater washing about the bottom of the boat. I permitted them to snatch some of it in the hollow of their palms. But as I gave the command "*En route*" I caught them exchanging significant glances. They thought I would have to go to sleep sometime! Aha! But I did not want to go to sleep. I was more awake than ever. It is they who went to sleep as they pulled, tumbling off the thwarts head over heels suddenly, one after another. I let them lie. All the stars were out. It was a quiet world. The sun rose. Another day. *Allez! En route!*

'They pulled badly. Their eyes rolled about and their tongues hung out. In the middle of the forenoon Mafile croaks out: "Let us make a rush at him, Simon. I would just as soon be shot at once as to die of thirst, hunger, and fatigue at the oar."

'But while he spoke he pulled; and Simon kept on pulling too. It made me smile. Ah! They loved their life, these two, in this evil world of theirs, just as I used to love my life, too, before they spoiled it for me with their phrases. I let them go on to the point of exhaustion, and only then I pointed at the sails of a ship on the horizon.

'Aha! You should have seen them revive and buckle to their work! For I kept them at it to pull right across that ship's path. They were changed. The sort of pity I had felt for them left me. They looked more like themselves every minute. They looked at me with the glances I remembered so well. They were happy. They smiled.

' "Well," says Simon, "the energy of that youngster has saved our lives. If he hadn't made us, we could never have pulled so far out into the track of ships. Comrade, I forgive you. I admire you."

'And Mafile growls from forward: "We owe you a famous debt of gratitude, comrade. You are cut out for a chief."

'Comrade, monsieur! Ah, what a good word! And they, such men as these two, had made it accursed. I looked at them. I remembered their lies, their promises, their menaces, and all my days of misery. Why could they not have left me alone after I came out of prison? I looked at them and thought that while they lived I could never be free. Never. Neither I nor others like me with warm hearts and weak heads. For I know I have not a strong head, monsieur. A black rage came upon me the rage of extreme intoxication – but not against the injustice of society. Oh, no!

' "I must be free!" I cried, furiously.

' "*Vive la liberté!*" yells that ruffian Mafile. "*Mort aux bourgeois* who send us to Cayenne! They shall soon know that we are free."

'The sky, the sea, the whole horizon, seemed to turn red, blood red all round the boat. My temples were beating so loud that I wondered they did not hear. How is it that they did not? How is it they did not understand?

'I heard Simon ask, "Have we not pulled far enough out now?"

' "Yes. Far enough," I said. I was sorry for him; it was the other I hated. He hauled in his oar with a loud sigh, and as he was raising his hand to wipe his forehead with the air of a man who has done his work, I pulled the trigger of my revolver and shot him like this off the knee, right through the heart.

'He tumbled down, with his head hanging over the side of the boat. I did not give him a second glance. The other cried out piercingly. Only one shriek of horror. Then all was still.

'He slipped off the thwart on to his knees and raised his clasped hands before his face in an attitude of supplication. "Mercy," he whispered, faintly. "Mercy for me! – comrade."

' "Ah, comrade," I said, in a low tone. "Yes, comrade, of course. Well, then, shout *Vive l'anarchie*."

'He flung up his arms, his face up to the sky and his mouth wide open in a great yell of despair. "*Vive l'anarchie! Vive –* "

'He collapsed all in a heap, with a bullet through his head.

'I flung them both overboard. I threw away the revolver, too. Then I sat down quietly. I was free at last! At last. I did not even look towards the ship; I did not care; indeed, I think I must have gone to sleep, because all of a sudden there were shouts and I found the ship almost on top of me. They hauled me on board and secured the boat astern. They were all blacks, except the captain, who was a mulatto. He alone knew a few words of French. I could not find out where they were going nor who they were. They gave me something to eat every day; but I did not like the way they used to discuss me in their language. Perhaps they were deliberating about throwing me overboard in order to keep possession of the boat. How do I know? As we were passing this island I asked whether it was inhabited. I understood from the mulatto that there was a house on it. A farm, I fancied, they meant. So I asked them to put me ashore on the beach and keep the boat for their trouble. This, I imagine, was just what they wanted. The rest you know.'

After pronouncing these words he lost suddenly all control over himself. He paced to and fro rapidly, till at last he broke into a run; his arms went like a windmill and his ejaculations became very much like raving. The burden of them was that he 'denied nothing, nothing!' I could only let him go on, and sat out of his way, repeating, '*Calmez vous, Calmez vous,*' at intervals, till his agitation exhausted itself.

I must confess, too, that I remained there long after he had crawled under his mosquito-net. He had entreated me not to leave him; so, as one sits up with a nervous child, I sat up with him – in the name of humanity – till he fell asleep.

On the whole, my idea is that he was much more of an anarchist than he confessed to me or to himself; and that, the special features of his case apart, he was very much like many other anarchists. Warm heart and weak head – that is the word of the riddle; and it is a fact that the bitterest contradictions and the deadliest conflicts of the world are carried on in every individual breast capable of feeling and passion.

From personal enquiry I can vouch that the story of the convict mutiny was in every particular as stated by him.

When I got back to Horta from Cayenne and saw the 'Anarchist' again, he did not look well. He was more worn, still more frail, and very livid indeed under the grimy smudges of his calling. Evidently the meat of the company's main herd (in its unconcentrated form) did not agree with him at all.

It was on the pontoon in Horta that we met; and I tried to induce him to leave the launch moored where she was and follow me to Europe there and then. It would have been delightful to think of the excellent manager's surprise and disgust at the poor fellow's escape. But he refused with unconquerable obstinacy!

'Surely you don't mean to live always here!' I cried. He shook his head.

'I shall die here,' he said. Then added moodily, 'Away from *them*.'

Sometimes I think of him lying open-eyed on his horseman's gear in the low shed full of tools and scraps of iron – the anarchist slave of the Marañon estate, waiting with resignation for that sleep which 'fled' from him, as he used to say, in such an unaccountable manner

The Informer

Mr X came to me, preceded by a letter of introduction from a good friend of mine in Paris, specifically to see my collection of Chinese bronzes and porcelain.

My friend in Paris is a collector, too. He collects neither porcelain, nor bronzes, nor pictures, nor medals, nor stamps, nor anything that could be profitably dispersed under an auctioneer's hammer. He would reject, with genuine surprise, the name of a collector. Nevertheless, that's what he is by temperament. He collects acquaintances. It is delicate work. He brings to it the patience, the passion, the determination of a true collector of curiosities. His collection does not contain any royal personages. I don't think he considers them sufficiently rare and interesting; but, with that exception, he has met with and talked to everyone worth knowing on any conceivable ground. He observes them, listens to them, penetrates them, measures them, and puts the memory away in the galleries of his mind. He has schemed, plotted, and travelled all over Europe in order to add to his collection of distinguished personal acquaintances.

As he is wealthy, well connected, and unprejudiced, his collection is pretty complete, including objects (or should I say subjects?) whose value is unappreciated by the vulgar, and often unknown to popular fame. Of those specimens my friend is naturally the most proud.

He wrote to me of X: 'He is the greatest rebel (*révolté*) of modern times. The world knows him as a revolutionary writer whose savage irony has laid bare the rottenness of the most respectable institutions. He has scalped every venerated head, and has mangled at the stake of his wit every received opinion and every recognised principle of conduct and policy. Who does not remember his flaming red revolutionary pamphlets? Their sudden swarmings used to overwhelm the powers of every Continental police like a plague of crimson gadflies. But this extreme writer has been also the active inspirer of secret societies, the mysterious unknown Number One of desperate conspiracies suspected and unsuspected, matured or baffled. And the world at large has never had an inkling of that fact! This accounts for him going about amongst us to this day, a veteran of many subterranean campaigns, standing aside now, safe within his reputation of merely the greatest destructive publicist that ever lived.'

Thus wrote my friend, adding that Mr X was an enlightened connoisseur of bronzes and china, and asking me to show him my collection.

X turned up in due course. My treasures are disposed in three large rooms without carpets and curtains. There is no other furniture than the *étagères* and the glass cases whose contents shall be worth a fortune to my heirs. I allow no fires to be lighted, for fear of accidents, and a fire-proof door separates them from the rest of the house.

It was a bitter cold day. We kept on our overcoats and hats. Middle-sized and spare, his eyes alert in a long, Roman-nosed countenance, X walked on his neat little feet, with short steps, and looked at my collection intelligently. I hope I looked at him intelligently, too. A snow-white moustache and imperial made his nut-brown complexion appear darker than it really was. In his fur coat and shiny tall hat that terrible man looked fashionable. I believe he belonged to a noble family, and could have called himself Vicomte X de la Z if he chose. We talked nothing but bronzes and porcelain. He was remarkably appreciative. We parted on cordial terms.

Where he was staying I don't know. I imagine he must have been a lonely man. Anarchists, I suppose, have no families – not, at any rate, as we understand that social relation. Organisation into families may answer to a need of human nature, but in the last instance it is based on law, and therefore must be something odious and impossible to an anarchist. But, indeed, I don't understand anarchists. Does a man of that – of that – persuasion still remain an anarchist when alone, quite alone and going to bed, for instance? Does he lay his head on the pillow, pull his bedclothes over him, and go to sleep with the necessity of the *chambardement général*, as the French slang has it, of the general blow-up, always present to his mind? And if so how can he? I am sure that if such a faith (or such a fanaticism) once mastered my thoughts I would never he able to compose myself sufficiently to sleep or eat or perform any of the routine acts of daily life. I would want no wife, no children; I could have no friends, it seems to me; and as to collecting bronzes or china, that, I should say, would be quite out of the question. But I don't know. All I know is that Mr X took his meals in a very good restaurant which I frequented also.

With his head uncovered, the silver top-knot of his brushed-up hair completed the character of his physiognomy, all bony ridges and sunken hollows, clothed in a perfect impassiveness of expression. His meagre brown hands emerging from large white cuffs came and went breaking bread, pouring wine, and so on, with quiet mechanical precision. His head and body above the tablecloth had a rigid immobility. This firebrand, this great agitator, exhibited the least possible amount of warmth and animation. His voice was rasping, cold, and monotonous in a low key. He could not be called a talkative personality; but with his detached calm manner he appeared as ready to keep the conversation going as to drop it at any moment.

And his conversation was by no means commonplace. To me, I own, there was some excitement in talking quietly across a dinner-table with a man whose venomous pen-stabs had sapped the vitality of at least one monarchy. That much was a matter of public knowledge. But I knew more. I knew of him – from my friend – as a certainty what the guardians of social order in Europe had at most only suspected, or dimly guessed at.

He had had what I may call his underground life. And as I sat, evening after evening, facing him at dinner, a curiosity in that direction would naturally arise in my mind. I am a quiet and peaceable product of civilisation, and know no passion other than the passion for collecting things which are rare, and must remain exquisite even if approaching to the monstrous. Some Chinese bronzes are monstrously precious. And here (out of my friend's collection), here I had before me a kind of rare monster. It is true that this monster was polished and in a sense even exquisite. His beautiful unruffled manner was that. But then he was not of bronze. He was not even Chinese, which would have enabled one to contemplate him calmly across the gulf of racial difference. He was alive and European; he had the manner of good society, wore a coat and hat like mine, and had pretty near the same taste in cooking. It was too frightful to think of.

One evening he remarked, casually, in the course of conversation, 'There's no amendment to be got out of mankind except by terror and violence.'

You can imagine the effect of such a phrase out of such a man's mouth upon a person like myself, whose whole scheme of life had been based upon a suave and delicate discrimination of social and artistic values. Just imagine! Upon me, to whom all sorts and forms of violence appeared as unreal as the giants, ogres, and seven-headed hydras whose activities affect, fantastically, the course of legends and fairy-tales!

I seemed suddenly to hear above the festive bustle and clatter of the brilliant restaurant the mutter of a hungry and seditious multitude.

I suppose I am impressionable and imaginative. I had a disturbing vision of darkness, full of lean jaws and wild eyes, amongst the hundred electric lights of the place. But somehow this vision made me angry, too. The sight of that man, so calm, breaking bits of white bread, exasperated me. And I had the audacity to ask him how it was that the starving proletariat of Europe to whom he had been preaching revolt and violence had not been made indignant by his openly luxurious life. 'At all this,' I said, pointedly, with a glance round the room and at the bottle of champagne we generally shared between us at dinner.

He remained unmoved.

'Do I feed on their toil and their heart's blood? Am I a speculator or a capitalist? Did I steal my fortune from a starving people? No! They know this very well. And they envy me nothing. The miserable mass of the people is generous to its leaders. What I have acquired has come to me through my writings; not from the millions of pamphlets distributed gratis to the hungry and the oppressed, but from the hundreds of thousands of copies sold to the well-fed bourgeois. You know that my writings were at one time the rage, the fashion – the thing to read with wonder and horror, to turn your eyes up at my pathos . . . or else, to laugh in ecstasies at my wit.'

'Yes,' I admitted. 'I remember, of course; and I confess frankly that I could never understand that infatuation.'

'Don't you know yet,' he said, 'that an idle and selfish class loves to see mischief being made, even if it is made at its own expense? Its own life being all a matter of pose and gesture, it is unable to realise the power and the danger of a real movement and of words that have no sham meaning. It is all fun and sentiment. It is sufficient, for instance, to point out the attitude of the old French aristocracy towards the philosophers whose words were preparing the Great Revolution. Even in England, where you have some common-sense, a demagogue has only to shout loud enough and long enough to find some backing in the very class he is shouting at. You, too, like to see mischief being made. The demagogue carries the amateurs of emotion with him. Amateurism in this, that, and the other thing is a delightfully easy way of killing time, and feeding one's own vanity – the silly vanity of being abreast with the ideas of the day after tomorrow. Just as good and otherwise harmless people will join you in ecstasies over your collection without having the slightest notion in what its marvellousness really consists.'

I hung my head. It was a crushing illustration of the sad truth he advanced. The world is full of such people. And that instance of the French aristocracy before the Revolution was extremely telling, too. I could not traverse his statement, though its cynicism – always a distasteful trait – took off much of its value to my mind. However, I admit I was impressed. I felt the need to say something which would not be in the nature of assent and yet would not invite discussion.

'You don't mean to say,' I observed, airily, 'that extreme revolutionists have ever been actively assisted by the infatuation of such people?'

'I did not mean exactly that by what I said just now. I generalised. But since you ask me, I may tell you that such help has been given to revolutionary activities, more or less consciously, in various countries. And even in this country.'

'Impossible!' I protested with firmness. 'We don't play with fire to that extent.'

'And yet you can better afford it than others, perhaps. But let me observe that most women, if not always ready to play with fire, are generally eager to play with a loose spark or so.'

'Is this a joke?' I asked, smiling.

'If it is, I am not aware of it,' he said, woodenly. 'I was thinking of an instance. Oh! mild enough in a way . . .'

I became all expectation at this. I had tried many times to approach him on his underground side, so to speak. The very word had been pronounced between us. But he had always met me with his impenetrable calm.

'And at the same time,' Mr X continued, 'it will give you a notion of the difficulties that may arise in what you are pleased to call underground work. It is sometimes difficult to deal with them. Of course there is no hierarchy amongst the affiliated. No rigid system.'

My surprise was great, but short-lived. Clearly, amongst extreme anarchists there could be no hierarchy; nothing in the nature of a law of precedence. The idea of anarchy ruling among anarchists was comforting, too. It could not possibly make for efficiency.

Mr X startled me by asking, abruptly, 'You know Hermione Street?'

I nodded doubtful assent. Hermione Street has been, within the last three years, improved out of any man's knowledge. The name exists still, but not one brick or stone of the old Hermione Street is left now.

It was the old street he meant, for he said: 'There was a row of two-storeyed brick houses on the left, with their backs against the wing of a great public building – you remember. Would it surprise you very much to hear that one of these houses was for a time the centre of anarchist propaganda and of what you would call underground action?'

'Not at all,' I declared. Hermione Street had never been particularly respectable, as I remembered it.

'The house was the property of a distinguished government official,' he added, sipping his champagne.

'Oh, indeed!' I said, this time not believing a word

'Of course he was not living there,' Mr X continued. 'But from ten till four he sat next door to it, the dear man, in his well-appointed private room in the wing of the public building I've mentioned. To be strictly accurate, I must explain that the house in Hermione Street did not really belong to him. It belonged to his grown-up children – a daughter and a son. The girl, a fine figure, was by no means vulgarly pretty. To more personal charm than mere youth could account for, she added the seductive appearance of enthusiasm, of independence, of courageous thought. I suppose she put on these appearances as she put on her picturesque dresses and for the same reason: to assert her individuality at any cost. You know, women would go to any length almost for such a purpose. She went to a great length. She had acquired all the appropriate gestures of revolutionary convictions – the gestures of pity, of anger, of indignation against the anti-humanitarian vices of the social class to which she belonged herself. All this sat on her striking personality as well as her slightly original costumes. Very slightly original; just enough to mark a protest against the philistinism of the overfed taskmasters of the poor. Just enough, and no more. It would not have done to go too far in that direction – you understand. But she was of age, and nothing stood in the way of her offering her house to the revolutionary workers.'

'You don't mean it!' I cried.

'I assure you,' he affirmed, 'that she made that very practical gesture. How else could they have got hold of it? The cause is not rich. And, moreover, there would have been difficulties with any ordinary house-agent, who would have wanted references and so on. The group she came in contact with while exploring the poor quarters of the town (you know the gesture of charity and personal service which was so fashionable some years ago) accepted with gratitude. The first advantage was that Hermione Street is, as you know, well away from the suspect part of the town specially watched by the police.

'The ground floor consisted of a little Italian restaurant, of the flyblown sort. There was no difficulty in buying the proprietor out. A woman and a man belonging to the group took it on. The man had been a cook. The comrades could get their meals there, unnoticed amongst the other customers. This was another advantage. The first floor was occupied by a shabby Variety Artists' Agency – an agency for performers in inferior music-halls, you know. A fellow called Bomm, I remember. He was not disturbed. It was rather favourable than otherwise to have a lot of foreign-looking people, jugglers, acrobats, singers of both sexes, and so on, going in and out all day long. The police paid no attention to new faces, you see. The top floor happened, most conveniently, to stand empty then.'

X interrupted himself to attack impassively, with measured

movements, a *bombe glacée* which the waiter had just set down on the table. He swallowed carefully a few spoonfuls of the iced sweet, and asked me, 'Did you ever hear of Stone's Dried Soup?'

'Hear of what?'

'It was,' X pursued, evenly, 'a comestible article once rather prominently advertised in the dailies, but which never, somehow, gained the favour of the public. The enterprise fizzled out, as you say here. Parcels of their stock could be picked up at auctions at considerably less than a penny a pound. The group bought some of it, and an agency for Stone's Dried Soup was started on the top floor. A perfectly respectable business. The stuff, a yellow powder of extremely unappetizing aspect, was put up in large square tins, of which six went to a case. If anybody ever came to give an order, it was, of course, executed. But the advantage of the powder was this, that things could be concealed in it very conveniently. Now and then a special case got put on a van and sent off to be exported abroad under the very nose of the policeman on duty at the corner. You understand?'

'I think I do,' I said, with an expressive nod at the remnants of the *bombe* melting slowly in the dish.

'Exactly. But the cases were useful in another way, too. In the basement, or in the cellar at the back, rather, two printing-presses were established. A lot of revolutionary literature of the most inflammatory kind was got away from the house in Stone's Dried Soup cases. The brother of our anarchist young lady found some occupation there. He wrote articles, helped to set up type and pull off the sheets, and generally assisted the man in charge, a very able young fellow called Sevrin.

'The guiding spirit of that group was a fanatic of social revolution. He is dead now. He was an engraver and etcher of genius. You must have seen his work. It is much sought after by certain amateurs now. He began by being revolutionary in his art, and ended by becoming a revolutionist, after his wife and child had died in want and misery. He used to say that the bourgeois, the smug, overfed lot, had killed them. That was his real belief. He still worked at his art and led a double life. He was tall, gaunt, and swarthy, with a long, brown beard and deep-set eyes. You must have seen him. His name was Horne.'

At this I was really startled. Of course years ago I used to meet Horne about. He looked like a powerful, rough gipsy, in an old top hat, with a red muffler round his throat and buttoned up in a long, shabby overcoat. He talked of his art with exaltation, and gave one the impression of being strung up to the verge of insanity. A small group of connoisseurs appreciated his work. Who would have thought that this man . . . Amazing! And yet it was not, after all, so difficult to believe.

'As you see,' X went on, 'this group was in a position to pursue its work of propaganda, and the other kind of work, too, under very advantageous conditions. They were all resolute, experienced men of a superior stamp. And yet we became struck at length by the fact that plans prepared in Hermione Street almost invariably failed.'

'Who were "we"?' I asked, pointedly.

'Some of us in Brussels – at the centre,' he said, hastily. 'Whatever vigorous action originated in Hermione Street seemed doomed to failure. Something always happened to baffle the best-planned manifestations in every part of Europe. It was a time of general activity. You must not imagine that all our failures are of a loud sort, with arrests and trials. That is not so. Often the police work quietly, almost secretly, defeating our combinations by clever counter-plotting. No arrests, no noise, no alarming of the public mind and inflaming the passions. It is a wise procedure. But at that time the police were too uniformly successful from the Mediterranean to the Baltic. It was annoying and began to look dangerous. At last we came to the conclusion that there must be some untrustworthy elements amongst the London groups. And I came over to see what could be done quietly.

'My first step was to call upon our young Lady Amateur of anarchism at her private house. She received me in a flattering way. I judged that she knew nothing of the chemical and other operations going on at the top of the house in Hermione Street. The printing of anarchist literature was the only "activity" she seemed to be aware of there. She was displaying very strikingly the usual signs of severe enthusiasm, and had already written many sentimental articles with ferocious conclusions. I could see she was enjoying herself hugely, with all the gestures and grimaces of deadly earnestness. They suited her big-eyed, broad-browed face and the good carriage of her shapely head, crowned by a magnificent lot of brown hair done in an unusual and becoming style. Her brother was in the room, too, a serious youth, with arched eyebrows and wearing a red necktie, who struck me as being absolutely in the dark about everything in the world, including himself. By and by a tall young man came in. He was clean-shaved with a strong bluish jaw and something of the air of a taciturn actor or of a fanatical priest: the type with thick black eyebrows – you know. But he was very presentable indeed. He shook hands at once vigorously with each of us. The young lady came up to me and murmured sweetly, "Comrade Sevrin."

'I had never seen him before. He had little to say to us, but sat down by the side of the girl, and they fell at once into earnest conversation. She leaned forward in her deep armchair, and took her nicely rounded chin in her beautiful white hand. He looked attentively into her eyes. It was the attitude of love-making, serious, intense, as if on the brink of the grave. I suppose she felt it necessary to round and complete her assumption of advanced ideas, of revolutionary lawlessness, by making believe to be in love with an anarchist. And this one, I repeat, was extremely presentable, notwithstanding his fanatical black-browed aspect. After a few stolen glances in their direction, I had no doubt that he was in earnest. As to the lady, her gestures were unapproachable, better than the very thing itself in the blended suggestion of dignity, sweetness, condescension, fascination, surrender, and reserve. She interpreted her conception of what that precise sort of love-making should be with consummate art. And so far, she, too, no doubt, was in earnest. Gestures – but so perfect!

'After I had been left alone with our Lady Amateur I informed her guardedly of the object of my visit. I hinted at our suspicions. I wanted to hear what she would have to say, and half expected some perhaps unconscious revelation. All she said was, "That's serious," looking delightfully concerned and grave. But there was a sparkle in her eyes which meant plainly, "How exciting!" After all, she knew little of anything except of words. Still, she undertook to put me in communication with Horne, who was not easy to find unless in Hermione Street, where I did not wish to show myself just then.

'I met Horne. This was another kind of a fanatic altogether. I exposed to him the conclusion we in Brussels had arrived at, and pointed out the significant series of failures. To this he answered with irrelevant exaltation: "I have something in hand that shall strike terror into the heart of these gorged brutes."

'And then I learned that, by excavating in one of the cellars of the house, he and some companions had made their way into the vaults under the great public building I have mentioned before. The blowing up of a whole wing was a certainty as soon as the materials were ready.

'I was not so appalled at the stupidity of that move as I might have been had not the usefulness of our centre in Hermione Street become already very problematical. In fact, in my opinion it was much more of a police trap by this time than anything else.

'What was necessary now was to discover what, or rather who, was wrong, and I managed at last to get that idea into Horne's head. He glared, perplexed, his nostrils working as if he were sniffing treachery in the air.

'And here comes a piece of work which will no doubt strike you as a sort of theatrical expedient. And yet what else could have been done? The problem was to find out the untrustworthy member of the group. But no suspicion could be fastened on one more than another. To set a watch upon them all was not very practicable. Besides, that proceeding often fails. In any case, it takes time, and the danger was pressing. I felt certain that the premises in Hermione Street would be ultimately raided, though the police had evidently such confidence in the informer that the house, for the time being, was not even watched. Horne was positive on that point. Under the circumstances it was an unfavourable symptom. Something had to be done quickly.

'I decided to organise a raid myself upon the group. Do you understand? A raid of other trusty comrades personating the police. A conspiracy within a conspiracy. You see the object of it, of course. When apparently about to be arrested I hoped the informer would betray himself in some way or other; either by some unguarded act or simply by his unconcerned demeanour, for instance. Of course there was the risk of complete failure and the no lesser risk of some fatal accident in the course of resistance, perhaps, or in the efforts at escape. For, as you will easily see, the Hermione Street group had to be actually and completely taken unawares, as I was sure they would be by the real police before very long. The informer was amongst them, and Horne alone could be let into the secret of my plan.

'I will not enter into the detail of my preparations. It was not very easy to arrange, but it was done very well, with a really convincing effect. The sham police invaded the restaurant, whose shutters were immediately put up. The surprise was perfect. Most of the Hermione Street party were found in the second cellar, enlarging the hole communicating with the vaults of the great public building. At the first alarm, several comrades bolted through impulsively into the aforesaid vault, where, of course, had this been a genuine raid, they would have been hopelessly trapped. We did not bother about them for the moment. They were harmless enough. The top floor caused considerable anxiety to Horne and myself. There, surrounded by tins of Stone's Dried Soup, a comrade, nicknamed the Professor (he was an ex-science student), was engaged in perfecting some new detonators. He was an abstracted, self-confident, sallow little man, armed with large round spectacles, and we were afraid that under a mistaken impression he would blow himself up and wreck the house about our ears. I rushed upstairs and found him already at the door, on the alert, listening, as he said, to "suspicious noises down below". Before I had quite finished explaining to him what was going on he shrugged his shoulders disdainfully and turned away to his balances and test-tubes. His was the true spirit of an extreme revolutionist. Explosives were his faith, his hope, his weapon, and his shield. He perished a couple of years afterwards in a secret laboratory through the premature explosion of one of his improved detonators.

'Hurrying down again, I found an impressive scene in the gloom of the big cellar. The man who personated the inspector (he was no stranger to the part) was speaking harshly, and giving bogus orders to his bogus subordinates for the removal of his prisoners. Evidently nothing enlightening had happened so far. Horne, saturnine and swarthy, waited with folded arms, and his patient, moody expectation had an air of stoicism well in keeping with the situation. I detected in the shadows one of the Hermione Street group surreptitiously chewing up and swallowing a small piece of paper. Some compromising scrap, I suppose; perhaps just a note of a few names and addresses. He was a true and faithful "companion". But the fund of secret malice which lurks at the bottom of our sympathies caused me to feel amused at that perfectly uncalled for performance.

'In every other respect the risky experiment, the theatrical *coup*, if you like to call it so, seemed to have failed. The deception could not be kept up much longer; the explanation would bring about a very embarrassing and even grave situation. The man who had eaten the paper would be furious. The fellows who had bolted away would be angry, too.

'To add to my vexation, the door communicating with the other cellar, where the printing-presses were, flew open, and our young lady revolutionist appeared, a black silhouette in a close-fitting dress and a large hat, with the blaze of gas flaring in there at her back. Over her shoulder I perceived the arched eyebrows and the red necktie of her brother.

'The last people in the world I wanted to see then! They had gone that evening to some amateur concert for the delectation of the poor people, you know; but she had insisted on leaving early, on purpose to call in Hermione Street on the way home, under the pretext of having some work to do. Her usual task was to correct the proofs of the Italian and French editions of the *Alarm Bell* and the *Firebrand* . . . '

'Heavens!' I murmured. I had been shown once a few copies of these publications. Nothing, in my opinion, could have been less fit for the eyes of a young lady. They were the most advanced things of the sort; advanced, I mean, beyond all bounds of reason and decency. One of them preached the dissolution of all social and domestic ties; the other advocated systematic murder. To think of a young girl calmly tracking printers' errors all along the sort of abominable sentences I remembered was intolerable to my sentiment of womanhood. Mr X, after giving me a glance, pursued steadily.

'I think, however, that she came mostly to exercise her fascinations upon Sevrin, and to receive his homage in her queenly and condescending way. She was aware of both – her power and his homage – and enjoyed them with, I dare say, complete innocence. We have no ground in expediency or morals to quarrel with her on that account. Charm in woman and exceptional intelligence in man are a law unto themselves. Is it not so?'

I refrained from expressing my abhorrence of that licentious doctrine because of my curiosity.

'But what happened then?' I hastened to ask.

X went on crumbling slowly a small piece of bread with a careless left hand.

'What happened, in effect,' he confessed, 'is that she saved the situation.'

'She gave you an opportunity to end your rather sinister farce,' I suggested.

'Yes,' he said, preserving his impassive bearing. 'The farce was bound to end soon. And it ended in a very few minutes. And it ended well. Had she not come in, it might have ended badly. Her brother, of course, did not count. They had slipped into the house quietly some time before. The printing-cellar had an entrance of its own. Not finding anyone there, she sat down to her proofs, expecting Sevrin to return to his work at any moment. He did not do so. She grew impatient, heard through the door the sounds of a disturbance in the other cellar and naturally came in to see what was the matter.

'Sevrin had been with us. At first he had seemed to me the most amazed of the whole raided lot. He appeared for an instant as if paralysed with astonishment. He stood rooted to the spot. He never moved a limb. A solitary gas-jet flared near his head; all the other lights had been put out at the first alarm. And presently, from my dark corner, I observed on his shaven actor's face an expression of puzzled, vexed watchfulness. He knitted his heavy eyebrows. The corners of his mouth dropped scornfully. He was angry. Most likely he had seen through the game, and I regretted I had not taken him from the first into my complete confidence.

'But with the appearance of the girl he became obviously alarmed. It was plain. I could see it grow. The change of his expression was swift and startling. And I did not know why. The reason never occurred to me. I was merely astonished at the extreme alteration of the man's face. Of course he had not been aware of her presence in the other cellar;

but that did not explain the shock her advent had given him. For a moment he seemed to have been reduced to imbecility. He opened his mouth as if to shout, or perhaps only to gasp. At any rate, it was somebody else who shouted. This somebody else was the heroic comrade whom I had detected swallowing a piece of paper. With laudable presence of mind he let out a warning yell.

' "It's the police! Back! Back! Run back, and bolt the door behind you."

'It was an excellent hint; but instead of retreating the girl continued to advance, followed by her long-faced brother in his knickerbocker suit, in which he had been singing comic songs for the entertainment of a joyless proletariat. She advanced not as if she had failed to understand – the word "police" has an unmistakable sound – but rather as if she could not help herself. She did not advance with the free gait and expanding presence of a distinguished amateur anarchist amongst poor, struggling professionals, but with slightly raised shoulders, and her elbows pressed close to her body, as if trying to shrink within herself. Her eyes were fixed immovably upon Sevrin. Sevrin the man, I fancy; not Sevrin the anarchist. But she advanced. And that was natural. For all their assumption of independence, girls of that class are used to the feeling of being specially protected, as, in fact, they are. This feeling accounts for nine-tenths of their audacious gestures. Her face had gone completely colourless. Ghastly. Fancy having it brought home to her so brutally that she was the sort of person who must run away from the police! I believe she was pale with indignation, mostly, though there was, of course, also the concern for her intact personality, a vague dread of some sort of rudeness. And, naturally, she turned to a man, to the man on whom she had a claim of fascination and homage – the man who could not conceivably fail her at any juncture.'

'But,' I cried, amazed at this analysis, 'if it had been serious, real, I mean – as she thought it was – what could she expect him to do for her?'

X never moved a muscle of his face.

'Goodness knows. I imagine that this charming, generous, and independent creature had never known in her life a single genuine thought; I mean a single thought detached from small human vanities, or whose source was not in some conventional perception. All I know is that after advancing a few steps she extended her hand towards the motionless Sevrin. And that at least was no gesture. It was a natural movement. As to what she expected him to do, who can tell? The impossible. But whatever she expected, it could not have come up, I am safe to say, to what he had made up his mind to do, even before that entreating hand had appealed to him so directly. It had not been necessary. From the moment he had seen her enter that cellar, he had made up his mind to sacrifice his future usefulness, to throw off the impenetrable, solidly fastened mask it had been his pride to wear – '

'What do you mean?' I interrupted, puzzled. 'Was it Sevrin, then, who was – '

'He was. The most persistent, the most dangerous, the craftiest, the most systematic of informers. A genius amongst betrayers. Fortunately for us, he was unique. The man was a fanatic, I have told you. Fortunately, again, for us, he had fallen in love with the accomplished and innocent gestures of that girl. An actor in desperate earnest himself, he must have believed in the absolute value of conventional signs. As to the grossness of the trap into which he fell, the explanation must be that two sentiments of such absorbing magnitude cannot exist simultaneously in one heart. The danger of that other and unconscious comedian robbed him of his vision, of his perspicacity, of his judgment. Indeed, it did at first rob him of his self-possession. But he regained that through the necessity – as it appeared to him imperiously – to do something at once. To do what? Why, to get her out of the house as quickly as possible. He was desperately anxious to do that. I have told you he was terrified. It could not be about himself. He had been surprised and annoyed at a move quite unforeseen and premature. I may even say he had been furious. He was accustomed to arrange the last scene of his betrayals with a deep, subtle art which left his revolutionist reputation untouched. But it seems clear to me that at the same time he had resolved to make the best of it, to keep his mask resolutely on. It was only with the discovery of her being in the house that everything – the forced calm, the restraint of his fanaticism, the mask – all came off together in a kind of panic. Why panic, do you ask? The answer is very simple. He remembered – or, I dare say, he had never forgotten – the Professor alone at the top of the house, pursuing his researches, surrounded by tins upon tins of Stone's Dried Soup. There was enough in some few of them to bury us all where we stood under a heap of bricks. Sevrin, of course, was aware of that. And we must believe, also, that he knew the exact character of the man. He had gauged so many such characters! Or perhaps he only gave the Professor credit for what he himself was capable of. But, in any case, the effect was produced. And suddenly he raised his voice in authority.

' "Get the lady away at once."

'It turned out that he was as hoarse as a crow; result, no doubt, of the intense emotion. It passed off in a moment. But these fateful words issued forth from his contracted throat in a discordant, ridiculous croak. They required no answer. The thing was done.

However, the man personating the inspector judged it expedient to say roughly: "She shall go soon enough, together with the rest of you."

'These were the last words belonging to the comedy part of this affair.

'Oblivious of everything and everybody, Sevrin strode towards him and seized the lapels of his coat. Under his thin bluish cheeks one could see his jaws working with passion.

' "You have men posted outside. Get the lady taken home at once. Do you hear? Now. Before you try to get hold of the man upstairs."

' "Oh! There is a man upstairs," scoffed the other, openly. "Well, he shall be brought down in time to see the end of this."

'But Sevrin, beside himself, took no heed of the tone.

' "Who's the imbecile meddler who sent you blundering here? Didn't you understand your instructions? Don't you know anything? It's incredible. Here – "

'He dropped the lapels of the coat and, plunging his hand into his breast, jerked feverishly at something under his shirt. At last he produced a small square pocket of soft leather, which must have been hanging like a scapulary from his neck by the tape whose broken ends dangled from his fist.

' "Look inside," he spluttered, flinging it in the other's face. And instantly he turned round towards the girl. She stood just behind him, perfectly still and silent. Her set, white face gave an illusion of placidity. Only her staring eyes seemed bigger and darker.

'He spoke rapidly, with nervous assurance. I heard him distinctly promise her to make everything as clear as daylight presently. But that was all I caught. He stood close to her, never attempting to touch her even with the tip of his little finger – and she stared at him stupidly. For a moment, however, her eyelids descended slowly, pathetically, and then, with the long black eyelashes lying on her white cheeks, she looked ready to fall down in a swoon. But she never even swayed where she stood. He urged her loudly to follow him at once, and walked towards the door at the bottom of the cellar stairs without looking behind him. And, as a matter of fact, she did move after him a pace or two. But, of course, he was not allowed to reach the door. There were angry exclamations, a short, fierce scuffle. Flung away violently, he came flying backwards upon her, and fell. She threw out her arms in a gesture of dismay and stepped aside, just clear of his head, which struck the ground heavily near her shoe.

'He grunted with the shock. By the time he had picked himself up, slowly, dazedly, he was awake to the reality of things. The man into whose hands he had thrust the leather case had extracted therefrom a narrow strip of bluish paper. He held it up above his head, and, as after the scuffle an expectant uneasy stillness reigned once more, he threw it down disdainfully with the words, "I think, comrades, that this proof was hardly necessary".'

'Quick as thought, the girl stooped after the fluttering slip. Holding it spread out in both hands, she looked at it; then, without raising her eyes, opened her fingers slowly and let it fall.

'I examined that curious document afterwards. It was signed by a very high personage, and stamped and countersigned by other high officials in various countries of Europe. In his trade – or shall I say, in his mission? – that sort of talisman might have been necessary, no doubt. Even to the police itself – all but the heads – he had been known only as Sevrin the noted anarchist.

'He hung his head, biting his lower lip. A change had come over him, a sort of thoughtful, absorbed calmness. Nevertheless, he panted. His sides worked visibly, and his nostrils expanded and collapsed in weird contrast with his sombre aspect of a fanatical monk in a meditative attitude, but with something, too, in his face of an actor intent upon the terrible exigencies of his part. Before him Horne declaimed, haggard and bearded, like an inspired denunciatory prophet from a wilderness. Two fanatics. They were made to understand each other. Does this surprise you? I suppose you think that such people would be foaming at the mouth and snarling at each other?'

I protested hastily that I was not surprised in the least; that I thought nothing of the kind; that anarchists in general were simply inconceivable to me mentally, morally, logically, sentimentally, and even physically. X received this declaration with his usual woodenness and went on.

'Horne had burst out into eloquence. While pouring out scornful invective, he let tears escape from his eyes and roll down his black beard unheeded. Sevrin panted quicker and quicker. When he opened his mouth to speak, everyone hung on his words.

' "Don't be a fool, Horne," he began. "You know very well that I have done this for none of the reasons you are throwing at me." And in a moment he became outwardly as steady as a rock under the other's lurid stare. "I have been thwarting, deceiving, and betraying you – from conviction."

'He turned his back on Horne, and addressing the girl, repeated the words: "From conviction."

'It's extraordinary how cold she looked. I suppose she could not think of any appropriate gesture. There can have been few precedents indeed for such a situation.

' "Clear as daylight," he added. "Do you understand what that means? From conviction."

'And still she did not stir. She did not know what to do. But the luckless wretch was about to give her the opportunity for a beautiful and correct gesture.

' "I have felt in me the power to make you share this conviction," he protested, ardently. He had forgotten himself; he made a step towards her – perhaps he stumbled. To me he seemed to be stooping low as if to touch the hem of her garment. And then the appropriate gesture came. She snatched her skirt away from his polluting contact and averted her head with an upward tilt. It was magnificently done, this gesture of conventionally unstained honour, of an unblemished high-minded amateur.

'Nothing could have been better. And he seemed to think so, too, for once more he turned away. But this time he faced no one. He was again panting frightfully, while he fumbled hurriedly in his waistcoat pocket, and then raised his hand to his lips. There was something furtive in this movement, but directly afterwards his bearing changed. His laboured breathing gave him a resemblance to a man who had just run a desperate race; but a curious air of detachment, of sudden and profound indifference, replaced the strain of the striving effort. The race was over. I did not want to see what would happen next. I was only too well aware. I tucked the young lady's arm under mine without a word, and made my way with her to the stairs.

'Her brother walked behind us. Half-way up the short flight she seemed unable to lift her feet high enough for the steps, and we had to pull and push to get her to the top. In the passage she dragged herself along, hanging on my arm, helplessly bent like an old woman. We issued into an empty street through a half-open door, staggering like besotted revellers. At the corner we stopped a four-wheeler, and the ancient driver looked round from his box with morose scorn at our efforts to get her in. Twice during the drive I felt her collapse on my shoulder in a half-faint. Facing us, the youth in knickerbockers remained as mute as a fish, and, till he jumped out with the latch-key, sat more still than I would have believed it possible.

'At the door of their drawing-room she left my arm and walked in first, catching at the chairs and tables. She unpinned her hat, then, exhausted with the effort, her cloak still hanging from her shoulders, flung herself into a deep armchair, sideways, her face half buried in a cushion. The good brother appeared silently before her with a glass of water. She motioned it away. He drank it himself and walked off to a distant corner – behind the grand piano, somewhere. All was still in this room where I had seen, for the first time, Sevrin, the anti-anarchist, captivated and spellbound by the consummate and hereditary grimaces that in a certain sphere of life take the place of feelings with an excellent effect. I suppose her thoughts were busy with the same memory. Her shoulders shook violently. A pure attack of nerves. When it quieted down she affected firmness, "What is done to a man of that sort? What will they do to him?"

' "Nothing. They can do nothing to him," I assured her, with perfect truth. I was pretty certain he had died in less than twenty minutes from the moment his hand had gone to his lips. For if his fanatical anti-anarchism went even as far as carrying poison in his pocket, only to rob his adversaries of legitimate vengeance, I knew he would take care to provide something that would not fail him when required.

'She drew an angry breath. There were red spots on her cheeks and a feverish brilliance in her eyes.

' "Has ever anyone been exposed to such a terrible experience? To think that he had held my hand! That man!" Her face twitched, she gulped down a pathetic sob. "If I ever felt sure of anything, it was of Sevrin's high-minded motives."

'Then she began to weep quietly, which was good for her. Then through her flood of tears, half resentful, "What was it he said to me? – 'From conviction!' It seemed a vile mockery. What could he mean by it?"

' "That, my dear young lady," I said, gently, "is more than I or anybody else can ever explain to you." '

Mr X flicked a crumb off the front of his coat.

'And that was strictly true as to her. Though Horne, for instance, understood very well; and so did I, especially after we had been to Sevrin's lodging in a dismal back street of an intensely respectable quarter. Horne was known there as a friend, and we had no difficulty in being admitted, the slatternly maid merely remarking, as she let us in, that "Mr Sevrin had not been home that night." We forced open a couple of drawers in the way of duty, and found a little useful information. The most interesting part was his diary; for this man, engaged in such deadly work, had the weakness to keep a record of the most damnatory kind. There were his acts and also his thoughts laid bare to us. But the dead don't mind that. They don't mind anything.

' "From conviction." Yes. A vague but ardent humanitarianism had urged him in his first youth into the bitterest extremity of negation and revolt. Afterwards his optimism flinched. He doubted and became lost. You have heard of converted atheists. These turn often into dangerous fanatics, but the soul remains the same. After he had got acquainted with the girl, there are to be met in that diary of his very queer politico-amorous rhapsodies. He took her sovereign grimaces with deadly seriousness. He longed to convert her. But all this cannot interest you. For the rest, I don't know if you remember – it is a good many years ago now – the journalistic sensation of the "Hermione Street Mystery"; the finding of a man's body in the cellar of an empty house; the inquest; some arrests; many surmises – then silence – the usual end for many obscure martyrs and confessors. The fact is, he was not enough of an optimist. You must be a savage, tyrannical, pitiless, thick-and-thin optimist, like Horne, for instance, to make a good social rebel of the extreme type.'

He rose from the table. A waiter hurried up with his overcoat; another held his hat in readiness.

'But what became of the young lady?' I asked.

'Do you really want to know?' he said, buttoning himself in his fur coat carefully. 'I confess to the small malice of sending her Sevrin's diary. She went into retirement; then she went to Florence; then she went into retreat in a convent. I can't tell where she will go next. What does it matter? Gestures! Gestures! Mere gestures of her class.'

He fitted on his glossy high hat with extreme precision, and casting a rapid glance round the room, full of well-dressed people, innocently dining, muttered between his teeth: 'And nothing else! That is why their kind is fated to perish.'

I never met Mr X again after that evening. I took to dining at my club. On my next visit to Paris I found my friend all impatience to hear of the effect produced on me by this rare item of his collection. I told him all the story, and he beamed on me with the pride of his distinguished specimen.

'Isn't X well worth knowing?' he bubbled over in great delight. 'He's unique, amazing, absolutely terrific.'

His enthusiasm grated upon my finer feelings. I told him curtly that the man's cynicism was simply abominable.

'Oh, abominable! abominable!' assented my friend, effusively. 'And then, you know, he likes to have his little joke sometimes,' he added in a confidential tone.

I fail to understand the connection of this last remark. I have been utterly unable to discover where in all this the joke comes in.

Il Conde

Vedi Napoli e poi mori

The first time we got into conversation was in the National Museum in Naples, in the rooms on the ground floor containing the famous collection of bronzes from Herculaneum and Pompeii: that marvellous legacy of antique art whose delicate perfection has been preserved for us by the catastrophic fury of a volcano.

He addressed me first, over the celebrated Resting Hermes which we had been looking at side by side. He said the right things about that wholly admirable piece. Nothing profound. His taste was natural rather than cultivated. He had obviously seen many fine things in his life and appreciated them: but he had no jargon of a dilettante or the connoisseur. A hateful tribe. He spoke like a fairly intelligent man of the world, a perfectly unaffected gentleman.

We had known each other by sight for some few days past. Staying in the same hotel – good, but not extravagantly up to date – I had noticed him in the vestibule going in and out. I judged he was an old and valued client. The bow of the hotel-keeper was cordial in its deference, and he acknowledged it with familiar courtesy. For the servants he was *Il Conde*. There was some squabble over a man's parasol – yellow silk with white lining sort of thing – the waiters had discovered abandoned outside the dining-room door. Our gold-laced door-keeper recognised it and I heard him directing one of the lift boys to run after *Il Conde* with it. Perhaps he was the only count staying in the hotel, or perhaps he had the distinction of being *the* count *par excellence*, conferred upon him because of his tried fidelity to the house.

Having conversed at the Museo – and by the by he had expressed his dislike of the busts and statues of Roman emperors in the gallery of marbles: their faces were too vigorous, too pronounced for him – having conversed already in the morning I did not think I was intruding when in the evening, finding the dining-room very full, I proposed to share his little table. Judging by the quiet urbanity of his consent he did not think so either. His smile was very attractive.

He dined in an evening waistcoat and a 'smoking' (he called it so) with a black tie. All this of very good cut, not new – just as these things should be. He was, morning or evening, very correct in his dress. I have no doubt that his whole existence had been correct, well ordered and conventional, undisturbed by startling events. His white hair brushed upwards off a lofty forehead gave him the air of an idealist, of an imaginative man. His white moustache, heavy but carefully trimmed and arranged, was not unpleasantly tinted a golden yellow in the middle. The faint scent of some very good perfume, and of good cigars (that last an odour quite remarkable to come upon in Italy) reached me across the table. It was in his eyes that his age showed most. They were a little weary with creased eyelids. He must have been sixty or a couple of years more. And he was communicative. I would not go so far as to call it garrulous – but distinctly communicative.

He had tried various climates, of Abbazia, of the Riviera, of other places, too, he told me; but the only one which suited him was the climate of the Gulf of Naples. The ancient Romans, who, he pointed out to me, were men expert in the art of living, knew very well what they were doing when they built their villas on these shores, in Baiae, in Vico, in Capri. They came down to this seaside in search of health, bringing with them their trains of mimes and flute-players to amuse their leisure. He thought it extremely probable that the Romans of the higher classes were specially predisposed to painful rheumatic affections.

This was the only personal opinion I heard him express. It was based on no special erudition. He knew no more of the Romans than an average informed man of the world is expected to know. He argued from personal experience. He had suffered himself from a painful and dangerous rheumatic affection till he found relief in this particular spot of Southern Europe.

This was three years ago, and ever since he had taken up his quarters on the shores of the gulf, either in one of the hotels in Sorrento or hiring a small villa in Capri. He had a piano, a few books; picked up transient acquaintances of a day, week, or month in the stream of travellers from all Europe. One can imagine him going out for his walks in the streets and lanes, becoming known to beggars, shopkeepers, children, country people; talking amiably over the walls to the *contadini* – and coming back to his rooms or his villa to sit before the piano, with his white hair brushed up and his thick orderly moustache, 'to make a little music for myself'. And, of course, for a change there was Naples near by – life, movement, animation, opera. A little amusement, as he said, is necessary for health. Mimes and flute-players, in fact. Only unlike the magnates of ancient Rome, he had no affairs of the city to call him away from these moderate delights. He had no affairs at all. Probably he had never had any grave affairs to attend to in his life. It was a kindly existence, with its joys and sorrows regulated by the course of Nature – marriages, births, deaths – ruled by the prescribed usages of good society and protected by the State.

He was a widower; but in the months of July and August he ventured to cross the Alps for six weeks on a visit to his married daughter. He told me her name. It was that of a very aristocratic family. She had a castle – in Bohemia, I think. This is as near as I ever came to ascertaining his nationality. His own name, strangely enough, he never mentioned. Perhaps he thought I had seen it on the published list. Truth to say, I never looked. At any rate, he was a good European – he spoke four languages to my certain knowledge – and a man of fortune. Not of great fortune evidently and appropriately. I imagine that to be extremely rich would have appeared to him improper, *outré* – too blatant altogether. And obviously, too, the fortune was not of his making. The making of a fortune cannot be achieved without some roughness. It is a matter of temperament. His nature was too kindly for strife. In the course of conversation he mentioned his estate quite by the way, in reference to that painful and alarming rheumatic affection. One year, staying incautiously beyond the Alps as late as the middle of September, he had been laid up for three months in that lonely country house with no one but his valet and the caretaking couple to attend to him. Because, as he expressed it, he 'kept no establishment there'. He had only gone for a couple of days to confer with his land agent. He promised himself never to be so imprudent in the future. The first weeks of September would find him on the shores of his beloved gulf.

Sometimes in travelling one comes upon such lonely men, whose only business is to wait for the unavoidable. Deaths and marriages have made a solitude round them, and one really cannot blame their endeavours to make the waiting as easy as possible. As he remarked to me, 'At my time of life freedom from physical pain is a very important matter.'

It must not be imagined that he was a wearisome hypochondriac. He was really much too well-bred to be a nuisance. He had an eye for the small weaknesses of humanity. But it was a good-natured eye. He made a restful, easy, pleasant companion for the hours between dinner and bedtime. We spent three evenings together, and then I had to leave Naples in a hurry to look after a friend who had fallen seriously ill in Taormina. Having nothing to do, *Il Conde* came to see me off at the station. I was somewhat upset, and his idleness was always ready to take a kindly form. He was by no means an indolent man.

He went along the train peering into the carriages for a good seat for me, and then remained talking cheerily from below. He declared he would miss me that evening very much and announced his intention of going after dinner to listen to the band in the public garden, the Villa Nazionale. He would amuse himself by hearing excellent music and looking at the best society. There would be a lot of people, as usual.

I seem to see him yet – his raised face with a friendly smile under the thick moustaches, and his kind, fatigued eyes. As the train began to move, he addressed me in two languages: first in French, saying, *'Bon voyage'*; then, in his very good, somewhat emphatic English, encouragingly, because he could see my concern: 'All will – be well – yet!'

My friend's illness having taken a decidedly favourable turn, I returned to Naples on the tenth day. I cannot say I had given much thought to *Il Conde* during my absence, but entering the dining-room I looked for him in his habitual place. I had an idea he might have gone back to Sorrento to his piano and his books and his fishing. He was great friends with all the boatmen, and fished a good deal with lines from a boat. But I made out his white head in the crowd of heads, and even from a distance noticed something unusual in his attitude. Instead of sitting erect, gazing all round with alert urbanity, he drooped over his plate. I stood opposite him for some time before he looked up, a little wildly, if such a strong word can be used in connection with his correct appearance.

'Ah, my dear sir! Is it you?' he greeted me. 'I hope all is well.'

He was very nice about my friend. Indeed, he was always nice, with the niceness of people whose hearts are genuinely humane. But this time it cost him an effort. His attempts at general conversation broke down into dullness. It occurred to me he might have been indisposed. But before I could frame the enquiry he muttered: 'You find me here very sad.'

'I am sorry for that,' I said. 'You haven't had bad news, I hope?'

It was very kind of me to take an interest. No. It was not that. No bad news, thank God. And he became very still as if holding his breath. Then, leaning forward a little, and in an odd tone of awed embarrassment, he took me into his confidence.

'The truth is that I have had a very – a very – how shall I say? – abominable adventure happen to me.'

The energy of the epithet was sufficiently startling in that man of moderate feelings and toned-down vocabulary. The word unpleasant I should have thought would have fitted amply the worst experience likely to befall a man of his stamp. And an adventure, too. Incredible! But it is in human nature to believe the worst; and I confess I eyed him stealthily, wondering what he had been up to. In a moment, however, my unworthy suspicions vanished. There was a fundamental refinement of nature about the man which made me dismiss all idea of some more or less disreputable scrape.

'It is very serious. Very serious.' He went on, nervously. 'I will tell you after dinner, if you will allow me.'

I expressed my perfect acquiescence by a little bow, nothing more. I wished him to understand that I was not likely to hold him to that offer, if he thought better of it later on. We talked of indifferent things, but with a sense of difficulty quite unlike our former easy, gossipy intercourse. The hand raising a piece of bread to his lips, I noticed, trembled slightly. This symptom, in regard of my reading of the man, was no less than startling.

In the smoking-room he did not hang back at all. Directly we had taken our usual seats he leaned sideways over the arm of his chair and looked straight into my eyes earnestly.

'You remember,' he began, 'that day you went away? I told you then I would go to the Villa Nazionale to hear some music in the evening.'

I remembered. His handsome old face, so fresh for his age, unmarked by any trying experience, appeared haggard for an instant. It was like the passing of a shadow. Returning his steadfast gaze, I took a sip of my black coffee. He was systematically minute in his narrative, simply in order, I think, not to let his excitement get the better of him.

After leaving the railway station, he had an ice, and read the paper in a café. Then he went back to the hotel, dressed for dinner, and dined with a good appetite. After dinner he lingered in the hall (there were chairs and tables there) smoking his cigar; talked to the little girl of the Primo Tenore of the San Carlo theatre, and exchanged a few words with that 'amiable lady', the wife of the Primo Tenore. There was no performance that evening, and these people were going to the Villa also. They went out of the hotel. Very well.

At the moment of following their example – it was half-past nine already – he remembered he had a rather large sum of money in his pocket-book. He entered, therefore, the office and deposited the greater part of it with the bookkeeper of the hotel. This done, he took a *carozella* and drove to the seashore. He got out of the cab and entered the Villa on foot from the Largo di Vittoria end.

He stared at me very hard. And I understood then how really impressionable he was. Every small fact and event of that evening stood out in his memory as if endowed with mystic significance. If he did not mention to me the colour of the pony which drew the *carozella*, and the aspect of the man who drove, it was a mere oversight arising from his agitation, which he repressed manfully.

He had then entered the Villa Nazionale from the Largo di Vittoria end. The Villa Nazionale is a public pleasure-ground laid out in grass plots, bushes, and flower-beds between the houses of the Riviera di Chiaja and the waters of the bay. Alleys of trees, more or less parallel, stretch its whole length – which is considerable. On the Riviera di Chiaja side the electric tramcars run close to the railings. Between the garden and the sea is the fashionable drive, a broad road bordered by a low wall, beyond which the Mediterranean splashes with gentle murmurs when the weather is fine.

As life goes on late at night in Naples, the broad drive was all astir with a brilliant swarm of carriage lamps moving in pairs, some creeping slowly, others running rapidly under the thin, motionless line of electric lamps defining the shore. And a brilliant swarm of stars hung above the land humming with voices, piled up with houses, glittering with lights – and over the silent flat shadows of the sea.

The gardens themselves are not very well lit. Our friend went forward in the warm gloom, his eyes fixed upon a distant luminous region extending nearly across the whole width of the Villa, as if the air had glowed there with its own cold, bluish, and dazzling light. This magic spot, behind the black trunks of trees and masses of inky foliage, breathed out sweet sounds mingled with bursts of brassy roar, sudden clashes of metal, and grave, vibrating thuds.

As he walked on, all these noises combined together into a piece of elaborate music whose harmonious phrases came persuasively through a great disorderly murmur of voices and shuffling of feet on the gravel of that open space. An enormous crowd immersed in the electric light, as if in a bath of some radiant and tenuous fluid shed upon their heads by luminous globes, drifted in its hundreds round the band. Hundreds more sat on chairs in more or less concentric circles, receiving unflinchingly the great waves of sonority that ebbed out into the darkness. The Count penetrated the throng, drifted with it in tranquil enjoyment, listening and looking at the faces. All people of good society: mothers with their daughters, parents and children, young men and young women all talking, smiling, nodding to each other. Very many pretty faces, and very many pretty toilettes. There was, of course, a quantity of diverse types: showy old fellows with white moustaches, fat men, thin men, officers in uniform; but what predominated, he told me, was the South Italian type of young man, with a colourless, clear complexion, red lips, jet-black little moustache and liquid black eyes so wonderfully effective in leering or scowling.

Withdrawing from the throng, the Count shared a little table in front of the café with a young man of just such a type. Our friend had some lemonade. The young man was sitting moodily before an empty glass. He looked up once, and then looked down again. He also tilted his hat forward. Like this – The Count made the gesture of a man pulling his hat down over his brow, and went on: 'I think to myself: he is sad; something is wrong with him; young men have their troubles. I take no notice of him, of course. I pay for my lemonade, and go away.'

Strolling about in the neighbourhood of the band, the Count thinks he saw twice that young man wandering alone in the crowd. Once their eyes met. It must have been the same young man, but there were so many there of that type that he could not be certain. Moreover, he was not very much concerned except in so far that he had been struck by the marked, peevish discontent of that face.

Presently, tired of the feeling of confinement one experiences in a crowd, the Count edged away from the band. An alley, very sombre by contrast, presented itself invitingly with its promise of solitude and coolness. He entered it, walking slowly on till the sound of the orchestra became distinctly deadened. Then he walked back and turned about once more. He did this several times before he noticed that there was somebody occupying one of the benches.

The spot being midway between two lamp-posts the light was faint.

The man lolled back in the corner of the seat, his legs stretched out, his arms folded and his head drooping on his breast. He never stirred, as though he had fallen asleep there, but when the Count passed by next time he had changed his attitude. He sat leaning forward. His elbows were propped on his knees, and his hands were rolling a cigarette. He never looked up from that occupation.

The Count continued his stroll away from the band. He returned slowly, he said. I can imagine him enjoying to the full, but with his usual tranquillity, the balminess of this southern night and the sounds of music softened delightfully by the distance.

Presently, he approached for the third time the man on the garden seat, still leaning forward with his elbows on his knees. It was a dejected pose. In the semi-obscurity of the alley his high shirt collar and his cuffs made small patches of vivid whiteness. The Count said that he had noticed him getting up brusquely as if to walk away, but almost before he was aware of it the man stood before him asking in a low, gentle tone whether the *signore* would have the kindness to oblige him with a light.

The Count answered this request by a polite 'Certainly', and dropped his hands with the intention of exploring both pockets of his trousers for the matches.

'I dropped my hands,' he said, 'but I never put them in my pockets. I felt a pressure there – '

He put the tip of his finger on a spot close under his breastbone, the very spot of the human body where a Japanese gentleman begins the operations of the Hara-kiri, which is a form of suicide following upon dishonour, upon an intolerable outrage to the delicacy of one's feelings.

'I glance down,' the Count continued in an awestruck voice, 'and what do I see? A knife! A long knife – '

'You don't mean to say,' I exclaimed, amazed, 'that you have been held up like this in the Villa at half-past ten o'clock, within a stone's throw of a thousand people!'

He nodded several times, staring at me with all his might.

'The clarionet,' he declared, solemnly, 'was finishing his solo, and I assure you I could hear every note. Then the band crashed *fortissimo*, and that creature rolled its eyes and gnashed its teeth hissing at me with the greatest ferocity, "Be silent! No noise or – "

I could not get over my astonishment.

'What sort of knife was it?' I asked, stupidly.

'A long blade. A stiletto – perhaps a kitchen knife. A long narrow blade. It gleamed. And his eyes gleamed. His white teeth, too. I could see them. He was very ferocious. I thought to myself: "If I hit him he will kill me." How could I fight with him? He had the knife and I had nothing. I am nearly seventy, you know, and that was a young man. I seemed even to recognise him. The moody young man of the café. The young man I met in the crowd. But I could not tell. There are so many like him in this country.'

The distress of that moment was reflected in his face. I should think that physically he must have been paralysed by surprise. His thoughts, however, remained extremely active. They ranged over every alarming possibility. The idea of setting up a vigorous shouting for help occurred to him, too. But he did nothing of the kind, and the reason why he refrained gave me a good opinion of his mental self-possession. He saw in a flash that nothing prevented the other from shouting, too.

'That young man might in an instant have thrown away his knife and pretended I was the aggressor. Why not? He might have said I attacked him. Why not? It was one incredible story against another! He might have said anything – bring some dishonouring charge against me – what do I know? By his dress he was no common robber. He seemed to belong to the better classes. What could I say? He was an Italian – I am a foreigner. Of course, I have my passport, and there is our consul – but to be arrested, dragged at night to the police office like a criminal.'

He shuddered. It was in his character to shrink from scandal, much more than from mere death. And certainly for many people this would have always remained – considering certain peculiarities of Neapolitan manners – a deucedly queer story. The Count was no fool. His belief in the respectable placidity of life having received this rude shock, he thought that now anything might happen. But also a notion came into his head that this young man was perhaps merely an infuriated lunatic.

This was for me the first hint of his attitude towards this adventure. In his exaggerated delicacy of sentiment he felt that nobody's self-esteem need be affected by what a madman may choose to do to one. It became apparent, however, that the Count was to be denied that consolation. He enlarged upon the abominably savage way in which that young man rolled his glistening eyes and gnashed his white teeth. The band was going now through a slow movement of solemn braying by all the trombones, with deliberately repeated bangs of the big drum.

'But what did you do?' I asked, greatly excited.

'Nothing,' answered the Count. 'I let my hands hang down very still. I told him quietly I did not intend making a noise. He snarled like a dog, then said in an ordinary voice:

' *"Vostro portofolio."*

'So I naturally,' continued the Count – and from this point acted the whole thing in pantomime. Holding me with his eyes, he went through all the motions of reaching into his inside breast pocket, taking out a pocket-book, and handing it over. But that young man, still bearing steadily on the knife, refused to touch it.

He directed the Count to take the money out himself, received it into his left hand, motioned the pocketbook to be returned to the pocket, all this being done to the sweet thrilling of flutes and clarionets sustained by the emotional drone of the hautboys. And the 'young man', as the Count called him, said: 'This seems very little.'

'It was, indeed, only 340 or 360 lire,' the Count pursued. 'I had left my money in the hotel, as you know. I told him this was all I had on me. He shook his head impatiently and said:

' *"Vostro orologio."*

The Count gave me the dumb show of pulling out his watch, detaching it. But, as it happened, the valuable gold half-chronometer he possessed had been left at a watchmaker's for cleaning. He wore that evening (on a leather guard) the Waterbury fifty-franc thing he used to take with him on his fishing expeditions. Perceiving the nature of this booty, the well-dressed robber made a contemptuous clicking sound with his tongue like this, 'Tse-Ah!' and waved it away hastily. Then, as the Count was returning the disdained object to his pocket, he demanded, with a threateningly increased pressure of the knife on the epigastrum by way of reminder:

' "*Vostri anelli.*"

'One of the rings,' went on the Count, 'was given me many years ago by my wife; the other is the signet ring of my father. I said, "No. *That* you shall not have!" '

Here the Count reproduced the gesture corresponding to that declaration by clapping one hand upon the other, and pressing both thus against his chest. It was touching in its resignation. 'That you shall not have,' he repeated, firmly, and closed his eyes, fully expecting – I don't know whether I am right in recording that such an unpleasant word had passed his lips – fully expecting to feel himself being – I really hesitate to say – being disembowelled by the push of the long, sharp blade resting murderously against the pit of his stomach – the very seat, in all human beings, of anguishing sensations.

Great waves of harmony went on flowing from the band.

Suddenly the Count felt the nightmarish pressure removed from the sensitive spot. He opened his eyes. He was alone. He had heard nothing. It is probable that 'the young man' had departed, with light steps, some time before, but the sense of the horrid pressure had lingered even after the knife had gone. A feeling of weakness came over him. He had just time to stagger to the garden seat. He felt as though he had held his breath for a long time. He sat all in a heap, panting with the shock of the reaction.

The band was executing, with immense bravura, the complicated finale. It ended with a tremendous crash. He heard it unreal and remote, as if his ears had been stopped, and then the hard clapping of a thousand, more or less, pairs of hands, like a sudden hail-shower passing away. The profound silence which succeeded recalled him to himself.

A tramcar resembling a long glass box wherein people sat with their heads strongly lighted, ran along swiftly within sixty yards of the spot where he had been robbed. Then another rustled by, and yet another going the other way. The audience about the band had broken up, and were entering the alley in small conversing groups. The Count sat up straight and tried to think calmly of what had happened to him. The vileness of it took his breath away again. As far as I can make it out he was disgusted with himself. I do not mean to say with his behaviour. Indeed, if his pantomimic rendering of it for my information was to be trusted, it was simply perfect. No, it was not that. He was not ashamed. He was shocked at being the selected victim, not of robbery so much as of contempt. His tranquillity had been wantonly desecrated. His lifelong, kindly nicety of outlook had been defaced.

Nevertheless, at that stage, before the iron had time to sink deep, he was able to argue himself into comparative equanimity. As his agitation calmed down somewhat, he became aware that he was frightfully hungry. Yes, hungry. The sheer emotion had made him simply ravenous. He left the seat and, after walking for some time, found himself outside the gardens and before an arrested tramcar, without knowing very well how he came there. He got in as if in a dream, by a sort of instinct. Fortunately he found in his trouser pocket a copper to satisfy the conductor. Then the car stopped, and as everybody was getting out he got out too. He recognised the Piazza San Ferdinando, but apparently it did not occur to him to take a cab and drive to the hotel. He remained in distress on the piazza like a lost dog, thinking vaguely of the best way of getting something to eat at once.

Suddenly he remembered his twenty-franc piece. He explained to me that he had that piece of French gold for something like three years. He used to carry it about with him as a sort of reserve in case of accident. Anybody is liable to have his pocket picked – a quite different thing from a brazen and insulting robbery.

The monumental arch of the Galleria Umberto faced him at the top of a noble flight of stairs. He climbed these without loss of time, and directed his steps towards the Café Umberto. All the tables outside were occupied by a lot of people who were drinking. But as he wanted something to eat, he went inside into the café, which is divided into aisles by square pillars set all round with long looking-glasses. The Count sat down on a red plush bench against one of these pillars, waiting for his risotto. And his mind reverted to his abominable adventure.

He thought of the moody, well-dressed young man, with whom he had exchanged glances in the crowd around the bandstand, and who, he felt confident, was the robber. Would he recognise him again? Doubtless. But he did not want ever to see him again. The best thing was to forget this humiliating episode.

The Count looked round anxiously for the coming of his risotto, and, behold! to the left against the wall – there sat the young man. He was alone at a table, with a bottle of some sort of wine or syrup and a carafe of iced water before him. The smooth olive cheeks, the red lips, the little jet-black moustache turned up gallantly, the fine black eyes a little heavy and shaded by long eyelashes, that peculiar expression of cruel discontent to be seen only in the busts of some Roman emperors – it was he, no doubt at all. But that was a type. The Count looked away hastily. The young officer over there reading a paper was like that, too. Same type. Two young men farther away playing draughts also resembled –

The Count lowered his head with the fear in his heart of being everlastingly haunted by the vision of that young man. He began to eat his risotto. Presently he heard the young man on his left call the waiter in a bad-tempered tone.

At the call, not only his own waiter, but two other idle waiters belonging to a quite different row of tables, rushed towards him with obsequious alacrity, which is not the general characteristic of the waiters in the Café Umberto. The young man muttered something and one of the waiters walking rapidly to the nearest door called out into the Galleria: 'Pasquale! O! Pasquale!'

Everybody knows Pasquale, the shabby old fellow who, shuffling between the tables, offers for sale cigars, cigarettes, picture postcards, and matches to the clients of the café. He is in many respects an engaging scoundrel. The Count saw the grey-haired, unshaven ruffian enter the café, the glass case hanging from his neck by a leather strap, and, at a word from the waiter, make his shuffling way with a sudden spurt to the young man's table. The young man was in need of a cigar with which Pasquale served him fawningly. The old pedlar was going out, when the Count, on a sudden impulse, beckoned to him.

Pasquale approached, the smile of deferential recognition combining oddly with the cynical searching expression of his eyes. Leaning his case on the table, he lifted the glass lid without a word. The Count took a box of cigarettes and urged by a fearful curiosity, asked as casually as he could –

'Tell me, Pasquale, who is that young *signore* sitting over there?'

The other bent over his box confidentially.

'That, *Signor Conde*,' he said, beginning to rearrange his wares busily and without looking up, 'that is a young *cavaliere* of a very good family from Bari. He studies in the university here, and is the chief, *capo*, of an association of young men – of very nice young men.'

He paused, and then, with mingled discretion and pride of knowledge, murmured the explanatory word 'Camorra' and shut down the lid. 'A very powerful Camorra,' he breathed out. 'The professors themselves respect it greatly . . . *una lira e cinquanta centesimi, Signor Conde.*'

Our friend paid with the gold piece. While Pasquale was making up the change, he observed that the young man, of whom he had heard so much in a few words, was watching the transaction covertly. After the old vagabond had withdrawn with a bow, the Count settled with the waiter and sat still. A numbness, he told me, had come over him.

The young man paid, too, got up, and crossed over, apparently for the purpose of looking at himself in the mirror set in the pillar nearest to the Count's seat. He was dressed all in black with a dark green bow tie. The Count looked round, and was startled by meeting a vicious glance out of the corners of the other's eyes. The young *cavaliere* from Bari (according to Pasquale; but Pasquale is, of course, an accomplished liar) went on arranging his tie, settling his hat before the glass, and meantime he spoke just loud enough to be heard by the Count. He spoke through his teeth with the most insulting venom of contempt and gazing straight into the mirror.

'Ah! So you had some gold on you – you old liar – you old *birba* – you *furfante*! But you are not done with me yet.'

The fiendishness of his expression vanished like lightning, and he lounged out of the café with a moody, impassive face.

The poor Count, after telling me this last episode, fell back trembling in his chair. His forehead broke into perspiration. There was a wanton insolence in the spirit of this outrage which appalled even me. What it was to the Count's delicacy I won't attempt to guess. I am sure that if he had not been too refined to do such a blatantly vulgar thing as dying from apoplexy in a café, he would have had a fatal stroke there and then. All irony apart, my difficulty was to keep him from seeing the full extent of my commiseration. He shrank from every excessive sentiment, and my commiseration was practically unbounded. It did not surprise me to hear that he had been in bed a week. He had got up to make his arrangements for leaving Southern Italy for good and all.

And the man was convinced that he could not live through a whole year in any other climate!

No argument of mine had any effect. It was not timidity, though he did say to me once: 'You do not know what a Camorra is, my dear sir. I am a marked man.' He was not afraid of what could be done to him. His delicate conception of his dignity was defiled by a degrading experience. He couldn't stand that. No Japanese gentleman, outraged in his exaggerated sense of honour, could have gone about his preparations for Hara-kiri with greater resolution. To go home really amounted to suicide for the poor Count.

There is a saying of Neapolitan patriotism, intended for the information of foreigners, I presume: 'See Naples and then die.' *Vedi Napoli e poi mori.* It is a saying of excessive vanity, and everything excessive was abhorrent to the nice moderation of the poor Count. Yet, as I was seeing him off at the railway station, I thought he was behaving with singular fidelity to its conceited spirit. *Vedi Napoli!* . . . He had seen it! He had seen it with startling thoroughness – and now he was going to his grave. He was going to it by the *train de luxe* of the International Sleeping Car Company, *via* Trieste and Vienna. As the four long, sombre coaches pulled out of the station I raised my hat with the solemn feeling of paying the last tribute of respect to a funeral *cortège*. *Il Conde*'s profile, much aged already, glided away from me in stony immobility, behind the lighted pane of glass – *Vedi Napoli e poi mori!*

The Secret Sharer

I

On my right hand there were lines of fishing-stakes resembling a mysterious system of half-submerged bamboo fences, incomprehensible in its division of the domain of tropical fishes, and crazy of aspect as if abandoned forever by some nomad tribe of fishermen now gone to the other end of the ocean; for there was no sign of human habitation as far as the eye could reach. To the left a group of barren islets, suggesting ruins of stone walls, towers, and blockhouses, had its foundations set in a blue sea that itself looked solid, so still and stable did it lie below my feet; even the track of light from the westering sun shone smoothly, without that animated glitter which tells of an imperceptible ripple. And when I turned my head to take a parting glance at the tug which had just left us anchored outside the bar, I saw the straight line of the flat shore joined to the stable sea, edge to edge, with a perfect and unmarked closeness, in one levelled floor half brown, half blue under the enormous dome of the sky. Corresponding in their insignificance to the islets of the sea, two small clumps of trees, one on each side of the only fault in the impeccable joint, marked the mouth of the river Meinam we had just left on the first preparatory stage of our homeward journey; and, far back on the inland level, a larger and loftier mass, the grove surrounding the great Paknam pagoda, was the only thing on which the eye could rest from the vain task of exploring the monotonous sweep of the horizon. Here and there gleams as of a few scattered pieces of silver marked the windings of the great river; and on the nearest of them, just within the bar, the tug steaming right into the land became lost to my sight, hull and funnel and masts, as though the impassive earth had swallowed her up without an effort, without a tremor. My eye followed the light cloud of her smoke, now here, now there, above the plain, according to the devious curves of the stream, but always fainter and farther away, till I lost it at last behind the mitre-shaped hill of the great pagoda. And then I was left alone with my ship, anchored at the head of the Gulf of Siam.

She floated at the starting-point of a long journey, very still in an immense stillness, the shadows of her spars flung far to the eastward by the setting sun. At that moment I was alone on her decks. There was not a sound in her – and around us nothing moved, nothing lived, not a canoe on the water, not a bird in the air, not a cloud in the sky. In this breathless pause at the threshold of a long passage we seemed to be measuring our fitness for a long and arduous enterprise, the appointed task of both our existences to be carried out, far from all human eyes, with only sky and sea for spectators and for judges.

There must have been some glare in the air to interfere with one's sight, because it was only just before the sun left us that my roaming eyes made out beyond the highest ridge of the principal islet of the group something which did away with the solemnity of perfect solitude. The tide of darkness flowed on swiftly; and with tropical suddenness a swarm of stars came out above the shadowy earth, while I lingered yet, my hand resting lightly on my ship's rail as if on the shoulder of a trusted friend. But, with all that multitude of celestial bodies staring down at one, the comfort of quiet communion with her was gone for good. And there were also disturbing sounds by this time – voices, footsteps forward; the steward flitted along the maindeck, a busily ministering spirit; a hand-bell tinkled urgently under the poop-deck . . .

I found my two officers waiting for me near the supper table, in the lighted cuddy. We sat down at once, and as I helped the chief mate, I said: 'Are you aware that there is a ship anchored inside the islands? I saw her mastheads above the ridge as the sun went down.'

He raised sharply his simple face, overcharged by a terrible growth of whisker, and emitted his usual ejaculations: 'Bless my soul, sir! You don't say so!'

My second mate was a round-cheeked, silent young man, grave beyond his years, I thought; but as our eyes happened to meet I detected a slight quiver on his lips. I looked down at once. It was not my part to encourage sneering on board my ship. It must be said, too, that I knew very little of my officers. In consequence of certain events of no particular significance, except to myself, I had been appointed to the command only a fortnight before. Neither did I know much of the hands forward. All these people had been together for eighteen months or so, and my position was that of the only stranger on board. I mention this because it has some bearing on what is to follow. But what I felt most was my being a stranger to the ship; and if all the truth must be told, I was somewhat of a stranger to myself. The youngest man on board (barring the second mate), and untried as yet by a position of the fullest responsibility, I was willing to take the adequacy of the others for granted. They had simply to be equal to their tasks; but I wondered how far I should turn out faithful to that ideal conception of one's own personality every man sets up for himself secretly.

Meantime the chief mate, with an almost visible effect of collaboration on the part of his round eyes and frightful whiskers, was trying to evolve a theory of the anchored ship. His dominant trait was to take all things into earnest consideration. He was of a painstaking turn of mind. As he used to say, he 'liked to account to himself' for practically everything that came in his way, down to a miserable scorpion he had found in his cabin a week before. The why and the wherefore of that scorpion – how it got on board and came to select his room rather than the pantry (which was a dark place and more what a scorpion would be partial to), and how on earth it managed to drown itself in the inkwell of his writing-desk – had exercised him infinitely. The ship within the islands was much more easily accounted for; and just as we were about to rise from table he made his pronouncement. She was, he doubted not, a ship from home lately arrived. Probably she drew too much water to cross the bar except at the top of spring tides. Therefore she went into that natural harbour to wait for a few days in preference to remaining in an open roadstead.

'That's so,' confirmed the second mate, suddenly, in his slightly hoarse voice. 'She draws over twenty feet. She's the Liverpool ship *Sephora* with a cargo of coal. Hundred and twenty-three days from Cardiff.'

We looked at him in surprise.

'The tugboat skipper told me when he came on board for your letters, sir,' explained the young man. 'He expects to take her up the river the day after tomorrow.'

After thus overwhelming us with the extent of his information he slipped out of the cabin. The mate observed regretfully that he 'could not account for that young fellow's whims'. What prevented him telling us all about it at once, he wanted to know.

I detained him as he was making a move. For the last two days the crew had had plenty of hard work, and the night before they had had very little sleep. I felt painfully that I – a stranger – was doing something unusual when I directed him to let all hands turn in without setting an anchor-watch. I proposed to keep on deck myself till one o'clock or thereabouts. I would get the second mate to relieve me at that hour.

'He will turn out the cook and the steward at four,' I concluded, 'and then give you a call. Of course at the slightest sign of any sort of wind we'll have the hands up and make a start at once.'

He concealed his astonishment. 'Very well, sir.' Outside the cuddy he put his head in the second mate's door to inform him of my unheard-of caprice to take a five hours' anchor-watch on myself. I heard the other raise his voice incredulously – 'What? The captain himself?' Then a few more murmurs, a door closed, then another. A few moments later I went on deck.

My strangeness, which had made me sleepless, had prompted that unconventional arrangement, as if I had expected in those solitary hours of the night to get on terms with the ship of which I knew nothing, manned by men of whom I knew very little more. Fast alongside a wharf, littered like any ship in port with a tangle of unrelated things, invaded by unrelated shore people, I had hardly seen her yet properly. Now, as she lay cleared for sea, the stretch of her maindeck seemed to me very fine under the stars. Very fine, very roomy for her size, and very inviting. I descended the poop and paced the waist, my mind picturing to myself the coming passage through the Malay Archipelago, down the Indian Ocean, and up the Atlantic. All its phases were familiar enough to me, every characteristic, all the alternatives which were likely to face me on the high seas – everything! . . . except the novel responsibility of command. But I took heart from the reasonable thought that the ship was like other ships, the men like other men, and that the sea was not likely to keep any special surprises expressly for my discomfiture.

Arrived at that comforting conclusion, I bethought myself of a cigar and went below to get it. All was still down there. Everybody at the after end of the ship was sleeping profoundly. I came out again on the quarter-deck, agreeably at ease in my sleeping-suit on that warm breathless night, barefooted, a glowing cigar in my teeth, and, going forward, I was met by the profound silence of the fore end of the ship. Only as I passed the door of the forecastle I heard a deep, quiet, trustful sigh of some sleeper inside. And suddenly I rejoiced in the great security of the sea as compared with the unrest of the land, in my choice of that untempted life presenting no disquieting problems, invested with an elementary moral beauty by the absolute straightforwardness of its appeal and by the singleness of its purpose.

The riding-light in the fore-rigging burned with a clear, untroubled, as if symbolic, flame, confident and bright in the mysterious shades of the night. Passing on my way aft along the other side of the ship, I observed that the rope side-ladder, put over, no doubt, for the master of the tug when he came to fetch away our letters, had not been hauled in as it should have been. I became annoyed at this, for exactitude in small matters is the very soul of discipline. Then I reflected that I had myself peremptorily dismissed my officers from duty, and by my own act had prevented the anchor-watch being formally set and things properly attended to. I asked myself whether it was wise ever to interfere with the established routine of duties even from the kindest of motives. My action might have made me appear eccentric. Goodness only knew how that absurdly whiskered mate would 'account' for my conduct, and what the whole ship thought of that informality of their new captain. I was vexed with myself.

Not from compunction certainly, but, as it were mechanically, I proceeded to get the ladder in myself. Now a side-ladder of that sort is a light affair and comes in easily, yet my vigorous tug, which should have brought it flying on board, merely recoiled upon my body in a totally unexpected jerk. What the devil! . . . I was so astounded by the immovableness of that ladder that I remained stock-still, trying to account for it to myself like that imbecile mate of mine. In the end, of course, I put my head over the rail.

The side of the ship made an opaque belt of shadow on the darkling glassy shimmer of the sea. But I saw at once something elongated and pale floating very close to the ladder. Before I could form a guess a faint flash of phosphorescent light, which seemed to issue suddenly from the naked body of a man, flickered in the sleeping water with the elusive, silent play of summer lightning in a night sky. With a gasp I saw revealed to my stare a pair of feet, the long legs, a broad livid back immersed right up to the neck in a greenish cadaverous glow. One hand, awash, clutched the bottom rung of the ladder. He was complete but for the head. A headless corpse! The cigar dropped out of my gaping mouth with a tiny plop and a short hiss quite audible in the absolute stillness of all things under heaven. At that I suppose he raised up his face, a dimly pale oval in the shadow of the ship's side. But even then I could only barely make out down there the shape of his black-haired head. However, it was enough for the horrid, frost-bound sensation which had gripped me about the chest to pass off. The moment of vain exclamations was past, too. I only climbed on the spare spar and leaned over the rail as far as I could, to bring my eyes nearer to that mystery floating alongside.

As he hung by the ladder, like a resting swimmer, the sea-lightning played about his limbs at every stir; and he appeared in it ghastly, silvery, fish-like. He remained as mute as a fish, too. He made no motion to get out of the water, either. It was inconceivable that he should not attempt to come on board, and strangely troubling to suspect that perhaps he did not want to. And my first words were prompted by just that troubled incertitude.

'What's the matter?' I asked in my ordinary tone, speaking down to the face upturned exactly under mine.

'Cramp,' it answered, no louder. Then slightly anxious, 'I say, no need to call anyone.'

'I was not going to,' I said.

'Are you alone on deck?'

'Yes.'

I had somehow the impression that he was on the point of letting go the ladder to swim away beyond my ken – mysterious as he came. But, for the moment, this being appearing as if he had risen from the bottom of the sea (it was certainly the nearest land to the ship) wanted only to know the time. I told him. And he, down there, tentatively: 'I suppose your captain's turned in?'

'I am sure he isn't,' I said.

He seemed to struggle with himself, for I heard something like the low, bitter murmur of doubt. 'What's the good?' His next words came out with a hesitating effort.

'Look here, my man. Could you call him out quietly?'

I thought the time had come to declare myself.

'*I* am the captain.'

I heard a 'By Jove!' whispered at the level of the water. The phosphorescence flashed in the swirl of the water all about his limbs, his other hand seized the ladder.

'My name's Leggatt.'

The voice was calm and resolute. A good voice. The self-possession of that man had somehow induced a corresponding state in myself. It was very quietly that I remarked: 'You must be a good swimmer.'

'Yes. I've been in the water practically since nine o'clock. The question for me now is whether I am to let go this ladder and go on swimming till I sink from exhaustion, or – to come on board here.'

I felt this was no mere formula of desperate speech, but a real alternative in the view of a strong soul. I should have gathered from this that he was young; indeed, it is only the young who are ever confronted by such clear issues. But at the time it was pure intuition on my part. A mysterious communication was established already between us two – in the face of that silent, darkened tropical sea. I was young, too; young enough to make no comment. The man in the water began suddenly to climb up the ladder, and I hastened away from the rail to fetch some clothes.

Before entering the cabin I stood still, listening in the lobby at the foot of the stairs. A faint snore came through the closed door of the chief mate's room. The second mate's door was on the hook, but the darkness in there was absolutely soundless. He, too, was young and could sleep like a stone. Remained the steward, but he was not likely to wake up before he was called. I got a sleeping-suit out of my room and, coming back on deck, saw the naked man from the sea sitting on the main-hatch, glimmering white in the darkness, his elbows on his knees and his head in his hands. In a moment he had concealed his damp body in a sleeping-suit of the same grey-stripe pattern as the one I was wearing and followed me like my double on the poop. Together we moved right aft, barefooted, silent.

'What is it?' I asked in a deadened voice, taking the lighted lamp out of the binnacle, and raising it to his face.

'An ugly business.'

He had rather regular features; a good mouth; light eyes under somewhat heavy, dark eyebrows; a smooth, square forehead; no growth on his cheeks; a small, brown moustache, and a well-shaped, round chin. His expression was concentrated, meditative, under the inspecting light of the lamp I held up to his face; such as a man thinking hard in solitude might wear. My sleeping-suit was just right for his size. A well-knit young fellow of twenty-five at most. He caught his lower lip with the edge of white, even teeth.

'Yes,' I said, replacing the lamp in the binnacle. The warm, heavy tropical night closed upon his head again.

'There's a ship over there,' he murmured.

'Yes, I know. The *Sephora*. Did you know of us?'

'Hadn't the slightest idea. I am the mate of her – ' He paused and corrected himself. 'I should say I *was*.'

'Aha! Something wrong?'

'Yes. Very wrong indeed. I've killed a man.'

'What do you mean? Just now?'

'No, on the passage. Weeks ago. Thirty-nine south. When I say a man – '

'Fit of temper,' I suggested, confidently.

The shadowy, dark head, like mine, seemed to nod imperceptibly above the ghostly grey of my sleeping-suit. It was, in the night, as though I had been faced by my own reflection in the depths of a sombre and immense mirror.

'A pretty thing to have to own up to for a Conway boy,' murmured my double, distinctly.

'You're a Conway boy?'

'I am,' he said, as if startled. Then, slowly . . . 'Perhaps you too – '

It was so; but being a couple of years older I had left before he joined. After a quick interchange of dates a silence fell; and I thought suddenly

of my absurd mate with his terrific whiskers and the 'Bless my soul –
you don't say so' type of intellect.

My double gave me an inkling of his thoughts by saying: 'My
father's a parson in Norfolk. Do you see me before a judge and jury
on that charge? For myself I can't see the necessity. There are fellows
that an angel from heaven – And I am not that. He was one of those
creatures that are just simmering all the time with a silly sort of
wickedness. Miserable devils that have no business to live at all. He
wouldn't do his duty and wouldn't let anybody else do theirs. But
what's the good of talking! You know well enough the sort of ill-
conditioned snarling cur – '

He appealed to me as if our experiences had been as identical as our
clothes. And I knew well enough the pestiferous danger of such a
character where there are no means of legal repression. And I knew
well enough also that my double there was no homicidal ruffian. I did
not think of asking him for details, and he told me the story roughly in
brusque, disconnected sentences. I needed no more. I saw it all going
on as though I were myself inside that other sleeping-suit.

'It happened while we were setting a reefed foresail, at dusk. Reefed
foresail! You understand the sort of weather. The only sail we had left
to keep the ship running; so you may guess what it had been like for
days. Anxious sort of job, that. He gave me some of his cursed
insolence at the sheet. I tell you I was overdone with this terrific
weather that seemed to have no end to it. Terrific, I tell you – and a
deep ship. I believe the fellow himself was half crazed with funk. It
was no time for gentlemanly reproof, so I turned round and felled
him like an ox. He up and at me. We closed just as an awful sea made
for the ship. All hands saw it coming and took to the rigging, but I had
him by the throat, and went on shaking him like a rat, the men above
us yelling, "Look out! look out!" Then a crash as if the sky had fallen
on my head. They say that for over ten minutes hardly anything was
to be seen of the ship – just the three masts and a bit of the forecastle
head and of the poop all awash driving along in a smother of foam. It
was a miracle that they found us, jammed together behind the
forebits. It's clear that I meant business, because I was holding him by
the throat still when they picked us up. He was black in the face. It
was too much for them. It seems they rushed us aft together, gripped
as we were, screaming "Murder!" like a lot of lunatics, and broke into
the cuddy. And the ship running for her life, touch and go all the
time, any minute her last in a sea fit to turn your hair grey only a-
looking at it. I understand that the skipper, too, started raving like the
rest of them. The man had been deprived of sleep for more than a

week, and to have this sprung on him at the height of a furious gale nearly drove him out of his mind. I wonder they didn't fling me overboard after getting the carcass of their precious ship-mate out of my fingers. They had rather a job to separate us, I've been told. A sufficiently fierce story to make an old judge and a respectable jury sit up a bit. The first thing I heard when I came to myself was the maddening howling of that endless gale, and on that the voice of the old man. He was hanging on to my bunk, staring into my face out of his sou'wester.

' "Mr Leggatt, you have killed a man. You can act no longer as chief mate of this ship." '

His care to subdue his voice made it sound monotonous. He rested a hand on the end of the skylight to steady himself with, and all that time did not stir a limb, so far as I could see. 'Nice little tale for a quiet tea-party,' he concluded in the same tone.

One of my hands, too, rested on the end of the skylight; neither did I stir a limb, so far as I knew. We stood less than a foot from each other. It occurred to me that if old 'Bless my soul – you don't say so' were to put his head up the companion and catch sight of us, he would think he was seeing double, or imagine himself come upon a scene of weird witchcraft; the strange captain having a quiet confabulation by the wheel with his own grey ghost. I became very much concerned to prevent anything of the sort. I heard the other's soothing undertone.

'My father's a parson in Norfolk,' it said. Evidently he had forgotten he had told me this important fact before. Truly a nice little tale.

'You had better slip down into my stateroom now,' I said, moving off stealthily. My double followed my movements; our bare feet made no sound; I let him in, closed the door with care, and, after giving a call to the second mate, returned on deck for my relief.

'Not much sign of any wind yet,' I remarked when he approached.

'No, sir. Not much,' he assented, sleepily, in his hoarse voice, with just enough deference, no more, and barely suppressing a yawn.

'Well, that's all you have to look out for. You have got your orders.'

'Yes, sir.'

I paced a turn or two on the poop and saw him take up his position face forward with his elbow in the ratlines of the mizzen-rigging before I went below. The mate's faint snoring was still going on peacefully. The cuddy lamp was burning over the table on which stood a vase with flowers, a polite attention from the ship's provision merchant – the last flowers we should see for the next three months at the very least. Two bunches of bananas hung from the beam symmetrically, one on each side of the rudder-casing. Everything was as before in the ship – except that two of her captain's sleeping-suits were simultaneously in use, one motionless in the cuddy, the other keeping very still in the captain's stateroom.

It must be explained here that my cabin had the form of the capital letter L, the door being within the angle and opening into the short part of the letter. A couch was to the left, the bed-place to the right; my writing-desk and the chronometers' table faced the door. But anyone opening it, unless he stepped right inside, had no view of what I call the long (or vertical) part of the letter. It contained some lockers surmounted by a bookcase; and a few clothes, a thick jacket or two, caps, oilskin coat, and suchlike, hung on hooks. There was at the bottom of that part a door opening into my bathroom, which could be entered also directly from the saloon. But that way was never used.

The mysterious arrival had discovered the advantage of this particular shape. Entering my room, lighted strongly by a big bulkhead lamp swung on gimbals above my writing-desk, I did not see him anywhere till he stepped out quietly from behind the coats hung in the recessed part.

'I heard somebody moving about, and went in there at once,' he whispered.

I, too, spoke under my breath.

'Nobody is likely to come in here without knocking and getting permission.'

He nodded. His face was thin and the sunburn faded, as though he had been ill. And no wonder. He had been, I heard presently, kept under arrest in his cabin for nearly nine weeks. But there was nothing sickly in his eyes or in his expression. He was not a bit like me, really; yet, as we stood leaning over my bed-place, whispering side by side, with our dark heads together and our backs to the door, anybody bold enough to open it stealthily would have been treated to the uncanny sight of a double captain busy talking in whispers with his other self.

'But all this doesn't tell me how you came to hang on to our side-ladder,' I enquired, in the hardly audible murmurs we used, after he had told me something more of the proceedings on board the *Sephora* once the bad weather was over.

'When we sighted Java Head I had had time to think all those matters out several times over. I had six weeks of doing nothing else, and with only an hour or so every evening for a tramp on the quarter-deck.'

He whispered, his arms folded on the side of my bed-place, staring through the open port. And I could imagine perfectly the manner of this thinking out – a stubborn if not a steadfast operation; something of which I should have been perfectly incapable.

'I reckoned it would be dark before we closed with the land,' he continued, so low that I had to strain my hearing, near as we were to each other, shoulder touching shoulder almost. 'So I asked to speak to the old man. He always seemed very sick when he came to see me – as if he could not look me in the face. You know, that foresail saved the ship. She was too deep to have run long under bare poles. And it was I that managed to set it for him. Anyway, he came. When I had him in my cabin – he stood by the door looking at me as if I had the halter round my neck already – I asked him right away to leave my cabin door unlocked at night while the ship was going through Sunda Straits. There would be the Java coast within two or three miles, off Angier Point. I wanted nothing more. I've had a prize for swimming – my second year in the Conway.'

'I can believe it,' I breathed out.

'God only knows why they locked me in every night. To see some of their faces you'd have thought they were afraid I'd go about at night strangling people. Am I a murdering brute? Do I look it? By Jove! if I had been he wouldn't have trusted himself like that into my room. You'll say I might have chucked him aside and bolted out, there and then – it was dark already. Well, no. And for the same reason I wouldn't think of trying to smash the door. There would have been a rush to stop me at the noise, and I did not mean to get into a confounded scrimmage. Somebody else might have got killed – for I would not have broken out only to get chucked back, and I did not want any more of that work. He refused, looking more sick than ever. He was afraid of the men, and also of that old second mate of his who had been sailing with him for years – a grey-headed old humbug; and his steward, too, had been with him devil knows how long – seventeen years or more – a dogmatic sort of loafer who hated me like poison, just because I was the chief mate. No chief mate ever made more than one voyage in the *Sephora*, you know. Those two old chaps ran the ship. Devil only knows what the skipper wasn't afraid of (all his nerve went to pieces altogether in that hellish spell of bad weather we had) – of what the law would do to him – of his wife, perhaps. Oh, yes! she's on board. Though I don't think she would have meddled. She would have been only too glad to have me out of the ship in any way. The "brand of Cain" business, don't you see. That's all right. I was ready enough to go off wandering on the face of the earth – and that was price enough to pay for an Abel of that sort. Anyhow, he wouldn't listen to me. "This thing must take its course. I represent the law here." He was shaking like a leaf. "So you won't?" "No!" "Then I hope you will be able to sleep on that," I said, and turned my back on him. "I wonder that *you* can," cries he, and locks the door.

'Well, after that, I couldn't. Not very well. That was three weeks ago. We have had a slow passage through the Java Sea; drifted about Carimata for ten days. When we anchored here they thought, I suppose, it was all right. The nearest land (and that's five miles) is the ship's destination; the consul would soon set about catching me; and there would have been no object in bolting to these islets there. I don't suppose there's a drop of water on them. I don't know how it was, but tonight that steward, after bringing me my supper, went out to let me eat it, and left the door unlocked. And I ate it – all there was, too. After I had finished I strolled out on the quarter-deck. I don't know that I meant to do anything. A breath of fresh air was all I wanted, I believe. Then a sudden temptation came over me. I kicked off my slippers and was in the water before I had made up my mind fairly. Somebody heard the splash and they raised an awful hullabaloo. "He's gone! Lower the boats! He's committed suicide! No, he's swimming." Certainly I was swimming. It's not so easy for a swimmer like me to commit suicide by drowning. I landed on the nearest islet before the boat left the ship's side. I heard them pulling about in the dark, hailing, and so on, but after a bit they gave up. Everything quieted down and the anchorage became as still as death. I sat down on a stone and began to think. I felt certain they would start searching for me at daylight. There was no place to hide on those stony things – and if there had been, what would have been the good? But now I was clear of that ship, I was not going back. So after a while I took off all my clothes, tied them up in a bundle with a stone inside, and dropped them in the deep water on the outer side of that islet. That was suicide enough for me. Let them think what they liked, but I didn't mean to drown myself. I meant to swim till I sank – but that's not the same thing. I struck out for another of these little islands, and it was from that one that I first saw your riding-light. Something to swim for. I went on easily, and on the way I came upon a flat rock a foot or two above water. In the daytime, I dare say, you might make it out with a glass from your poop. I scrambled up on it and rested myself for a bit. Then I made another start. That last spell must have been over a mile.'

His whisper was getting fainter and fainter, and all the time he stared straight out through the porthole, in which there was not even a star to be seen. I had not interrupted him. There was something that made comment impossible in his narrative, or perhaps in himself; a sort of feeling, a quality, which I can't find a name for. And when he ceased, all I found was a futile whisper: 'So you swam for our light?'

'Yes – straight for it. It was something to swim for. I couldn't see any stars low down because the coast was in the way, and I couldn't see the land, either. The water was like glass. One might have been swimming in a confounded thousand-feet-deep cistern with no place for scrambling out anywhere; but what I didn't like was the notion of swimming round and round like a crazed bullock before I gave out; and as I didn't mean to go back . . . No. Do you see me being hauled back, stark naked, off one of these little islands by the scruff of the neck and fighting like a wild beast? Somebody would have got killed for certain, and I did not want any of that. So I went on. Then your ladder – '

'Why didn't you hail the ship?' I asked, a little louder.

He touched my shoulder lightly. Lazy footsteps came right over our heads and stopped. The second mate had crossed from the other side of the poop and might have been hanging over the rail, for all we knew.

'He couldn't hear us talking – could he?' My double breathed into my very ear, anxiously.

His anxiety was an answer, a sufficient answer, to the question I had put to him. An answer containing all the difficulty of that situation. I closed the porthole quietly, to make sure. A louder word might have been overheard.

'Who's that?' he whispered then.

'My second mate. But I don't know much more of the fellow than you do.'

And I told him a little about myself. I had been appointed to take charge while I least expected anything of the sort, not quite a fortnight ago. I didn't know either the ship or the people. Hadn't had the time in port to look about me or size anybody up. And as to the crew, all they knew was that I was appointed to take the ship home. For the rest, I was almost as much of a stranger on board as himself, I said. And at the moment I felt it most acutely. I felt that it would take very little to make me a suspect person in the eyes of the ship's company.

He had turned about meantime; and we, the two strangers in the ship, faced each other in identical attitudes.

'Your ladder – ' he murmured, after a silence. 'Who'd have thought of finding a ladder hanging over at night in a ship anchored out here! I felt just then a very unpleasant faintness. After the life I've been leading for nine weeks, anybody would have got out of condition. I wasn't capable of swimming round as far as your rudder-chains. And, lo and behold! there was a ladder to get hold of. After I gripped it I said to myself, 'What's the good?' When I saw a man's head looking over I thought I would swim away presently and leave him shouting – in whatever language it was. I didn't mind being looked at. I – I liked it. And then you speaking to me so quietly – as if you had expected me – made me hold on a little longer. It had been a confounded lonely time – I don't mean while swimming. I was glad to talk a little to somebody that didn't belong to the *Sephora*. As to asking for the captain, that was a mere impulse. It could have been no use, with all the ship knowing about me and the other people pretty certain to be round here in the morning. I don't know – I wanted to be seen, to talk with somebody, before I went on. I don't know what I would have said . . . "Fine night, isn't it?" or something of the sort.'

'Do you think they will be round here presently?' I asked with some incredulity.

'Quite likely,' he said, faintly.

He looked extremely haggard all of a sudden. His head rolled on his shoulders.

'H'm. We shall see then. Meantime get into that bed,' I whispered. 'Want help? There.'

It was a rather high bed-place with a set of drawers underneath. This amazing swimmer really needed the lift I gave him by seizing his leg. He tumbled in, rolled over on his back, and flung one arm across his eyes. And then, with his face nearly hidden, he must have looked exactly as I used to look in that bed. I gazed upon my other self for a while before drawing across carefully the two green serge curtains which ran on a brass rod. I thought for a moment of pinning them together for greater safety, but I sat down on the couch, and once there I felt unwilling to rise and hunt for a pin. I would do it in a moment. I was extremely tired, in a peculiarly intimate way, by the strain of stealthiness, by the effort of whispering and the general secrecy of this excitement. It was three o'clock by now and I had been on my feet since nine, but I was not sleepy; I could not have gone to sleep. I sat there, fagged out, looking at the curtains, trying to clear my mind of the confused sensation of being in two places at once, and greatly bothered by an exasperating knocking in my head. It was a relief to discover suddenly that it was not in my head at all, but on the outside of the door. Before I could collect myself the words 'Come in' were out of my mouth, and the steward entered with a tray, bringing in my morning coffee. I had slept, after all, and I was so frightened that I shouted, 'This way! I am here, steward,' as though he had been miles away. He put down the tray on the table next the couch and only then said, very quietly, 'I can see you are here, sir.' I felt him give me a keen look, but I dared not meet his eyes just then. He must have wondered why I had drawn the curtains of my bed before going to sleep on the couch. He went out, hooking the door open as usual.

I heard the crew washing decks above me. I knew I would have been told at once if there had been any wind. Calm, I thought, and I was doubly vexed. Indeed, I felt dual more than ever. The steward reappeared suddenly in the doorway. I jumped up from the couch so quickly that he gave a start.

'What do you want here?'

'Close your port, sir – they are washing decks.'

'It is closed,' I said, reddening.

'Very well, sir.' But he did not move from the doorway and returned my stare in an extraordinary, equivocal manner for a time. Then his eyes wavered, all his expression changed, and in a voice unusually gentle, almost coaxingly: 'May I come in to take the empty cup away, sir?'

'Of course!' I turned my back on him while he popped in and out. Then I unhooked and closed the door and even pushed the bolt. This sort of thing could not go on very long. The cabin was as hot as an oven, too. I took a peep at my double, and discovered that he had not moved, his arm was still over his eyes; but his chest heaved; his hair was wet; his chin glistened with perspiration. I reached over him and opened the port.

'I must show myself on deck,' I reflected.

Of course, theoretically, I could do what I liked, with no one to say nay to me within the whole circle of the horizon; but to lock my cabin door and take the key away I did not dare. Directly I put my head out of the companion I saw the group of my two officers, the second mate barefooted, the chief mate in long india-rubber boots, near the break of the poop, and the steward half-way down the poop-ladder talking to them eagerly. He happened to catch sight of me and dived, the second ran down on the main-deck shouting some order or other, and the chief mate came to meet me, touching his cap.

There was a sort of curiosity in his eye that I did not like. I don't know whether the steward had told them that I was 'queer' only, or downright drunk, but I know the man meant to have a good look at me. I watched him coming with a smile which, as he got into point-blank range, took effect and froze his very whiskers. I did not give him time to open his lips.

'Square the yards by lifts and braces before the hands go to breakfast.'

It was the first particular order I had given on board that ship; and I stayed on deck to see it executed, too. I had felt the need of asserting myself without loss of time. That sneering young cub got taken down a peg or two on that occasion, and I also seized the opportunity of having a good look at the face of every foremast man as they filed past me to go to the after braces. At breakfast time, eating nothing myself, I presided with such frigid dignity that the two mates were only too glad to escape from the cabin as soon as decency permitted; and all the time the dual working of my mind distracted me almost to the point of insanity. I was constantly watching myself, my secret self, as dependent on my actions as my own personality, sleeping in that bed, behind that door which faced me as I sat at the head of the table. It was very much like being mad, only it was worse because one was aware of it.

I had to shake him for a solid minute, but when at last he opened his eyes it was in the full possession of his senses, with an enquiring look.

'All's well so far,' I whispered. 'Now you must vanish into the bathroom.'

He did so, as noiseless as a ghost, and I then rang for the steward, and facing him boldly, directed him to tidy up my stateroom while I was having my bath – 'and be quick about it'. As my tone admitted of no excuses, he said, 'Yes, sir,' and ran off to fetch his dust-pan and brushes. I took a bath and did most of my dressing, splashing, and whistling softly for the steward's edification, while the secret sharer of my life stood drawn up bolt upright in that little space, his face looking very sunken in daylight, his eyelids lowered under the stern, dark line of his eyebrows drawn together by a slight frown.

When I left him there to go back to my room the steward was finishing dusting. I sent for the mate and engaged him in some insignificant conversation. It was, as it were, trifling with the terrific character of his whiskers; but my object was to give him an opportunity for a good look at my cabin. And then I could at last shut, with a clear conscience, the door of my stateroom and get my double back into the recessed part. There was nothing else for it. He had to sit still on a small folding stool, half smothered by the heavy coats hanging there. We listened to the steward going into the bathroom out of the saloon filling the water-bottles there, scrubbing the bath, setting things to rights, whisk, bang, clatter – out again into the saloon – turn the key – click. Such was my scheme for keeping my second self invisible. Nothing better could be contrived under the circumstances. And there we sat; I at my writing-desk ready to appear busy with some papers, he behind me, out of sight of the door. It would not have been prudent to talk in daytime; and I could not have stood the excitement of that queer sense of whispering to myself. Now and then, glancing over my shoulder, I saw him far back there, sitting rigidly on the low stool, his bare feet close together, his arms folded, his head hanging on his breast – and perfectly still. Anybody would have taken him for me.

I was fascinated by it myself. Every moment I had to glance over my shoulder. I was looking at him when a voice outside the door said:'Beg pardon, sir.'

'Well!' . . . I kept my eyes on him, and so, when the voice outside the door announced, 'There's a ship's boat coming our way, sir,' I saw him give a start – the first movement he had made for hours. But he did not raise his bowed head.

'All right. Get the ladder over.'

I hesitated. Should I whisper something to him? But what? His immobility seemed never to have been disturbed. What could I tell him he did not know already? . . . Finally I went on deck.

II

The skipper of the *Sephora* had a thin red whisker all round his face, and the sort of complexion that goes with hair of that colour; also the particular, rather smeary shade of blue in the eyes. He was not exactly a showy figure; his shoulders were high, his stature but middling – one leg slightly more bandy than the other. He shook hands, looking vaguely around. A spiritless tenacity was his main characteristic, I judged. I behaved with a politeness which seemed to disconcert him. Perhaps he was shy. He mumbled to me as if he were ashamed of what he was saying; gave his name (it was something like Archbold – but at this distance of years I am hardly sure), his ship's name, and a few other particulars of that sort, in the manner of a criminal making a reluctant and doleful confession. He had had terrible weather on the passage out – terrible – terrible – wife aboard, too.

By this time we were seated in the cabin and the steward brought in a tray with a bottle and glasses. 'Thanks! No.' Never took liquor. Would have some water, though. He drank two tumblerfuls. Terrible thirsty work. Ever since daylight had been exploring the islands round his ship.

'What was that for – fun?' I asked, with an appearance of polite interest.

'No!' He sighed. 'Painful duty.'

As he persisted in his mumbling and I wanted my double to hear every word, I hit upon the notion of informing him that I regretted to say I was hard of hearing.

'Such a young man, too!' he nodded, keeping his smeary blue, unintelligent eyes fastened upon me. What was the cause of it – some disease? he enquired, without the least sympathy and as if he thought that, if so, I'd got no more than I deserved.

'Yes; disease,' I admitted in a cheerful tone which seemed to shock him. But my point was gained, because he had to raise his voice to give me his tale. It is not worth while to record that version. It was just over two months since all this had happened, and he had thought so much about it that he seemed completely muddled as to its bearings, but still immensely impressed.

'What would you think of such a thing happening on board your own ship? I've had the *Sephora* for these fifteen years. I am a well-known shipmaster.'

He was densely distressed – and perhaps I should have sympathised with him if I had been able to detach my mental vision from the unsuspected sharer of my cabin as though he were my second self. There he was on the other side of the bulkhead, four or five feet from us, no more, as we sat in the saloon. I looked politely at Captain Archbold (if that was his name), but it was the other I saw, in a grey sleeping-suit, seated on a low stool, his bare feet close together, his arms folded, and every word said between us falling into the ears of his dark head bowed on his chest.

'I have been at sea now, man and boy, for seven-and-thirty years, and I've never heard of such a thing happening in an English ship. And that it should be my ship. Wife on board, too.'

I was hardly listening to him.

'Don't you think,' I said, 'that the heavy sea which, you told me, came aboard just then might have killed the man? I have seen the sheer weight of a sea kill a man very neatly, by simply breaking his neck.'

'Good God!' he uttered, impressively, fixing his smeary blue eyes on me. 'The sea! No man killed by the sea ever looked like that.' He seemed positively scandalised at my suggestion. And as I gazed at him, certainly not prepared for anything original on his part, he advanced his head close to mine and thrust his tongue out at me so suddenly that I couldn't help starting back.

After scoring over my calmness in this graphic way he nodded wisely. If I had seen the sight, he assured me, I would never forget it as long as I lived. The weather was too bad to give the corpse a proper sea burial. So next day at dawn they took it up on the poop, covering its face with a bit of bunting; he read a short prayer, and then, just as it was, in its oilskins and long boots, they launched it amongst those mountainous seas that seemed ready every moment to swallow up the ship herself and the terrified lives on board of her.

'That reefed foresail saved you,' I threw in.

'Under God – it did,' he exclaimed fervently. 'It was by a special mercy, I firmly believe, that it stood some of those hurricane squalls.'

'It was the setting of that sail which – ' I began.

'God's own hand in it,' he interrupted me. 'Nothing less could have done it. I don't mind telling you that I hardly dared give the order. It seemed impossible that we could touch anything without losing it, and then our last hope would have been gone.'

The terror of that gale was on him yet. I let him go on for a bit, then said, casually – as if returning to a minor subject: 'You were very anxious to give up your mate to the shore people, I believe?'

He was. To the law. His obscure tenacity on that point had in it something incomprehensible and a little awful; something, as it were, mystical, quite apart from his anxiety that he should not be suspected of 'countenancing any doings of that sort'. Seven-and-thirty virtuous years at sea, of which over twenty of immaculate command, and the last fifteen in the *Sephora*, seemed to have laid him under some pitiless obligation.

'And you know,' he went on, groping shamefacedly amongst his feelings, 'I did not engage that young fellow. His people had some interest with my owners. I was in a way forced to take him on. He looked very smart, very gentlemanly, and all that. But do you know – I never liked him, somehow. I am a plain man. You see, he wasn't exactly the sort for the chief mate of a ship like the *Sephora*.'

I had become so connected in thoughts and impressions with the secret sharer of my cabin that I felt as if I, personally, were being given to understand that I, too, was not the sort that would have done for the chief mate of a ship like the *Sephora*. I had no doubt of it in my mind.

'Not at all the style of man. You understand,' he insisted, superfluously, looking hard at me.

I smiled urbanely. He seemed at a loss for a while.

'I suppose I must report a suicide.'

'Beg pardon?'

'Sui–cide! That's what I'll have to write to my owners directly I get in.'

'Unless you manage to recover him before tomorrow,' I assented, dispassionately . . . 'I mean, alive.'

He mumbled something which I really did not catch, and I turned my ear to him in a puzzled manner.

He fairly bawled: 'The land – I say, the mainland is at least seven miles off my anchorage.'

'About that.'

My lack of excitement, of curiosity, of surprise, of any sort of pronounced interest, began to arouse his distrust. But except for the felicitous pretence of deafness I had not tried to pretend anything. I had felt utterly incapable of playing the part of ignorance properly, and therefore was afraid to try. It is also certain that he had brought some ready-made suspicions with him, and that he viewed my politeness as a strange and unnatural phenomenon. And yet how else could I have received him? Not heartily! That was impossible for psychological reasons, which I need not state here. My only object was to keep off his enquiries. Surlily? Yes, but surliness might have provoked a point-blank question. From its novelty to him and from its nature, punctilious courtesy was the manner best calculated to restrain the man. But there was the danger of his breaking through my defence bluntly. I could not, I think have met him by a direct lie, also for psychological (not moral) reasons. If he had only known how afraid I was of his putting my feeling of identity with the other to the test! But, strangely enough (I thought of it only afterward), I believe that he was not a little disconcerted by the reverse side of that weird situation, by something in me that reminded him of the man he was seeking – suggested a mysterious similitude to the young fellow he had distrusted and disliked from the first.

However that might have been, the silence was not very prolonged. He took another oblique step.

'I reckon I had no more than a two-mile pull to your ship. Not a bit more.'

'And quite enough, too, in this awful heat,' I said.

Another pause full of mistrust followed. Necessity, they say, is mother of invention, but fear, too, is not barren of ingenious suggestions. And I was afraid he would ask me point-blank for news of my other self.

'Nice little saloon, isn't it?' I remarked, as if noticing for the first time the way his eyes roamed from one closed door to the other. 'And very well fitted out, too. Here, for instance,' I continued, reaching over the back of my seat negligently and flinging the door open, 'is my bathroom.'

He made an eager movement, but hardly gave it a glance. I got up, shut the door of the bathroom, and invited him to have a look round, as if I were very proud of my accommodation. He had to rise and be shown round, but he went through the business without any raptures whatever.

'And now we'll have a look at my stateroom,' I declared, in a voice as loud as I dared to make it, crossing the cabin to the starboard side with purposely heavy steps.

He followed me in and gazed around. My intelligent double had vanished. I played my part.

'Very convenient – isn't it?'

'Very nice. Very comf . . .' He didn't finish, and went out brusquely as if to escape from some unrighteous wiles of mine. But it was not to be. I had been too frightened not to feel vengeful; I felt I had him on the run, and I meant to keep him on the run. My polite insistence must have had something menacing in it, because he gave in suddenly. And I did not let him off a single item: mate's room, pantry, storerooms, the very sail-locker which was also under the poop – he had to look into them all. When at last I showed him out on the quarter-deck he drew a long, spiritless sigh, and mumbled dismally that he must really be going back to his ship now. I desired my mate, who had joined us, to see to the captain's boat.

The man of whiskers gave a blast on the whistle which he used to wear hanging round his neck, and yelled, '*Sephora's* away!' My double down there in my cabin must have heard, and certainly could not feel more relieved than I. Four fellows came running out from somewhere forward and went over the side, while my own men, appearing on deck too, lined the rail. I escorted my visitor to the gangway ceremoniously, and nearly overdid it. He was a tenacious beast. On the very ladder he lingered, and in that unique, guiltily conscientious manner of sticking to the point: 'I say . . . you . . . you don't think that – '

I covered his voice loudly: 'Certainly not . . . I am delighted. Goodbye.'

I had an idea of what he meant to say, and just saved myself by the privilege of defective hearing. He was too shaken generally to insist, but my mate, close witness of that parting, looked mystified and his face took on a thoughtful cast. As I did not want to appear as if I wished to avoid all communication with my officers, he had the opportunity to address me.

'Seems a very nice man. His boat's crew told our chaps a very extraordinary story, if what I am told by the steward is true. I suppose you had it from the captain, sir?'

'Yes. I had a story from the captain.'

'A very horrible affair – isn't it, sir?'

'It is.'

'Beats all these tales we hear about murders in Yankee ships.'

'I don't think it beats them. I don't think it resembles them in the least.'

'Bless my soul – you don't say so! But of course I've no acquaintance whatever with American ships, not I, so I couldn't go against your knowledge. It's horrible enough for me . . . But the queerest part is that those fellows seemed to have some idea the man was hidden aboard here. They had really. Did you ever hear of such a thing?'

'Preposterous – isn't it?'

We were walking to and fro athwart the quarter-deck. No one of the crew forward could be seen (the day was Sunday), and the mate pursued: 'There was some little dispute about it. Our chaps took offence. "As if we would harbour a thing like that," they said. "Wouldn't you like to look for him in our coal-hole?" Quite a tiff. But they made it up in the end. I suppose he did drown himself. Don't you, sir?'

'I don't suppose anything.'

'You have no doubt in the matter, sir?'

'None whatever.'

I left him suddenly. I felt I was producing a bad impression, but with my double down there it was most trying to be on deck. And it was almost as trying to be below. Altogether a nerve-trying situation. But on the whole I felt less torn in two when I was with him. There was no one in the whole ship whom I dared take into my confidence. Since the hands had got to know his story, it would have been impossible to pass him off for anyone else, and an accidental discovery was to be dreaded now more than ever . . .

The steward being engaged in laying the table for dinner, we could talk only with our eyes when I first went down. Later in the afternoon we had a cautious try at whispering. The Sunday quietness of the ship was against us; the stillness of air and water around her was against us; the elements, the men were against us – everything was against us in our secret partnership; time itself – for this could not go on forever. The very trust in Providence was, I suppose, denied to his guilt. Shall I confess that this thought cast me down very much? And as to the chapter of accidents which counts for so much in the book of success, I could only hope that it was closed. For what favourable accident could be expected?

'Did you hear everything?' were my first words as soon as we took up our position side by side, leaning over my bed-place.

He had. And the proof of it was his earnest whisper, 'The man told you he hardly dared to give the order.'

I understood the reference to be to that saving foresail.

'Yes. He was afraid of it being lost in the setting.'

'I assure you he never gave the order. He may think he did, but he never gave it. He stood there with me on the break of the poop after the maintopsail blew away, and whimpered about our last hope – positively whimpered about it and nothing else – and the night coming on! To hear one's skipper go on like that in such weather was enough to drive any fellow out of his mind. It worked me up into a sort of desperation. I just took it into my own hands and went away from him, boiling, and – But what's the use telling you? *You* know! . . . Do you think that if I had not been pretty fierce with them I should have got the men to do anything? Not it! The bo's'n perhaps? Perhaps! It wasn't a heavy sea – it was a sea gone mad! I suppose the end of the world will be something like that; and a man may have the heart to see it coming once and be done with it – but to have to face it day after day I don't blame anybody. I was precious little better than the rest. Only – I was an officer of that old coal-waggon, anyhow – '

'I quite understand,' I conveyed that sincere assurance into his ear. He was out of breath with whispering; I could hear him pant slightly. It was all very simple. The same strung-up force which had given twenty-four men a chance, at least, for their lives, had, in a sort of recoil, crushed an unworthy mutinous existence.

But I had no leisure to weigh the merits of the matter – footsteps in the saloon, a heavy knock. 'There's enough wind to get under way with, sir.' Here was the call of a new claim upon my thoughts and even upon my feelings.

'Turn the hands up,' I cried through the door. 'I'll be on deck directly.'

I was going out to make the acquaintance of my ship. Before I left the cabin our eyes met – the eyes of the only two strangers on board. I pointed to the recessed part where the little camp-stool awaited him and laid my finger on my lips. He made a gesture – somewhat vague – a little mysterious, accompanied by a faint smile, as if of regret.

This is not the place to enlarge upon the sensations of a man who feels for the first time a ship move under his feet to his own independent word. In my case they were not unalloyed. I was not wholly alone with my command; for there was that stranger in my cabin. Or rather, I was not completely and wholly with her. Part of me was absent. That mental feeling of being in two places at once affected me physically as if the mood of secrecy had penetrated my very soul. Before an hour had elapsed since the ship had begun to move, having occasion to ask the mate (he stood by my side) to take a compass bearing of the Pagoda, I caught myself reaching up to his ear in whispers. I say I caught myself, but enough had escaped to startle the man. I can't describe it otherwise than by saying that he shied. A grave, preoccupied manner, as though he were in possession of some perplexing intelligence, did not leave him henceforth. A little later I moved away from the rail to look at the compass with such a stealthy gait that the helmsman noticed it – and I could not help noticing the unusual roundness of his eyes. These are trifling instances, though it's to no commander's advantage to be suspected of ludicrous eccentricities. But I was also more seriously affected. There are to a seaman certain words, gestures, that should in given conditions come as naturally, as instinctively as the winking of a menaced eye. A certain order should spring on to his lips without thinking; a certain sign should get itself made, so to speak, without reflection. But all unconscious alertness had abandoned me. I had to make an effort of will to recall myself back (from the cabin) to the conditions of the moment. I felt that I was appearing an irresolute commander to those people who were watching me more or less critically.

And, besides, there were the scares. On the second day out, for instance, coming off the deck in the afternoon (I had straw slippers on my bare feet) I stopped at the open pantry door and spoke to the steward. He was doing something there with his back to me. At the sound of my voice he nearly jumped out of his skin, as the saying is, and incidentally broke a cup.

'What on earth's the matter with you?' I asked, astonished.

He was extremely confused. 'Beg your pardon, sir. I made sure you were in your cabin.'

'You see I wasn't.'

'No, sir. I could have sworn I had heard you moving in there not a moment ago. It's most extraordinary . . . very sorry, sir.'

I passed on with an inward shudder. I was so identified with my secret double that I did not even mention the fact in those scanty, fearful whispers we exchanged. I suppose he had made some slight noise of some kind or other. It would have been miraculous if he hadn't at one time or another. And yet, haggard as he appeared, he looked always perfectly self-controlled, more than calm – almost invulnerable. On my suggestion he remained almost entirely in the bathroom, which, upon the whole, was the safest place. There could be really no shadow of an excuse for anyone ever wanting to go in there, once the steward had done with it. It was a very tiny place. Sometimes he reclined on the floor, his legs bent, his head sustained on one elbow. At others I would find him on the camp-stool, sitting in his grey sleeping-suit and with his cropped dark hair like a patient, unmoved convict. At night I would smuggle him into my bed-place, and we would whisper together, with the regular footfalls of the officer of the watch passing and repassing over our heads. It was an infinitely miserable time. It was lucky that some tins of fine preserves were stowed in a locker in my stateroom; hard bread I could always get hold of; and so he lived on stewed chicken, pâté de foie gras, asparagus, cooked oysters, sardines – on all sorts of abominable sham delicacies out of tins. My early morning coffee he always drank; and it was all I dared do for him in that respect.

Every day there was the horrible manoeuvring to go through so that my room and then the bathroom should be done in the usual way. I came to hate the sight of the steward, to abhor the voice of that harmless man. I felt that it was he who would bring on the disaster of discovery. It hung like a sword over our heads.

The fourth day out, I think (we were then working down the east side of the Gulf of Siam, tack for tack, in light winds and smooth water) – the fourth day, I say, of this miserable juggling with the unavoidable, as we sat at our evening meal, that man, whose slightest movement I dreaded, after putting down the dishes ran up on deck busily. This could not be dangerous. Presently he came down again; and then it appeared that he had remembered a coat of mine which I had thrown over a rail to dry after having been wetted in a shower which had passed over the ship in the afternoon. Sitting stolidly at the head of the table I became terrified at the sight of the garment on his arm. Of course he made for my door. There was no time to lose.

'Steward,' I thundered. My nerves were so shaken that I could not govern my voice and conceal my agitation. This was the sort of thing that made my terrifically whiskered mate tap his forehead with his forefinger. I had detected him using that gesture while talking on deck with a confidential air to the carpenter. It was too far to hear a word, but I had no doubt that this pantomime could only refer to the strange new captain.

'Yes, sir,' the pale-faced steward turned resignedly to me. It was this maddening course of being shouted at, checked without rhyme or reason, arbitrarily chased out of my cabin, suddenly called into it, sent flying out of his pantry on incomprehensible errands, that accounted for the growing wretchedness of his expression.

'Where are you going with that coat?'

'To your room, sir.'

'Is there another shower coming?'

'I'm sure I don't know, sir. Shall I go up again and see, sir?'

'No! never mind.'

My object was attained, as of course my other self in there would have heard everything that passed. During this interlude my two officers never raised their eyes off their respective plates; but the lip of that confounded cub, the second mate, quivered visibly.

I expected the steward to hook my coat on and come out at once. He was very slow about it; but I dominated my nervousness sufficiently not to shout after him. Suddenly I became aware (it could be heard plainly enough) that the fellow for some reason or other was opening the door of the bathroom. It was the end. The place was literally not big enough to swing a cat in. My voice died in my throat and I went stony all over. I expected to hear a yell of surprise and terror, and made a movement, but had not the strength to get on my legs. Everything remained still. Had my second self taken the poor wretch by the throat? I don't know what I would have done next moment if I had not seen the steward come out of my room, close the door, and then stand quietly by the sideboard.

'Saved,' I thought. 'But, no! Lost! Gone! He was gone!'

I laid my knife and fork down and leaned back in my chair. My head swam. After a while, when sufficiently recovered to speak in a steady voice, I instructed my mate to put the ship round at eight o'clock himself.

'I won't come on deck,' I went on. 'I think I'll turn in, and unless the wind shifts I don't want to be disturbed before midnight. I feel a bit seedy.'

'You did look middling bad a little while ago,' the chief mate remarked without showing any great concern.

They both went out, and I stared at the steward clearing the table. There was nothing to be read on that wretched man's face. But why did he avoid my eyes, I asked myself. Then I thought I should like to hear the sound of his voice.

'Steward!'

'Sir!' Startled as usual.

'Where did you hang up that coat?'

'In the bathroom, sir.' The usual anxious tone. 'It's not quite dry yet, sir.'

For some time longer I sat in the cuddy. Had my double vanished as he had come? But of his coming there was an explanation, whereas his disappearance would be inexplicable . . . I went slowly into my dark room, shut the door, lighted the lamp, and for a time dared not turn round. When at last I did I saw him standing bolt-upright in the narrow recessed part. It would not be true to say I had a shock, but an irresistible doubt of his bodily existence flitted through my mind. Can it be, I asked myself, that he is not visible to other eyes than mine? It was like being haunted. Motionless, with a grave face, he raised his hands slightly at me in a gesture which meant clearly, 'Heavens! what a narrow escape!' Narrow indeed. I think I had come creeping quietly as near insanity as any man who has not actually gone over the border. That gesture restrained me, so to speak.

The mate with the terrific whiskers was now putting the ship on the other tack. In the moment of profound silence which follows upon the hands going to their stations I heard on the poop his raised voice:

'Hard alee!' and the distant shout of the order repeated on the maindeck. The sails, in that light breeze, made but a faint fluttering noise. It ceased. The ship was coming round slowly; I held my breath in the renewed stillness of expectation; one wouldn't have thought that there was a single living soul on her decks. A sudden brisk shout, 'Mainsail haul!' broke the spell, and in the noisy cries and rush overhead of the men running away with the main-brace we two, down in my cabin, came together in our usual position by the bed-place.

He did not wait for my question. 'I heard him fumbling here and just managed to squat myself down in the bath,' he whispered to me. 'The fellow only opened the door and put his arm in to hang the coat up. All the same – '

'I never thought of that,' I whispered back, even more appalled than before at the closeness of the shave, and marvelling at that something unyielding in his character which was carrying him through so finely. There was no agitation in his whisper. Whoever was being driven distracted, it was not he. He was sane. And the proof of his sanity was continued when he took up the whispering again.

'It would never do for me to come to life again.'

It was something that a ghost might have said. But what he was alluding to was his old captain's reluctant admission of the theory of suicide. It would obviously serve his turn – if I had understood at all the view which seemed to govern the unalterable purpose of his action.

'You must maroon me as soon as ever you can get amongst these islands off the Cambodje shore,' he went on.

'Maroon you! We are not living in a boy's adventure tale,' I protested. His scornful whispering took me up.

'We aren't indeed! There's nothing of a boy's tale in this. But there's nothing else for it. I want no more. You don't suppose I am afraid of what can be done to me? Prison or gallows or whatever they may please. But you don't see me coming back to explain such things to an old fellow in a wig and twelve respectable tradesmen, do you? What can they know whether I am guilty or not – or of *what* I am guilty, either? That's my affair. What does the Bible say? "Driven off the face of the earth." Very well. I am off the face of the earth now. As I came at night so I shall go.'

'Impossible!' I murmured. 'You can't.'

'Can't? . . . Not naked like a soul on the Day of Judgment. I shall freeze on to this sleeping-suit. The Last Day is not yet – and . . . you have understood thoroughly. Didn't you?'

I felt suddenly ashamed of myself. I may say truly that I understood – and my hesitation in letting that man swim away from my ship's side had been a mere sham sentiment, a sort of cowardice.

'It can't be done now till next night,' I breathed out. 'The ship is on the off-shore tack and the wind may fail us.'

'As long as I know that you understand,' he whispered. 'But of course you do. It's a great satisfaction to have got somebody to understand. You seem to have been there on purpose.' And in the same whisper, as if we two whenever we talked had to say things to each other which were not fit for the world to hear, he added, 'It's very wonderful.'

We remained side by side talking in our secret way – but sometimes silent or just exchanging a whispered word or two at long intervals. And as usual he stared through the port. A breath of wind came now and again into our faces. The ship might have been moored in dock, so gently and on an even keel she slipped through the water, that did not murmur even at our passage, shadowy and silent like a phantom sea.

At midnight I went on deck, and to my mate's great surprise put the ship round on the other tack. His terrible whiskers flitted round me in silent criticism. I certainly should not have done it if it had been only a question of getting out of that sleepy gulf as quickly as possible. I believe he told the second mate, who relieved him, that it was a great want of judgment. The other only yawned. That intolerable cub shuffled about so sleepily and lolled against the rails in such a slack, improper fashion that I came down on him sharply.

'Aren't you properly awake yet?'

'Yes, sir! I am awake.'

'Well, then, be good enough to hold yourself as if you were. And keep a look-out. If there's any current we'll be closing with some islands before daylight.'

The east side of the gulf is fringed with islands, some solitary, others in groups. On the blue background of the high coast they seem to float on silvery patches of calm water, arid and grey, or dark green and rounded like clumps of evergreen bushes, with the larger ones, a mile or two long, showing the outlines of ridges, ribs of grey rock under the dank mantle of matted leafage. Unknown to trade, to travel, almost to geography, the manner of life they harbour is an unsolved secret. There must be villages – settlements of fishermen at least – on the largest of them, and some communication with the world is probably kept up by native craft. But all that forenoon, as we headed for them, fanned along by the faintest of breezes, I saw no sign of man or canoe in the field of the telescope I kept on pointing at the scattered group.

At noon I gave no orders for a change of course, and the mate's whiskers became much concerned and seemed to be offering themselves unduly to my notice.

At last I said: 'I am going to stand right in. Quite in – as far as I can take her.'

The stare of extreme surprise imparted an air of ferocity also to his eyes, and he looked truly terrific for a moment.

'We're not doing well in the middle of the gulf,' I continued, casually. 'I am going to look for the land breezes tonight.'

'Bless my soul! Do you mean, sir, in the dark amongst the lot of all them islands and reefs and shoals?'

'Well – if there are any regular land breezes at all on this coast one must get close inshore to find them, mustn't one?'

'Bless my soul!' he exclaimed again under his breath. All that afternoon he wore a dreamy, contemplative appearance which in him was a mark of perplexity. After dinner I went into my stateroom as if I meant to take some rest. There we two bent our dark heads over a half-unrolled chart lying on my bed.

'There,' I said. 'It's got to be Koh-ring. I've been looking at it ever since sunrise. It has got two hills and a low point. It must be inhabited. And on the coast opposite there is what looks like the mouth of a biggish river – with some town, no doubt, not far up. It's the best chance for you that I can see.'

'Anything. Koh-ring let it be.'

He looked thoughtfully at the chart as if surveying chances and distances from a lofty height – and following with his eyes his own figure wandering on the blank land of Cochin-China, and then passing off that piece of paper clean out of sight into uncharted regions. And it was as if the ship had two captains to plan her course for her. I had been so worried and restless running up and down that I had not had the patience to dress that day. I had remained in my sleeping-suit, with straw slippers and a soft floppy hat. The closeness of the heat in the gulf had been most oppressive, and the crew were used to see me wandering in that airy attire.

'She will clear the south point as she heads now,' I whispered into his ear. 'Goodness only knows when, though, but certainly after dark. I'll edge her in to half a mile, as far as I may be able to judge in the dark – '

'Be careful,' he murmured, warningly – and I realised suddenly that all my future, the only future for which I was fit, would perhaps go irretrievably to pieces in any mishap to my first command.

I could not stop a moment longer in the room. I motioned him to get out of sight and made my way on the poop. That unplayful cub had the watch. I walked up and down for a while thinking things out, then beckoned him over.

'Send a couple of hands to open the two quarter-deck ports,' I said, mildly.

He actually had the impudence, or else so forgot himself in his wonder at such an incomprehensible order, as to repeat: 'Open the quarter-deck ports! What for, sir?'

'The only reason you need concern yourself about is because I tell you to do so. Have them open wide and fastened properly.'

He reddened and went off, but I believe made some jeering remark to the carpenter as to the sensible practice of ventilating a ship's quarter-deck. I know he popped into the mate's cabin to impart the fact to him because the whiskers came on deck, as it were by chance, and stole glances at me from below – for signs of lunacy or drunkenness, I suppose.

A little before supper, feeling more restless than ever, I rejoined, for a moment, my second self. And to find him sitting so quietly was surprising, like something against nature, inhuman.

I developed my plan in a hurried whisper.

'I shall stand in as close as I dare and then put her round. I shall presently find means to smuggle you out of here into the sail-locker, which communicates with the lobby. But there is an opening, a sort of square for hauling the sails out, which gives straight on the quarter-deck and which is never closed in fine weather, so as to give air to the sails. When the ship's way is deadened in stays and all the hands are aft at the main-braces you shall have a clear road to slip out and get overboard through the open quarter-deck port. I've had them both fastened up. Use a rope's end to lower yourself into the water so as to avoid a splash – you know. It could be heard and cause some beastly complication.'

He kept silent for a while, then whispered, 'I understand.'

'I won't be there to see you go,' I began with an effort. 'The rest . . . I only hope I have understood, too.'

'You have. From first to last' – and for the first time there seemed to be a faltering, something strained in his whisper. He caught hold of my arm, but the ringing of the supper bell made me start. He didn't, though; he only released his grip.

After supper I didn't come below again till well past eight o'clock. The faint, steady breeze was loaded with dew; and the wet, darkened sails held all there was of propelling power in it. The night, clear and starry, sparkled darkly, and the opaque, lightless patches shifting slowly against the low stars were the drifting islets. On the port bow there was a big one more distant and shadowily imposing by the great space of sky it eclipsed.

On opening the door I had a back view of my very own self looking at a chart. He had come out of the recess and was standing near the table.

'Quite dark enough,' I whispered.

He stepped back and leaned against my bed with a level, quiet glance. I sat on the couch. We had nothing to say to each other. Over our heads the officer of the watch moved here and there. Then I heard him move quickly. I knew what that meant. He was making for the companion; and presently his voice was outside my door.

'We are drawing in pretty fast, sir. Land looks rather close.'

'Very well,' I answered. 'I am coming on deck directly.'

I waited till he was gone out of the cuddy, then rose. My double moved too. The time had come to exchange our last whispers, for neither of us was ever to hear each other's natural voice.

'Look here!' I opened a drawer and took out three sovereigns. 'Take this, anyhow. I've got six and I'd give you the lot, only I must keep a little money to buy some fruit and vegetables for the crew from native boats as we go through Sunda Straits.'

He shook his head.

'Take it,' I urged him, whispering desperately. 'No one can tell what –'

He smiled and slapped meaningly the only pocket of the sleeping-jacket. It was not safe, certainly. But I produced a large old silk handkerchief of mine, and tying the three pieces of gold in a corner, pressed it on him. He was touched, I suppose, because he took it at last and tied it quickly round his waist under the jacket, on his bare skin.

Our eyes met; several seconds elapsed, till, our glances still mingled, I extended my hand and turned the lamp out. Then I passed through the cuddy, leaving the door of my room wide open. . . . 'Steward!'

He was still lingering in the pantry in the greatness of his zeal, giving a rub-up to a plated cruet stand the last thing before going to bed. Being careful not to wake up the mate, whose room was opposite, I spoke in an undertone.

He looked round anxiously. 'Sir!'

'Can you get me a little hot water from the galley?'

'I am afraid, sir, the galley fire's been out for some time now.'

'Go and see.'

He fled up the stairs.

'Now,' I whispered, loudly, into the saloon – too loudly, perhaps, but I was afraid I couldn't make a sound. He was by my side in an instant – the double captain slipped past the stairs – through a tiny dark passage . . . a sliding door. We were in the sail-locker, scrambling on our knees over the sails. A sudden thought struck me. I saw myself wandering barefooted, bareheaded, the sun beating on my dark poll. I snatched off my floppy hat and tried hurriedly in the dark to ram it on my other self. He dodged and fended off silently. I wonder what he thought had come to me before he understood and suddenly desisted. Our hands met gropingly, lingered united in a steady, motionless clasp for a second . . . No word was breathed by either of us when they separated.

I was standing quietly by the pantry door when the steward returned.

'Sorry, sir. Kettle barely warm. Shall I light the spirit-lamp?'

'Never mind.'

I came out on deck slowly. It was now a matter of conscience to shave the land as close as possible – for now he must go overboard whenever the ship was put in stays. Must! There could be no going back for him. After a moment I walked over to leeward and my heart flew into my mouth at the nearness of the land on the bow. Under any other circumstances I would not have held on a minute longer. The second mate had followed me anxiously.

I looked on till I felt I could command my voice.

'She will weather,' I said then in a quiet tone.

'Are you going to try that, sir?' he stammered out incredulously.

I took no notice of him and raised my tone just enough to be heard by the helmsman.

'Keep her good full.'

'Good full, sir.'

The wind fanned my cheek, the sails slept, the world was silent. The strain of watching the dark loom of the land grow bigger and denser was too much for me. I had shut my eyes – because the ship must go closer. She must! The stillness was intolerable. Were we standing still?

When I opened my eyes the second view started my heart with a thump. The black southern hill of Koh-ring seemed to hang right over the ship like a towering fragment of the everlasting night. On that enormous mass of blackness there was not a gleam to be seen, not a sound to be heard. It was gliding irresistibly toward us and yet seemed already within reach of the hand. I saw the vague figures of the watch grouped in the waist, gazing in awed silence.

'Are you going on, sir,' enquired an unsteady voice at my elbow.

I ignored it. I had to go on.

'Keep her full. Don't check her way. That won't do now,' I said, warningly.

'I can't see the sails very well,' the helmsman answered me, in strange, quavering tones.

Was she close enough? Already she was, I won't say in the shadow of the land, but in the very blackness of it, already swallowed up as it were, gone too close to be recalled, gone from me altogether.

'Give the mate a call,' I said to the young man who stood at my elbow as still as death. 'And turn all hands up.'

My tone had a borrowed loudness reverberated from the height of the land. Several voices cried out together: 'We are all on deck, sir.'

Then stillness again, with the great shadow gliding closer, towering higher, without a light, without a sound. Such a hush had fallen on the ship that she might have been a bark of the dead floating in slowly under the very gate of Erebus.

'My God! Where are we?'

It was the mate moaning at my elbow. He was thunderstruck, and as it were deprived of the moral support of his whiskers. He clapped his hands and absolutely cried out, 'Lost!'

'Be quiet,' I said, sternly.

He lowered his tone, but I saw the shadowy gesture of his despair. 'What are we doing here?'

'Looking for the land wind.'

He made as if to tear his hair, and addressed me recklessly.

'She will never get out. You have done it, sir. I knew it'd end in something like this. She will never weather, and you are too close now to stay. She'll drift ashore before she's round. O my God!'

I caught his arm as he was raising it to batter his poor devoted head, and shook it violently.

'She's ashore already,' he wailed, trying to tear himself away.

'Is she? . . . Keep good full there!'

'Good full, sir,' cried the helmsman in a frightened, thin, childlike voice.

I hadn't let go the mate's arm and went on shaking it. 'Ready about, do you hear? You go forward' – shake – 'and stop there' – shake – 'and hold your noise' – shake – 'and see these head-sheets properly overhauled' – shake, shake – shake.

And all the time I dared not look toward the land lest my heart should fail me. I released my grip at last and he ran forward as if fleeing for dear life.

I wondered what my double there in the sail-locker thought of this commotion. He was able to hear everything – and perhaps he was able to understand why, on my conscience, it had to be thus close – no less. My first order 'Hard alee!' re-echoed ominously under the towering shadow of Koh-ring as if I had shouted in a mountain gorge. And then I watched the land intently. In that smooth water and light wind it was impossible to feel the ship coming-to. No! I could not feel her. And my second self was making now ready to slip out and lower himself overboard. Perhaps he was gone already . . . ?

The great black mass brooding over our very mastheads began to pivot away from the ship's side silently. And now I forgot the secret stranger ready to depart, and remembered only that I was a total stranger to the ship. I did not know her. Would she do it? How was she to be handled?

I swung the mainyard and waited helplessly. She was perhaps stopped, and her very fate hung in the balance, with the black mass of Koh-ring like the gate of the everlasting night towering over her taffrail. What would she do now? Had she way on her yet? I stepped to the side swiftly, and on the shadowy water I could see nothing except a faint phosphorescent flash revealing the glassy smoothness of the sleeping surface. It was impossible to tell – and I had not learned yet the feel of my ship. Was she moving? What I needed was something easily seen, a piece of paper, which I could throw overboard and watch. I had nothing on me. To run down for it I didn't dare. There was no time. All at once my strained, yearning stare distinguished a white object floating within a yard of the ship's side. White on the black water. A phosphorescent flash passed under it. What was that thing? . . . I recognised my own floppy hat. It must have fallen off his head . . . and he didn't bother. Now I had what I wanted – the saving mark for my eyes. But I hardly thought of my other self, now gone from the ship, to be hidden forever from all friendly faces, to be a fugitive and a vagabond on the earth, with no brand of the curse on his sane forehead to stay a slaying hand . . . too proud to explain.

And I watched the hat – the expression of my sudden pity for his mere flesh. It had been meant to save his homeless head from the dangers of the sun. And now – behold – it was saving the ship, by serving me for a mark to help out the ignorance of my strangeness. Ha! It was drifting forward, warning me just in time that the ship had gathered sternway.

'Shift the helm,' I said in a low voice to the seaman standing still like a statue.

The man's eyes glistened wildly in the binnacle light as he jumped round to the other side and spun round the wheel.

I walked to the break of the poop. On the overshadowed deck all hands stood by the forebraces waiting for my order. The stars ahead seemed to be gliding from right to left. And all was so still in the world that I heard the quiet remark 'She's round,' passed in a tone of intense relief between two seamen.

'Let go and haul.'

The foreyards ran round with a great noise, amidst cheery cries. And now the frightful whiskers made themselves heard giving various orders. Already the ship was drawing ahead. And I was alone with her. Nothing! no one in the world should stand now between us, throwing a shadow on the way of silent knowledge and mute affection, the perfect communion of a seaman with his first command.

Walking to the taffrail, I was in time to make out, on the very edge of a darkness thrown by a towering black mass like the very gateway of Erebus – yes, I was in time to catch an evanescent glimpse of my white hat left behind to mark the spot where the secret sharer of my cabin and of my thoughts, as though he were my second self, had lowered himself into the water to take his punishment: a free man, a proud swimmer striking out for a new destiny.

Prince Roman

'Events which happened seventy years ago are perhaps rather too far off to be dragged aptly into a mere conversation. Of course the year 1831 is for us an historical date, one of these fatal years when in the presence of the world's passive indignation and eloquent sympathies we had once more to murmur "*Vae Victis*" and count the cost in sorrow. Not that we were ever very good at calculating, either in prosperity or in adversity. That's a lesson we could never learn, to the great exasperation of our enemies who have bestowed upon us the epithet of Incorrigible . . . '

The speaker was of Polish nationality, that nationality not so much alive as surviving, which persists in thinking, breathing, speaking, hoping and suffering in its grave, railed in by a million of bayonets and triple-sealed with the seals of three great empires.

The conversation was about aristocracy. How did this, nowadays discredited, subject come up? It is some years ago now and the precise recollection has faded. But I remember that it was not considered practically as an ingredient in the social mixture; and I verily believe that we arrived at that subject through some exchange of ideas about patriotism – a somewhat discredited sentiment, because the delicacy of our humanitarians regards it as a relic of barbarism. Yet neither the great Florentine painter who closed his eyes in death thinking of his city, nor St Francis blessing with his last breath the town of Assisi were barbarians. It requires a certain greatness of soul to interpret patriotism worthily – or else a sincerity of feeling denied to the vulgar refinement of modern thought which cannot understand the august simplicity of a sentiment proceeding from the very nature of things and men.

The aristocracy we were talking about was the very highest, the great families of Europe, not impoverished, not converted, not liberalised, the most distinctive and specialised class of all classes, for which even ambition itself does not exist among the usual incentives to activity and regulators of conduct.

The undisputed right of leadership having passed away from them we judged that their great fortunes, their cosmopolitanism, brought about by wide alliances, their elevated station, in which there is so little to gain and so much to lose, must make their position difficult in times of political commotion or national upheaval. No longer born to command – which is the very essence of aristocracy – it becomes difficult for them to do ought else but hold aloof from the great movements of popular passion.

We had reached that conclusion when the remark about far off events was made and the date of 1831 mentioned. And the speaker continued:

'I don't mean to say that I knew Prince Roman at that remote time. I begin to feel pretty ancient, but I am not so ancient as that. In fact Prince Roman was married the very year my father was born. It was in 1828; the nineteenth century was young yet and the Prince was even younger than the century, but I don't know exactly by how much. In any case his was an early marriage. It was an ideal alliance from every point of view. The girl was young and beautiful, an orphan heiress of a great name and of a great fortune. The Prince, then an officer in the Guards and distinguished amongst his fellows by something reserved and reflective in his character, had fallen headlong in love with her beauty, her charm and the serious qualities of her mind and heart. He was a rather silent young man; but his glances, his bearing, his whole person expressed his absolute devotion to the woman of his choice, a devotion which she returned in her own frank and fascinating manner.

'The flame of this pure young passion promised to burn for ever; and for a season it lit up the dry, cynical atmosphere of the great world of St Petersburg. The Emperor Nicholas himself, the grandfather of the present man, the one who died from the Crimean war, the last perhaps of the autocrats with a mystical belief in the divine character of his mission, showed some interest in this pair of married lovers. It is true that Nicholas kept a watchful eye on all the doings of the great Polish nobles. The young people leading a life appropriate to their station were obviously wrapped up in each other; and society, fascinated by the sincerity of a feeling moving serenely among the artificialities of its anxious and fastidious agitation, watched them with benevolent indulgence and an amused tenderness.

'The marriage was the social event of 1828 in the capital. Just forty years afterwards I was staying in the country house of my mother's brother in our southern provinces.

'It was the dead of winter. The great lawn in front was as pure and smooth as an Alpine snowfield, a white and feathery level sparkling under the sun as if sprinkled with diamond-dust, declining gently to the lake – a long, sinuous piece of frozen water looking bluish and more solid than the earth. A cold brilliant sun glided low above an undulating horizon of great folds of snow in which the villages of Ukrainian peasants remained out of sight, like clusters of boats hidden in the hollows of a running sea. And everything was very still.

'I don't know now how I had managed to escape at eleven o'clock in the morning from the schoolroom. I was a boy of eight, the little girl, my cousin, a few months younger than myself, though hereditarily more quick-tempered, was less adventurous. So I had escaped alone; and presently I found myself in the great stone-paved hall, warmed by a monumental stove of white tiles, a much more pleasant locality than the schoolroom which for some reason or other, perhaps hygienic, was always kept at a low temperature.

'We children were aware that there was a guest staying in the house. He had arrived the night before just as we were being driven off to bed. We broke back through the line of beaters to rush and flatten our noses against the dark window panes; but we were too late to see him alight. We had only watched in a ruddy glare the big travelling carriage on sleigh-runners harnessed with six horses, a black mass against the snow, going off to the stables, preceded by a horseman carrying a blazing ball of tow and resin in an iron basket at the end of a long stick swung from his saddle bow. Two stable boys had been sent out early in the afternoon along the snow-tracks to meet the expected guest at dusk and light his way with these road torches. At that time, you must remember, there was not a single mile of railways in our southern provinces. My little cousin and I had no knowledge of trains and engines, except from picture-books, as of things rather vague, extremely remote, and not particularly interesting unless to grown-ups who travelled abroad.

'Our notion of princes, perhaps a little more precise, was mainly literary and had a glamour reflected from the light of fairy tales, in which princes always appear young, charming, heroic and fortunate. Yet, as well as any other children, we could draw a firm line between the real and the ideal. We knew that princes were historical person-ages. And there was some glamour in that fact too. But what had driven me to roam cautiously over the house like an escaped prisoner, was the hope of snatching an interview with a special friend of mine, the head forester, who generally came to make his report at that time of the day. I yearned for news of a certain wolf. You know, in a country where wolves are to be found, every winter almost brings forward an individual eminent by the audacity of his misdeeds, by his more perfect wolfishness, so to speak. I wanted to hear some new thrilling tale of that wolf – perhaps the dramatic story of his death . . .

'But there was no one in the hall.

'Deceived in my hopes I became suddenly very much depressed.

Unable to slip back in triumph to my studies I elected to stroll spiritlessly into the billiard-room where certainly I had no business. There was no one there either, and I felt very lost and desolate under its high ceiling, all alone with the massive English billiard-table which seemed, in heavy, rectilinear silence, to disapprove of that small boy's intrusion.

'As I began to think of retreat I heard footsteps in the adjoining drawing-room; and, before I could turn tail and flee, my uncle and his guest appeared in the doorway. To run away after having been seen would have been highly improper, so I stood my ground. My uncle looked surprised to see me; the guest by his side was a spare man, of average stature, buttoned up in a black frock coat and holding himself very erect with a stiffly soldier-like carriage. From the folds of a soft white cambric neck-cloth peeped the points of a collar close against each shaven cheek. A few wisps of thin grey hair were brushed smoothly across the top of his bald head. His face, which must have been beautiful in its day, had preserved in age the harmonious simplicity of its lines. What amazed me was its even, almost deathlike pallor. He seemed to me to be prodigiously old; a faint smile, a mere momentary alteration in the set of his thin lips acknowledged my blushing confusion; and I became greatly interested to see him reach into the inside breastpocket of his coat. He extracted therefrom a lead pencil and a block of detachable pages, which he handed to my uncle with an almost imperceptible bow.

'I was very much astonished, but my uncle received it as a matter of course. He wrote something at which the other glanced and nodded slightly. A thin wrinkled hand – the hand was older than the face – patted my cheek and then rested on my head lightly. An unringing voice, a voice as colourless as the face itself, issued from his sunken lips, while the eyes, dark and still, looked down at me kindly.

' "And how old is this shy little boy?"

'Before I could answer my uncle wrote down my age on the pad. I was deeply impressed. What was this ceremony? Was this personage too great to be spoken to? Again he glanced at the pad, and again gave a nod, and again that impersonal, mechanical voice was heard – "He resembles his grandfather."

'I remembered my paternal grandfather. He had died not long before. He, too, was prodigiously old. And to me it seemed perfectly natural that two such ancient and venerable persons should have known each other in the dim ages of creation before my birth. But my uncle obviously had not been aware of the fact. So obviously that the mechanical voice explained.

' "Yes, yes. Comrades in '31. He was one of those who knew. Old times, my dear sir, old times . . . "

'He made a gesture as if to put aside an importunate ghost. And now they were both looking down at me. I wondered whether anything was expected from me. To my round, questioning eyes my uncle remarked, "He's completely deaf." And the unrelated, inexpressive voice said – "Give me your hand."

'Acutely conscious of inky fingers I put it out timidly. I had never seen a deaf person before and was rather startled. He pressed it firmly and then gave me a final pat on the head.

'My uncle addressed me weightily.

' "You have shaken hands with Prince Roman S—. It's something for you to remember when you grow up."

'I was impressed by his tone. I had enough historical information to know vaguely that the Princes S— counted amongst the sovereign princes of Ruthenia till the union of all Ruthenian lands to the kingdom of Poland, when they became great Polish magnates, sometime at the beginning of the fifteenth century. But what concerned me most was the failure of the fairytale glamour. It was shocking to discover a prince who was deaf, bald, meagre, and so prodigiously old. It never occurred to me that this imposing and disappointing man had been young, rich, beautiful. I could not know that he had been happy in the felicity of an ideal marriage uniting two young hearts, two great names and two great fortunes; happy with a happiness which, as in fairy tales, seemed destined to last forever . . .

'But it did not last forever. It was fated not to last very long even by the measure of the days allotted to men's passage on this earth, where enduring happiness is only found in the conclusion of fairy tales. A daughter was born to them and shortly afterwards the health of the young princess began to fail. For a time she bore up with smiling intrepidity, sustained by the feeling that now her existence was necessary for the happiness of two lives. But at last the husband, thoroughly alarmed by the rapid changes in her appearance, obtained an unlimited leave and took her away from the capital, to his parents in the country.

'The old prince and princess were extremely frightened at the state of their beloved daughter-in-law. Preparations were at once made for a journey abroad. But it seemed as if it were already too late; and the invalid herself opposed the project with gentle obstinacy. Thin and pale in the great armchair, where the insidious and obscure nervous malady made her appear smaller and more frail every day without effacing the smile of her eyes or the charming grace of her wasted face, she clung to her native land and wished to breathe her native air. Nowhere else could she expect to get well so quickly, nowhere else would it be so easy for her to die.

'She died before her little girl was two years old. The grief of the husband was terrible and the more alarming to his parents because perfectly silent and dry-eyed. After the funeral, while the immense bareheaded crowd of peasants surrounding the private chapel in the grounds was dispersing, the Prince, waving away his friends and relations, remained alone to watch the masons of the estate closing the family vault. When the last stone was in position he uttered a groan, the first sound of pain which had escaped from him for days, and walking away with lowered head shut himself up again in his apartments.

'His father and mother feared for his reason. His outward tranquillity was appalling to them. They had nothing to trust to but that very youth which made his despair so self-absorbed and so intense. Old Prince John, fretful and anxious, repeated, "Poor Roman should be roused somehow. He's so young." But they could find nothing to rouse him with. And the old princess, wiping her eyes, wished in her heart he were young enough to come and cry at her knee.

'In time Prince Roman making an effort would join now and again the family circle. But it was as if his heart and his mind had been buried in the family vault with the wife he had lost. He took to wandering in the woods with a gun, watched over secretly by one of the keepers, who would report in the evening that "His Serenity has never fired a shot all day". Sometimes walking to the stables in the morning he would order in subdued tones a horse to be saddled, wait switching his boot till it was led up to him, then mount without a word and ride out of the gates at a walking pace. He would be gone all day. People saw him on the roads looking neither to the right nor to the left, white-faced, sitting rigidly in the saddle like a horseman of stone on a living mount.

'The peasants working in the fields, the great unhedged fields, looked after him from the distance; and sometimes some sympathetic old woman on the threshold of a low, thatched hut, was moved to make the sign of the cross in the air behind his back; as though he were one of themselves, a simple village soul struck by a sore affliction.

'He rode looking straight ahead, seeing no one, as if the earth were empty and all mankind buried in that grave which had opened so suddenly in his path to swallow up his happiness. What were men to him with their sorrows, joys, labours and passions, from which she who had been all the world to him had been cut off so early?

'They did not exist; and he would have felt as completely lonely and abandoned as a man in the toils of a cruel nightmare if it had not been for this countryside where he had been born and had spent his happy boyish years. He knew it well – every slight rise crowned with trees amongst the ploughed fields, every dell concealing a village. The dammed streams made a chain of lakes set in the green meadows. Far away to the north the great Lithuanian forest faced the sun, no higher than a hedge; and to the south, the way to the plains, the vast brown spaces of the earth touched the blue sky.

'And this familiar landscape associated with the days without thought and without sorrow, this land the charm of which he felt without even looking at it, soothed his pain, like the presence of an old friend who sits silent and disregarded by one in some dark hour of life.

'One afternoon, it happened that the Prince, after turning his horse's head for home, remarked a low dense cloud of dark dust cutting off slantwise a part of the view. He reined in on a knoll and peered. There were slender gleams of steel here and there in that cloud, and it contained moving forms which revealed themselves at last as a long line of peasant carts full of soldiers, moving slowly in double file under the escort of mounted Cossacks.

'It was like an immense reptile creeping over the fields; its head dipped out of sight in a slight hollow and its tail went on writhing and growing shorter as though the monster were eating its way slowly into the very heart of the land.

'The Prince directed his way through a village lying a little off the track. The roadside inn, with its stable, byre and barn under one enormous thatched roof, resembled a deformed, hunchbacked, ragged giant, sprawling amongst the small huts of the peasants. The inn-keeper, a portly, dignified Jew, clad in a black satin coat reaching down to his heels and girt with a red sash, stood at the door stroking his long silvery beard.

'He watched the Prince approach and bowed gravely from the waist, not expecting to be noticed even, since it was well known that their young lord had no eyes for anything or anybody in his grief. It was quite a shock for him when the Prince pulled up and asked: "What's all this, Yankel?"

' "That is, please your Serenity, that is a convoy of footsoldiers; they are hurrying down to the south."

'He glanced right and left cautiously, but as there was no one near but some children playing in the dust of the village street, he came up close to the stirrup.

' "Doesn't your Serenity know? It has begun already down there. All the landowners great and small are out in arms, and even the common people have risen. Only yesterday the saddler from Grodek" (it was a tiny market-town near by) "went through here with his two apprentices on his way to join. He left even his cart with me. I gave him a guide through our neighbourhood. You know, your Serenity, our people they travel a lot and they see all that's going on, and they know all the roads."

'He tried to keep down his excitement, for the Jew Yankel, innkeeper and tenant of all the mills on the estate, was a Polish patriot.

'And in a still lower voice: "I was already a married man when the French and all the other nations passed this way with Napoleon. Tse! Tse! That was a great harvest for death, Nu! Perhaps this time God will help."

'The Prince nodded. "Perhaps – " and falling into deep meditation he let his horse take him home.

'That night he wrote a letter and early in the morning sent a mounted express to the post town. During the day he came out of his taciturnity, to the great joy of the family circle, and conversed with his father of recent events – the revolt in Warsaw, the flight of the Grand Duke Constantine, the first slight successes of the Polish army (at that time there was a Polish army), the risings in the provinces. Old Prince John, moved and uneasy, speaking from a purely aristocratic point of view, mistrusted the popular origins of the movement, regretted its democratic tendencies, and did not believe in the possibility of success.

'He was sad, inwardly agitated.

' "I am judging all this calmly. There are secular principles of legitimity and order which have been violated in this reckless enterprise for the sake of most subversive illusions. Though of course the patriotic impulses of the heart . . . "

'Prince Roman had listened in a thoughtful attitude. He took advantage of the pause to tell his father quietly that he had sent that morning a letter to St Petersburg resigning his commission in the Guards.

'The old prince remained silent. He thought that he ought to have been consulted. His son was also ordnance officer to the Emperor and he knew that the Tzar would never forget this appearance of defection in a Polish noble. In a discontented tone he pointed out to his son that as it was he had an unlimited leave. The right thing would have been to keep quiet. They had too much tact at court to recall a man of his name. Or at worst some distant mission might have been asked for – to the Caucasus for instance – away from this unhappy struggle which was wrong in principle and therefore destined to fail.

' "Presently you shall find yourself without any interest in life and with no occupation. And you shall need something to occupy you, my poor boy. You have acted rashly, I fear."

'Prince Roman murmured,

' "I thought it better."

'His father faltered under his steady gaze.

' "Well, well – perhaps! But as ordnance officer to the Emperor and in favour with all the Imperial family . . . "

' "Those people had never been heard of when our house was already illustrious," the young man let fall disdainfully.

'This was the sort of remark to which the old prince was sensible. "Well – perhaps it is better," he conceded at last.

'The father and son parted affectionately for the night. The next day Prince Roman seemed to have fallen back into the depths of his indifference. He rode out as usual. He remembered that the day before he had seen a reptile-like convoy of soldiery bristling with bayonets crawling over the face of that land which was his. The woman he loved had been his too. Death had robbed him of her. Her loss had been to him a moral shock. It had opened his heart to a greater sorrow, his mind to a vaster thought, his eyes to all the past, and to the existence of another love fraught with pain but as mysteriously imperative as that lost one to which he had entrusted his happiness.

'That evening he retired earlier than usual and rang for his personal servant.

' "Go and see if there is light yet in the quarters of the Master-of-the Horse. If he is still up ask him to come and speak to me."

'While the servant was absent on this errand the Prince tore up hastily some papers, locked the drawers of his desk, and hung a medallion containing the miniature of his wife round his neck against his breast.

'The man the Prince was expecting belonged to that past which the death of his love had called to life. He was of a family of small nobles who for generations had been adherents, servants and friends of the Princes S—. He remembered the times before the last partition, and had taken part in the struggles of the last hour. He was a typical old Pole of that class, with a great capacity for emotion, for blind enthusiasm; with martial instincts and simple beliefs; and even with the old-time habit of larding his speech with Latin words. And his kindly shrewd eyes, his ruddy face, his lofty brow and his thick, grey, pendent moustache were also very typical of his kind

' "Listen, Master Francis," the Prince said familiarly and without preliminaries. "Listen, old friend. I am going to vanish from here quietly. I go where something louder than my grief and yet something with a voice very like it calls me. I confide in you alone. You will say what's necessary when the time comes."

'The old man understood. His extended hands trembled exceedingly. But as soon as he found his voice he thanked God aloud for letting him live long enough to see the descendant of the illustrious family in its youngest generation give an example, *coram gentibus*, of the love of his country and of valour in the field. He doubted not of his dear Prince attaining a place in council and in war worthy of his high birth; he saw already that *in fulgore* of family glory *affulget patride serenitas*. At the end of the speech he burst into tears and fell into the Prince's arms.

'The Prince quieted the old man, and when he had him seated in an armchair and comparatively composed he said: "Don't misunderstand me, Master Francis. You know how I loved my wife. A loss like that opens one's eyes to unsuspected truths. There is no question here of leadership and glory. I mean to go alone and to fight obscurely in the ranks. I am going to offer my country what is mine to offer, that is my life, as simply as the saddler from Grodek who went through yesterday with his apprentices . . . "

'The old man cried out at this. That could never be. He could not allow it. But he had to give way before the arguments and the express will of the Prince.

' "Ha! If you say that it is a matter of feeling and conscience – so be it. But you cannot go utterly alone. Alas! that I am too old to be of any use. *Cripit verba dolor*, my dear Prince, at the thought that I am over seventy and of no more account in the world than a cripple in the church porch. It seems that to sit at home and pray to God for the nation and for you is all I am fit for. But there is my son, my youngest boy, Peter. He will make a worthy companion for you. And as it happens he's staying with me here. There has not been for ages a Prince S— hazarding his life without a companion of our name to ride by his side. You must have by you somebody who knows who you are if only to let your parents and your old servant hear what is happening to you. And when does your Princely Mightiness mean to start?"

' "In an hour," said the Prince; and the old man hurried off to warn his son.

'Prince Roman took up a candlestick and walked quietly along a dark corridor in the silent house. The head-nurse said afterwards that waking up suddenly she saw the Prince looking at his child, one hand shading the light from its eyes. He stood and gazed at her for some time, and then putting the candlestick on the floor bent over the cot and kissed lightly the little girl, who did not wake. He went out noiselessly taking the light away with him. She saw his face perfectly well, but she could read nothing of his purpose in it. It was pale but perfectly calm, and after he turned away from the cot he never looked back at it once.

'The only other trusted person, besides the old man and his son Peter, was the Jew Yankel. When he asked the Prince where precisely he wanted to be guided the Prince answered, "To the nearest party." A grandson of the Jew, a lanky youth, conducted the two young men by little known paths, across woods and morasses, and led them in sight of the few fires of a small detachment camped in a hollow. Some invisible horses neighed, a voice in the dark cried "Who goes there?" . . . and the young Jew departed hurriedly, explaining that he must make haste home to be in time for keeping the Sabbath.

'Thus, humbly and in accord with the simplicity of the vision of duty he saw when death had removed the brilliant bandage of happiness from his eyes, did Prince Roman bring his offering to his country. His companion made himself known as the son of the Master-of-the-Horse to the Princes S— and declared him to be a relation, a distant cousin from the same parts as himself and, as people presumed, of the same name. In truth no one enquired much. Two more young men, clearly of the right sort, had joined. Nothing more natural.

'Prince Roman did not remain long in the south. One day while scouting with several others, they were ambushed near the entrance of a village by some Russian infantry. The first discharge laid low a good many and the rest scattered in all directions. The Russians, too, did not stay, being afraid of a return in force. After some time, the peasants coming to view the scene extricated Prince Roman from under his dead horse. He was unhurt but his faithful companion had been one of the first to fall. The Prince helped the peasants to bury him and the other dead.

'Then alone, not certain where to find the body of partisans which was constantly moving about in all directions, he resolved to try and join the main Polish army facing the Russians on the borders of Lithuania. Disguised in peasant clothes, in case of meeting some marauding Cossacks, he wandered a couple of weeks before he came upon a village occupied by a regiment of Polish cavalry on outpost duty.

'On a bench, before a peasant hut of a better sort, sat an elderly officer whom he took for the Colonel. The Prince approached respectfully, told his story shortly and stated his desire to enlist; and when asked his name by the officer, who had been looking him over carefully, he gave on the spur of the moment the name of his dead companion.

'The elderly officer thought to himself: Here's the son of some peasant proprietor of the liberated class. He liked his appearance. "And can you read and write, my good fellow?" he asked.

' "Yes, your honour, I can," said the Prince.

' "Good. Come along inside the hut, the regimental adjutant is there. He will enter your name and administer the oath to you."

The adjutant stared very hard at the newcomer but said nothing. When all the forms had been gone through and the recruit gone out, he turned to his superior officer.

' "Do you know who that is?"

' "Who? That Peter? A likely chap."

' "That's Prince Roman S—."

' "Nonsense."

'But the adjutant was positive. He had seen the Prince several times, about two years before, in the Castle in Warsaw. He had even spoken to him once at a reception of officers held by the Grand Duke. "He's changed. He seems much older, but I am certain of my man. I have a good memory for faces."

'The two officers looked at each other in silence. "He's sure to be recognised sooner or later," murmured the adjutant.

'The Colonel shrugged his shoulders. "It's no affair of ours – if he has a fancy to serve in the ranks. As to being recognised it's not so likely. All our officers and men come from the other end of Poland."

'He meditated gravely for a while, then smiled. "He told me he could read and write. There's nothing to prevent me making him a sergeant at the first opportunity. He's sure to shape all right."

'Prince Roman as a non-commissioned officer surpassed the Colonel's expectations. Before long Sergeant Peter became famous for his resourcefulness and courage. It was not the reckless courage of a desperate man; it was a self-possessed, as if conscientious, valour which nothing could dismay; a boundless but equable devotion, unaffected by time, by reverses, by the discouragement of endless retreats, by the bitterness of waning hopes and the horrors of pestilence added to the toils and perils of war. It was in this year that the cholera made its first appearance in Europe. It devastated the camps of both armies, affecting the firmest minds with the terror of a mysterious death stalking silently between the piled-up arms and around the bivouac fires.

'A sudden shriek would wake up the harassed soldiers and they would see in the glow of embers one of themselves writhe on the ground like a worm trodden on by an invisible foot. And before the dawn broke he would be stiff and cold. Parties so visited have been known to rise like one man, abandon the fire and run off into the night in mute panic. Or a comrade talking to you on the march would stammer suddenly in the middle of a sentence, roll affrighted eyes, and fall down with distorted face and blue lips, breaking the ranks with the convulsions of his agony. Men were struck in the saddle, on sentry duty, in the firing line, carrying orders, serving the guns. I have been told that in a battalion forming under fire with perfect steadiness for the assault of a village, three cases occurred within five minutes at the head of the column; and the attack could not be delivered because the leading companies scattered all over the fields like chaff before the wind.

'Sergeant Peter, young as he was, had a great influence over his men. It was said that the number of desertions in the squadron in which he served was less than in any other in the whole of that cavalry division. Such was supposed to be the compelling example of one man's quiet intrepidity in facing every form of danger and terror.

'However that may be, he was liked and trusted generally. When the end came and the remnants of that army corps, hard pressed on all sides, were preparing to cross the Prussian frontier, Sergeant Peter had enough influence to rally round him a score of troopers. He managed to escape with them at night from the hemmed-in army. He led this band through two hundred miles of country covered by numerous Russian detachments and ravaged by the cholera. But this was not to avoid captivity, to go into hiding and try to save themselves. No. He led them into a fortress which was still occupied by the Poles, and where the last stand of the vanquished revolution was to be made.

'This looks like mere fanaticism. But fanaticism is human. Man has adored ferocious divinities. There is ferocity in every passion, even in love itself. The religion of undying hope resembles the mad cult of despair, of death, of annihilation. The difference lies in the moral motive springing from the secret needs and the unexpressed aspiration of the believers. It is only to vain men that all is vanity; and all is deception only to those who have never been sincere with themselves.

'It was in the fortress that my grandfather found himself together with Sergeant Peter. My grandfather was a neighbour of the S— family in the country, but he did not know Prince Roman, who, however, knew his name perfectly well. The Prince introduced himself one night as they both sat on the ramparts, leaning against a gun carriage.

'The service he wished to ask for was, in case of his being killed, to have the intelligence conveyed to his parents.

'They talked in low tones, the other servants of the piece lying about near them. My grandfather gave the required promise, and then asked frankly – for he was greatly interested by the disclosure so unexpectedly made: "But tell me, Prince, why this bequest. Have you any evil forebodings as to yourself?"

' "Not in the least; I was thinking of my people. They have no idea where I am," answered Prince Roman. "I'll engage to do as much for you, if you like. It's certain that half of us at least shall be killed before the end, so there's an even chance of one of us surviving the other."

'My grandfather told him where, as he supposed, his wife and children were then. From that moment till the end of the siege the two were much together. On the day of the great assault my grandfather received a severe wound. The town was taken. Next day the citadel itself, its hospital full of dead and dying, its magazines empty, its defenders having burnt their last cartridge, opened its gates.

'During all the campaign the Prince, exposing his person conscientiously on every occasion, had not received a scratch. No one had recognised him, or at any rate had betrayed his identity. Till then, as long as he did his duty, it had mattered nothing who he was.

'Now, however, the position was changed. As ex-guardsman and as late ordnance officer to the Emperor, this rebel ran a serious risk of being given special attention in the shape of a firing squad at ten paces. For more than a month he remained lost in the miserable crowd of prisoners packed in the casemates of the citadel, with just enough food to keep body and soul together but otherwise allowed to die from wounds, privation and disease at the rate of forty or so a day.

'The position of the fortress being central, new parties, captured in the open in the course of a thorough pacification, were being sent in frequently. Amongst such newcomers there happened to be a young man, a personal friend of the Prince from his schooldays. He recognised him, and in the extremity of his dismay cried aloud, "My God! Roman, you here!"

'It is said that years of life embittered by remorse paid for this momentary lack of self-control. All this happened in the main quadrangle of the citadel. The warning gesture of the Prince came too late. An officer of the gendarmes on guard had heard the exclamation. The incident appeared to him worth inquiring into. The investigation which followed was not very arduous because the Prince, asked categorically for his real name, owned up at once.

'The intelligence of the Prince S— being found amongst the prisoners was sent to St Petersburg. His parents were already there living in sorrow, incertitude and apprehension. The capital of the Empire was the safest place to reside in for a noble whose son had disappeared so mysteriously from home in a time of rebellion. The old people had not heard from him, or of him, for months. They took care not to contradict the rumours of suicide from despair circulating in the great world, which remembered the interesting love-match, the charming and frank happiness brought to an end by death. But they hoped secretly that their son survived, and that he had been able to cross the frontier with that part of the army which had surrendered to the Prussians.

'The news of his captivity was a crushing blow. Directly, nothing could be done for him. But the greatness of their name, of their position, their relations and connections in the highest spheres, enabled his parents to act indirectly; and they moved heaven and earth, as the saying is, to save their son from the "consequences of his madness", as poor Prince John did not hesitate to express himself. Great personages were approached by society leaders, high dignitaries were interviewed, powerful officials were induced to take an interest in that affair. The help of every possible secret influence was enlisted. Some private secretaries got heavy bribes. The mistress of a certain senator obtained a large sum of money.

'But, as I have said, in such a glaring case no direct appeal could be made and no open steps taken. All that could be done was to incline by private representation the mind of the President of the Military Commission to the side of clemency. He ended by being impressed by the hints and suggestions, some of them from very high quarters, which he received from St Petersburg. And, after all, the gratitude of such great nobles as the Princes S— was something worth having from a worldly point of view. He was a good Russian, but he was also a good-natured man. Moreover, the hate of Poles was not at that time a cardinal article of patriotic creed as it became some thirty years later. He felt well disposed at first sight towards that young man, bronzed, thin-faced, worn out by months of hard campaigning, the hardships of the siege and the rigours of captivity.

'The Commission was composed of three officers. It sat in the citadel in a bare, vaulted room behind a long black table. Some clerks occupied the two ends, and, besides the gendarmes who brought in the Prince, there was no one else there.

'Within those four sinister walls shutting out from him all the sights and sounds of liberty, all hopes of the future, all consoling illusions – alone in the face of his enemies erected for judges – who can tell how much love of life there was in Prince Roman? How much remained of that sense of duty, revealed to him in sorrow? How much of his awakened love for his native country? That country which demands to be loved as no other country has ever been loved, with the mournful affection one bears to the unforgotten dead and with the unextinguishable fire of a hopeless passion which only a living, breathing, warm ideal can kindle in our breasts for our pride, for our weariness, for our exultation, for our undoing.

'There is something monstrous in the thought of such an exaction till it stands before us embodied in the shape of a fidelity without fear and without reproach. Nearing the supreme moment of his life the Prince could only have had the feeling that it was about to end. He answered the questions put to him clearly, concisely . . . with the most profound indifference. After all those tense months of action to talk was a weariness to him. But he concealed it, lest his foes should suspect in his manner the apathy of discouragement or the numbness of a crushed spirit. The details of his conduct could have no importance one way or another; with his thoughts these men had nothing to do. He preserved a scrupulously courteous tone. He had refused the permission to sit down.

'What happened at this preliminary examination is only known from the presiding officer. Pursuing the only possible course in that glaringly bad case he tried from the first to bring to the Prince's mind the line of defence he wished him to take. He absolutely framed his questions so as to put the right answers in the culprit's mouth, going so far as to suggest the very words – how, distracted by excessive grief after his young wife's death, rendered irresponsible for his conduct by his despair, in a moment of blind recklessness, without realising the highly reprehensible nature of the act, nor yet its danger and its dishonour, he went off to join the nearest rebels on a sudden impulse. And that now, penitently . . .

'But Prince Roman was silent. The military judges looked at him hopefully. In silence he reached for a pen and wrote on a sheet of paper he found under his hand: "I joined the national rising from conviction."

'He pushed the paper across the table. The president took it up, showed it in turn to his two colleagues sitting to the right and left, then looking fixedly at Prince Roman let it fall from his hand. And the silence remained unbroken till he spoke to the gendarmes ordering them to remove the prisoner.

'Such was the written testimony of Prince Roman in the supreme moment of his life. I have heard that the princes of the S— family, in all its branches, adopted the last two words, "from conviction", for the device under the armorial bearings of their house. I don't know whether the report is true. My uncle could not tell me. He remarked only that, naturally, it was not to be seen on Prince Roman's own seal.

'He was condemned for life to Siberian mines. Emperor Nicholas, who always took personal cognisance of all sentences on Polish nobility, wrote with his own hand in the margin: "The authorities are severely warned to take care that this convict walks in chains like any other criminal every step of the way."

'It was a sentence of deferred death. Very few survived entombment in these mines for more than three years. Yet as he was reported as still alive at the end of that time he was allowed, on a petition of his parents and by way of exceptional grace, to serve as common soldier in the Caucasus. All communication with him was forbidden. He had no civil rights. For all practical purposes except that of suffering he was a dead man. The little child he had been so careful not to wake up when he kissed her in her cot, inherited all the fortune after Prince John's death. Her existence saved those immense estates from confiscation.

'It was twenty-five years before Prince Roman, stone deaf, his health broken, was permitted to return to Poland. His daughter, married splendidly to a Polish-Austrian *grand seigneur* and moving in the cosmopolitan sphere of the highest European aristocracy, lived mostly abroad in Nice and Vienna. He, settling down on one of her estates, not the one with the palatial residence but another where there was a modest little house, saw very little of her.

'But Prince Roman did not shut himself up as if his work were done. There was hardly anything done in the private and public life of the neighbourhood in which Prince Roman's advice and assistance were not called upon, and never in vain. It was well said that his days did not belong to himself but to his fellow citizens. And especially he was the particular friend of all returned exiles, helping them with purse and advice, arranging their affairs and finding them means of livelihood.

'I heard from my uncle many tales of his devoted activity, in which he was always guided by a simple wisdom, a high sense of honour and the most scrupulous conception of private and public probity. He remains a living figure for me because of that meeting in a billiard-room, when, in my anxiety to hear about a particularly wolfish wolf, I came in momentary contact with a man who was pre-eminently a man amongst all men capable of feeling deeply, of believing steadily, of loving ardently.

'I remember to this day the grasp of Prince Roman's bony, wrinkled hand closing on my small inky paw, and my uncle's half-serious, half-amused way of looking down at his trespassing nephew.

'They moved on and forgot that little boy. But I did not move; I gazed after them, not so much disappointed as disconcerted by this Prince so utterly unlike a prince in a fairy tale. They moved very slowly across the room. Before reaching the other door the Prince stopped; and I heard him – I seem to hear him now – saying: "I wish you would write to Vienna about filling up that post. He's a most deserving fellow – and your recommendation would be decisive."

'My uncle's face turned to him expressed genuine wonder. It said as plainly as any speech could say: what better recommendation than a father's can be needed? The Prince was quick at reading expressions. Again he spoke with the toneless accent of a man who has not heard his own voice for years, for whom the soundless world is like an abode of silent shades.

'And to this day I remember the very words.

' "I ask you because, you see, my daughter and my son-in-law don't believe me to be a good judge of men. They think that I let myself be guided too much by mere sentiment."

The Tale

Outside the large single window the crepuscular light was dying out slowly in a great square gleam without colour, framed rigidly in the gathering shades of the room.

It was a long room. The irresistible tide of the night ran into the most distant part of it, where the whispering of a man's voice, passionately interrupted and passionately renewed, seemed to plead against the answering murmurs of infinite sadness.

At last no answering murmur came. His movement when he rose slowly from his knees by the side of the deep, shadowy couch holding the shadowy suggestion of a reclining woman revealed him tall under the low ceiling, and sombre all over except for the crude discord of the white collar under the shape of his head and the faint, minute spark of a brass button here and there on his uniform.

He stood over her a moment masculine and mysterious in his immobility before he sat down on a chair near by. He could see only the faint oval of her upturned face and, extended on her black dress, her pale hands, a moment before abandoned to his kisses and now as if too weary to move.

He dared not make a sound, shrinking as a man would do from the prosaic necessities of existence. As usual, it was the woman who had the courage. Her voice was heard first – almost conventional – while her being vibrated yet with conflicting emotions.

'Tell me something,' she said.

The darkness hid his surprise and then his smile. Had he not just said to her everything worth saying in the world – and that not for the first time!

'What am I to tell you?' he asked, in a voice creditably steady. He was beginning to feel grateful to her for that something final in her tone which had eased the strain.

'Why not tell me a tale?'

'A tale!' He was really amazed.

'Yes. Why not?'

These words came with a slight petulance, the hint of a loved woman's capricious will, which is capricious only because it feels itself to be a law, embarrassing sometimes and always difficult to elude.

'Why not?' he repeated, with a slightly mocking accent, as though he had been asked to give her the moon. But now he was feeling a little angry with her for that feminine mobility that slips out of an emotion as easily as out of a splendid gown.

He heard her say a little unsteadily, with a sort of fluttering intonation which made him think suddenly of a butterfly's flight: 'You used to tell – your – your simple and – and professional – tales very well at one time. Or well enough to interest me. You had a – a sort of art – in the days – the days before the war.'

'Really?' he said, with involuntary gloom. 'But now, you see, the war is going on,' he continued in such a dead, equable tone that she felt a slight chill fall over her shoulders. And yet she persisted. For there's nothing more unswerving in the world than a woman's caprice.

'It could be a tale not of this world,' she explained.

'You want a tale of the other, the better world?' he asked, with matter-of-fact surprise. 'You must evoke for that task those who have already gone there.'

'No. I don't mean that. I mean another – some other – world. In the universe – not in heaven.'

'I am relieved. But you forget that I have only a five days' leave.'

'Yes. And I've also taken a five days' leave from – from my duties.'

'I like that word.'

'What word?'

'Duty.'

'It is horrible sometimes.'

'Oh, that's because you think it's narrow. But it isn't. It contains infinities, and – and so - '

'What is this jargon?'

He disregarded the interjected scorn. 'An infinity of absolution, for instance,' he continued. 'But as to this "another world" – who's going to look for it and for the tale that is in it?'

'You,' she said, with a strange, almost rough, sweetness of assertion.

He made a shadowy movement of assent in his chair, the irony of which not even the gathered darkness could render mysterious.

'As you will. In that world, then, there was once upon a time a Commanding Officer and a Northman. Put in the capitals, please, because they had no other names. It was a world of seas and continents and islands – '

'Like the earth,' she murmured, bitterly.

'Yes. What else could you expect from sending a man made of our common, tormented clay on a voyage of discovery? What else could he find? What else could you understand or care for, or feel the existence of even? There was comedy in it and slaughter.'

'Always like the earth,' she murmured.

'Always. And since I could find in the universe only what was deeply rooted in the fibres of my being there was love in it too. But we won't talk of that.'

'No. We won't,' she said, in a neutral tone which concealed perfectly her relief – or her disappointment. Then after a pause she added: 'It's going to be a comic story.'

'Well – ' he paused too. 'Yes. In a way. In a very grim way. It will be human, and, as you know, comedy is but a matter of the visual angle. And it won't be a noisy story. All the long guns in it will be dumb – as dumb as so many telescopes.'

'Ah, there are guns in it, then! And may I ask – where?'

'Afloat. You remember that the world of which we speak had its seas. A war was going on in it. It was a funny world and terribly in earnest. Its war was being carried on over the land, over the water, under the water, up in the air, and even under the ground. And many young men in it, mostly in wardrooms and messrooms, used to say to each other – pardon the unparliamentary word – they used to say, "It's a damned bad war, but it's better than no war at all." Sounds flippant, doesn't it?'

He heard a nervous, impatient sigh in the depths of the couch while he went on without a pause: 'And yet there is more in it than meets the eye. I mean more wisdom. Flippancy, like comedy, is but a matter of visual first-impression. That world was not very wise. But there was in it a certain amount of common working sagacity. That, however, was mostly worked by the neutrals in diverse ways, public and private, which had to be watched; watched by acute minds and also by actual sharp eyes. They had to be very sharp indeed, too, I assure you.'

'I can imagine,' she murmured, appreciatively.

'What is there that you can't imagine?' he pronounced, soberly. 'You have the world in you. But let us go back to our Commanding Officer, who, of course, commanded a ship of a sort. My tales if often professional (as you remarked just now) have never been technical. So I'll just tell you that the ship was of a very ornamental sort once, with lots of grace and elegance and luxury about her. Yes, once! She was like a pretty woman who had suddenly put on a suit of sackcloth and stuck revolvers in her belt. But she floated lightly, she moved nimbly, she was quite good enough.'

'That was the opinion of the Commanding Officer?' said the voice from the couch.

'It was. He used to be sent out with her along certain coasts to see – what he could see. Just that. And sometimes he had some preliminary information to help him, and sometimes he had not. And it was all one, really. It was about as useful as information trying to convey the locality and intentions of a cloud, of a phantom taking shape here and there and impossible to seize, would have been.

'It was in the early days of the war. What at first used to amaze the Commanding Officer was the unchanged face of the waters, with its familiar expression, neither more friendly nor more hostile. On fine days the sun strikes sparks upon the blue; here and there a peaceful smudge of smoke hangs in the distance, and it is impossible to believe that the familiar clear horizon traces the limit of one great circular ambush.

'Yes, it is impossible to believe, till someday you see a ship, not your own ship (that isn't so impressive), but some ship in company, blow up all of a sudden and plop under almost before you know what has happened to her. Then you begin to believe. Henceforth you go out for the work to see – what you can see, and you keep on at it with the conviction that some day you will die from something you have not seen. One envies the soldiers at the end of the day, wiping the sweat and blood from their faces, counting the dead fallen to their hands, looking at the devastated fields, the torn earth that seems to suffer and bleed with them. One does, really. The final brutality of it – the taste of primitive passion – the ferocious frankness of the blow struck with one's hand – the direct call and the straight response. Well, the sea gave you nothing of that, and seemed to pretend that there was nothing the matter with the world.'

She interrupted, stirring a little.

'Oh, yes. Sincerity – frankness – passion – three words of your gospel. Don't I know them!'

'Think! Isn't it ours – believed in common?' he asked, anxiously, yet without expecting an answer, and went on at once. 'Such were the feelings of the Commanding Officer. When the night came trailing over the sea, hiding what looked like the hypocrisy of an old friend, it was a relief. The night blinds you frankly – and there are circumstances when the sunlight may grow as odious to one as falsehood itself. Night is all right.

'At night the Commanding Officer could let his thoughts get away – I won't tell you where. Somewhere where there was no choice but between truth and death. But thick weather, though it blinded one, brought no such relief. Mist is deceitful, the dead luminosity of the fog is irritating. It seems that you *ought* to see.

'One gloomy, nasty day the ship was steaming along her beat in sight of a rocky, dangerous coast that stood out intensely black like an Indian-ink drawing on grey paper. Presently the Second in Command spoke to his chief. He thought he saw something on the water, to seaward. Small wreckage, perhaps.

' "But there shouldn't be any wreckage here, sir," he remarked.

' "No," said the Commanding Officer. "The last reported submarined ships were sunk a long way to the westward. But one never knows. There may have been others since then not reported nor seen. Gone with all hands."

'That was how it began. The ship's course was altered to pass the object close; for it was necessary to have a good look at what one could see. Close, but without touching; for it was not advisable to come in contact with objects of any form whatever floating casually about. Close, but without stopping or even diminishing speed; for in those times it was not prudent to linger on any particular spot, even for a moment. I may tell you at once that the object was not dangerous in itself. No use in describing it. It may have been nothing more remarkable than, say, a barrel of a certain shape and colour. But it was significant.

'The smooth bow-wave hove it up as if for a closer inspection, and then the ship, brought again to her course, turned her back on it with indifference, while twenty pairs of eyes on her deck stared in all directions trying to see – what they could see.

'The Commanding Officer and his Second in Command discussed the object with understanding. It appeared to them to be not so much a proof of the sagacity as of the activity of certain neutrals. This activity had in many cases taken the form of replenishing the stores of certain submarines at sea. This was generally believed, if not absolutely known. But the very nature of things in those early days pointed that way. The object, looked at closely and turned away from with apparent indifference, put it beyond doubt that something of the sort had been done somewhere in the neighbourhood.

'The object in itself was more than suspect. But the fact of its being left in evidence roused other suspicions. Was it the result of some deep and devilish purpose? As to that all speculation soon appeared to be a vain thing. Finally the two officers came to the conclusion that it was left there most likely by accident, complicated possibly by some unforeseen necessity; such, perhaps, as the sudden need to get away quickly from the spot, or something of that kind.

'Their discussion had been carried on in curt, weighty phrases, separated by long, thoughtful silences. And all the time their eyes roamed about the horizon in an everlasting, almost mechanical effort of vigilance. The younger man summed up grimly: "Well, it's evidence. That's what this is. Evidence of what we were pretty certain of before. And plain, too."

' "And much good it will do to us," retorted the Commanding Officer. "The parties are miles away; the submarine, devil only knows where, ready to kill; and the noble neutral slipping away to the eastward, ready to lie!"

'The Second in Command laughed a little at the tone. But he guessed that the neutral wouldn't even have to lie very much. Fellows like that, unless caught in the very act, felt themselves pretty safe. They could afford to chuckle. That fellow was probably chuckling to himself. It's very possible he had been before at the game and didn't care a rap for the bit of evidence left behind. It was a game in which practice made one bold and successful too.

'And again he laughed faintly. But his Commanding Officer was in revolt against the murderous stealthiness of methods and the atrocious callousness of complicities that seemed to taint the very source of men's deep emotions and noblest activities; to corrupt their imagination which builds up the final conceptions of life and death. He suffered – '

The voice from the sofa interrupted the narrator.

'How well I can understand that in him!'

He bent forward slightly.

'Yes. I too. Everything should be open in love and war. Open as the day, since both are the call of an ideal which it is so easy, so terribly easy, to degrade in the name of Victory.'

He paused: then went on: 'I don't know that the Commanding Officer delved so deep as that into his feelings. But he did suffer from them – a sort of disenchanted sadness. It is possible, even, that he suspected himself of folly. Man is various. But he had no time for much introspection, because from the south-west a wall of fog had advanced upon his ship. Great convolutions of vapours flew over, swirling about masts and funnel, which looked as if they were beginning to melt. Then they vanished.

'The ship was stopped, all sounds ceased, and the very fog became motionless, growing denser and as if solid in its amazing dumb immobility. The men at their stations lost sight of each other. Footsteps sounded stealthy; rare voices, impersonal and remote, died out without resonance. A blind white stillness took possession of the world.

'It looked, too, as if it would last for days. I don't mean to say that the fog did not vary a little in its density. Now and then it would thin out mysteriously, revealing to the men a more or less ghostly presentment of their ship. Several times the shadow of the coast itself swam darkly before their eyes through the fluctuating opaque brightness of the great white cloud clinging to the water.

'Taking advantage of these moments, the ship had been moved cautiously nearer the shore. It was useless to remain out in such thick weather. Her officers knew every nook and cranny of the coast along their beat. They thought that she would be much better in a certain cove. It wasn't a large place, just ample room for a ship to swing at her anchor. She would have an easier time of it till the fog lifted up.

'Slowly, with infinite caution and patience, they crept closer and closer, seeing no more of the cliffs than an evanescent dark loom with a narrow border of angry foam at its foot. At the moment of anchoring the fog was so thick that for all they could see they might have been a thousand miles out in the open sea. Yet the shelter of the land could be felt. There was a peculiar quality in the stillness of the air. Very faint, very elusive, the wash of the ripple against the encircling land reached their ears, with mysterious sudden pauses.

'The anchor dropped, the leads were laid in. The Commanding Officer went below into his cabin. But he had not been there very long when a voice outside his door requested his presence on deck. He thought to himself: "What is it now?" He felt some impatience at being called out again to face the wearisome fog.

'He found that it had thinned again a little and had taken on a gloomy hue from the dark cliffs which had no form, no outline, but asserted themselves as a curtain of shadows all round the ship, except in one bright spot, which was the entrance from the open sea. Several officers were looking that way from the bridge. The Second in Command met him with the breathlessly whispered information that there was another ship in the cove.

'She had been made out by several pairs of eyes only a couple of minutes before. She was lying at anchor very near the entrance – a mere vague blot on the fog's brightness. And the Commanding Officer by staring in the direction pointed out to him by eager hands ended by distinguishing it at last himself. Indubitably a vessel of some sort.

' "It's a wonder we didn't run slap into her when coming in," observed the Second in Command.

' "Send a boat on board before she vanishes," said the Commanding Officer. He surmised that this was a coaster. It could hardly be anything else. But another thought came into his head suddenly. "It is a wonder," he said to his Second in Command, who had rejoined him after sending the boat away.

'By that time both of them had been struck by the fact that the ship so suddenly discovered had not manifested her presence by ringing her bell.

' "We came in very quietly, that's true," concluded the younger officer. "But they must have heard our leadsmen at least. We couldn't have passed her more than fifty yards off. The closest shave! They may even have made us out, since they were aware of something coming in. And the strange thing is that we never heard a sound from her. The fellows on board must have been holding their breath."

' "Aye," said the Commanding Officer, thoughtfully.

'In due course the boarding-boat returned, appearing suddenly alongside, as though she had burrowed her way under the fog. The officer in charge came up to make his report, but the Commanding Officer didn't give him time to begin.

'He cried from a distance: "Coaster, isn't she?"

' "No, sir. A stranger – a neutral," was the answer.

' "No. Really! Well, tell us all about it. What is she doing here?"

'The young man stated then that he had been told a long and complicated story of engine troubles. But it was plausible enough from a strictly professional point of view and it had the usual features: disablement, dangerous drifting along the shore, weather more or less thick for days, fear of a gale, ultimately a resolve to go in and anchor anywhere on the coast, and so on. Fairly plausible.

' "Engines still disabled?" enquired the Commanding Officer.

' "No, sir. She has steam on them."

'The Commanding Officer took his Second aside. "By Jove!" he said, "you were right! They were holding their breaths as we passed them. They were."

'But the Second in Command had his doubts now.

' "A fog like this does muffle small sounds, sir," he remarked. "And what could his object be, after all?"

' "To sneak out unnoticed," answered the Commanding Officer.

' "Then why didn't he? He might have done it, you know. Not exactly unnoticed, perhaps. I don't suppose he could have slipped his cable without making some noise. Still, in a minute or so he would have been lost to view – clean gone before we had made him out fairly. Yet he didn't."

'They looked at each other. The Commanding Officer shook his head. Such suspicions as the one which had entered his head are not defended easily. He did not even state it openly. The boarding officer finished his report. The cargo of the ship was of a harmless and useful character. She was bound to an English port. Papers and everything in perfect order. Nothing suspicious to be detected anywhere.

'Then passing to the men, he reported the crew on deck as the usual lot. Engineers of the well-known type, and very full of their achievement in repairing the engines. The mate surly. The master rather a fine specimen of a Northman, civil enough, but appeared to have been drinking. Seemed to be recovering from a regular bout of it.

' "I told him I couldn't give him permission to proceed. He said he wouldn't dare to move his ship her own length out in such weather as this, permission or no permission. I left a man on board though."

' "Quite right."

'The Commanding Officer, after communing with his suspicions for a time, called his Second aside.

' "What if she were the very ship which had been feeding some infernal submarine or other?" he said in an undertone.

'The other started. Then, with conviction: "She would get off scot-free. You couldn't prove it, sir."

' "I want to look into it myself."

' "From the report we've heard I am afraid you couldn't even make a case for reasonable suspicion, sir."

' "I'll go on board all the same."

'He had made up his mind. Curiosity is the great motive power of hatred and love. What did he expect to find? He could not have told anybody – not even himself.

'What he really expected to find there was the atmosphere, the atmosphere of gratuitous treachery, which in his view nothing could excuse; for he thought that even a passion of unrighteousness for its own sake could not excuse that. But could he detect it? Sniff it? Taste it? Receive some mysterious communication which would turn his invincible suspicions into a certitude strong enough to provoke action with all its risks?

'The master met him on the after-deck, loomed up in the fog amongst the blurred shapes of the usual ships' fittings. He was a robust Northman, bearded, and in the force of his age. A round leather cap fitted his head closely. His hands were rammed deep into the pockets of his short leather jacket. He kept them there while he explained that at sea he lived in the chart-room, and led the way there, striding carelessly. Just before reaching the door under the bridge he staggered a little, recovered himself, flung it open, and stood aside, leaning his shoulder as if involuntarily against the side of the house, and staring vaguely into the fog-filled space. But he followed the Commanding Officer at once, flung the door to, snapped on the electric light, and hastened to thrust his hands back into his pockets, as though afraid of being seized by them either in friendship or in hostility.

'The place was stuffy and hot. The usual chart-rack overhead was full, and the chart on the table was kept unrolled by an empty cup standing on a saucer half-full of some spilt dark liquid. A slightly nibbled biscuit reposed on the chronometer-case. There were two settees, and one of them had been made up into a bed with a pillow and some blankets, which were now very much tumbled. The Northman let himself fall on it, his hands still in his pockets.

' "Well, here I am," he said, with a curious air of being surprised at the sound of his own voice.

'The Commanding Officer from the other settee observed the handsome flushed face. Drops of fog hung on the yellow beard and moustaches of the Northman. The much darker eyebrows ran together in a puzzled frown, and suddenly he jumped up.

' "What I mean is that I don't know where I am. I really don't," he burst out, with extreme earnestness. "Hang it all! I got turned around somehow. The fog has been after me for a week. More than a week. And then my engines broke down. I will tell you how it was."

'He burst out into loquacity. It was not hurried, but it was insistent. It was not continuous for all that. It was broken by the most queer, thoughtful pauses. Each of these pauses lasted no more than a couple of seconds, and each had the profundity of an endless meditation. When he began again nothing betrayed in him the slightest consciousness of these intervals. There was the same fixed glance, the same unchanged earnestness of tone. He didn't know. Indeed, more than one of these pauses occurred in the middle of a sentence.

'The Commanding Officer listened to the tale. It struck him as more plausible than simple truth is in the habit of being. But that, perhaps, was prejudice. All the time the Northman was speaking the Commanding Officer had been aware of an inward voice, a grave murmur in the depth of his very own self, telling another tale, as if on purpose to keep alive in him his indignation and his anger with that baseness of greed or of mere outlook which lies often at the root of simple ideas.

'It was the story that had been already told to the boarding officer an hour or so before. The Commanding Officer nodded slightly at the Northman from time to time. The latter came to an end and turned his eyes away. He added, as an afterthought: "Wasn't it enough to drive a man out of his mind with worry? And it's my first voyage to this part, too. And the ship's my own. Your officer has seen the papers. She isn't much, as you can see for yourself. Just an old cargo-boat. Bare living for my family."

'He raised a big arm to point at a row of photographs plastering the bulkhead. The movement was ponderous, as if the arm had been made of lead.

'The Commanding Officer said, carelessly: "You will be making a fortune yet for your family with this old ship."

' "Yes, if I don't lose her," said the Northman, gloomily.

' "I mean – out of this war," added the Commanding Officer.

'The Northman stared at him in a curiously unseeing and at the same time interested manner, as only eyes of a particular blue shade can stare.

' "And you wouldn't be angry at it," he said, "would you? You are too much of a gentleman. We didn't bring this on you. And suppose we sat down and cried. What good would that be? Let those cry who made the trouble," he concluded, with energy. "Time's money, you say. Well – *this* time *is* money. Oh! isn't it!"

'The Commanding Officer tried to keep under the feeling of immense disgust. He said to himself that it was unreasonable. Men were like that – moral cannibals feeding on each other's misfortunes. He said aloud: "You have made it perfectly plain how it is that you are here. Your log-book confirms you very minutely. Of course, a log-book may be cooked. Nothing easier."

'The Northman never moved a muscle. He was gazing at the floor; he seemed not to have heard. He raised his head after a while.

' "But you can't suspect me of anything," he muttered, negligently.

'The Commanding Officer thought: "Why should he say this?"

'Immediately afterwards the man before him added: "My cargo is for an English port."

'His voice had turned husky for the moment. The Commanding Officer reflected: "That's true. There can be nothing. I can't suspect him. Yet why was he lying with steam up in this fog – and then, hearing us come in, why didn't he give some sign of life? Why? Could it be anything else but a guilty conscience? He could tell by the leadsmen that this was a man-of-war."

'Yes – why? The Commanding Officer went on thinking: "Suppose I ask him and then watch his face. He will betray himself in some way. It's perfectly plain that the fellow *has* been drinking. Yes, he has been drinking; but he will have a lie ready all the same." The Commanding Officer was one of those men who are made morally and almost physically uncomfortable by the mere thought of having to beat down a lie. He shrank from the act in scorn and disgust, which was invincible because more temperamental than moral.

'So he went out on deck instead and had the crew mustered formally for his inspection. He found them very much what the report of the boarding officer had led him to expect. And from their answers to his questions he could discover no flaw in the log-book story.

'He dismissed them. His impression of them was – a picked lot; have been promised a fistful of money each if this came off; all slightly anxious, but not frightened. Not a single one of them likely to give the show away. They don't feel in danger of their life. They know England and English ways too well!

'He felt alarmed at catching himself thinking as if his vaguest suspicions were turning into a certitude. For, indeed, there was no shadow of reason for his interference. There was nothing to give away.

'He returned to the chart-room. The Northman had lingered behind there; and something subtly different in his bearing, more bold in his blue, glassy stare, induced the Commanding Officer to conclude that the fellow had snatched at the opportunity to take another swig at the bottle he must have had concealed somewhere.

'He noticed, too, that the Northman on meeting his eyes put on an elaborately surprised expression. At least, it seemed elaborated. Nothing could be trusted. And the Englishman felt himself with astonishing conviction faced by an enormous lie, solid like a wall, with no way round to get at the truth, whose ugly murderous face he seemed to see peeping over at him with a cynical grin.

' "I dare say," he began, suddenly, "you are wondering at my proceedings, though I am not detaining you, am I? You wouldn't dare to move in thick fog?"

' "I don't know where I am," the Northman ejaculated, earnestly. "I really don't."

'He looked around as if the very chart-room fittings were strange to him. The Commanding Officer asked him whether he had not seen any unusual objects floating about while he was at sea.

' "Objects! What objects? We were groping blind in the fog for days."

' "We had a few clear intervals," said the Commanding Officer. "And I'll tell you what we have seen and the conclusion I've come to about it."

'He told him in a few words. He heard the sound of a sharp breath indrawn through closed teeth. The Northman with his hand on the table stood absolutely motionless and dumb. He stood as if thunderstruck. Then he produced a fatuous smile.

'Or at least so it appeared to the Commanding Officer. Was this significant, or of no meaning whatever? He didn't know, he couldn't tell. All the truth had departed out of the world as if drawn in, absorbed in this monstrous villainy this man was – or was not – guilty of.

' "Shooting's too good for people that conceive neutrality in this pretty way," remarked the Commanding Officer, after a silence.

' "Yes, yes, yes," the Northman assented, hurriedly – then added an unexpected and dreamy-voiced, "Perhaps."

'Was he pretending to be drunk, or only trying to appear sober? His glance was straight, but it was somewhat glazed. His lips outlined themselves firmly under his yellow moustache. But they twitched. Did they twitch? And why was he drooping like this in his attitude?

' "There's no perhaps about it," pronounced the Commanding Officer sternly.

'The Northman had straightened himself. And unexpectedly he looked stern too.

' "No. But what about the tempters? Better kill that lot off. There's about four, five, six million of them," he said, grimly; but in a moment changed into a whining key. "But I had better hold my tongue. You have some suspicions."

' "No, I've no suspicions," declared the Commanding Officer.

'He never faltered. At that moment he had the certitude. The air of the chart-room was thick with guilt and falsehood braving the discovery, defying simple right, common decency, all humanity of feeling, every scruple of conduct.

'The Northman drew a long breath. "Well, we know that you English are gentlemen. But let us speak the truth. Why should we love you so very much? You haven't done anything to be loved. We don't love the other people, of course. They haven't done anything for that either. A fellow comes along with a bag of gold . . . I haven't been in Rotterdam my last voyage for nothing."

' "You may be able to tell something interesting, then, to our people when you come into port," interjected the Officer.

' "I might. But you keep some people in your pay at Rotterdam. Let them report. I am a neutral – am I not? . . . Have you ever seen a poor man on one side and a bag of gold on the other? Of course, I couldn't be tempted. I haven't the nerve for it. Really I haven't. It's nothing to me. I am just talking openly for once."

' "Yes. And I am listening to you," said the Commanding Officer quietly.

'The Northman leaned forward over the table. "Now that I know you have no suspicions, I talk. You don't know what a poor man is. I do. I am poor myself. This old ship, she isn't much, and she is mortgaged, too. Bare living, no more. Of course, I wouldn't have the nerve. But a man who has nerve! See. The stuff he takes aboard looks like any other cargo – packages, barrels, tins, copper tubes – what not. He doesn't see it work. It isn't real to him. But he sees the gold. That's real. Of course, nothing could induce me. I suffer from an internal disease. I would either go crazy from anxiety – or – or – take to drink or something. The risk is too great. Why – ruin!"

' "It should be death." The Commanding Officer got up, after this curt declaration, which the other received with a hard stare oddly combined with an uncertain smile. The Officer's gorge rose at the atmosphere of murderous complicity which surrounded him, denser, more impenetrable, more acrid than the fog outside.

' "It's nothing to me," murmured the Northman, swaying visibly.

' "Of course not," assented the Commanding Officer, with a great effort to keep his voice calm and low. The certitude was strong within him. "But I am going to clear all you fellows off this coast at once. And I will begin with you. You must leave in half an hour."

'By that time the Officer was walking along the deck with the Northman at his elbow.

' "What! In this fog?" the latter cried out, huskily.

' "Yes, you will have to go in this fog."

' "But I don't know where I am. I really don't."

'The Commanding Officer turned round. A sort of fury possessed him. The eyes of the two men met. Those of the Northman expressed a profound amazement.

' "Oh, you don't know how to get out." The Commanding Officer spoke with composure, but his heart was beating with anger and dread. "I will give you your course. Steer south-by-east-half-east for about four miles and then you will be clear to haul to the eastward for your port. The weather will clear up before very long."

' "Must I? What could induce me? I haven't the nerve."

' "And yet you must go. Unless you want to – "

' "I don't want to," panted the Northman. "I've enough of it."

'The Commanding Officer got over the side. The Northman remained still as if rooted to the deck. Before his boat reached his ship the Commanding Officer heard the steamer beginning to pick up her anchor. Then, shadowy in the fog, she steamed out on the given course.

' "Yes," he said to his officers, "I let him go." '

The narrator bent forward towards the couch, where no movement betrayed the presence of a living person.

'Listen,' he said, forcibly. 'That course would lead the Northman straight on a deadly ledge of rock. And the Commanding Officer gave it to him. He steamed out – ran on it – and went down. So he had spoken the truth. He did not know where he was. But it proves nothing. Nothing either way. It may have been the only truth in all his story. And yet . . . He seems to have been driven out by a menacing stare – nothing more.'

He abandoned all pretence.

'Yes, I gave that course to him. It seemed to me a supreme test. I believe – no, I don't believe. I don't know. At the time I was certain. They all went down; and I don't know whether I have done stern retribution – or murder; whether I have added to the corpses that litter the bed of the unreadable sea the bodies of men completely innocent or basely guilty. I don't know. I shall never know.'

He rose. The woman on the couch got up and threw her arms round his neck. Her eyes put two gleams in the deep shadow of the room. She knew his passion for truth, his horror of deceit, his humanity.

'Oh, my poor, poor – '

'I shall never know,' he repeated, sternly, disengaged himself, pressed her hands to his lips, and went out.

WORDSWORTH CLASSICS

GENERAL EDITORS *Marcus Clapham & Clive Reynard*

JANE AUSTEN
Emma
Mansfield Park
Northanger Abbey
Persuasion
Pride and Prejudice
Sense and Sensibility

ARNOLD BENNETT
Anna of the Five Towns
The Old Wives' Tale

R. D. BLACKMORE
Lorna Doone

M. E. BRADDON
Lady Audley's Secret

ANNE BRONTË
Agnes Grey
The Tenant of
Wildfell Hall

CHARLOTTE BRONTË
Jane Eyre
The Professor
Shirley
Villette

EMILY BRONTË
Wuthering Heights

JOHN BUCHAN
Greenmantle
The Island of Sheep
John Macnab
Mr Standfast
The Thirty-Nine Steps
The Three Hostages

SAMUEL BUTLER
Erewhon
The Way of All Flesh

LEWIS CARROLL
Alice in Wonderland

M. CERVANTES
Don Quixote

ANTON CHEKHOV
Selected Stories

G. K. CHESTERTON
The Club of Queer
Trades

Father Brown:
Selected Stories
The Man Who Was
Thursday
The Napoleon of
Notting Hill

ERSKINE CHILDERS
The Riddle of the Sands

SELECTED BY
REX COLLINGS
Classic Victorian and
Edwardian Ghost Stories

WILKIE COLLINS
The Moonstone
The Woman in White

JOSEPH CONRAD
Almayer's Folly
Heart of Darkness
Lord Jim
Nostromo
Sea Stories
The Secret Agent
Selected Short Stories
Victory

J. FENIMORE COOPER
The Last of the Mohicans

STEPHEN CRANE
The Red Badge of
Courage

EDITED BY
DAVID STUART DAVIES
Shadows of
Sherlock Holmes

THOMAS DE QUINCEY
Confessions of an English
Opium Eater

DANIEL DEFOE
Moll Flanders
Robinson Crusoe

CHARLES DICKENS
Barnaby Rudge
Bleak House
Christmas Books
David Copperfield
Dombey and Son

Ghost Stories
Great Expectations
Hard Times
Little Dorrit
Martin Chuzzlewit
The Mystery of
Edwin Drood
Nicholas Nickleby
Old Curiosity Shop
Oliver Twist
Our Mutual Friend
Pickwick Papers
A Tale of Two Cities

BENJAMIN DISRAELI
Sybil

FYODOR DOSTOEVSKY
Crime and Punishment
The Idiot

SIR ARTHUR CONAN
DOYLE
The Adventures of
Sherlock Holmes
The Case-Book of
Sherlock Holmes
The Return of
Sherlock Holmes
The Lost World &
Other Stories
Sir Nigel
The White Company

EDITED BY
DAVID STUART DAVIES
The Best of
Sherlock Holmes

GEORGE DU MAURIER
Trilby

ALEXANDRE DUMAS
The Count of
Monte Cristo
The Three Musketeers

MARIA EDGEWORTH
Castle Rackrent

GEORGE ELIOT
Adam Bede
Daniel Deronda

WORDSWORTH CLASSICS

WORDSWORTH CLASSICS

DISTRIBUTION

AUSTRALIA & PAPUA NEW GUINEA
Peribo Pty Ltd
58 Beaumont Road, Mount Kuring-Gai
NSW 2080, Australia
Tel: (02) 457 0011 Fax: (02) 457 0022

CZECH REPUBLIC
Bohemian Ventures s r. o.,
Delnicka 13, 170 00 Prague 7
Tel: 042 2 877837 Fax: 042 2 801498

FRANCE
Copernicus Diffusion
81 Rue des Entrepreneurs, Paris 75015
Tel: 01 53 95 38 00 Fax: 01 53 95 38 01

GERMANY & AUSTRIA
Taschenbuch-Vertrieb
Ingeborg Blank GmbH
Lager und Buro Rohrmooser Str 1
85256 Vierkirchen/Pasenbach
Tel: 08139-8130/8184 Fax: 08139-8140

Tradis Verlag und Vertrieb GmbH (Bookshops)
Postfach 90 03 69, D-51113 Köln
Tel: 022 03 31059 Fax: 022 03 39340

GREAT BRITAIN
Wordsworth Editions Ltd
Cumberland House, Crib Street
Ware, Hertfordshire SG12 9ET
Tel: 01920 465167 Fax: 01920 462267

INDIA
Rupa & Co
Post Box No 7071,
7/16 Makhanlal Street, Ansari Road,
Daryaganj, New Delhi – 110 002
Tel: 3278586 Fax: (011) 3277294

IRELAND
Easons & Son Limited
Furry Park Industrial Estate
Santry 9, Eire
Tel: 003531 8733811 Fax: 003531 8733945

ISRAEL
Sole Agent —**Timmy Marketing Limited**
Israel Ben Zeev 12, Ramont Gimmel, Jerusalem
Tel: 972-2-5865266 Fax: 972-2-5860035
Sole Distributor – Sefer ve Sefel Ltd
Tel & Fax: 972-2-6248237

ITALY
Logos — Edizioni e distribuzione libri
Via Curtatona 5/J
41100 Modena, Italy
Tel: 059-418820/418821 Fax: 059-280123

NEW ZEALAND & FIJI
Allphy Book Distributors Ltd
4-6 Charles Street, Eden Terrace, Auckland,
Tel: (09) 3773096 Fax: (09) 3022770

MALAYSIA & BRUNEI
Vintrade SDN BHD
5 & 7 Lorong Datuk Sulaiman 7
Taman Tun Dr Ismail
60000 Kuala Lumpur, Malaysia
Tel: (603) 717 3333 Fax: (603) 719 2942

MALTA & GOZO
Agius & Agius Ltd
42A South Street, Valletta VLT 11
Tel: 234038 - 220347 Fax: 241175

PHILIPPINES
I J Sagun Enterprises
P O Box 4322 CPO Manila
2 Topaz Road, Greenheights Village,
Taytay, Rizal
Tel: 631 80 61 TO 66

SOUTH AFRICA
Chapter Book Agencies
Postnet Private bag X10016
Edenvale, 1610 Gauteng
South Africa
Tel: (++27) 11 425 5990
Fax: (++27) 11 425 5997

SLOVAK REPUBLIC
Slovak Ventures s r. o.,
Stefanikova 128, 949 01 Nitra
Tel/Fax: 042 87 525105/6/7

SPAIN
Ribera Libros, S.L.
Poligono Martiartu, Calle 1 - no 6
48480 Arrigorriaga, Vizcaya
Tel: 34 4 6713607 (Almacen)
        34 4 4418787 (Libreria)
Fax: 34 4 6713608 (Almacen)
        34 4 4418029 (Libreria)

UNITED STATES OF AMERICA
NTC/Contemporary Publishing Company
4225 West Touhy Avenue
Lincolnwood (Chicago)
Illinois 60646-4622
USA
Tel: (847) 679 5500 Fax: (847) 679 2494

DIRECT MAIL
Bibliophile Books
5 Thomas Road, London E14 7BN,
Tel: 0171-515 9222 Fax: 0171-538 4115
***Order hotline 24 hours* Tel: 0171-515 9555**
Cash with order + £2.50 p&p (UK)